Life Changing SECRETS

from the 3 Masters of Success

Life Changing

SECRETS

from the 3 *Masters of Success*

NAPOLEON HILL

•

DALE CARNEGIE

•

DR JOSEPH MURPHY

MANJUL

Manjul Publishing House

First published in India by

MANJUL

Manjul Publishing House
• C-16, Sector 3, Noida, Uttar Pradesh 201301, India
Website: www.manjulindia.com
Registered Office:
•10, Nishat Colony, Bhopal 462 003 - India
Distribution Centres
Ahmedabad, Bengaluru, Bhopal, Kolkata, Chennai,
Hyderabad, Mumbai, New Delhi, Pune

This edition first published in 2014
Eighth impression 2024

ISBN 978-81-8322-481-9

Printed and bound in India by Thomson Press (India) Limited.

Contents

About this Book

Think and Grow Rich by Napoleon Hill.

Power of Your Subconscious Mind, by Dr Joseph Murphy.

Public Speaking and Influencing People by Dale Carnegie.

Together these three books have sold over 100,000,000 copies worldwide. Generations of readers have successfully applied insights from these books to achieve personal and professional success in every area of their lives.

This book won't tell you what to desire or what to pursue. It simply lays out practical ways to use the power of your mind to pursue your personal goals and to reach them. In short, this book is about the way the world really works. Certain unseen principles control the translation of our desires to reality. These lie in the power of *your* mind. They are laid out here clearly and straightforwardly: follow the process – success will be yours.

Life Changing Secrets from the 3 Masters of Success is more than just a blueprint for your own personal success. It is a description of the way the world really works. By presenting the core principles of these authors together, in one volume, was the best way to highlight the big picture that has been lost in translation over the years. No expert or institution has the real answers you seek. The answers already exist in the power of your mind, a power available to all people at this very moment. These authors do not elevate themselves as gurus or experts. They show you how your own mind is already the expert on its own success. Look inward to start with your own true desire – that desire will lead to an idea, which will lead to concrete opportunities. You will discover those opportunities, coupled with hard work, will lead to your own true success – the way you define it, not anyone else.

A practical, cause-and-effect approach is what Napoleon Hill used in his book *Think and Grow Rich*. Dr Joseph Murphy, leader of one of the most broad-based self-help movements of the twentieth century, wrote a book called *The Power of Your Subconscious Mind*. While Hill's *Think and Grow Rich* applied the principle of the power of our minds to the single context of building wealth, Dr Murphy found that these same principles that stem from the power of the mind – such as desire, self-confidence, positive thinking, setting specific goals, imagining your ideal end result in specific terms like perseverance and generosity – apply just as powerfully and practically to any aspect of our lives.

Dale Carnegie wrote many classic self-help books including the immensely practical book called *Public Speaking and Influencing People*, to show how to apply these same principles of the mind to learning the skill that drives success in any field perhaps more than any other, the power of persuasion to increase influence over others.

In this book Dale Carnegie shows you how to: develop poise, gain self-confidence, improve your memory, make your meaning clear, influence other people to your way of thinking, and win arguments without making enemies. *Public Speaking and Influencing People* also offers hundreds of practical and valuable tips on influencing the important people in your life: your friends, your customers, your business associates, your employers.

This anthology of proven principles helps make success possible. These principles have nothing to do with geography or ethnicity; these same principles, if broadly and consistently applied anywhere, would make individual lives, families, communities and entire nations successful and influential in the best possible way, regardless of geography or wealth or social standing or opportunity. America didn't become a world power because of the advantage of wealth or political might – it started with neither of these. Nor was it dependence on strong, caretaker institutions – quite the opposite. America's success began with an *idea*. This idea was that all peoples are created equal and this equality is based in the qualities of the mind. That is, because we are all equal, we all have the inherent right to life, liberty and the pursuit of happiness. That's the American idea. It's true no matter where one happens to live or what one happens to have. The world beyond America's borders deserves to have these principles laid out clearly and practically as well, without any nationalistic rhetoric.

Part I

THINK AND GROW RICH

Turn Your Ideas into Financial Abundance

Napoleon Hill

Introduction

Think – and grow rich. This is not a new idea. Dozens of self-help books, published for decades, are based on this principle: the way you think about your life and your potential has a greater effect than any material advantage you may have. Even in the business world, the often-untapped power of our minds is key, with the potential to be a game-changer. Harness the power of the subconscious and the sky may be the limit for personal success. As Internet commerce grows by leaps and bounds, many entrepreneurs are starting businesses with nothing more than an idea. Yet to build a thriving business, you need a step-by-step process to convert that idea into business opportunities and convert those business opportunities into a steady stream of income. You might be surprised to know that you'll find that process laid out fully in Napoleon Hill's *Think and Grow Rich*, first published in 1937. Immediately after the Great Depression, many Americans found themselves stuck after experiencing years of poverty. Many were on the brink of ever-deeper despair, despondency and dependence. Yet some became rich – and not just rich, but fabulously wealthy. Many of us in the 21st century might scoff, 'The oil magnates? The monopolists? The slumlords? Sure, anyone can get rich if they're selfish enough and ruthless enough to take advantage of others to use them for their own gain.' Andrew Carnegie, one of those fabulously rich oil magnates, hired a young man named Napoleon Hill to set the record straight as he saw it. Hill was asked to interview hundreds of well-known, wealthy individuals, then write a book based on their secrets of success. In fact, this was not a compilation of many secrets, but one secret, a kind of 'magic formula,' that lay at the foundation of their success. In the preface to the resulting book, *Think and Grow Rich*, Hill wrote: 'It was Mr Carnegie's idea that the magic formula, which gave him a stupendous fortune, ought to be placed within reach of people who do not have time to investigate how men make money and it was his hope that I might test and demonstrate the soundness of the formula through the experience of men and women in every calling.' Carnegie further said that 'this formula should be taught in all public schools and colleges, and...if properly taught it would so revolutionise the entire educational system that the time spent in school could be reduced to half.' Carnegie told Hill the secret before he ever started interviewing, so it really wasn't a secret at all. Yet whether we call it a secret, a magic formula, or a common denominator, Hill found that the wealth of every person he interviewed, including Thomas Edison, Henry Ford, Charles Schwab and Andrew Carnegie himself, did not depend on ruthlessness, greed, inherited wealth or influence. Rather, he found 13 other common traits in all of those whom he interviewed. And these 13 all came down, he said, to the power of the mind. His conclusion? 'All achievement begins with an idea.' Read in today's context, these principles provide a step-by-step process, surprisingly fresh and timely, for the growing spirit of service-based entrepreneurism. Although the title *Think and Grow Rich* might conjure up images of greed for some, Hill wrote in a time very different from our own. For instance, after the Great Depression, 'growing rich' was an unquestioned good for the vast majority of Americans then living in abject poverty and losing hope. Moreover, at this time in American life, one might assume that most people wanted to do right by each other. Today, no one can take that for granted. Quite the contrary. After the 2008 economic collapse sparked by greed, people across the globe are rightly craving 'enlightened' businesses and 'green' entrepreneurism. We've seen the results of outsized corporate greed and for most of us, ostentatious material wealth, as a goal is no longer what it once was. We don't just want to 'grow rich'; we want to create meaningful work for others and ourselves and build (or be part of) sustainable and global businesses that do well and continue to do well. Actually, Napoleon Hill made this very point long ago: If you make money by shortchanging others, you're less likely to keep it. The 20th century has proven his point well. Too many of us have just failed to heed the lesson. Still, the time in which this book was written is much like our own in many ways. New technologies are changing everything: back then it was electricity and the automobile; now it's the Internet and the iPhone. The potential for riches is vast – and what Napoleon Hill said years ago is just as valid today: 'If the thing you wish to do is right and you believe in it, go ahead and do it.' And change the world – and your bank account – for the better.

Author's Preface

In every chapter of this book, mention has been made of the moneymaking secret that has made fortunes for more than five hundred exceedingly wealthy people whom I have carefully analysed over many years.

Andrew Carnegie brought the secret to my attention, more than a quarter of a century ago. The canny, lovable old Scotsman carelessly tossed it into my mind, when I was but a boy. Then he sat back in his chair, with a merry twinkle in his eyes and watched carefully to see if I had brains enough to understand the full significance of what he had said to me.

When he saw that I had grasped the idea, he asked if I would be willing to spend twenty years or more, preparing myself to take it to the world, to men and women who, without the secret, might go through life as failures. I said I would. With Mr Carnegie's cooperation, I have kept my promise.

This book contains the secret. It has been put to a practical test by thousands of people, in almost every walk of life. It was Mr Carnegie's idea that the magic formula, which gave him a stupendous fortune, ought to be placed within reach of people who do not have time to investigate how men make money. It was his hope that I might test and demonstrate the soundness of the formula through the experience of men and women in every calling. He believed the formula should be taught in all public schools and colleges and expressed the opinion that if it were properly taught it would so revolutionise the entire educational system that the time spent in school could be reduced to less than half.

His experience with Charles M Schwab and other young men of Mr Schwab's type, convinced Mr Carnegie that much of that which is taught in the schools is of no value whatsoever in connection with the business of earning a living or accumulating riches. He had arrived at this decision, because he had taken into his business one young man after another, many of them with but little schooling. By coaching them in the use of this formula, he developed in them rare leadership. Moreover, his coaching made fortunes for everyone of them who followed his instructions.

In the chapter on Faith, you will read the astounding story of the organisation of the giant United States Steel Corporation, as it was conceived and carried out by one of the young men through whom Mr Carnegie proved that his formula will work for all who are ready for it. This single application of the secret, by that young man – Charles M Schwab – made him a huge fortune in both money and *opportunity*. Roughly speaking, this particular application of the formula was worth six hundred million dollars.[1]

These facts – and they are facts well known to almost everyone who knew Mr Carnegie – give you a fair idea of what the reading of this book may bring to you, provided you *know what it is that you want*.

Even before it had undergone twenty years of practical testing, the secret was passed on to more than one hundred thousand

[1]In 1937 US dollars.

men and women who have used it for their personal benefit, as Mr Carnegie planned that they should. Some have made fortunes with it. Others have used it successfully in creating harmony in their homes.

The secret to which I refer has been mentioned no fewer than a hundred times, throughout this book. It has not been directly named, for it seems to work more successfully when it is merely uncovered and left in sight, where *those who are ready and searching for it*, may pick it up. That is why Mr Carnegie tossed it to me so quietly, without giving me its specific name.

If you are *ready* to put it to use, you will recognise this secret at least once in every chapter. I would feel privileged to tell you how you will know if you are ready, but that would deprive you of much of the benefit you will receive when you make the discovery in your own way.

While this book was being written, my own son, who was then finishing the last year of his college work, picked up the manuscript of Chapter Two, read it and discovered the secret for himself. He used the information so effectively that he went directly into a responsible position at a beginning salary greater than the average man ever earns. His story has been briefly described in Chapter Two. When you read it, perhaps you will dismiss any feeling you may have had, at the beginning of the book that it promised too much. Also if you have ever been discouraged, if you have had difficulties to surmount – something took the very soul out of you, if you have tried and failed, if you were ever handicapped by illness or physical affliction, this story of my son's discovery and use of the Carnegie formula may prove to be the very oasis in the 'Desert of Lost Hope' you have been searching.

President Woodrow Wilson extensively used this secret, during World War I. It was passed on to every soldier who fought in the war, carefully wrapped in the training received before going to the front. President Wilson told me it was a strong factor in raising the funds needed for the war.

A peculiar thing about this secret is that those who once acquire it and use it, find themselves literally swept on to success, with just a little effort and they never again submit to failure! If you doubt this, study the names of those who have used it, wherever they have been mentioned, check their records for yourself and be convinced.

There is no such thing as something for nothing!

The secret to which I refer cannot be had without a price, although the price is far less than its value. Those who are not intentionally searching for it cannot have it at any price. It cannot be given away; it cannot be purchased for money because it comes in two parts. One part is already in possession of those who are ready for it.

The secret serves equally well, all who are ready for it. Education has nothing to do with it. Long before I was born, the secret had found its way into the possession of Thomas A Edison. He used it so intelligently that he became the world's leading inventor, although he had only three months of schooling.

The secret was passed on to a business associate of Mr Edison. He used it so effectively that he accumulated a great fortune and retired from active business while still a young man. You will find his story at the beginning of the first chapter. It should convince you that riches are not beyond your reach, that you can still be what you wish to be, that money, fame, recognition and happiness can be had by all who are ready and determined to have these blessings.

How do I know these things? You should have the answer before you finish this book. You may find it in the very first chapter or on the last page.

While I was performing the twenty-year task of research, which I had undertaken at Mr Carnegie's request, I analysed hundreds of well-known men, many of whom admitted that they had accumulated their vast fortunes through the aid of the Carnegie secret. Among these men were:

Henry Ford, Theodore Roosevelt, William Wrigley, John Wanamaker, James J Hill, Wilbur Wright, William Jennings Bryan, Woodrow Wilson, William Howard Taft, Elbert H Gary, King Gillette, Alexander Bell, John D Rockefeller, Thomas A Edison, F W Woolworth, Clarence Darrow.

These names represent but a small fraction of the hundreds of well-known Americans whose achievements, financially and otherwise, prove that those who understand and apply the Carnegie secret, reach high stations in life. I have never known anyone who was inspired to use the secret, who did not achieve noteworthy success in his chosen calling. I have never known any person to distinguish himself or to accumulate riches of any consequence, without possession of the secret. From these two facts I draw the conclusion that the secret is more important, as a part of the knowledge essential for self-determination, than any, which one receives through what is popularly known as 'education.'

What is education, anyway? This has been answered in full detail. As far as schooling is concerned, many of these men had very little. John Wanamaker once told me that what little schooling he had, he acquired in very much the same manner as a modern locomotive takes on water, by 'scooping it up as it runs.' Henry Ford never reached high school, let alone college. I am not attempting to minimise the value of schooling, but I am trying to express my earnest belief that those who master and apply the secret will reach high stations, accumulate riches to bargain with life on their own terms, even if their schooling has been meagre.

Somewhere, as you read, the secret to which I refer will jump from the page and stand boldly before you, *if you are ready for it*! When it appears, you will recognise it. Whether you receive the sign in the first or the last chapter, stop for a moment when it presents itself – celebrated, for that occasion will mark the most important turning point of your life.

We pass now, to Chapter One and to the story of my very dear friend, who has generously acknowledged having seen the mystic sign and whose business achievements are evidence enough that he celebrated. As you read his story and the others, remember that they deal with the important problems of life, such as all people experience.

The problems arising from one's endeavour to earn a living, to find hope, courage, contentment and peace of mind; to accumulate riches and to enjoy freedom of body and spirit.

Remember, too, as you go through the book that it deals with facts and not with fiction its purpose being to convey a great universal truth through which all who are *ready* may learn, not only *what to do, but also how to do it*! and receive, as well, *the needed stimulus to make a start*.

As a final word of preparation, before you begin the first chapter, may I offer one brief suggestion that may provide a clue by which the Carnegie secret may be recognised? It is this – *All achievement, all earned riches have their beginning in an idea*! If you are ready for the secret, you already possess one half of it, therefore, you will readily recognise the other half the moment it reaches your mind.

Napoleon Hill, 1937

ONE

The Power of Thought

Truly, 'thoughts are things,' and powerful things at that, when they are mixed with definiteness of purpose, persistence and a *Burning Desire* for their translation into riches or other material objects.

Edwin C Barnes discovered how true it is that men really do *Think and Grow Rich*. His discovery did not come about at one sitting. It came little by little, beginning with a *burning desire* to become a business associate of the great Thomas Edison.

One of the chief characteristics of Barnes' *Desire* was that it was definite. He wanted to work *with* Edison, not *for* him. Observe, carefully, the description of how he went about translating his *Desire* into reality. You will then have a better understanding of the thirteen principles, which lead to riches.

When this *Desire*, or impulse of thought, first flashed into his mind he was in no position to act upon it. Two difficulties stood in his way. He did not know Mr Edison and he did not have enough money to pay his railroad fare to Orange, New Jersey. These difficulties were sufficient to have discouraged the majority of men from making any attempt to carry out the desire. Yet his was no ordinary desire! He was so determined to find a way to carry out his desire that he finally decided to travel by 'blind baggage,' rather than be defeated. (To the uninitiated, this means that he went to East Orange on a freight train).

He presented himself at Mr Edison's laboratory and announced he had come to go into business with the inventor. In speaking of the first meeting between Barnes and Edison, years later, Mr Edison said, 'He stood there before me, looking like an ordinary tramp, but there was something in the expression of his face which conveyed the impression that he was determined to get what he had come after. I had learned, from years of experience with men, that when a man really desires a thing so deeply that he is willing to stake his entire future on a single turn of the wheel in order to get it, he is sure to win. I gave him the opportunity he asked for, because I saw he had made up his mind to stand by until he succeeded. Subsequent events proved that no mistake was made.'

Just what young Barnes said to Mr Edison on that occasion was far less important than what he thought. Edison, himself, said so! It could not have been the young man's appearance that got him his start in the Edison office, for that was definitely against him. It was what he thought that counted.

If the significance of this statement could be conveyed to every person who reads it, there would be no need for the remainder of this book.

Barnes did not get his partnership with Edison on his first interview. He did get a chance to work in the Edison offices, at a very nominal wage, doing work that was unimportant to Edison, but most important to Barnes, because it gave him an opportunity to display his 'merchandise' where his intended 'partner' could see it.

Months went by. Apparently nothing happened to bring the coveted goal, which Barnes had set up in his mind as his Definite major purpose. But something important was happening in Barnes' mind. He was constantly intensifying his *Desire* to become the business associate of Edison.

Psychologists have correctly said, 'When one is truly ready for a thing, it puts in its appearance.' Barnes was ready for a business association with Edison; moreover, he was determined to remain ready until he got that which he was seeking.

He did not say to himself, 'Ah well, what's the use? I guess I'll change my mind and try for a salesman's job' But, he did say, 'I came here to go into business with Edison and I'll accomplish this end if it takes the remainder of my life.' He meant it! What a different story men would have to tell if only they would adopt a definite purpose as well as stand by that purpose until it had time to become an all-consuming obsession!

Maybe young Barnes did not know it at the time, but his bulldog determination, his persistence in standing back of a single desire, was destined to mow down all opposition and bring him the opportunity he was seeking.

When the opportunity came, it appeared in a different form and from a different direction than Barnes had expected. That is one of the tricks of opportunity. It has a sly habit of slipping in by the back door. Often it comes disguised in the form of misfortune or temporary defeat. Perhaps this is why so many fail to recognise opportunity.

Mr Edison had just perfected a new office device, known at that time, as the Edison Dictating Machine (later called the Ediphone). His salesmen were not enthusiastic about the machine. They did not believe it could be sold without great effort. Barnes saw his opportunity. It had crawled in quietly, hidden in a queer looking machine that interested no one but Barnes and the inventor.

Barnes knew he could sell the Edison Dictating Machine. He

suggested this to Edison, then promptly got his chance. He did sell the machine. In fact, he sold it so successfully that Edison gave him a contract to distribute and market it all over the nation. Out of that business association grew the slogan, 'Made by Edison and installed by Barnes.' Out of this business alliance Barnes made himself rich in money, but he accomplished something infinitely greater, he proved that one really may 'Think and Grow Rich.'

How much actual cash that original *Desire* of Barnes' had been worth to him, I have no way of knowing. Perhaps it has brought him two or three million dollars, but the amount, whatever it is, becomes insignificant when compared with the greater asset he acquired in the form of definite knowledge that an intangible impulse of thought can be transformed into its physical counterpart by the application of known principles.

Barnes literally thought himself into a partnership with the great Edison! He thought himself into a fortune. He had nothing to start with, except the capacity to know *what he wanted and the determination to stand by that desire until he realised it*.

He had no money to begin with. He had only a little education. He had no influence. Yet he did have initiative, faith and the will to win. With these intangible forces he made himself number one man with the greatest inventor who ever lived.

Now, let us look at a different situation to study a man who had plenty of tangible evidence of riches, but lost it, because he stopped three feet short of the goal he was seeking.

THREE FEET FROM GOLD

One of the most common causes of failure is the habit of quitting when one is overtaken by temporary defeat. Every person is guilty of this mistake at one time or another.

R U Darby, who later became one of the most successful insurance salesmen in the country, tells the story of his uncle, who was caught by the 'gold fever' in the gold-rush days and went west to *dig and grow rich*. He had never heard that more gold has been mined from the brains of men than has ever been taken from the earth. He staked a claim and went to work with pick and shovel. The going was hard, but his lust for gold was definite.

After weeks of labour, he was rewarded by the discovery of the shining ore. He needed machinery to bring the ore to the surface. Quietly, he covered up the mine, retraced his footsteps to his home in Williamsburg, Maryland and told his relatives and a few neighbours of the 'strike.' They got together money for the needed machinery, had it shipped. Darby and his Uncle went back to work the mine.

The first car of ore was mined and shipped to a smelter. The returns proved they had one of the richest mines in Colorado! A few more cars of that ore would clear the debts. Then would come the big killing in profits.

Down went the drills! Up went the hopes of Darby and his uncle! Then something happened! The vein of gold ore disappeared! They had come to the end of the rainbow and the pot of gold was no longer there! They drilled on, desperately trying to pick up the vein again, all to no avail.

Finally, they decided to quit. They sold the machinery to a junk man for a few hundred dollars and took the train back home. Some 'junk' men are dumb, but not this one! He called in a mining engineer to look at the mine and do a little calculating. The engineer advised that the project had failed, because the owners were not familiar with 'fault lines.' His calculations showed that the vein would be found *just three feet from where the Darbys had stopped drilling*! That is exactly where it was found!

The 'Junk' man took millions of dollars in ore from the mine, because he knew enough to seek expert counsel before giving up. Most of the money, which went into the machinery, was procured through the efforts of R U Darby, who was then a very young man. The money came from his relatives and neighbours, because of their faith in him. He paid back every dollar of it, although he tooks years in doing so.

Long afterward, Mr Darby recovered his loss many times over, when he made the discovery that desire can be transformed into gold. The discovery came after he went into the business of selling life insurance.

Remembering that he lost a huge fortune, because he *stopped* three feet from gold, Darby profited by the experience in his chosen work, by the simple method of saying to himself, 'I stopped three feet from gold, but I will never stop because men say 'no' when I ask them to buy insurance.' He owes his 'stick ability' to the lesson he learned from his 'quit ability' in the gold mining business.

Before success comes to most people, they are sure to meet with much temporary defeat and perhaps, some failure. When faced with defeat the easiest and most logical thing to do is to *quit*. That is exactly what the majority of people do.

More than five hundred of the most successful people this country has ever known, told the author their greatest success came just one step beyond the point at which defeat had overtaken them. Failure is a trickster with a keen sense of irony and cunning. It takes great delight in tripping one when success is almost within reach. But what of the man who has neither the time, nor the inclination to study failure in search of knowledge that may lead to success? Where and how is he to learn the art of converting defeat into stepping stones to opportunity?

In answer to these questions, this book was written.

The answer called for a description of thirteen principles, but remember, as you read, the answer you may be seeking, to the questions which have caused you to ponder over the strangeness of life, may be found in your own mind, through some idea, plan, or purpose which may spring into your mind as you read.

One sound idea is all that one needs to achieve success. The principles described in this book, contain the best and the most practical of all that is known, concerning ways and means of creating useful ideas.

Before we go any further in our approach to the description of these principles, we believe you are entitled to receive this important suggestion:

When riches begin to come – they come so quickly, in such great abundance, that one wonders where they have been hiding during all those lean years. This is an astounding statement and all the more so, when we take into consideration the popular belief, that riches come only to those who work hard and long.

When you begin to think and grow rich, you will observe that riches begin with a state of mind, with definiteness of purpose, with little or no hard work. You and every other person, ought to be interested in knowing how to acquire that state of mind, which will attract riches. I spent twenty-five years in research, analysing more than 25,000 people, because I, too, wanted to know 'how wealthy men become that way.'

Without that research, this book could not have been written.

Here take notice of a very significant truth: The business depression started in 1929 and continued on to an all time record of destruction, until sometime after President Roosevelt entered office. Then the depression began to fade into nothingness. Just as an electrician in a theatre raises the lights so gradually that darkness is transmuted into light before you realise it, so did the spell of fear in the minds of the people gradually fade away and become faith.

Observe very closely, as soon as you master the principles of this philosophy and begin to follow the instructions for applying those principles, your financial status will begin to improve and everything you touch will begin to transmute itself into an asset for your benefit. Impossible? Not at all!

One of the main weaknesses of mankind is the average man's familiarity with the word 'impossible.' He knows all the rules that will *not* work. He knows all the things that *cannot* be done. This book was written for those who seek the rules that have made others successful and are willing to stake everything on those rules.

A great many years ago I purchased a fine dictionary. The first thing I did with it was to turn to the word 'impossible,' and neatly clip it out of the book. That would not be an unwise thing for you to do.

Success comes to those who become *Success Conscious.*

Failure comes to those who carelessly allow themselves to become *Failure Conscious.*

The object of this book is to help all who seek it, to learn the art of changing their minds from *Failure Consciousness to Success Consciousness.*

Another weakness found in altogether too many people, is the habit of measuring everything and everyone, by their own impressions and beliefs. Some who will read this, will believe that no one can *Think and Grow Rich*. They cannot think in terms of riches, because their thought habits have been soaked in poverty, want, misery, failure and defeat.

Millions of people look at the achievements of Henry Ford

to envy him, because of his good fortune or luck or genius – whatever it is that they credit for Ford's fortune. Perhaps one person in every hundred thousand knows the secret of Ford's success and those who do know are too modest or too reluctant, to speak of it, because of its simplicity. A single transaction will illustrate the 'secret' perfectly.

When Ford decided to produce his now famous V-8 motor, he chose to build an engine with the entire eight cylinders cast in one block and instructed his engineers to produce a design for the engine. The design was placed on paper, but the engineers believed that it was simply impossible to cast an eight-cylinder gas engine block in one piece. Ford said, 'Produce it anyway.'

'But,' they replied, 'it's impossible!'

'Go ahead,' Ford commanded, 'and stay on the job until you succeed no matter how much time is required.'

The engineers went ahead. There was nothing else for them to do, if they were to remain on the Ford staff. Six months went by, nothing happened. Another six months passed and still nothing happened. The engineers tried every conceivable plan to carry out the orders, but the thing seemed out of the question; 'impossible!'

At the end of the year Ford checked with his engineers and again they informed him they had found no way to carry out his orders.

'Go right ahead,' said Ford, 'I want it and I'll have it.'

They went ahead and then, as if by a stroke of magic, the secret was discovered. The Ford *Determination* had won once more!

This story may not be described with minute accuracy, but the sum and substance of it is correct. Deduce from it, you who wish to *Think and Grow Rich*, the secret of the Ford millions, if you can. You'll not have to look very far.

Henry Ford is a success, because he understands and applies

the principles of success. One of these is *Desire*: knowing what one wants. Remember this Ford story as you read and pick out the lines in which the secret of his stupendous achievement has been described. If you can do this, if you can lay your finger on the particular group of principles that made Henry Ford rich, you can equal his achievements in almost any calling for which you are suited.

You Are 'The Master of Your Fate, the Captain of Your Soul,'

When, the English poet, W C Henley wrote the prophetic lines, 'I am the Master of my Fate, I am the Captain of my Soul,' he should have informed us that the reason we are the Masters of our Fate, the Captains of our Souls, because we have the power to control our thoughts.

He should have told us that the ether in which this little earth floats, in which we move and have our being, is a form of energy moving at an inconceivably high rate of vibration and that the ether is filled with a form of universal power which *adapts* itself to the nature of the thoughts we hold in our minds; and *influences* us, in natural ways, to transmute our thoughts into their physical equivalent.

If the poet had told us of this great truth, we would know *why it is* that we are the Masters of our Fate, the Captains of our Souls. He should have told us, with great emphasis, that this power makes no attempt to discriminate between destructive thoughts and constructive thoughts, that it will urge us to translate into physical reality thoughts of poverty, just as quickly as it will influence us to act upon thoughts of riches.

He should have told us, too, that our brains become magnetised with the dominating thoughts which we hold in our minds. By means with which no man is familiar, these 'magnets' attract to us the forces, the people, the circumstances of life, which harmonise with the nature of our dominating thoughts.

He should have told us, that before we can accumulate riches in great abundance, we must magnetise our minds with intense *desire* for riches, that we must become 'money conscious' until the *desire* for money drives us to create definite plans for acquiring it.

We are now ready to examine the first of these principles. Maintain a spirit of open-mindedness and remember as you read, they are the invention of no one man. The principles were gathered from the life experiences of more than 500 men who actually accumulated riches in huge amounts; men who began in poverty, with but little education, without influence. The principles worked for these men. You can put them to work for your own enduring benefit.

You will find it easy, not hard, to do.

Before you read the next chapter, I want you to know that it conveys factual information that might easily change your entire financial destiny, as it has so definitely brought changes of stupendous proportions to two people described.

I want you to know, also, that the relationship between these two men and myself is such that I could have taken no liberties with the facts, even if I had wished to do so. One of them has been my closest personal friend for almost twenty-five years; the other is my own son. The unusual success of these two men, success that they generously accredit to the principle described in the next chapter, more than justifies this personal reference as a means of emphasising the far-flung power of this principle.

TWO

Desire: The Starting Point of All Achievement

When Edwin C Barnes climbed down from the freight train in Orange, NJ, more than thirty years ago, he may have resembled a tramp, but his thoughts were those of a king!

As he made his way from the railroad tracks to Thomas A Edison's office, his mind was at work. He saw himself *standing in Edison's presence.* He heard himself asking Mr Edison for an opportunity to carry out the one *consuming obsession of his life, a burning desire* to become the business associate of the great inventor.

Barnes' desire was not a hope! It was not a wish! It was a keen, pulsating *desire*, which transcended everything else. It was *definite.*

The desire was not new when he approached Edison. It had been Barnes' dominating desire for a long time. In the beginning, when the desire first appeared in his mind, it may have been, probably was, only a wish, but it was no mere wish when he appeared before Edison with it.

A few years later, Edwin C Barnes again stood before Edison, in the same office where he first met the inventor. This time his *desire* had been translated into reality. He was in business with Edison. The dominating *dream of his life* had become a reality. Today, people who know Barnes envy him because of the 'break' life yielded him. They see him in the days of his triumph, without taking the trouble to investigate the cause of his success.

Barnes succeeded because he chose a definite goal, placed all his energy, all his will power and all his effort, everything back of that goal. He did not become the partner of Edison the day he arrived. He was content to start in the most menial work, as long as it provided an opportunity to take even one step toward his cherished goal.

Five years passed before the chance he had been seeking made its appearance. During all those years not one ray of hope, not one promise of attainment of his *desire* had been held out to him. To everyone, except himself, he appeared only another cog in the Edison business wheel, but in his own mind, *he was the partner of Edison every minute of the time*, from the very day that he first went to work there.

It is a remarkable illustration of the power of a Definite Desire. Barnes won his goal, because he wanted to be a business associate of Mr Edison, more than he wanted anything else. He created a plan by which to attain that purpose. But he burned all his bridges behind him. He stood by his *desire* until it became the dominating obsession of his life and finally, a fact.

When he went to Orange, he did not say to himself, 'I will try to induce Edison to give me a job of some sort.' He said, 'I will see Edison and put him on notice that I have come to go into business with him.'

He did not say, 'I will work there for a few months and if I get no encouragement, I will quit and get a job somewhere else.'

He did say, 'I will start anywhere. I will do anything Edison tells me to do, but before I am through, I will be his associate.' He did not say, 'I will keep my eyes open for another opportunity, in case I fail to get what I want in the Edison organisation.' He said, 'There is but ONE thing in this world that I am determined to have and that is a business association with Thomas A Edison. I will burn all bridges behind me and stake my *entire future* on my ability to get what I want.'

He left himself no possible way of retreat. He had to win or perish! That is all there is to the Barnes story of success!

A long while ago, a great warrior faced a situation necessary for him to make a decision to insured his success on the battlefield. He was about to send his armies against a powerful foe, whose men outnumbered his own. He loaded his soldiers into boats, sailed to the enemy's country, unloaded soldiers and equipment, then gave the order to burn the ships that had carried them. Addressing his men before the first battle, he said, 'You see the boats going up in smoke. That means that we cannot leave these shores alive unless we win! We now have no choice – we win or we perish! They won. Every person who wins in any undertaking must be willing to burn his ships and cut all sources of retreat. Only by so doing can one be sure of maintaining that state of mind known as a *burning desire to win*, essential to success.

The morning after the great Chicago fire, a group of merchants stood on State Street, looking at the smoking remains of what had been their stores. They had a conference to decide if they would try to rebuild or leave Chicago and start over in a more promising section of the country. They reached a decision – all except one – to leave Chicago.

The merchant who decided to stay and rebuild pointed a finger at the remains of his store and said, 'Gentlemen, on that very spot I will build the world's greatest store, no matter how many times it may burn down.' The store was built. It stands there today, a towering monument to the power of that state of mind known as a *burning desire*. The easy thing for Marshal Field to do would have been exactly what his fellow merchants did. When the going was hard and the future looked dismal, they pulled up and went where the going seemed easier.

Mark well this difference between Marshal Field and the other merchants, because it is the same difference, which distinguishes Edwin C Barnes from thousands of other young men who have worked in the Edison organisation. It is the same difference, which distinguishes practically all who succeed from those who fail.

Every human being who reaches the age of understanding of money – wishes for it. Wishing will not bring riches. But desiring riches with obsession, then planning definite ways and means to acquire riches and backing those plans with persistence which does not recognise failure – will bring riches.

The method by which *desire* for riches can be transformed into its financial equivalent, consists of six definite, practical steps:

First Fix in your mind the exact amount of money you desire. It is not sufficient merely to say, 'I want plenty of money.' Be definite as to the amount. (There is a psychological reason for definiteness, which will be described, in a subsequent chapter.)

Second Determine exactly what you intend to give in return for the money you desire. (There is no such reality as 'something for nothing.)

Third Establish a definite date when you intend to possess the money you desire.

Fourth Create a definite plan for carrying out your desire and begin at once, whether you are ready or not, to put this plan into action.

Fifth Write out a clear, concise statement of the amount of money you intend to acquire, name the time limit for its acquisition, state what you intend to give in return for the money and describe clearly the plan through which you intend to accumulate it.

Sixth Read your written statement aloud, twice daily, once just before retiring at night and once after rising in the morning. *As you read, see and feel and believe yourself already in possession of the money.*

It is important that you follow the instructions described in these six steps. It is especially important that you observe and follow the instructions in the sixth paragraph.

You may complain that it is impossible for you to 'see yourself in possession of money' before you actually have it. Here is where a *burning desire* will come to your aid. If you truly *desire* money so keenly that your desire is an obsession, you will have no difficulty in convincing yourself that you will acquire it. The object is to want money and to become so determined to have it that you *convince* yourself you will have it.

Only those who become 'money conscious' ever accumulate great riches. 'Money consciousness' means that the mind has become so thoroughly saturated with the *desire* for money, that one can see one's self already in possession of it. To the uninitiated, who has not been schooled in the working principles of the human mind, these instructions may appear impractical. It may be helpful, to all who fail to recognise the soundness of the six steps, to know that the information they convey, was received from Andrew Carnegie, who began as an ordinary labourer in the steel mills, but managed, despite his humble beginning, to make these principles yield him a fortune of considerably more than one hundred million dollars. It may be of further help to know that the six steps here recommended were carefully scrutinised by Thomas A Edison, who placed his stamp of approval upon them as being, not only the steps essential for the accumulation of money, but necessary for the attainment of any definite goal. The steps call for no 'hard labour.' They call for no sacrifice. They do not require one to become ridiculous, or credulous. To apply them calls for no great amount of education. But the successful application of these six steps does call for sufficient imagination to enable one to see and to understand, that accumulation of money cannot be left to chance, good fortune and luck. One must realise that all who have accumulated great fortunes first did a certain amount of dreaming, hoping, wishing, *desiring* and *planning* before they acquired money. You may as well know, right here, that you can never have riches in great quantities, *unless* you can work yourself into a white heat of *desire* for money and actually *believe* you will possess it.

You may as well know, also that every great leader, from the dawn of civilisation down to the present, was a dreamer. If you do not see great riches in your imagination, you will never see them in your bank balance. Never, in the history of America has there been so great an opportunity for practical dreamers as today. We who are in this race for riches, should be encouraged to know that this dynamic world in which we live is demanding new ideas, new ways of doing things, new leaders, new inventions, new methods of teaching, new methods of marketing, new books, new literature, new applications for computers, new cures for diseases and new approaches to every aspect of business and life. Behind all this demand for new and better things, there is one quality which one must possess to win and that is *definiteness of purpose*, the knowledge of what one wants and a burning *desire* to possess it. To accomplish this requires practical dreamers who can and will put their dreams into action. The practical dreamers have always been and always will be the patternmakers of civilisation. We who desire to accumulate riches, should remember the real leaders of the world always have been people who harnessed and put into practical use, the intangible, unseen forces of unborn opportunity. They have converted those forces, (or impulses of thought), into skyscrapers, cities, factories, airplanes, automobiles, better health care and every form of convenience that makes life more pleasant.

Tolerance and an open mind are practical necessities of the dreamer of today. Those who are afraid of new ideas are doomed before they start. Never has there been a time more favourable to pioneers than the present. True, there is no wild and woolly west to be conquered, as in the days of the covered wagon; but there is a vast business, financial and industrial world to be remolded and redirected along new and better lines.

In planning to acquire your share of the riches, let no one influence you to scorn the dreamer. To win the big stakes in this ever changing world, you must catch the spirit of the great pioneers of the past, whose dreams have given to civilisation all that it has of value, the spirit which serves as the life-blood of our own country – your opportunity and mine, to develop and market our talents. Let us not forget, Columbus dreamed of an unknown world, staked his life on the existence of such a world and discovered it! Copernicus, the great astronomer, dreamed of a multiplicity of worlds and revealed them! No one denounced him as 'impractical' after he had triumphed. Instead, the world worshipped his shrine, thus proving once more that, '*Success requires no apologies, failure permits no alibis*.'

If the thing you wish to do is right and you believe in it, go ahead and do it! Put your dream across and never mind what 'they' say if you meet with temporary defeat, for 'they,' perhaps, do not know that, *Every failure brings with it the seed of an equivalent success.*

Henry Ford, poor and uneducated, dreamed of a horseless carriage, went to work with what tools he possessed, without waiting for opportunity to favour him and now evidence of his dream belts the entire earth. He has put more wheels into operation than any man who ever lived, because he was not afraid to back his dreams. Thomas Edison dreamed of a lamp that could be operated by electricity, began where he stood to put his dream into action and despite more than ten thousand failures, he stood by that dream until he made it a physical reality. Practical dreamers *Do Not Quit*!

Before passing to the next chapter, kindle anew in your mind the fire of hope, faith, courage and tolerance. If you have these states of mind and a working knowledge of the principles described, all else that you need will come to you, when you are *Ready* for it. Let Emerson state the thought in these words, 'Every proverb, every book and every byword that belongs to thee for aid and comfort shall surely come home through open or winding passages. Every friend whom not thy fantastic will, but the great and tender soul in thee craveth, shall lock thee in his embrace.'

There is a difference between *wishing* for a thing and being *ready* to receive it. No one is ready for a thing, until he believes he can acquire it. The state of mind must be *belief*, not mere hope or wish. Open-mindedness is essential for belief. Closed minds do not inspire faith, courage and belief.

Remember, no more effort is required to aim high in life, to demand abundance and prosperity, than is required to accept misery and poverty.

Desire Outwits Mother Nature

As a fitting climax to this chapter, I wish to introduce one of the most unusual persons I have ever known. I first saw him a few minutes after he was born. He came into the world without any physical sign of ears. The doctor admitted, when pressed for an opinion, that the child might be deaf and mute for life.

I challenged the doctor's opinion. I had the right to do so; I was the child's father. I, too, reached a decision and rendered an opinion, but I expressed the opinion silently, in the secrecy of my own heart. I decided that my son would hear and speak. Nature could send me a child without ears, but Nature could not induce me to accept the reality of the affliction. In my own mind I knew that my son would hear and speak. How? I was sure there must be a way and I knew I would find it. I thought of the words of the immortal Emerson, 'The whole course of things goes to teach us faith. We need only obey. There is guidance for each of us and by lowly listening, we shall hear the right word.'

The right word? *Desire*! More than anything else, I *desired* that my son should not be a deaf mute. From that desire I never receded, not for a second. Many years previously, I had written, 'Our only limitations are those we set up in our own minds.' For the first time, I wondered if that statement were true. Lying on the bed in front of me was a newly born child, without the natural equipment of hearing. Even though he might hear and speak, he was obviously disfigured for life. Surely, this was a limitation, which that child had not set up in his own mind. What could I do about it? Somehow I would find a way to transplant into that child's mind my own *burning desire* for ways and means of conveying sound to his brain without the aid of ears.

As soon as the child was old enough to cooperate, I would

fill his mind so completely with a *burning desire* to hear, that Nature would, by methods of her own, translate it into physical reality. All this thinking took place in my own mind, but I spoke of it to no one. Every day I renewed the pledge I had made to myself, not to accept a deaf-mute son.

As he grew older and began to take notice of things around him, we observed that he had a slight degree of hearing. When he reached the age when children usually begin talking, he made no attempt to speak, but we could tell by his actions that he could hear certain sounds slightly. That was all I wanted to know! I was convinced that if he could hear, even slightly, he might develop still greater hearing capacity. Then something happened which gave me hope. It came from an entirely unexpected source. We bought a record player. When the child heard the music for the first time, he went into ecstasies and promptly appropriated the machine. He soon showed a preference for certain records, among them, 'It's a Long Way to Tipperary.' On one occasion, he played that piece over and over, for almost two hours, standing in front of the record player, with his teeth clamped on the edge of the case. The significance of this self-formed habit of his did not become clear to us until years afterward, for we had never heard of the principle of 'bone conduction' of sound at that time.

Shortly after he appropriated the record player, I discovered that he could hear me quite clearly when I spoke with my lips touching his mastoid bone – at the base of the brain. These discoveries placed in my possession the necessary media by which I began to translate into reality my burning desire to help my son develop hearing and speech. By that time he was making stabs at speaking certain words. The outlook was far from encouraging, but *desire backed by faith* knows no such word as impossible.

Having determined that he could hear the sound of my voice

plainly, I began, immediately to transfer to his mind the desire to hear and speak. I soon discovered that the child enjoyed bedtime stories, so I went to work, creating stories designed to develop in him self-reliance, imagination and a keen desire to hear and to be normal. There was one story in particular, which I emphasised by giving it some new and dramatic colouring each time it was told. It was designed to plant in his mind the thought that his affliction was not a liability, but an asset of great value.

Despite the fact that all the philosophy I had examined clearly indicated that: *Every adversity brings with it the seed of an equivalent advantage*, I must confess that I had not the slightest idea how this affliction could ever become an asset. However, I continued my practice of wrapping that philosophy in bedtime stories, hoping the time would come when he would find some plan by which his handicap could be made to serve some useful purpose. Reason told me plainly, that there was no adequate compensation for the lack of ears and natural hearing equipment. *Desire* to *faith*, pushed reason aside and inspired me to carry on.

As I analyse the experience in retrospect, I can see now, that my son's faith in me had much to do with the astounding results. He did not question anything I told him. I sold him the idea that he had a distinct advantage over his older brother and that this advantage would reflect itself in many ways. For example, the teachers in school would observe that he had no ears. Just because of this, they would show him special attention and treat him with extraordinary kindness. They always did. His mother saw to that, by visiting the teachers and arranging with them to give the child the extra attention necessary. I sold him the idea, too, that when he became old enough to sell newspapers, (his older brother had already become a newspaper merchant), he would have a big advantage over his brother, for the reason that people would pay him extra money for his wares, because they could see that he was a bright, industrious boy, despite the fact he had no ears.

We could notice that, gradually, the child's hearing was improving. Moreover, he had not the slightest tendency to be self-conscious, because of his affliction. When he was about seven, he showed the first evidence that our method of nurturing his mind was bearing fruit. For several months he begged for the privilege of selling newspapers, but his mother would not give her consent. She was afraid that his deafness made it unsafe for him to go on the street alone.

Finally, he took matters in his own hands. One afternoon, when he was left at home with the servants, he climbed through the kitchen window, jumped to the ground and set out on his own. He borrowed six cents in capital from the neighbourhood shoemaker, invested it in papers, sold out, reinvested and kept repeating until late in the evening. After balancing his accounts along with paying back the six cents he had borrowed from his banker, he had a net profit of forty-two cents. When we got home that night, we found him in bed asleep, with the money tightly clenched in his hand. His mother opened his hand, removed the coins and cried. Of all things! Crying over her son's first victory seemed so inappropriate. My reaction was the reverse. I laughed heartily, for I knew that my endeavour to plant in the child's mind an attitude of faith in himself had been successful. His mother saw, in his first business venture, a little deaf boy who had gone out in the streets and risked his life to earn money. I saw a brave, ambitious, self-reliant little businessman whose stock in himself had been increased a hundred per cent, because he had gone into business on his own initiative and had won. The transaction pleased me, because I knew that he had given evidence of a trait of resourcefulness that would go with him all through life.

Later events proved this to be true. When his older brother wanted something, he would lie down on the floor, kick his feet in the air, cry for it – and get it. When the 'little deaf boy' wanted something, he would plan a way to earn the money, then buy it for himself. He still follows that plan! Truly, my own son has taught me that handicaps can be converted into stepping-stones on which one may climb toward some worthy goal, unless they are accepted as obstacles, then used as alibis.

The little deaf boy went through the grades, high school and college without being able to hear his teachers, except when they shouted loudly, at close range. He did not go to a school for the deaf. We would not permit him to learn the sign language. We were determined that he should live a normal life. He would associate with normal children. We stood by that decision, although it cost us many heated debates with school officials.

While he was in high school, he tried an electrical hearing aid, but it was of no value to him; due, we believed, to a condition that was disclosed when the child was six, by Dr J Gordon Wilson, of Chicago, when he operated on one side of the boy's head and discovered that there was no sign of natural hearing equipment.

During his last week in college, (eighteen years after the operation), something happened, which marked the most important turning point of his life. Through what seemed to be mere chance, he came into possession of another electrical hearing device, which was sent to him on trial. He was slow about testing it, due to his disappointment with a similar device. Finally he picked the instrument up and more or less carelessly, placed it on his head, hooked up the battery. Lo! As if by a stroke of magic, his lifelong *desire for normal hearing became a reality*! For the first time in his life he heard practically as well as any person with normal hearing.

'God moves in mysterious ways, His wonders to perform.' Overjoyed because of the changed world that had been brought to him through his hearing device, he rushed to the telephone, called his mother and heard her voice perfectly. The next day he plainly heard the voices of his professors in class, for the first time in his life! Previously he could hear them only when they shouted, at short range. He heard the radio. He heard the talking pictures. For the first time in his life, he could converse freely with other people, without the necessity of their having to speak loudly. Truly, he had come into possession of a changed world. We had refused to accept Nature's error. By *persistent desire*, we had induced Nature to correct that error, through the only practical means available.

Desire had commenced to pay dividends, but the victory was not yet complete. The boy still had to find a definite and practical way to convert his handicap into an equivalent asset.

Hardly realising the significance of what had already been accomplished but intoxicated with the joy of his newly discovered world of sound, he wrote a letter to the manufacturer of the hearing aid, enthusiastically describing his experience. Something in his letter; something, perhaps which was not written on the lines, but between them; caused the company to invite him to New York. When he arrived, he was escorted through the factory and while talking with the Chief Engineer, telling him about his changed world, a hunch, an idea or an inspiration – call it what you wish – flashed into his mind. It was this impulse of thought which converted his affliction into an asset, destined to pay dividends in both money and happiness to thousands for all time to come.

The sum and substance of that impulse of thought was this: It occurred to him that he might be of help to the millions of deaf people who go through life without the benefit of hearing devices, if he could find a way to tell them the story of his Changed World. Then and there, he reached a decision to devote the remainder of his life to rendering useful service to the hard of hearing. For an entire month, he carried on an intensive research. He analysed the entire marketing system of the manufacturer of the hearing device and created ways and means of communicating with the hard of hearing – all over the world for the purpose of sharing with them his newly discovered 'Changed World.' When this was done, he wrote a two-year plan, based upon his findings. When he presented the plan to the company, he was instantly given a position, for the purpose of carrying out his ambition. Little did he dream, when he went to work, that he was destined to bring hope and practical relief to thousands of deafened people who, without his help, would have been doomed forever to deaf mutism.

Shortly after he became associated with the manufacturer of his hearing aid, he invited me to attend a class conducted by his company, for the purpose of teaching deaf mutes to hear and to speak. I had never heard of such a form of education, therefore I visited the class, skeptical but hopeful that my time would not be entirely wasted. Here I saw a demonstration, which gave me a greatly enlarged vision of what I had done to arouse and keep alive in my son's mind the *desire* for normal hearing. I saw deaf mutes actually being taught to hear and to speak, through application of the self-same principle I had used, more than twenty years previously, in saving my son from deaf mutism.

Thus, through some strange turn of the Wheel of Fate, my son, Blair and I had been destined to aid in correcting deaf mutism for those as yet unborn. We are the only living human beings, as far as I know, who have established definitely the fact that deaf mutism can be corrected to the extent of restoring to normal life those who suffer with this affliction. It has been done for one; it will be done for others.

There is no doubt in my mind that Blair would have been a deaf mute all his life, if his mother and I had not managed to shape his mind as we did. The doctor who attended at his birth told us, confidentially, the child might never hear or speak.

When Blair was an adult, Dr Irving Voorhees, a noted specialist on such cases, examined him very thoroughly. He was astounded when he learned how well my son could hear as well as speak. He said his examination indicated, 'Theoretically, the boy should not be able to hear at all.' But the lad does hear, despite the fact that X-ray pictures show there is no opening in the skull, whatsoever, from where his ears should be to the brain.

When I planted in his mind the *desire* to hear and talk, to live as a normal person, there went with that impulse some strange influence which caused Nature to become the bridge-builder. The bridge to span the gulf of silence between his brain and the outer world, by some means which the keenest medical specialists have not been able to interpret. Also it would be sacrilege for me to even conjecture as to how Nature performed this miracle. It would be unforgivable if I neglected to tell the world as much as I know of the humble part I assumed in the strange experience. It is my duty and a privilege to say I believe and not without reason, that nothing is impossible to the person who backs *desire* with enduring *faith*. I have no doubt that a *burning desire* has devious ways of transmuting itself into its physical equivalent. Blair desired normal hearing; now he has it! He was born with a handicap, which might easily have sent one with a less defined *desire* to the street with a bundle of pencils and a tin cup. That handicap now promises to serve as the medium by which he will render useful service to many millions of hard of hearing, also, to give him useful employment at adequate financial compensation the remainder of his life. The little 'white lies' I planted in his mind when he was a child, by leading him to *believe* his affliction would become a great asset, which he could capitalize, has justified itself. There is nothing, right or wrong, which *belief*, plus *burning desire*, cannot make real. These qualities are free to everyone.

In all my experience in dealing with men and women who had personal problems, I never handled a single case, which more definitely demonstrates the power of *desire*. Authors sometimes make the mistake of writing of subjects of which they have but superficial, or very elementary knowledge. It has been my good fortune to have had the privilege of testing the soundness of the *power of desire*, through the affliction of my own son. Perhaps it was fortunate that the experience came as it did, for surely no one is better prepared than he, to serve as an example of what happens when *desire* is put to the test. If Mother Nature bends to the will of desire, is it logical that mere men can defeat a burning desire? Strange and imponderable is the power of the human mind! We do not understand the method by which it uses every circumstance, every individual, every physical thing within its reach, as a means of transforming *desire* into its physical counterpart. Perhaps science will uncover this secret.

I planted in my son's mind the *desire* to hear and to speak as any normal person hears and speaks. That *desire* has now become a reality. I planted in his mind the *desire* to convert his greatest handicap into his greatest asset. That *desire* has been realised.

The modus operandi by which this astounding result was achieved is not hard to describe. It consisted of three very definite facts; first, I mixed faith with the *desire* for normal hearing, which

I passed on to my son. Second, I communicated my desire to him in every conceivable way available, through persistent, continuous effort, over a period of years. Third, *he believed me*! I believe in the power of *desire* backed by *faith*, because I have seen this power lift people from lowly beginnings to places of power and wealth. I have seen it rob the grave of its victims; I have seen it serve as the medium by which people staged a comeback after having been defeated in a hundred different ways; I have seen it provide my own son with a normal, happy, successful life, despite Nature's sending him into the world without ears.

How can one harness and use the power of *desire*? This has been answered through this and the subsequent chapters of this book.

I wish to convey the thought that all achievement, no matter what may be its nature – or its purpose – must begin with an intense, *burning desire* for something definite. Through some strange and powerful principle of 'mental chemistry' nature wraps up in the impulse of *strong desire* 'that something' which recognises no such word as impossible and accepts no such reality as failure.

THREE

Faith: Visualisation and Belief in Attainment of Desire

Faith is the chief chemist of the mind. When *Faith* is blended with the vibration of thought, the subconscious mind instantly picks up the vibration, translates it into its spiritual equivalent and transmits it to infinite intelligence, as in the case of prayer. The emotions of *faith*, *love* and *sex* are the most powerful of all the major positive emotions. When the three are blended, they have the effect of 'colouring' the vibration of thought so that it instantly reaches the subconscious mind, where it is changed into its spiritual equivalent, the only form that induces a response from infinite intelligence.

Love and faith are psychic; related to the spiritual side of man. Sex is purely biological and related only to the physical. The mixing or blending, of these three emotions has the effect of opening a direct line of communication between the finite, thinking mind of man and infinite intelligence.

HOW TO DEVELOP FAITH

Faith is a state of mind that may be induced or created by affirmation or repeated instructions to the subconscious mind, through the principle of autosuggestion. As an illustration, consider the purpose for which you are, presumably, reading this book. The object is, naturally, to acquire the ability to transform the intangible thought impulse of *desire* into its physical counterpart, *money*. By following the instructions laid down in the chapters on autosuggestion and the subconscious mind, as summarised in the chapter on autosuggestion, you may *convince* the subconscious mind that you believe you will receive that for which you ask and it will act upon that belief, which your subconscious mind passes back to you in the form of '*faith*,' followed by definite plans for procuring that which you desire.

The method to develop *faith*, where it does not already exist, is extremely difficult to describe. Almost as difficult, in fact, as it would be to describe the colour of red to a blind man who has never seen colour and has nothing with which to compare what you describe to him. Faith is a state of mind that you may develop at will, after you have mastered the thirteen principles, because it is a state of mind, which develops voluntarily, through application and use of these principles. Repetition of affirmation of orders to your subconscious mind is the only known method of voluntary development of the emotion of faith. Perhaps the meaning may be made clearer through the following explanation as to the way people sometimes become criminals. Stated in the words of a famous criminologist, 'When people first come into contact with crime, they abhor it. If they remain in contact with crime for a time, they become accustomed to it and endure it. If they remain in contact with it long enough, they finally embrace it and become influenced by it.' This is the equivalent of saying that any impulse of thought which is repeatedly passed on to the subconscious mind is, finally, accepted and acted upon by the subconscious mind, which proceeds to translate that impulse into its physical equivalent, by the most practical procedure available. In connection with this, consider again the statement: all thoughts which have been emotionalised, (given feeling) and mixed with faith, begin immediately to translate themselves into their physical equivalent or counterpart.

The emotions, or the 'feeling' portion of thoughts, are the factors that give thoughts vitality, life and action. The emotions of faith, love and sex, when mixed with any thought impulse, give it greater action than any of these emotions can do singly. Not only thought impulses which have been mixed with *faith*, but also those that have been mixed with any of the positive emotions, or any of the negative emotions, may reach and influence the subconscious mind. It is clear the subconscious mind will translate into its physical equivalent, a thought impulse of a negative or destructive nature, just as readily as it will act upon thought impulses of a positive or constructive nature. This accounts for the strange phenomenon that so many millions of people experience, referred to as 'misfortune,' or 'bad luck.' There are millions of people who *believe* themselves 'doomed' to poverty and failure, because of some strange force over which they *believe* they have no control. They are the creators of their own 'misfortunes,' because of this negative *belief*, which is picked up by the subconscious mind and translated into its physical equivalent.

This is an appropriate place at which to suggest again that you may benefit, by passing on to your subconscious mind, any *desire* that you wish translated into its physical or monetary equivalent, in a state of expectancy or *belief* that the transformation will actually take place. Your *belief* or *faith*, is the element that determines the action of your subconscious mind. There is nothing to hinder you from 'deceiving' your subconscious mind when giving it instructions through autosuggestion, as I deceived my son's subconscious mind. To make this 'deceit' more realistic, conduct yourself just as you would, if you were *already in possession of the material thing which you are demanding*, when you call upon your subconscious mind. The subconscious mind will transmute into its physical equivalent, by the most direct and practical media available, any order that is given to it in a state of *belief*, or *faith* that the order will be carried out. Surely, enough has been stated to give a starting point from which one may, through experiment and practice, acquire the ability to mix *faith* with any order given to the subconscious mind. Perfection will come through practice. It cannot come by merely reading instructions. If it were true that one may become a criminal by association with crime, (and this is a known fact), it is equally true that one may develop faith by voluntarily suggesting to the subconscious mind that one has faith. The mind comes, finally, to take on the nature of the influences that dominate it. Understand this truth and you will know why it is essential for you to encourage the positive emotions as dominating forces of your mind and discourage and eliminate negative emotions. A mind dominated by positive emotions, becomes a favourable abode for the state of mind known as faith. A mind so dominated may, at will, give the subconscious mind instructions, which it will accept and act upon immediately.

FAITH IS A STATE OF MIND WHICH MAY BE INDUCED BY AUTOSUGGESTION

All through the ages, the religionists have admonished struggling humanity to 'have faith' in this, that and the other dogma or creed, but they have failed to tell people HOW to have faith.

They have not stated that faith is a state of mind and that it may be induced by self-suggestion.

In language which any normal human being can understand, we will describe all that is known about the principle through which *faith* may be developed, where it does not already exist. Have *faith* in yourself; Faith in the Infinite. Before we begin, you should be reminded again that:

Faith is the 'eternal elixir' which gives life, power and action to the impulse of thought!

This sentence is worth reading a second time and a third and a fourth. It is worth reading aloud!

Faith is the starting point of all accumulation of riches!

Faith is the basis of all 'miracles,' and all mysteries that cannot be analysed by the rules of science!

Faith is the only known antidote for *Failure*!

Faith is the element, the 'chemical' which, when mixed with prayer, gives one direct communication with Infinite Intelligence.

Faith is the element that transforms the ordinary vibration of thought, created by the finite mind of man, into the spiritual equivalent.

Faith is the only agency through which the cosmic force of Infinite Intelligence can be harnessed and used.

Every one of the above statements is capable of proof! The proof is simple and easily demonstrated. It is wrapped up in the principle of autosuggestion. Let us center our attention, therefore, upon the subject of self-suggestion and find out what it is and what it is capable of achieving. It is a well-known fact that one comes, finally, to *believe* whatever one repeats to one's self, whether the statement be true or false. If a person repeats a lie over and over, the lie will eventually be accepted as truth. Moreover, it will be *believed* to be the truth. Each of us is what we are, because of the *dominating thoughts* which we permit to occupy our minds. Thoughts which are deliberately placed in our own mind and encouraged with sympathy and with which are mixed any one or more of the emotions, constitute the motivating forces, which direct and control our every movement, act and deed!

Thoughts which are mixed with any of the feelings of emotions, constitute a 'magnetic' force which attracts, from the vibrations of the ether, other similar or related thoughts. A thought when 'magnetised' with emotion may be compared to a seed that, when planted in fertile soil, germinates, grows and multiplies itself over and over again, until that which was originally one small seed, becomes countless millions of seeds of the *same brand*!

The ether is a great cosmic mass of eternal forces of vibration. It is made up of both destructive vibrations and constructive vibrations. It carries, at all times, vibrations of fear, poverty, disease, failure, misery along with vibrations of prosperity, health, success and happiness, just as surely as it carries the sound of hundreds of orchestrations of music and hundreds of human voices, all of which maintain their own individuality and means of identification, through the medium of radio.

From the great storehouse of the ether, the human mind is constantly attracting vibrations that harmonise with whatever *dominates* the human mind. Any thought, idea, plan or purpose, which one holds in one's mind attracts – from the vibrations of the ether – a host of its relatives, adds these 'relatives' to its own force and grows until it becomes the dominating, *motivating master* of the individual in whose mind it has been housed.

Now, let us go back to the starting point and become informed as to how the original seed of an idea, plan or purpose may be planted in the mind. The information is easily conveyed: any idea, plan or purpose may be placed in the mind through repetition of thought. This is why you are asked to write out a statement of your major purpose or *definite chief aim*, commit it to memory and repeat it, in audible words, day after day, until these vibrations of sound have reached your subconscious mind.

We are what we are, because of the vibrations of thought that we pick up and register, through the stimuli of our daily environment. Resolve to throw off the influences of any unfortunate environment and to build your own life to *order*. Taking inventory of mental assets and liabilities, you will discover that your greatest weakness is lack of self-confidence. This handicap can be surmounted and timidity translated into courage, through the aid of the principle of autosuggestion. The application of this principle may be made through a simple arrangement of positive thought impulses stated in writing, memorised and repeated, until they become a part of the working equipment of the subconscious faculty of your mind.

SELF-CONFIDENCE FORMULA

First I know that I have the ability to achieve the object of my definite purpose in life, therefore, I demand of myself persistent, continuous action toward its attainment and I here and now promise to render such action.

Second I realise the dominating thoughts of my mind will eventually reproduce themselves in outward, physical action and gradually transform themselves into physical reality, therefore, I will concentrate my thoughts for thirty minutes daily, upon the task of thinking of the person I intend to become, thereby creating in my mind a clear mental picture of that person.

Third I know through the principle of autosuggestion, any desire that I persistently hold in my mind will eventually seek expression through some practical means of attaining the object back of it; therefore, I will devote ten minutes daily to demanding of myself the development of *self-confidence*.

Fourth I have clearly written down a description of my *definite chief aim* in life and I will never stop trying, until I shall have developed sufficient self-confidence for its attainment.

Fifth I fully realise that no wealth or position can long endure, unless built upon truth and justice, therefore, I will engage in no transaction that does not benefit all whom it affects. I will succeed by attracting to myself the forces I wish to use and the cooperation of other people. I will induce others to serve me, because of my willingness to serve others. I will eliminate hatred, envy, jealousy, selfishness and cynicism by developing love for all humanity. Simply because I know that a negative attitude toward others can never bring me success. I will cause others to believe in me, because I will believe in them and in myself. I will sign my name to this formula, commit it to memory and repeat it aloud once a day, with full *faith* that it will gradually influence my *thoughts* and *actions* so that I will become a self-reliant and successful person. The basis of this formula is a law of Nature that no one has yet been able to explain. It has baffled the scientists of all ages. The psychologists have named this law 'autosuggestion,' and let it go at that. The name by which one calls this law is of little importance. The important fact about it is – it *works* for the glory and success of humankind, *if* it is used constructively. On the other hand, if used destructively, it will destroy just as readily. In this statement may be found a very significant truth, namely; that those who go down in defeat and end their lives in poverty, misery and distress, do so because of negative application of the principle of autosuggestion. The cause may be found in the fact that *all impulses of thought have a tendency to clothe themselves in their physical equivalent*. The subconscious mind, (the chemical laboratory in which all thought impulses are combined and made ready for translation into physical reality), makes no distinction between constructive and destructive thought impulses. It works with the material we feed it, through our thought impulses. The subconscious mind will translate into reality a thought driven by *fear* just as readily as it will translate into reality a thought driven by *courage* or *faith*. The pages of medical history are rich with illustrations of cases of 'suggestive suicide.' A person may commit suicide through negative suggestion, just as effectively as by any other means. In a Midwestern city, a man by the name of Joseph Grant, a bank official, 'borrowed' a large sum of the bank's money, without the consent of the directors. He lost the money through gambling. One afternoon, the Bank Examiner came and began to check the accounts. Grant left the bank, took a room in a local hotel and when they found him, three days later, he was lying in bed, wailing and moaning, repeating over and over these words, 'My God, this will kill me! I cannot stand the disgrace.' In a short time he was dead. The doctors pronounced the case one of 'mental suicide.' Just as electricity will turn the wheels of industry and render useful service if used constructively; or snuff out life if wrongly used, so will the law of autosuggestion lead you to peace and prosperity, or down into the valley of misery, failure and death, according to your degree of understanding and application of it. If you fill your mind with *fear*, doubt and disbelief in your ability to connect with and use the forces of Infinite Intelligence, the law of autosuggestion will take this spirit of unbelief and use it as a pattern by which your subconscious mind will translate it into its physical equivalent. *This statement is as true as the statement that two and two are four!* Like the wind that carries one ship east and another west, the law of autosuggestion will lift you up or pull you down, according to the way you set your sails of thought. Somewhere in your make-up (perhaps in the cells of your brain) there lies sleeping, the seed of achievement that, if aroused and put into action, would carry you to heights, such as you may never have hoped to attain. Just as a master musician may cause the most beautiful strains of music to pour forth from the strings of a violin, so may you arouse the genius which lies asleep in your brain and cause it to drive you upward to whatever goal you may wish to achieve. Abraham Lincoln was a failure at everything he tried, until he was well past the age of forty. He was a Mr Nobody from Nowhere, until a great experience came into his life, aroused the sleeping genius within his heart and brain and gave the world one of its really great men. That 'experience' was mixed with the emotions of sorrow and love. It came to him through Ann Rutledge, the only woman whom he ever truly loved. It is a known fact that the emotion of love is closely akin to the state of mind known as faith. For this reason love comes very near to translating one's thought impulses into their spiritual equivalent. During his work of research, the author discovered, from the analysis of the lifework and achievements of hundreds of men of outstanding accomplishment, that there was the influence of a woman's love behind nearly every one of them. The emotion of love, in the human heart and brain, creates a favourable field of magnetic attraction, which causes an influx of the higher and finer vibrations that are afloat in the ether. Let us consider the power of faith, as it is demonstrated, by a man who is well known to all of civilisation, Mahatma Gandhi, of

India. In this man the world experienced one of the most astounding examples known to civilisation, of the possibilities of faith. Gandhi wielded more potential power than any man living in his time and this, despite the fact that he had none of the orthodox tools of power, such as money, battleships, soldiers and materials of warfare. Gandhi had no money, he had no home, he didn't even own a suit of clothes, but *he did have power*. How did he gain that power? *He created it out of his understanding of the principle of faith, through his ability to transplant that faith into the minds of two hundred million people.* Gandhi accomplished, through the influence of *faith*, what the strongest military power on earth could not and never would accomplish through soldiers and military equipment. He accomplished the astounding feat of influencing two hundred million minds to *coalesce and move in unison, as a single mind*. What other force on earth, except faith could do as much? The watchword of the future will be *human happiness and contentment*. When this state of mind is attained, the production will take care of itself, more effectively than anything that has ever been accomplished where people did not and could not mix faith and individual interest with their labour. Because of the need for faith and cooperation in operating business and industry, it will be both interesting and profitable to analyse an event that provides an excellent understanding of the method by which industrialists and leaders of business accumulate great fortunes, by giving before they try to get. The event chosen for this illustration dates back to 1900, when the United States Steel Corporation was being formed. As you read the story, keep in mind these fundamental facts and you will understand how ideas have been converted into huge fortunes. First, the huge United States Steel Corporation was born in the mind of Charles M Schwab, in the form of an idea he created through his imagination! Second, he mixed faith with his idea. Third, he formulated a plan for the transformation of his idea into physical and financial reality. Fourth, he put his plan into action with his famous speech at the University Club. Fifth, he applied and followed through on his plan with persistence and backed it with firm decision until it had been fully carried out. Sixth, he prepared the way for success by a burning desire for success. If you are one of those who have often wondered how great fortunes are accumulated, this story of the creation of the United States Steel Corporation will be enlightening. If you have any doubt that men can think and grow rich, this story should dispel that doubt, because you can plainly see in the story of the United States Steel, the application of a major portion of the thirteen principles described in this book. John Lowell, in the *New York World Telegram*, with whose courtesy it is here reprinted, dramatically told this astounding description of the power of an idea.

A PRETTY AFTER-DINNER SPEECH FOR A BILLION DOLLARS

'When, on the evening of December 12, 1900, some eighty of the nation's financial nobility gathered in the banquet hall of the University Club on Fifth Avenue to do honour to a young man from out of the West, not half a dozen of the guests realised they were to witness the most significant episode in American industrial history. 'J. Edward Simmons and Charles Stewart Smith, their hearts full of gratitude for the lavish hospitality bestowed on them by Charles M Schwab during a recent visit to Pittsburgh, had arranged the dinner to introduce the thirty-eight-year-old steel man to eastern banking society. But they didn't expect him to stampede the convention. They warned him, in fact, that the bosoms within New York's stuffed shirts would not be responsive to oratory and that, if he didn't want to bore the Stilimans and Harrimans and Vanderbilts, he had better limit himself to fifteen or twenty minutes of polite vaporings and let it go at that.

'Even John Pierpont Morgan, sitting on the right hand of Schwab as became his imperial dignity, intended to grace the banquet table with his presence only briefly. And so far as the press and public were concerned, the whole affair was of so little moment that no mention of it found its way into print the next day.

'So the two hosts and their distinguished guests ate their way through the usual seven or eight courses. There was little conversation and what there was of it, was restrained. Few of the bankers and brokers had met Schwab, whose career had flowered along the banks of the Monongahela and none knew him well. But before the evening was over, they – and with them Money Master Morgan – were to be swept off their feet and a billion dollar baby, the United States Steel Corporation, was to be conceived.
'It is perhaps unfortunate, for the sake of history, that no record of Charlie Schwab's speech at the dinner ever was made. He repeated some parts of it at a later date during a similar meeting of Chicago bankers. And still later, when the government brought suit to dissolve the Steel Trust, he gave his own version, from the witness stand, of the remarks that stimulated Morgan into a frenzy of financial activity. 'It is probable, however, that it was a 'homely' speech, somewhat ungrammatical (for the niceties of language never bothered Schwab), full of epigrams and threaded with wit. But aside from that it had a galvanic force and effect upon the five billion of estimated capital that was represented by the diners. After it was over and the gathering was still under its spell, although Schwab had talked for ninety minutes, Morgan

led the orator to a recessed window where, dangling their legs from the high, uncomfortable seat, they talked for an hour more. 'The magic of the Schwab personality had been turned on, full force, but what was more important and lasting was the full-fledged, clear-cut program he laid down for the aggrandisement of steel. Many other men had tried to interest Morgan in slapping together a steel trust after the pattern of the biscuit, wire and hoop, sugar, rubber, whisky, oil or chewing gum combinations. John W Gates, the gambler, had urged it, but Morgan distrusted him. The Moore boys, Bill and Jim, Chicago stockjobbers who had glued together a match trust and a cracker corporation, had urged it and failed. Elbert H Gary, the sanctimonious country lawyer, wanted to foster it, but he wasn't big enough to be impressive. Until Schwab's eloquence took J P Morgan to the heights from which he could visualise the solid results of the most daring financial undertaking ever conceived, the project was regarded as a delirious dream of easy-money crackpots. 'The financial magnetism that began, a generation ago, to attract thousands of small and sometimes inefficiently managed companies into large and competition-crushing combinations, had become operative in the steel world through the devices of that jovial business pirate, John W Gates. Gates already had formed the American Steel and Wire Company out of a chain of small concerns and together with Morgan had created the Federal Steel Company. The National Tube and American Bridge companies were two more Morgan concerns and the Moore Brothers had forsaken the match and cookie business to form the 'American' group Tin Plate, Steel Hoop, Sheet Steel-and the National Steel Company.

'But by the side of Andrew Carnegie's gigantic vertical trust, a trust owned and operated by fifty-three partners, those other combinations were picayune [of little value]. They might combine to their heart's content but the whole lot of them couldn't make a dent in the Carnegie organisation and Morgan knew it. 'The eccentric old Scot knew it, too. From the magnificent heights of Skibo Castle he had viewed, first with amusement and then with resentment, the attempts of Morgan's smaller companies to cut into his business. When the attempts became too bold, Carnegie's temper was translated into anger and retaliation. He decided to duplicate every mill owned by his rivals. Hitherto, he hadn't been interested in wire, pipe, hoops, or sheet. Instead, he was content to sell such companies the raw steel and let them work it into whatever shape they wanted. Now, with Schwab as his chief and able lieutenant, he planned to drive his enemies to the wall.

'So it was that in the speech of Charles M Schwab, Morgan saw the answer to his problem of combination. A trust without Carnegie – giant of them all – would be no trust at all, a plum pudding, as one writer said, without the plums. Schwab's speech on the night of December 12, 1900, undoubtedly carried the inference, though not the pledge, that the vast Carnegie enterprise could be brought under the Morgan tent. He talked of the world future for steel, of reorganisation for efficiency, of specialisation, of the scrapping of unsuccessful mills and concentration of effort on the flourishing properties, of economies in the ore traffic, of economies in overhead and administrative departments, of capturing foreign markets.

'More than that, he told the buccaneers among them wherein lay the errors of their customary piracy. Their purposes, he inferred, had been to create monopolies, raise prices and pay themselves fat dividends out of privilege. Schwab condemned the system in his heartiest manner. The shortsightedness of such a policy, he told his hearers, [audience] lay in the fact that it restricted the market in an era when everything cried for expansion. By cheapening the cost of steel, he argued, an ever-expanding market would be created; more uses for steel would be devised and a good portion of the world trade could be captured. Actually, though he did not know it, Schwab was an apostle of modern mass production.

'So the dinner at the University Club came to an end. Morgan went home, to think about Schwab's rosy predictions. Schwab went back to Pittsburgh to run the steel business for Andrew Carnegie, while Gary and the rest went back to their stock tickers, to fiddle around in anticipation of the next move.

'It was not long coming. It took Morgan about one week to digest the feast of reason Schwab had placed before him. When he had assured himself that no financial indigestion was to result, he sent for Schwab – and found that young man rather coy. Mr Carnegie, Schwab indicated, might not like it if he found his trusted company president had been flirting with the Emperor of Wall Street, the street upon which Carnegie was resolved never to tread. Then it was suggested by John W Gates the go-between, that if Schwab 'happened' to be in the Bellevue Hotel in Philadelphia, J P Morgan might also 'happen' to be there. When Schwab arrived, however, Morgan was inconveniently ill at his New York home and so, on the elder man's pressing invitation, Schwab went to New York and presented himself at the door of the financier's library.

'Now certain economic historians have professed the belief that from the beginning to the end of the drama, the stage was set by Andrew Carnegie – that the dinner to Schwab, the famous speech, the Sunday night conference between Schwab and the Money King, were events arranged by the canny Scot. The truth is exactly the opposite. When Schwab was called in to consummate the deal, he didn't even know whether 'the little boss,' as Andrew was called, would so much as listen to an offer to sell, particularly to a group of men whom Andrew regarded as being endowed with something less than holiness. But Schwab did take into the conference with him, in his own handwriting, six sheets of figures, representing to his mind the physical worth and the potential earning capacity of every steel company he regarded as an essential star in the new metal firmament.

'Four men pondered over these figures all night. The chief, of course, was Morgan, steadfast in his belief in the Divine Right of Money. With him was his aristocratic partner, Robert Bacon, a scholar and a gentleman. The third was John W Gates whom Morgan scorned as a gambler and used as a tool. The fourth was Schwab, who knew more about the processes of making and selling steel than any whole group of men then living. Throughout that conference, the Pittsburgher's figures were never questioned. If he said a company was worth so much, then it was worth that much and no more. He was insistent, too, upon including in the combination only those concerns he nominated. He had conceived a corporation in which there would be no duplication, not even to satisfy the greed of friends who wanted to unload their companies upon the broad Morgan shoulders. Thus he left out, by design, a number of the larger concerns upon which many of Wall Street had cast hungry eyes. 'When dawn came, Morgan rose and straightened his back. Only one question remained.

'''Do you think you can persuade Andrew Carnegie to sell?' he asked.'

'I can try,' said Schwab.

'If you can get him to sell, I will undertake the matter,' said Morgan.

'So far so good. But would Carnegie sell? How much would he demand? (Schwab thought about $320,000,000). What would he take payment in? Common or preferred stocks? Bonds? Cash?

Nobody could raise a third of a billion dollars in cash.

'There was a golf game in January on the frost cracking heath of the St Andrews links in Westchester, with Andrew bundled up in sweaters against the cold and Charlie talking volubly, as usual, to keep his spirits up. But no word of business was mentioned until the pair sat down in the cozy warmth of the Carnegie cottage. Then, with the same persuasiveness that had hypnotised eighty millionaires at the University Club, Schwab poured out the glittering promises of retirement in comfort, of untold millions to satisfy the old man's social caprices. Carnegie capitulated, wrote a figure on a slip of paper, handed it to Schwab and said, "All right, that's what we'll sell for."

'The figure was approximately $400,000,000 and was reached by taking the $320,000,000 mentioned by Schwab as a basic figure and adding to it $80,000,000 to represent the increased capital value over the previous two years.

'Later, on the deck of a trans-Atlantic liner, the Scotsman said ruefully to Morgan, 'I wish I had asked you for $100,000,000 more.' 'If you had asked for it, you'd have gotten it,' Morgan told him cheerfully.

There was an uproar, of course. A British correspondent cabled that the foreign steel world was 'appalled' by the gigantic combination. President Hadley, of Yale, declared that unless trusts were regulated the country might expect 'an emperor in Washington within the next twenty-five years.' But that able stock manipulator, Keene, went at his work of shoving the new stock at the public so vigorously that all the excess water-estimated by some at nearly $600,000,000 – was absorbed in a twinkling. So Carnegie had his millions and the Morgan syndicate had $62,000,000 for all its 'trouble,' and all the 'boys,' from Gates to Gary, had their millions. 'The thirty-eight-year-old Schwab had his reward. He was made president of the new corporation and remained in control until 1930.' The dramatic story of 'Big Business' which you have just finished was included in this book, because it is a perfect illustration of the method by which desire can be transformed into its physical equivalent! I imagine some readers will question the statement that a mere, intangible desire can be converted into its physical equivalent. Doubtless some will say, 'You cannot convert nothing into something!' The answer is in the story of United States Steel. That giant organisation was created in the mind of one man. The plan by which the organisation was provided with the steel mills that gave it financial stability was created in the mind of the same man. His faith, his desire, his imagination, his persistence were the real ingredients that went into United States Steel. The steel mills and mechanical equipment acquired by the corporation, After it had been brought into legal existence, were incidental, but careful analysis will disclose the fact that the appraised value of the properties acquired by the corporation increased in value by an estimated six hundred million dollars, by the mere transaction which consolidated them under one management. In other words, Charles M Schwab's idea, plus the faith with which he conveyed it to the minds of J P Morgan and the others, was marketed for a profit of approximately $600,000,000. Not an insignificant sum for a single idea! What happened to some of the people who took their share of the millions of dollars of profit made by this transaction, is a matter with which we are not now concerned. The important feature of the astounding achievement is that it serves as unquestionable evidence of the soundness of the philosophy described in this book, because this philosophy was the basis of the entire transaction. Moreover, the practicability of the philosophy has been established by the fact that the United States Steel Corporation prospered and became one of the richest and most powerful corporations in America, employing thousands of people, developing new uses for steel and opening new markets; thus proving that the $600,000,000 in profit which the Schwab idea produced was earned.

Riches begin in the form of thought! Only the person in whose mind the thought is put into motion limits the amount, faith removes limitations! Remember this when you are ready to bargain with *life* for whatever it is that you ask as your price for having passed this way. Remember, also, that the man who created the United States Steel Corporation was practically unknown at the time. He was merely Andrew Carnegie's 'Man Friday' until he gave birth to his famous idea. After that, he quickly rose to a position of power, fame and riches.

FOUR

Autosuggestion: The Medium for Influencing the Subconscious Mind

Autosuggestion is a term that applies to all suggestions and all self-administered stimuli that reach one's mind through the five senses. Stated in another way, autosuggestion is self-suggestion. It is the agency of communication between that part of the mind where conscious thought takes place and that, which serves as the seat of action for the subconscious mind. Through the dominating thoughts which one permits to remain in the conscious mind, (whether these thoughts be negative or positive, is immaterial), the principle of autosuggestion voluntarily reaches the subconscious mind and influences it with these thoughts.

No thought, whether it is negative or positive, can enter the subconscious mind without the aid of the principle of autosuggestion, with the exception of thoughts picked up from the ether. Stated differently, all sense impressions which are perceived through the five senses, are stopped by the conscious thinking mind and may be either passed on to the subconscious mind, or rejected, at will. The conscious faculty serves, therefore, as an outer guard to the approach of the subconscious. Nature has so built us that we have absolute control over the material, which reaches our subconscious mind, through our five senses, although this is not meant to be construed as a statement that we always exercises this control. In the great majority of instances, we do not exercise it, which explains why so many people go through life in poverty. Recall what has been said about the subconscious mind resembling a fertile garden spot, in which weeds will grow in abundance, if the seeds of more desirable crops are not sown – autosuggestion is the agency of control through which an individual may voluntarily feed the subconscious mind on thoughts of a creative nature. By neglect, permit thoughts of a destructive nature to find their way into this rich garden of the mind.

You were instructed, in the last of the six steps described in the chapter on Desire, to read aloud twice daily the written statement of your Desire For Money and to see and feel yourself already in possession of the money! By following these instructions, you communicate the object of your desire directly to your subconscious mind in a spirit of absolute faith. Through repetition of this procedure, you voluntarily create thought habits that are favourable to your efforts to transmute desire into its monetary equivalent. Go back to these six steps described in chapter two and read them again, very carefully, before you proceed further. Then (when you come to it), read very carefully the four instructions for the organisation of your 'Master Mind' group, described in Chapter Seven on Organised Planning. By comparing these two sets of instructions with that which has been stated on autosuggestion, you, of course, will see that the instructions involve the application of the principle of autosuggestion. Remember, therefore, when reading aloud the statement of your desire (through which you are endeavouring to develop a 'money consciousness') that the mere reading of the words is of no consequence – unless you mix emotion or feeling with your words. If you repeat a million times the famous Emil Coué formula, 'Day by day, in every way, I am getting better and better,' without mixing emotion and faith with your words, you will experience no desirable results. Your subconscious mind recognises and acts upon only thoughts that have been well mixed with emotion or feeling. This is a fact of such importance as to warrant repetition in practically every chapter, because the lack of understanding of this is the main reason the majority of people who try to apply the principle of autosuggestion get no desirable results. Plain, unemotional words do not influence the subconscious mind. You will get no appreciable results until you learn to reach your subconscious mind with thoughts or spoken words that have been well emotionalised with belief. Do not become discouraged, if you cannot control and direct your emotions the first time you try to do so. Remember, there is no such possibility as something for nothing. Ability to reach and influence your subconscious mind has its price and you must pay that price. You cannot cheat, even if you desire to do so. The price of ability to influence your subconscious mind is everlasting persistence in applying the principles described here. You cannot develop the desired ability for a lower price. You and you alone, must decide whether or not the reward for which you are striving (the 'money consciousness'), is worth the price you must pay for it in effort. 'Wisdom and 'cleverness.' alone, will not attract and retain money except in a few very rare instances, where the law of averages favours the attraction of money through these sources. The method of attracting money described here does not depend upon the law of averages. Moreover, the method plays no favourites. It will work for one person as effectively as it will for another. Where failure is experienced, it is the individual, not the method, which has failed. If you try and fail, make another effort and still another, until you succeed. Your ability to use the principle of autosuggestion will depend, very largely, upon your capacity to concentrate upon a given desire until that desire becomes a burning obsession.

When you begin to carry out the instructions in connection with the six steps described in the second chapter, it will be necessary for you to make use of the principle of concentration. Let us here offer suggestions for the effective use of concentration. When you begin to carry out the first of the six steps, which instructs you to 'fix in your own mind the exact amount of money you desire,' hold your thoughts on that amount of money by concentration, or fixation of attention, with your eyes closed, until you can actually see the physical appearance of the money. Do this at least once each day. As you go through these exercises, follow the instructions given in the chapter on faith and see yourself actually in possession of the money! Here is a most significant fact – the subconscious mind takes any orders given it in a spirit of absolute faith and acts upon those orders, although the orders often have to be presented over and over again, through repetition, before they are interpreted by the subconscious mind. Following the preceding statement, consider the possibility of playing a perfectly legitimate 'trick' on your subconscious mind, by making it believe, because you believe it, that you must have the amount of money you are visualising, that this money is already awaiting your claim, that the subconscious mind *must* hand over to you practical plans for acquiring the money which is yours. Hand over the thought suggested in the preceding paragraph to your imagination and see what your imagination can, or will do, to create practical plans for the accumulation of money through transmutation of your desire. Do not wait for a definite plan, through which you intend to exchange services or merchandise in return for the money you are visualising, but begin at once to see yourself in possession of the money, demanding and expecting meanwhile, that your subconscious mind will hand over the plan, or plans you need. Be on the alert for these plans and when they appear, put them into action immediately. When the plans appear, they will probably 'flash' into your mind through the sixth sense, in the form of an 'inspiration.' This inspiration may be considered a direct message from Infinite Intelligence. Treat it with respect and act upon it as soon as you receive it. Failure to do this will be fatal to your success. In the fourth of the six steps, you were instructed to 'Create a definite plan for carrying out your desire and begin at once to put this plan into action.' You should follow this instruction in the manner described in the preceding paragraph. Do not trust to your 'reason' when creating your plan for accumulating money through the transformation of desire. Your reason is faulty. Moreover, your reasoning faculty may be lazy. If you depend entirely upon it to serve you, it may disappoint you. When visualising the money you intend to accumulate, (with closed eyes), see yourself rendering the service, or delivering the merchandise you intend to give in return for this money. This is important!

SUMMARY OF INSTRUCTIONS

The fact that you are reading this book is an indication that you earnestly seek knowledge. It is also an indication that you are a student of this subject. If you are only a student, there is a chance that you may learn much that you did not know, but you will learn only by assuming an attitude of humility. If you choose to follow some of the instructions but neglect, or refuse to follow others – you 'will fail! To get satisfactory results, you must follow *all* instructions in a spirit of faith. The instructions given in connection with the six steps in the second chapter will now be summarised and blended with the principles covered by this chapter, as follows:

First. Go into some quiet spot (preferably in bed at night) where you will not be disturbed or interrupted, close your eyes and repeat aloud, (so you may hear your own words) the written statement of the amount of money you intend to accumulate, the time limit for its accumulation and a description of the service or merchandise you intend to give in return for the money. As you carry out these instructions, *see yourself all ready in possession of the money.*

For example suppose that you intend to accumulate $100,000 by the first of January, five years hence, that you intend to give personal services in return for the money, in the capacity of a sales representative. Your written statement of your purpose should be similar to the following:

'By the first day of January (choose your year), I will have in my possession $100,000, which will come to me in various amounts from time to time during the interim. 'In return for this money I will give the most efficient service of which I am capable, rendering the fullest possible quantity and the best possible quality of service as a sales representative of (describe the service or merchandise you intend to sell).

'I believe that I will have this money in my possession. My faith is so strong that I can now see this money before my eyes. I can touch it with my hands. It is now awaiting transfer to me at the time and in the proportion that I deliver the service I intend to render in return for it. I am awaiting a plan by which to accumulate this money and I will follow that plan, when it is received.'

Second Repeat this program night and morning until you can see, (in your imagination) the money you intend to accumulate.

Third Place a written copy of your statement where you can see it night and morning and read it just before retiring and upon arising until it has been memorised. Remember, as you carry out these instructions, that you are applying the principle of autosuggestion, for the purpose of giving orders to your subconscious mind. Remember, also, that your subconscious mind will act only upon instructions that are emotionalised and handed over to it with 'feeling.' Faith is the strongest and most productive of the emotions. Follow the instructions given in the chapter on faith. These instructions may, at first, seem abstract. Do not let this disturb you. Follow the instructions, no matter how abstract or impractical they may, at first, appear to be. The time will soon come, if you do as you have been instructed, in spirit as well as in act, when a whole new universe of power will unfold to you.

Skepticism, in connection with all new ideas, is characteristic of all human beings. But if you follow the instructions outlined, your skepticism will soon be replaced by belief and this, in turn, will soon become crystallised into absolute faith. Then you will have arrived at the point where you may truly say, 'I am the master of my fate, I am the captain of my soul!'

Many philosophers have made the statement, that people have control over their own earthly destinies, but most of them have failed to say why they have control. The reason that one may control one's own earthly status and especially one's financial status, is thoroughly explained in this chapter. People may control themselves and their environment, because they have the power to influence their own subconscious minds and through it, gain the cooperation of Infinite Intelligence. You are now reading the chapter that represents the keystone to the arch of this philosophy. The instructions contained in this chapter must be understood and applied with persistence, if you succeed in transforming desire into money.

The actual performance of transforming desire into money, involves the use of autosuggestion as an agency by which one may reach and influence, the subconscious mind. The other principles are simply tools with which to apply autosuggestion. Keep this thought in mind and you will, at all times, be conscious of the important part the principle of autosuggestion is to play in your efforts to accumulate money through the methods described in this book.

Carry out these instructions as though you were a small child. Inject into your efforts something of the faith of a child. The author has been most careful, to see that no impractical instructions were included, because of his sincere desire to be helpful. After you have read the entire book, come back to this chapter and follow in spirit and in action, this instruction:

Read the entire chapter aloud once every night, that is until you become thoroughly convinced that the principle of autosuggestion is sound, that it will accomplish for you all that has been claimed for it.

Follow the foregoing instruction to the letter and it will open the way for a complete understanding and mastery of the principles of success.

FIVE

Specialised Knowledge: Personal Experiences or Observations

There are two kinds of knowledge. One is general and the other is specialised. General knowledge, no matter how great in quantity or variety it may be, is of but little use in the accumulation of money. The faculties of the great universities possess, in the aggregate, practically every form of general knowledge known to civilisation. They specialise on teaching knowledge, but they do not specialise on the organisation, or the use of knowledge.

Knowledge will not attract money, unless it is organised and intelligently directed, through practical plans of action, to the definite end of accumulation of money. Lack of understanding of this fact has been the source of confusion to millions of people who falsely believe that 'knowledge is power.' it is nothing of the sort! Knowledge is only potential power. It becomes power only when and if, it is organised into definite plans of action and directed to a definite end. This 'missing link' in all systems of education known to civilisation today, may be found in the failure of educational institutions to teach their students how to organise and use knowledge after they acquire it. Many people make the mistake of assuming that, because Henry Ford had but little 'schooling,' he is not a man of 'education.' Those who make this mistake do not know Henry Ford, nor do they understand the real meaning of the word 'educate.' That word is derived from the Latin word 'educo,' meaning to educe, to draw out, to develop from within.

An educated person is not, necessarily, one who has an abundance of general or specialised knowledge. Educated people have developed the faculties of their minds that they may acquire anything they want, or its equivalent, without violating the rights of others. Henry Ford comes well within the meaning of this definition. During the First World War, a Chicago newspaper published certain editorials in which, among other statements, Henry Ford was called 'an ignorant pacifist.' Mr Ford objected to the statements and brought suit against the paper for libeling him. When the suit was tried in the courts, the attorneys for the paper pleaded justification and placed Mr Ford, himself, on the witness stand, for the purpose of proving to the jury that he was ignorant. The attorneys asked Mr Ford a great variety of questions, all of them intended to prove, by his own evidence that, while he might possess considerable specialised knowledge pertaining to the manufacture of automobiles, he was, in the main, ignorant. Mr Ford was plied with such questions as the following:

'Who was Benedict Arnold?' and 'How many soldiers did the British send over to America to put down the Rebellion of 1776?' In answer to the last question, Mr Ford replied, 'I do not know the exact number of soldiers the British sent over, but I have heard that it was a considerably larger number than ever went back.'

Finally, Mr Ford became tired of this line of questioning and in reply to a particularly offensive question, he leaned over, pointed his finger at the lawyer who had asked the question and said, 'If I should really want to answer the foolish question you have just asked, or any of the other questions you have been asking me, let me remind you that I have a row of electric push-buttons on my desk and by pushing the right button, I can summon to my aid people who can answer any question I desire to ask concerning the business to which I am devoting most of my efforts. Now, will you kindly tell me, why I should clutter up my mind with general knowledge, for the purpose of being able to answer questions, when I have people around me who can supply any knowledge I require?'

There certainly was good logic to that reply.

That answer floored the lawyer. Every person in the courtroom realised it was the answer, not of an ignorant man, but of a man of education. Any person is educated who knows where to get knowledge when needed and how to organise that knowledge into definite plans of action. Through the assistance of his 'Master Mind' group, Henry Ford had at his command all the specialised knowledge he needed to enable him to become one of the wealthiest men in America. It was not essential that he have this knowledge in his own mind. Surely no person who has sufficient inclination and intelligence to read a book of this nature can possibly miss the significance of this illustration.

Before you can be sure of your ability to transform desire into its monetary equivalent, you will require specialised knowledge of the service, merchandise, or profession that you intend to offer in return for fortune. Perhaps you may need much more specialised knowledge than you have the ability or the inclination to acquire and if this should be true, you may bridge your weakness through the aid of your 'Master Mind' group.

Andrew Carnegie stated that he, personally, knew nothing

about the technical end of the steel business; moreover, he did not particularly care to know anything about it. The specialised knowledge that he required for the manufacture and marketing of steel, he found available through the individual units of his Master Mind group. The accumulation of great fortunes calls for power. Power is acquired through highly organised and intelligently directed specialised knowledge, but that knowledge does not, necessarily, have to be in the possession of the person who accumulates the fortune. The preceding paragraph should give hope and encouragement to the individual with ambition to accumulate a fortune, who has not possessed him or herself of the necessary 'education' to supply such specialised knowledge as may be required.

People sometimes go through life suffering from 'inferiority complexes,' because they do not have formal education. The person who can organise and direct a 'Master Mind' group of people who possess knowledge useful in the accumulation of money, is just as much an educated person as any one in the group. Remember this, if you suffer from a feeling of inferiority, because your schooling has been limited.

IT PAYS TO KNOW HOW TO PURCHASE KNOWLEDGE

First of all, decide the sort of specialised knowledge you require and the purpose for which it is needed. To a large extent your major purpose in life, the goal toward which you are working, will help determine what knowledge you need. With this question settled, your next move requires that you have accurate information concerning dependable sources of knowledge. The more important of these are:

- One's own experience and education
- Experience and education available through cooperation of others
- Colleges and Universities
- The Internet
- Public Libraries
- Special Training Courses

As knowledge is acquired it must be organised and put into use, for a definite purpose, through practical plans. Knowledge has no value except whatever can be gained from its application toward some worthy end. This is one reason why college degrees are not guarantees of successful careers. If you contemplate taking additional schooling, first determine the purpose for which you want the knowledge you are seeking, then learn where this particular sort of knowledge can be obtained, from reliable sources. Successful people, in all callings, never stop acquiring specialised knowledge related to their major purpose, business, or profession. Those who are not successful usually make the mistake of believing that the knowledge acquiring period ends when one finishes school. The truth is that schooling does but little more than to put one in the way of learning how to acquire practical knowledge. The person who stops studying merely because he has finished school is forever hopelessly doomed to mediocrity, no matter what may be his calling. The way of success is the way of continuous pursuit of knowledge.

SIX

Imagination: The Workshop of the Mind

The imagination is literally the workshop where all plans fashioned by man are created.

The impulse, the desire, is given shape, form and action through the aid of the imaginative faculty of the mind.

It has been said that one can create anything that he can imagine. Of all the ages of civilisation, this is the most favourable for the development of the imagination because it is an age of rapid change. On every hand one may contact stimuli that develop the imagination. Through the aid of his imaginative faculty, humankind has discovered and harnessed, more of Nature's forces during the past fifty years than during the entire history of the human race, previous to that time. We have conquered the air so completely, that the birds are a poor match for us in flying. We have harnessed the ether and made it serve as a means of instantaneous communication with any part of the world. We have analysed and weighed the sun at a distance of millions of miles and have determined, through the aid of imagination, the elements of which it consists. We have discovered that our own brain is both a broadcasting and a receiving station for the vibration of thought. We are beginning now to learn how to make practical use of this discovery. We have increased the speed of locomotion, until we may now travel at a speed of more than six hundred miles an hour. We may breakfast in New York and lunch in San Francisco. Our only limitation, within reason, lies in the development and use of our imagination. We have not yet reached the apex of development in the use of our imaginative faculty. We have merely discovered that we have an imagination and have commenced to use it in a very elementary way.

TWO FORMS OF IMAGINATION

The imaginative faculty functions in two forms. One is known as 'synthetic imagination,' and the other as 'creative imagination.'

Synthetic imagination: Through this faculty, one may arrange old concepts, ideas or plans into new combinations. This faculty creates nothing. It merely works with the material of experience, education and observation with which it is fed. It is the faculty used most by the inventor, with the exception of the 'genius' who draws upon the creative imagination, when he cannot solve his problem through synthetic imagination. Creative imagination: through the faculty of creative imagination, the finite mind of humankind has direct communication with Infinite Intelligence. It is the faculty through which 'hunches' and 'inspirations' are received. It is by this faculty that all basic, or new ideas are developed. It is through this faculty that thought vibrations from the minds of others are received. It is through this faculty that one individual may 'tune in,' or communicate with the subconscious minds of others.

The creative imagination works automatically, in the manner

described in subsequent pages. This faculty functions only when the conscious mind is vibrating at an exceedingly rapid rate, as for example, when the conscious mind is stimulated through the emotion of a strong desire.

The creative faculty becomes more alert, more receptive to vibrations from the sources mentioned, in proportion to its development through *use*. This statement is significant! Ponder over it before passing on.

Keep in mind as you follow these principles that the entire story of how one may convert desire into money cannot be told in one statement. The story will be complete, only when one has mastered, assimilated and begun to make use of all the principles. The great leaders of business, industry, finance and the great artists, musicians, poets and writers became great, because they developed the faculty of creative imagination. Both the synthetic and creative faculties of imagination become more alert with use, just as any muscle or organ of the body develops through use. Desire is only a thought, an impulse. It is nebulous and ephemeral. It is abstract and of no value, until it has been transformed into its physical counterpart. While the synthetic imagination is the one which will be used most frequently, in the process of transforming the impulse of desire into money, you must keep in mind the fact, that you may face circumstances and situations which demand use of the creative imagination as well. Your imaginative faculty may have become weak through inaction. It can be revived and made alert through use. This faculty does not die, though it may become inactive through lack of use. Centre your attention, for the time being, on the development of the synthetic imagination, because this is the faculty that you will use more often in the process of converting desire into money. Transformation of the intangible impulse, of desire, into the tangible reality, of money, calls for the use of a plan or plans. These plans must be formed with the aid of the imagination and mainly, with the synthetic faculty. Read the entire book through, then come back to this chapter and begin at once to put your imagination to work on the building of a plan or plans, for the transformation of your desire into money. Detailed instructions for the building of plans have been given in almost every chapter. Carry out the instructions best suited to your needs. Reduce your plan to writing, if you have not already done so. The moment you complete this, you will have definitely given concrete form to the intangible desire. Read the preceding sentence once more. Read it aloud, very slowly and as you do so, remember that the moment you reduce the statement of your desire a plan for its realisation, into writing, you have actually taken the first of a series of steps that will enable you to convert the thought into reality.

The Earth on which you live, you, yourself and every other material thing are the result of evolutionary change, through which microscopic bits of matter have been organised and arranged in an orderly fashion.

Moreover – this statement is of stupendous importance – this Earth, every one of the billions of individual cells of your body and every atom of matter, *began as an intangible form of energy.*

Desire is a thought impulse! Thought impulses are forms of energy. When you begin with the thought impulse, desire to accumulate money, you are drafting into your service the same 'stuff' that nature used in creating this Earth and every material form in the universe, including the body and brain in which the thought impulses function. As far as science has been able to determine, the entire universe consists of but two elements – matter and energy.

Through the combination of energy and matter, has been created everything perceptible from the largest star that floats in the heavens, down to and including humankind.

You are now engaged in the task of trying to profit by Nature's method. You are (sincerely and earnestly, we hope) trying to adapt yourself to nature's laws by endeavouring to convert desire into its physical and monetary equivalent. You can do it! It has been done before!

You can build a fortune through the aid of laws that are unchangeable. But, first, you must become familiar with these laws and learn to use them. Through repetition and by approaching the description of these principles from every conceivable angle, the author hopes to reveal to you the secret through which great fortunes has been accumulated. Strange and paradoxical as it may seem, the 'secret' is not a secret. Nature, herself, advertises it on the Earth on which we live, the stars, the planets suspended within our view, in the elements above and around us, in every blade of grass and every form of life within our vision. Nature advertises this 'secret' in the terms of biology, in the conversion of a tiny cell, so small that it may be lost on the point of a pin, into the human being now reading this line. The conversion of desire into its physical equivalent is, certainly, no more miraculous!

HOW TO MAKE PRACTICAL USE OF IMAGINATION

Ideas are the beginning points of all fortunes. Ideas are products of the imagination. Let us examine a few well-known ideas that have resulted in huge fortunes. It is hoped that these illustrations will convey definite information concerning the method by which imagination is used to accumulate riches.

THE ENCHANTED KETTLE

Many years ago, an old country doctor drove to town, hitched his horse, quietly slipped into a drug store by the back door and began 'dickering' with the young drug clerk. His mission was destined to yield great wealth to many people. It was destined to bring to the South the most far-flung benefit since the Civil War.

For more than an hour, behind the prescription counter, the old doctor and the clerk talked in low tones. Then the doctor left. He went out to the buggy and brought back a large, old-fashioned kettle, a big wooden paddle (used for stirring the contents of the kettle) and deposited them in the back of the store.

The clerk inspected the kettle, reached into his inside pocket, took out a roll of bills and handed it over to the doctor. The roll contained exactly $500.00 – the clerk's entire savings! The doctor handed over a small slip of paper on which was written a secret formula. The words on that small slip of paper were worth a King's ransom! *But not to the doctor!* Those magic words were needed to start the kettle to boiling, but neither the doctor nor the young clerk knew what fabulous fortunes were destined to flow from that kettle. The old doctor was glad to sell them for five hundred dollars. The money would pay off his debts and give him freedom of mind. The clerk was taking a big chance by staking his entire life's savings on a mere scrap of paper and an old kettle! He never dreamed his investment would start a kettle to overflowing with gold that would surpass the miraculous performance of Aladdin's lamp.

What the clerk really purchased was an *idea*!

The old kettle and the wooden paddle and the secret message on a slip of paper were incidental. The strange performance of that kettle began to take place after the new owner mixed with the secret instructions an ingredient of which the doctor knew nothing. Read this story carefully, give your imagination a test! See if you can discover what it was that the young man added to the secret message, which caused the kettle to overflow with gold. Remember, as you read, that this is not a story from Arabian Nights. Here you have a story of facts, stranger than fiction, facts which began in the form of an idea. Let us take a look at the vast fortunes of gold this idea has produced. It has paid and still pays huge fortunes to men and women all over the world, who distribute the contents of the kettle to millions of people.

The Old Kettle is now one of the world's largest consumers of sugar, thus providing jobs of a permanent nature to thousands of men and women engaged in growing sugar cane and in refining and marketing sugar.

The Old Kettle consumes, annually, millions of glass bottles, providing jobs to huge numbers of glass workers. The Old Kettle gives employment to an army of clerks, copy writers and advertising experts throughout the nation. It has brought fame and fortune to scores of artists who have created magnificent pictures describing the product. The Old Kettle has converted a small Southern city into the business capital of the South, which now benefits, directly or indirectly, every business and practically every resident of the city. The influence of this idea now benefits every civilised country in the world, pouring out a continuous stream of gold to all who touch it.

Gold from the kettle built and maintains one of the most prominent colleges of the South, where thousands of young people receive the training essential for success. The Old Kettle has done other marvelous things.

All through the depression of the 1930s, when factories banks and business houses were folding up and quitting by the thousands, the owner of this Enchanted Kettle went marching on, *giving continuous employment* to an army of men and women all over the world and paying out extra portions of gold to those who, long ago, *had faith in the idea.* If the product of that old brass kettle could talk it would tell thrilling tales of romance in every language: romances of love, romances of business, romances of professional men and women who are daily being stimulated by it.

The author is sure of at least one such romance, for he was a part of it and it all began not far from the very spot on which the drug clerk purchased the old kettle. It was here that the author met his wife and it was she who first told him of the Enchanted Kettle. It was the product of that Kettle they were drinking when he asked her to accept him 'for better or worse.'

Now that you know the content of the Enchanted Kettle is a world famous drink, it is fitting that the author confess that the home city of the drink supplied him with a wife, also that the drink itself provides him with stimulation of thought without intoxication and thereby it serves to give the refreshment of mind which an author must have to do his best work.

Whoever you are, wherever you may live, whatever occupation you may be engaged in, just remember in the future, every time you see the words 'Coca-Cola,' that its vast empire of wealth and influence grew out of a single *idea*. The mysterious ingredient the drug clerk – Asa Candler – mixed with the secret formula was…*imagination*!

Stop and think of that, for a moment. Remember, also, that the thirteen steps to riches, described in this book, were the media through which the influence of Coca-Cola has been extended to every city, town, village and crossroads of the world and that *any idea* you may create, as sound and *meritorious* as Coca-Cola, has the possibility of duplicating the stupendous record of this worldwide thirst-killer. Truly, thoughts are things and their scope of operation is the world, itself.

WHAT I WOULD DO IF I HAD A MILLION DOLLARS

This story proves the truth of that old saying, 'where there's a will, there's a way.' That beloved educator and clergyman, Frank W Gunsaulus, who began his preaching career in the stockyards region of South Chicago, told it to me.

While Dr Gunsaulus was going through college, he observed many defects in our educational system, defects which he believed he could correct, if he were the head of a college. His deepest desire was to become the directing head of an educational institution in which young men and women would be taught to 'learn by doing.'

He made up his mind to organise a new college in which he could carry out his ideas, without being handicapped by orthodox methods of education. He needed a million dollars to put the project across! Where was he to lay his hands on so large a sum of money? That was the question that absorbed most of this ambitious young preacher's thought.

But he couldn't seem to make any progress.

Every night he took that thought to bed with him. He got up with it in the morning. He took it with him everywhere he went. He turned it over and over in his mind until it became a consuming obsession with him. A million dollars is a lot of money. He recognised that fact, but he also recognised the truth that the only limitation is what one sets up in one's own mind. Being a philosopher as well as a preacher, Dr Gunsaulus recognised, as do all who succeed in life, that definiteness of purpose is the starting point where one must begin. He recognised, too, that definiteness of purpose takes on animation, life and power when backed by a burning desire to translate that purpose into its material equivalent.

He knew all these great truths, yet he did not know where or how to lay his hands on a million dollars. The natural procedure would have been to give up and quit, by saying, 'Ah well, my idea is a good one, but I cannot do anything with it, because I never can procure the necessary million dollars.' That is exactly what the majority of people would have said, but it is not what Dr Gunsaulus said. What he said and what he did are so important that I now introduce him and let him speak for himself.

'One Saturday afternoon I sat in my room thinking of ways and means of raising the money to carry out my plans. For nearly two years, I had been thinking, but I had done nothing but think!'

The time had come for action!

'I made up my mind, then and there, that I would get the necessary million dollars within a week. How? I was not concerned about that. The main thing of importance was the decision to get the money within a specified time and I want to tell you that the moment I reached a definite decision to get the money within a specified time, a strange feeling of assurance came over me, such as I had never before experienced. Something inside him seemed to say, 'Why didn't you reach that decision a long time ago? The money was waiting for you all the time!' 'Things began to happen in a hurry. I called the newspapers and announced I would preach a sermon the following morning, entitled, 'What I would do if I had a million dollars.'

'I went to work on the sermon immediately, but I must tell you, frankly, the task was not difficult, because I had been preparing that sermon for almost two years. The spirit behind it was a part of me!

'Long before midnight I had finished writing the sermon. I went to bed and slept with a feeling of confidence, for *I could see myself already in possession of the million dollars.*

The next morning I arose early, went into the bathroom, read the sermon, then knelt on my knees and asked that my sermon might come to the attention of someone who would supply the needed money.

'While I was praying I again had that feeling of assurance that the money would be forthcoming. In my excitement, I walked out without my sermon and did not discover the oversight until I was in my pulpit and about ready to begin delivering it. 'It was too late to go back for my notes and what a blessing that I couldn't go back! Instead, my own subconscious mind yielded the material I needed. When I arose to begin my sermon, I closed my eyes and spoke with all my heart and soul of my dreams. I not only talked to my audience, but I fancy I talked also to God. I told them what I would do with a million dollars if that amount were placed in my hands. I described the plan I had in mind for organising a great educational institution, where young people would learn to do practical things and at the same time develop their minds.

'When I had finished and sat down, a man slowly arose from his seat, about three rows from the rear and made his way toward the pulpit. I wondered what he was going to do. He came into the pulpit, extended his hand and said, 'Reverend, I liked your sermon. I believe you can do everything you said you would, if you had a million dollars. To prove that I believe in you and your sermon, if you will come to my office tomorrow morning, I will give you the million dollars. My name is Phillip D Armour.'

Young Gunsaulus went to Mr Armour's office and the million dollars was presented to him. With the money, he founded the

Armour Institute of Technology. That is more money than the majority of preachers ever see in an entire lifetime, yet the thought impulse behind the money was created in the young preacher's mind in a fraction of a minute. The necessary million dollars came as a result of an idea. Behind the idea was a desire that young Gunsaulus had been nursing in his mind for almost two years. Observe this important fact... *He got the money within thirty-six hours after he reached a definite decision in his own mind to get it and decided upon a definite plan for getting it*! There was nothing new or unique about young Gunsaulus' vague thinking about a million dollars and weakly hoping for it. Others before him and many since his time, have had similar thoughts. But there was something very unique and different about the decision he reached on that memorable Saturday, when he put vagueness into the background and definitely said, 'I will get that money within a week!' God seems to throw Himself on the side of people who know exactly what they want, if they are determined to get just that! Moreover, the principle through which Dr Gunsaulus got his million dollars is still alive! It is available to you! This universal law is as workable today as it was when the young preacher made use of it so successfully. This book describes, step by step, the thirteen elements of this great law and suggests how they may be put to use. Observe that Asa Candler and Dr Frank Gunsaulus had one characteristic in common. Both knew the astounding truth that ideas can be transmuted into cash through the power of definite purpose, plus definite plans. If you are one of those who believe that hard work and honesty, alone, will bring riches, perish the thought! It is not true! Riches, when they come in huge quantities, are never the result of *hard* work! Riches come, if they come at all, in response to definite demands, based upon the application of definite principles and not by chance or luck.

Generally speaking, an idea is an impulse of thought that impels action, by an appeal to the imagination. All master sales reps know that ideas can be sold where merchandise cannot. Ordinary sales reps do not know this – that is why they are 'ordinary.'

There is no standard price on ideas. The creator of ideas makes his own price. If he is smart, gets it. The moving picture industry created a whole flock of millionaires. Most of them were men who couldn't create ideas – but – they had the imagination to recognise ideas when they saw them.

Andrew Carnegie knew very little about making steel – I have Carnegie's own word for this – but he made practical use of two of the principles described in this book and made the steel business yield him a fortune.

The story of practically every great fortune starts with the day when a creator of ideas and a seller of ideas got together and worked in harmony. Carnegie surrounded himself with experts who could do all that he could not do, people who created ideas and men who put ideas into operation and made themselves and the others fabulously rich.

Millions of people go through life hoping for favourable 'breaks.' Perhaps a favourable break can get one an opportunity, but the safest plan is not to depend upon luck. It was a favourable 'break' that gave me the biggest opportunity of my life – but twenty-five years of determined effort had to be devoted to that opportunity before it became an asset. The 'break' consisted of my good fortune in meeting and gaining the cooperation of Andrew Carnegie. On that occasion Carnegie planted in my mind the idea of organising the principles of achievement into a philosophy of success. Thousands of people have profited by the discoveries made in the twenty-five years of research and several fortunes have been accumulated through the application of the philosophy. The beginning was simple. It was an idea that anyone might have developed.

The favourable break came through Carnegie, but what about the *determination, definiteness of purpose* and the *desire to attain the goal and the persistent effort of twenty-five years?* It was no ordinary *desire* that survived disappointment, discouragement, temporary defeat, criticism and the constant reminding of 'waste of time.' It was a *burning desire*! An obsession! When Mr Carnegie first planted the idea in my mind, it was coaxed, nursed and enticed to remain alive. Gradually, the idea became a giant under its own power and it coaxed, nursed and drove me. Ideas are like that. First you give life and action and guidance to ideas and then they take on a power of their own to sweep all else aside.

SEVEN

Organised Planning: The Crystallisation of Desire into Action

You have learned that everything that is created or acquired, begins in the form of desire, that desire is taken on the first lap of its journey, from the abstract to the concrete, into the workshop of the imagination, where plans for its transition are created and organised.

In Chapter Two, you were instructed to take six definite, practical steps, as your first move in translating the desire for money into its monetary equivalent. One of these steps is the formation of a definite, practical plan, or plans, through which this transformation may be made. You will now be instructed how to build plans which will be practical:

1. Form allies yourself with a group of as many people as you may need for the creation and carrying out of your plan, or plans for the accumulation of money-making use of the 'Master Mind' principle described in chapter 10. (Compliance with this instruction is absolutely essential. Do not neglect it.)

2. Before forming your 'Master Mind' alliance, decide what advantages and benefits, you may offer the individual members of your group, in return for their cooperation. No one will work indefinitely without some form of compensation. No intelligent person will either request or expect another to work without adequate compensation, although this may not always be in the form of money.
3. Arrange to meet with the members of your 'Master Mind' group at least twice a week and more often if possible, until you have jointly perfected the necessary plan or plans for the accumulation of money.
4. Maintain perfect harmony between yourself and every member of your 'Master Mind' group. If you fail to carry out this instruction to the letter, you may expect to meet with failure. The 'Master Mind' principle cannot obtain where perfect harmony does not prevail. Keep in mind these facts:
    a. You are engaged in an undertaking of major importance to you. To be sure of success, you must have plans that are faultless.
    b. You must have the advantage of the experience, education, native ability and imagination of other minds. This is in harmony with the methods followed by every person who has accumulated a great fortune.

No individual has sufficient experience, education, native ability and knowledge to insure the accumulation of a great fortune, without the cooperation of other people. Every plan you adopt, in your endeavour to accumulate wealth, should be the joint creation of yourself and every other member of your 'Master Mind' group. You may originate your own plans, either in whole or in part, but see that those plans are checked and approved by the members of your 'master mind' alliance. If the first plan which you adopt does not work successfully, replace it with a new plan, if this new plan fails to work, replace it, in turn with still another and so on, until you find a plan which does work. Right here is the point at which the majority of people meet with failure, because of their lack of persistence in creating new plans to take the place of those which fail.

The most intelligent person living cannot succeed in accumulating money – nor in any other undertaking – without plans that are practical and workable. Just keep this fact in mind and remember when your plans fail, that temporary defeat is not permanent failure. It may only mean that your plans have not been sound. Build other plans. Start all over again.

Thomas A Edison 'failed' ten thousand times before he perfected the incandescent electric light bulb. That is – he met with temporary defeat ten thousand times, before his efforts were crowned with success. Temporary defeat should mean only one thing, the certain knowledge that there is something wrong with your plan. Millions of people go through life in misery and poverty, because they lack a sound plan through which to accumulate a fortune. Henry Ford accumulated a fortune, not because of his superior mind, but because he adopted and followed a *plan* which proved to be sound. A thousand people could be pointed out, with a better education than Ford's, yet they live in poverty, because they do not possess the *right* plan for the accumulation of money.

James J Hill met with temporary defeat when he first endeavoured to raise the necessary capital to build a railroad from the East to the West, but he turned defeat into victory through new plans.

We see people who have accumulated great fortunes, but we

often recognise only their triumph, overlooking the temporary defeats that they had to surmount before 'arriving.' *no follower of this philosophy can reasonably expect to accumulate a fortune without experiencing 'temporary defeat.'* When defeat comes, accept it as a signal that your plans are not sound, rebuild those plans and set sail once more toward your coveted goal. If you give up before your goal has been reached, you are a 'quitter.'

A QUITTER NEVER WINS – AND – A WINNER NEVER QUITS.

Lift this sentence out, write it on a piece of paper in letters an inch high and place it where you will see it every night before you go to sleep and every morning before you go to work. When you begin to select members for your 'Master Mind' group, endeavour to select those who do not take defeat seriously. Some people foolishly believe that only money can make money. This is not true! *Desire*, transformed into its monetary equivalent, through the principles laid down here, is the agency through which money is 'made.' Money, of itself, is nothing but inert matter. It cannot move, think or talk, but it can 'hear' when one who *desires* it, calls it to come!

PLANNING THE SALE OF SERVICES

The remainder of this chapter has been given over to a description of ways and means of marketing personal services. The information here conveyed will be of practical help to any person having any form of personal services to market, but it will be of priceless benefit to those who aspire to leadership in their chosen occupations.

Intelligent planning is essential for success in any undertaking designed to accumulate riches. Here will be found detailed instructions to those who must begin the accumulation of riches by selling personal services.

It should be encouraging to know that practically all the great fortunes began in the form of compensation for personal services or from the sale of ideas. What else, except ideas and personal services, would one not possessed of property have to give in return for riches?

Broadly speaking, there are two types of people in the world. One type is known as *leaders* and the other as *followers*. Decide at the outset whether you intend to become a leader in your chosen calling, or remain a follower. The difference in compensation is vast. The follower cannot reasonably expect the compensation to which a leader is entitled, although many followers make the mistake of expecting such pay. It is no disgrace to be a follower. On the other hand, it is no credit to remain a follower. Most great leaders began in the capacity of followers. They became great leaders because they were *Intelligent Followers*. With few exceptions, people who cannot follow a leader intelligently cannot become efficient leaders. People, who can follow a leader most efficiently, are usually those who develop into leaders most rapidly. An intelligent follower has many advantages, among them the opportunity to acquire knowledge from the leader.

THE MAJOR ATTRIBUTES OF LEADERSHIP

The following are important factors of leadership:

1. *Unwavering courage* based upon knowledge of self and of one's occupation. No follower wishes to be dominated by a leader who lacks self-confidence and courage. Such a leader very long will dominate no intelligent follower.

2. *Self-control* People, who cannot control themselves, can never control others. Self-control sets a mighty example for one's followers, which the more intelligent will emulate.
3. *A keen sense of justice* Without a sense of fairness and justice, no leader can command and retain the respect of his or her followers.
4. *Decision-maker* People who waver in decisions, shows that they are not sur of themselves. They cannot led others successfully.
5. *Planner* The successful leader must plan the work, also work the plan. A leader, who moves by guesswork, without practical, definite plans, is comparable to a ship without a rudder. Sooner or later it will land on the rocks
6. *The habit of doing more than paid for*. One of the penalties of leadership is the necessity of willingness of the leaders, to do more than they require from followers.
7. *A pleasing personality* No slovenly, careless person can become a successful leader. Leadership calls for respect. Followers will not respect leaders who do not grade high on all of the factors of a pleasing personality.
8. *Sympathy and understanding* Successful leaders must be in sympathy with their followers. Moreover, they must understand them and their problems.
9. *Mastery of detail* Successful leadership calls for mastery of details of the leader's position.
10. *Willingness to assume full responsibility* Successful leaders must be willing to assume responsibility for the mistakes and the shortcomings of their followers. If they try to shift this responsibility, they will not remain leaders. If followers make mistakes and become incompetent, it is the leader who has failed.

11. *Cooperation* Successful leaders must understand and apply the principle of cooperative effort and be able to induce followers to do the same. Leadership calls for power, which calls for cooperation.

There are two forms of leadership. The first, by far the most effective, is 'leadership by consent' with the sympathy of the followers. The second is 'leadership by force', without the consent and sympathy of the followers. History is filled with evidence that leadership by force cannot endure. The downfall and disappearance of 'dictators' and kings is significant. It means that people will not follow forced leadership indefinitely.

The world has entered a new era of relationship between leaders and followers, which very clearly call for new leaders and a new brand of leadership in business and industry. Those who belong to the old school of leadership-by-force must acquire an understanding of the new brand of leadership (cooperation) or be relegated to the rank and file of the followers. There is no other way out for them.

The relationship of employer and employee or of leader and follower, in the future, will be one of mutual cooperation, based upon an equitable division of the profits of business. In the future, the relationship of employer and employee will be more like a partnership than it has been in the past. Hitler, Stalin and Saddam Hussein are examples of leadership by force. Their leadership passed. Without much difficulty, one might point to the prototypes of these ex-leaders, among the business, financial and labour leaders of America who have been dethroned or slated to go. *Leadership-by-consent* of the followers is the only brand that can endure!

People may follow the forced leadership temporarily, but

they will not do so willingly. The new brand of *leadership* will embrace the eleven factors of leadership, described in this chapter, as well as some other factors. People, who make these the basis of his leadership, will find abundant opportunity to lead in any walk of life.

THE 10 MAJOR CAUSES OF FAILURE IN LEADERSHIP

We come now to the major faults of leaders who fail, because it is just as essential to know what not to do, as it is to know what to do.

1. *Inability to organise details* Efficient leadership calls for ability to organise and to master details. No genuine leader is ever 'too busy' to do anything which may be required as a leader. Whether a leader or follower is 'too busy' to change plans, or to give attention to any emergency, it is an indication of inefficiency. The successful leader must be the master of all details connected with the position. That means, of course, that the habit of relegating details to capable lieutenants must be acquired.
2. *Unwillingness to render humble service* Truly great leaders are willing, when occasion demands, to perform any sort of labour that they would ask another to perform. 'The greatest among ye shall be the servant of all' is a truth that all able leaders observe and respect.
3. *Expectation of pay for what they 'know' instead of what they do with they know*. The world does not pay for what people 'know.' It pays them for what they do or induce others to do.
4. *Fear of competition from followers* The leader who fears that one of his followers may take his position is practically

sure to realise that fear sooner or later. Able leaders train understudies to whom they may delegate, at will. Only in this way may leaders multiply themselves and prepare to be at many places and give attention to many things at one time. It is an eternal truth that people receive more pay for their ability to get others to perform, than they could possibly earn by their own efforts. Efficient leaders may, through knowledge of their jobs and the magnetism of their personalities, greatly increase the efficiency of others and induce them to render more service and better service than they could render without by themselves.

5. *Lack of imagination* Without imagination, leaders are incapable of meeting emergencies and of creating plans by which to guide followers efficiently.
6. *Selfishness* Leaders who claim all the honour for the work of their followers are sure to be met by resentment. Really great leaders claim none of the honours. They are contented to see the honours, when there are any, go to their followers, because they know that most people will work harder for commendation and recognition than they will for money alone.
7. *Intemperance* Followers do not respect an intemperate leader. Moreover, intemperance in any of its various forms destroys the endurance and the vitality of all who indulge in it.
8. *Disloyalty* Perhaps this should have come at the head of the list. Leaders who are not loyal to their trust and to their associates – those above and below them, cannot long maintain their leadership. Disloyalty marks one as being less than the dust of the earth and brings down on one's head the contempt they deserve. Lack of loyalty is one of the major causes of failure in every walk of life.

9. *Emphasis of the 'authority' of leadership* Efficient leaders lead by encouraging and not by trying to instill fear in the hearts of their followers. Leaders who try to impress followers with their 'authority' come within the category of leadership through *force. Real leaders*, have no need to advertise that fact except by their conduct, sympathy, understanding, fairness and a demonstration of knowledge of the job.
10. *Emphasis of title* Competent leaders require no 'title' to gain the respect of their followers. Leaders who make too much over the title generally have little else to emphasise. The doors to the office of real leaders are open to all who wish to enter. Their working quarters are free from formality or ostentation.

These are among the more common of the causes of failure in leadership. Any one of these faults is sufficient to induce failure. Study the list carefully if you aspire to leadership and make sure that you are free of these faults.

SOME FERTILE FIELDS IN WHICH 'NEW LEADERSHIP' WILL BE REQUIRED

Before leaving this chapter, your attention is called to a few of the fertile fields in which there has been a decline of leadership and in which the new type of leader may find an abundance of opportunity.

First, in the field of politics there is a most insistent demand for new leaders; a demand that indicates nothing less than an emergency. Too many politicians have, seemingly, become high-grade, legalised racketeers. They have increased taxes and debauched the machinery of industry and business until the people can no longer stand the burden.

Second, the financial business is undergoing a reform. The leaders in this field have almost entirely lost the confidence of the public. Already financial executives have sensed the need of reform. They have begun it.

Third, industry calls for new leaders. The old type of leaders thought and moved in terms of dividends instead of thinking and moving in terms of human equations! The Future leaders in industry, to endure, must regard himself as a quasi-public official whose duty it is to manage their trust in such a way that it will work hardship on no individual or group of individuals. Exploitation of workers is a thing of the past. Let those who aspire to leadership in the field of business, industry and labour remember this.

Fourth, religious leaders of the future will be forced to give more attention to the temporal needs of their followers, in the solution of their economic and personal problems of the present with less attention to the dead past as also the yet unborn future.

Fifth, in the professions of law, medicine and education, a new brand of leadership and to some extent, new leaders will become a necessity. This is especially true in the field of education. Leaders in that field must, in the future, find ways and means of teaching people how to apply the knowledge they receive in school. They must deal more with practice and less with theory.

Sixth, new leaders will be required in the field of journalism. The media of the future, to be conducted successfully, must be divorced from 'special privilege' and relieved from the subsidy of advertising.

These are but a few of the fields where opportunities for new leaders and a new brand of leadership are now available. The world is undergoing a rapid change. This means that the media, from where changes in human habits are promoted, must be adapted to the changes. The media here described, are the ones that, more than any others, determine the trend of civilisation.

HOW TO GET THE EXACT POSITION YOU DESIRE

Everyone enjoys doing the kind of work for which he or she is best suited. An artist loves to work with paints, mechanics with their hands, a writer loves to write. Those with less definite talents have their preferences for certain fields of business and industry. If America does anything well, it offers a full range of occupations, tilling the soil, manufacturing, marketing, as well as the full gambit of professions.

First Decide *exactly* what kind of a job you want. If the job doesn't already exist, perhaps you can create it.

Second Choose the company or individual for whom you wish to work.

Third Study your prospective employer as to policies, personnel and chances of advancement.

Fourth By analysis of yourself, your talents and capabilities, figure *what you can offer.* Plan ways and means of giving advantages, services, developments, along with ideas that you believe you can successfully deliver.

Fifth Forget about 'a job.' Forget whether or not there is an opening. Forget the usual routine of 'have you got a job for me?' Concentrate on what you can give.

Sixth Once you have your plan in mind, arrange with an experienced writer to help you put it on paper in neat form, with full detail.

Seventh Present it to the proper person with authority to make the decision. Every company is looking for people who can give something of value, whether it is ideas, services or 'connections.' Every company has room for the person who has a definite plan of action that brings value addition to the business of the organisation.

This procedure may take a few days or weeks of extra time, but the difference in income, in advancement recognition will save years of hard work at a low pay. It has many advantages, the main one being that it will often save from one to five years of time in reaching a chosen goal.

Every person who starts or 'gets in' half way up the ladder, does so by deliberate and careful planning, (excepting, of course, the Boss' son).

THE NEW WAY OF MARKETING SERVICES

'Jobs' Are Now 'Partnerships'

Men and women, who market their services to the best advantage in the future, must recognise the stupendous change that has taken place in connection with the relationship between employer and employee.

The time will come when the 'Golden Rule,' and not the 'Rule of Gold' will be the dominating factor in the marketing of merchandise as well as personal services. The future relationship between employers and their employees will be more in the nature of a partnership consisting of:

a. The employer
b. The employee
c. The public they serve

This new way of marketing personal services is called new for many reasons, first, both the employer and the employee of the future will be considered as fellow-employees whose business it will be to serve the public efficiently. Earlier employers and employees have bartered among themselves, driving the best bargains they could with one another. They did not consider that the final analysis they were, in reality, *bargaining at the expense of the third party: the public they served.* In the future both employers and employees will recognise that they are *no longer privileged to drive bargains at the expense of those whom they serve.* The real employer of the future will be the public. Every person seeking to market personal services effectively should keep this uppermost in mind.

'Courtesy' and 'Service' are the watchwords of merchandising today and apply to the person who is marketing personal services even more directly than to the employer whom he serves, because, in the final analysis, both the employer and his employee are employed by the public they serve. If they fail to serve well, they pay by the loss of their privilege to serve.

WHAT IS YOUR 'QQS' RATING?

The causes of success in marketing services effectively and permanently, have been clearly described. Unless those causes are studied, analysed, understood and applied, no one can market one's services effectively and permanently. It is up to you to sell your own personal services. The quality and the quantity of service rendered and the spirit in which it is rendered, determine to a large extent, the price and the duration of employment. To market personal services effectively, (which means a permanent market, at a satisfactory price, under pleasant conditions), one must adopt and follow the 'QQS' formula which means that quality, plus quantity, plus the proper spirit of cooperation, equals perfect marketing of service. Remember the 'QQS' formula, but do more – *apply it as a habit!*

Let us analyse the formula to make sure we understand exactly what it means.

1. Quality of service shall be construed to mean the performance of every detail, in connection with your position, in the most efficient manner possible, with the object of greater efficiency always in mind.
2. Quantity of service shall be understood to mean the *habit* of rendering all the service of which you are capable, at all times, with the purpose of increasing the amount of service rendered as greater skill is developed through practice and experience. Emphasis is again placed on the word habit.
3. Spirit of service shall be construed to mean the habit of agreeable, harmonious conduct that will induce cooperation from associates and fellow employees.

Adequacy of quality and quantity of service is not sufficient to maintain a permanent market for your services. The conduct or the spirit in which you deliver service, is a strong determining factor in connection with both the price you receive and the duration of employment. Andrew Carnegie stressed this point more than others in connection with his description of the factors that lead to success in the marketing of personal services. He emphasised again and again, the necessity for harmonious conduct. He stressed the fact that he would not retain any person, no matter how great a quantity, or how efficient the quality of his or her work, unless that person worked in a spirit of harmony. Mr Carnegie insisted upon everybody being agreeable. To prove that he placed a high value upon this quality, he permitted many people who conformed to his standards to become very wealthy. Those who did not conform had to make room for others. The importance of a pleasing personality has been stressed, because it is a factor that enables one to render service in the proper spirit. If one has a personality which pleases and renders service in a spirit of harmony, these assets often make up for deficiencies in both the quality and the quantity of service one renders. Nothing, however, can be successfully substituted for pleasing conduct.

THE CAPITAL VALUE OF YOUR SERVICES

The person whose income is derived entirely from the sale of personal services is no less than a merchant who sells commodities and it might well be added, such a person is subject to exactly the same rules of conduct as the merchant who sells merchandise.

This has been emphasised, because the majority of people who live by the sale of personal services make the mistake of considering themselves free from the rules of conduct and the responsibilities attached to those who are engaged in marketing commodities.

The new way of marketing services has practically forced both employer and employee into partnership alliances, through which both take into consideration the rights of the third party, *the public they serve*. The day of the 'go-getter' has been supplanted by the 'go-giver.' High-pressure methods in business finally blew the lid off. There will never be the need to put the lid back on, because, in the future, business will be conducted by methods that will require no pressure.

The actual capital value of your brains may be determined by the amount of income you can produce (by marketing your services). Multiplying your annual income by sixteen and two-thirds may make a fair estimate of the capital value of your services, as it is reasonable to estimate that your annual income represents six percent of your capital value. Money rents for 6% per annum. Money is worth no more than brains. It is often worth much less.

Competent 'brains,' if effectively marketed, represent a much more desirable form of capital than that which is required to conduct a business dealing in commodities, because 'brains' are a form of capital which cannot be permanently depreciated through depressions, nor can this form of capital be stolen or spent. Moreover, the money that is essential for the conduct of business is as worthless as a sand dune, until it has been mixed with efficient 'brains.'

THE THIRTY MAJOR CAUSES OF FAILURE

How Many of These Are Holding You Back?

Life's greatest tragedy consists of men and women who earnestly try and fail! The tragedy lies in the overwhelmingly large majority of people who fail, as compared to the few who succeed.

I have had the privilege of analysing several thousand men and women, 98% of whom were classed as 'failures.' There is something radically wrong with a civilisation and a system of education, which permit 98% of the people to go through life as failures. But I did not write this book for the purpose of moralising on the rights and wrongs of the world; that would require a book a hundred times the size of this one.

My analysis work proved that there are thirty major reasons for failure and thirteen major principles through which people accumulate fortunes. In this chapter, a description of the thirty major causes of failure will be given. As you go over the list, check yourself by it, point by point, for the purpose of discovering how many of these causes of failure stand between you and success.

1. *Unfavourable hereditary background* There is but little, if anything, which can be done for people who are born with a deficiency in brainpower. This philosophy offers but one method of bridging this weakness – through the aid of the Master Mind. Observe with profit, however, that this is the *only* one of the thirty causes of failure that may not be easily corrected by any individual.
2. *Lack of a well-defined purpose in life* There is no hope of success for the person who does not have a central purpose, or definite goal at which to aim. Ninety-eight out of every hundred of those whom I have analysed, had no such aim. Perhaps this was the major cause of their failure.
3. *Lack of ambition to aim above mediocrity* We offer no hope for the person who is so indifferent as not to want to get ahead in life and who is not willing to pay the price.
4. *Insufficient education* This is a handicap that may be overcome with comparative ease. Experience has proven that the best-educated people are often those who are known as 'self-made,' or self-educated. It takes more than a college degree to make one a person of education. Any person who is educated is one who has learned to get whatever he or she wants in life without violating the rights of others. Education consists, not so much of knowledge, but of knowledge effectively and persistently applied. People are paid, not merely for what they know, but more particularly for what they do with what they know.
5. *Lack of self-discipline* Discipline comes through self-control. This means that one must control all negative qualities. Before

you can control conditions, you must first control yourself. Self-mastery is the hardest job you will ever tackle. If you do not conquer self, self will conquer you. You may see at one and the same time both your best friend and your greatest enemy, by stepping in front of a mirror.

6. *Ill health* No person may enjoy outstanding success without good health. Many of the causes of ill health are subject to mastery and control. These, in the main are:
    a. Overeating of foods not conducive to health
    b. Wrong habits of thought; giving expression to negatives
    c. Wrong use of and over indulgence in sex
    d. Lack of proper physical exercise
    e. An inadequate supply of fresh air, due to improper breathing
7. *Unfavourable environmental influences during childhood* 'As the twig is bent, so shall the tree grow.' Most people who have criminal tendencies acquire them as the result of bad environment and improper associates during childhood.
8. *Procrastination* This is one of the most common causes of failure. 'Old Man Procrastination' stands within the shadow of all people, awaiting an opportunity to spoil their chances of success. Most of us go through life as failures, because we are waiting for the 'time to be right' to start doing something worthwhile. Do not wait. The time will never be 'just right.' Start where you stand and work with whatever tools you may have at your command and better tools will be found as you go along.
9. *Lack of persistence* Most of us are good 'starters' but poor 'finishers' of everything we begin. Moreover, people are prone to give up at the first signs of defeat. There is no substitute for persistence. The persistent person, discovers that 'Old

Man Failure' finally becomes tired and goes away. Failure cannot cope with persistence.

10. *Negative personality* There is no hope of success for the person who repels people through a negative personality. Success comes through the application of power and power is attained through the cooperative efforts of other people. A negative personality will not induce cooperation.
11. *Lack of controlled sexual urge* Sex energy is the most powerful of all the stimuli that move people into action. Because it is the most powerful of the emotions, it must be controlled, through transformation and converted into other channels.
12. *Uncontrolled desire for 'something for nothing'* The gambling instinct drives millions of people to failure. Evidence of this may be found in a study of the dot.com fiasco of the early 2000s, during which millions of people tried to make money by investing in fly-by-night companies.
13. *Lack of a well defined power of decision* People who succeed reach decisions promptly and change them, if at all, very slowly. People who fail, reach decisions, if at all, very slowly and change them frequently and quickly. Indecision and procrastination are twins. Where one is found, the other may usually be found also. Kill off this pair before they completely tie you to the treadmill of failure.
14. *One or more of the six basic fears* These fears have been analysed for you in chapter 15. They must be mastered before you can market your services effectively.
15. *Wrong selection of a mate in marriage* This a most common cause of failure. The relationship of marriage brings people intimately into contact. Unless this relationship is harmonious, failure is likely to follow. Moreover, it will be a form of failure

that is marked by misery and unhappiness, destroying all signs of ambition.

16. *Over-caution* The person, who takes no chances, generally has to take whatever is left when others are through choosing. Over-caution is as bad as under-caution. Both are extremes to be guarded against. Life itself is filled with the element of chance.
17. *Wrong selection of associates in business* This is one of the most common causes of failure in business. In marketing personal services, one should use great care to select an employer who will be an inspiration and who is intelligent and successful. We emulate those with whom we associate most closely. Pick an employer who is worth emulating.
18. *Superstition and prejudice* Superstition is a form of fear. It is also a sign of ignorance. People who succeed keep open minds and are afraid of nothing.
19. *Wrong selection of a vocation* No one can succeed in a line of endeavour which he or she does not like. The most essential step in the marketing of personal services is that of selecting an occupation into which you can throw yourself wholeheartedly.
20. *Lack of concentration of effort* The 'jack-of-all-trades' seldom is good at any. Concentrate all of your efforts on one definite chief aim.
21. *The habit of indiscriminate spending* Spendthrifts cannot succeed, mainly because they stand eternally in fear of poverty. Form the habit of systematic saving by putting aside a definite percentage of your income. Money in the bank gives one a very safe foundation of courage when bargaining for the sale of personal services. Without money, one must take what one is offered and be glad to get it.

22. *Lack of enthusiasm* Without enthusiasm one cannot be convincing. Moreover, enthusiasm is contagious and the person, who has it, under control, is generally welcome in any group of people.
23. *Intolerance* The person with a 'closed' mind on any subject seldom gets ahead. Intolerance means that one has stopped acquiring knowledge. The most damaging forms of intolerance are those connected with religious, racial and political differences of opinion.
24. *Intemperance* The most damaging forms of intemperance are connected with eating, strong drink and sexual activities. Overindulgence in any of these is fatal to success.
25. *Inability to cooperate with others* More people lose their positions and their big opportunities in life, because of this fault, than for all other reasons combined. It is a fault which no well-informed business executive or leader will tolerate.
26. *Possession of power that was not acquired through self-effort* (Sons and daughters of wealthy families and others who inherit money that they did not earn). Power in the hands of one who did not acquire it gradually is often fatal to success. Quick riches are more dangerous than poverty.
27. *Intentional dishonesty* There is no substitute for honesty. One may be temporarily dishonest by force of circumstances over which one has no control, without permanent damage. But, there is no hope for people who are dishonest by choice. Sooner or later, their deeds will catch up with him and they will pay by loss of reputation and perhaps even loss of liberty.
28. *Egotism and vanity* These qualities serve as red lights that warn others to keep away. They are fatal to success.
29. *Guessing instead of thinking* Most people are too indifferent or lazy to acquire facts with which to think accurately. They

prefer to act on 'opinions' created by guesswork or snap-judgements.

30. *Lack of capital* This is a common cause of failure among those who start out in business for the first time, without sufficient reserve of capital to absorb the shock of their mistakes and to carry them over until they have established a reputation.
31. Under this, name any particular cause of failure from which you have suffered that has not been included in the foregoing list.

In these thirty major causes of failure is found a description of the tragedy of life, which obtains for practically every person who tries and fails. It will be helpful if you can induce someone who knows you well to go over this list with you and help to analyse you by the thirty causes of failure. It may be beneficial if you try this alone. Most people cannot see themselves as others see them. You may be one who cannot. The oldest of admonitions is 'Know thyself!' If you market merchandise successfully, you must know the merchandise. The same is true in marketing personal services. You should know all of your weaknesses in order that you may either bridge them or eliminate them entirely. You should know your strength in order that you may call attention to it when selling your services. You can know yourself only through accurate analysis.

Before you even start to negotiate for a readjustment of your salary in your present position or to seek employment elsewhere, be sure that you are worth more than you now receive.

It is one thing to want money – everyone wants more – but it is something entirely different to be worth more! Many people mistake their wants for their just dues. Your financial requirements or wants have nothing whatever to do with your worth. Your value is established entirely by your ability to render useful service or your capacity to induce others to render such service.

TAKE INVENTORY OF YOURSELF

28 Questions You Should Answer

Annual self-analysis is an essential in the effective marketing of personal services, as is annual inventory in merchandising. Moreover, the yearly analysis should disclose a *decrease in faults* and an *increase in virtues*. One goes ahead, stands still, or goes backward in life. One's object should be, of course, to go ahead. Annual self-analysis will disclose whether advancement has been made and if so, how much. It will also disclose any backward steps one may have made. The effective marketing of personal services requires one to move forward even if the progress is slow.

Your annual self-analysis should be made at the end of each year, so you can include in your New Year's Resolutions any improvements that the analysis indicates should be made. Take this inventory by asking yourself the following questions and by checking your answers with the aid of someone who will not permit you to deceive yourself as to their accuracy.

SELF-ANALYSIS QUESTIONNAIRE FOR PERSONAL INVENTORY

1. Have I attained the *goal* that I established as my objective for this year? (You should work with a definite yearly objective to be attained as a part of your major life objective).
2. Have I delivered service of the best possible *quality* of which I was capable or could I have improved any part of this service?

3. Have I delivered service in the greatest possible quantity of which I was capable?
4. Has the spirit of my conduct been harmonious and cooperative at all times?
5. Have I permitted the habit of procrastination to decrease my efficiency and if so, to what extent?
6. Have I improved my personality and if so, in what ways?
7. Have I been persistent in following my plans through to completion?
8. Have I reached decisions promptly and definitely on all occasions?
9. Have I permitted any one or more of the six basic fears to decrease my efficiency?
10. Have I been either 'over-cautious,' or 'under-cautious?'
11. Has my relationship with my associates in work been pleasant, or unpleasant? If it has been unpleasant, has the fault been partly or wholly mine?
12. Have I dissipated any of my energy through lack of concentration of effort?
13. Have I been open minded and tolerant in connection with all subjects?
14. In what way have I improved my ability to render service?
15. Have I been intemperate in any of my habits?
16. Have I expressed, either openly or secretly, any form of egotism?
17. Has my conduct toward my associates been such that it has induced them to respect me?
18. Have my opinions and decisions been based upon guesswork, or accuracy of analysis and thought?
19. Have I followed the habit of budgeting my time, my expenses and my income and have I been conservative in these budgets?

20. How much time have I devoted to unprofitable effort which I might have used to better advantage?
21. How may I re-budget my time and change my habits so I will be more efficient during the coming year?
22. Have I been guilty of any conduct that was not approved by my conscience?
23. In what ways have I rendered more service and better service than I was paid to render?
24. Have I been unfair to anyone and if so, in what way?
25. If I had been the purchaser of my own services for the year, would I be satisfied with my purchase?
26. Am I in the right vocation and if not, why not?
27. Has the purchaser of my services been satisfied with the service I have rendered and if not, why not?
28. What is my present rating on the fundamental principles of success? (Make this rating fairly and frankly and have it checked by someone who is courageous enough to do it accurately).

Having read and assimilated the information conveyed through this chapter, you are now ready to create a practical plan for marketing your personal services. An adequate description of every principle essential in planning the sale of personal services, including the major attributes of leadership; the most common causes of failure in leadership; a description of the fields of opportunity for leadership; the main causes of failure in all walks of life and the important questions, which should be used in self-analysis are given here.

This extensive and detailed presentation of accurate information has been included, because all who must begin the accumulation of riches by marketing personal services will need it. Those who have lost their fortunes and those who are just beginning to earn money, have nothing but personal services to offer in return for riches, therefore it is essential that they have available the practical information needed to market services to best advantage.

The information contained in this chapter will be of great value to all who aspire to attain leadership in any calling. It will be particularly helpful to those aiming to market their services as business or industrial executives.

Complete assimilation and understanding of the information here conveyed will be helpful in marketing one's own services and it will also help one to become more analytical and capable of judging people. The information will be priceless to personnel directors, employment managers and other executives charged with the selection of employees and the maintenance of efficient organisations. If you doubt this statement, test its soundness by answering in writing the twenty-eight self-analysis questions. That might be both interesting and profitable, even though you do not doubt the soundness of the statement.

WHERE AND HOW ONE MAY FIND OPPORTUNITIES TO ACCUMULATE RICHES

Now that we have analysed the principles by which riches may be accumulated, we naturally ask, 'where may one find favourable opportunities to apply these principles?' Very well, let us take an inventory to see what the USA offers the person seeking riches, great or small. To begin with, let us remember, all of us, that we live in a country where every law-abiding citizen enjoys freedom of thought and freedom of deed unequaled anywhere in the world. Most of us have never taken inventory of the advantages of this freedom. We have never compared our unlimited freedom with the curtailed freedom in other countries.

Here we have freedom of thought, freedom in the choice and enjoyment of education, freedom in religion, freedom in politics, freedom in the choice of a business, profession or occupation, freedom to accumulate and own without molestation, all the property we can accumulate, freedom to choose our place of residence, freedom in marriage, freedom through equal opportunity to all races, freedom of travel from one state to another, freedom in our choice of foods and freedom to aim for any station in life for which we have prepared ourselves, even for the presidency of the United States.

We have other forms of freedom, but this list will give a bird's eye view of the most important, which constitute opportunity of the highest order. This advantage of freedom is all the more conspicuous because the United States is the only country guaranteeing to every citizen, whether native born or naturalised, so broad and varied a list of freedom.

Next, let us recount some of the blessings that our widespread freedom has placed within our hands. Take the average American family for example (the family with an average income) to sum up the benefits available to every member of the family, in this land of opportunity and plenty!

a. Food. Next to freedom of thought and deed come food, clothing and shelter, the three basic necessities of life. Because of our universal freedom the average American family has available, at its very door, the choicest selection of food to be found anywhere in the world and at prices within its financial range.
b. Shelter. This family lives in a comfortable apartment, heated by steam, lighted with electricity, with gas for

cooking, all for a reasonable rate. The toast they had for breakfast was toasted on an electric toaster, the apartment is cleaned with a vacuum sweeper that is run by electricity. Hot and cold water is available, at all times, in the kitchen and the bathroom. The food is kept cool in a refrigerator that is run by electricity. The wife curls her hair, washes her clothes and irons them with easily operated electrical equipment, on power obtained by inserting a plug in the wall. The husband shaves with an electric shaver and they receive entertainment from all over the world, twenty-four hours a day, if they want it, by merely turning the dial of their television.

There are other conveniences in this apartment, but this list gives a fair idea of some of the concrete evidences of the freedom we, of America, enjoy. (And this is neither political nor economic propaganda).

c. Clothing. Anywhere in the United States, men and women can meet their clothing requirements. That is they can dress very comfortably at prices within the range of an average family's salary.

Only the three basic necessities of food, clothing and shelter have been mentioned. The average American citizen has other privileges and advantages available in return for modest effort, not exceeding eight hours per day of labour. Among these is the privilege of automobile transportation, with which one can go and come at will, at a small cost.

The average American has security of property rights not found in any other country in the world. Surplus money can be placed in a bank with the assurance that the government will protect it and make good if the bank fails. If an American citizen wants to travel from one state to another no passport is needed. Americans may go when they please and return at will. In most other countries, the people cannot travel with so much freedom and at so little cost.

THE 'MIRACLE' THAT HAS PROVIDED THESE BLESSINGS

We often hear politicians proclaiming the freedom of America, when they solicit votes, but seldom do they take the time or devote sufficient effort to the analysis of the source or nature of this 'freedom.' Having no axe to grind, no grudge to express, no ulterior motives to be carried out, I have the privilege of going into a frank analysis of that mysterious, abstract, greatly misunderstood 'Something' which gives to every citizen of America more blessings, more opportunities to accumulate wealth, more freedom of every nature, than may be found in any other country.

I have the right to analyse the source and nature of this unseen power, because I know and have known for more than a quarter of a century, many of the people who organised that power and many who are now responsible for its maintenance.

The name of this mysterious benefactor of mankind is Capital!

Capital consists not alone of money, but more particularly of highly organised, intelligent groups of people who plan ways and means of using money efficiently for the good of the public and profitably to themselves.

These groups consist of scientists, educators, chemists, inventors, business analysts, public relations experts, transportation experts, accountants, lawyers, doctors and both men and women who have highly specialised knowledge in all fields of industry and business. They pioneer, experiment and blaze trails in new fields of endeavour. They support colleges, hospitals and public schools, build good roads, publish newspapers, pay most of the cost of government and take care of the multitudinous detail essential to human progress. Stated briefly, the capitalists are the brains of civilisation, because they supply the entire fabric of which all education, enlightenment and human progress consists.

Money, without brains, always is dangerous. Properly used, it is the most important essential of civilisation. A simple breakfast for a New York family consisting of grapefruit juice, cereal, eggs, bread and butter and tea with sugar could not be provided at a reasonable price, if organised capital had not provided the machinery, the ships, the railroads and the huge armies of trained people to operate them.

Steamships and railroads do not spring up from the Earth and function automatically. They come in response to the call of civilisation, through the labour and ingenuity and organising ability of people who have imagination, faith, enthusiasm, decision and persistence! These people are known as capitalists. They are motivated by the desire to build, construct, achieve, render useful service, earn profits and accumulate riches. As they render services without which there would be no civilisation, they are able to earn great riches.

Just to keep the record simple and understandable, I will add that these capitalists are the selfsame people about most of us have heard soapbox orators speak. They are the same people to whom radicals, racketeers, dishonest politicians and grafting labour leaders refer as 'the predatory interests,' or 'Wall Street.'

I am not attempting to present a brief for or against any group of people or any system of economics. I am not attempting to condemn collective bargaining when I refer to 'grafting labour leaders,' nor do I aim to give a clean bill of health to all individuals known as capitalists.

The purpose of this book – A purpose to which I have faithfully devoted over a quarter of a century – is to present to all who want the knowledge, the most dependable philosophy through which individuals may accumulate riches in whatever amounts they desire.

I have here analysed the economic advantages of the capitalistic system for the two-fold purpose of showing:

1. All who seek riches must recognise and adapt themselves to the system that controls all approaches to fortunes, large or small and
2. The side of the picture opposite to that being shown by politicians and demagogues who deliberately cloud the issues they bring up, by referring to organised capital as if t were something poisonous. This is a capitalistic country. It was developed through the use of capital and we who claim the right to share the blessings of freedom and opportunity, we who seek to accumulate riches here, may as well know that neither riches nor opportunity would be available to us if organised capital had not provided these benefits.

If you are one of those who believe that riches can be accumulated by the mere act of people who organise themselves into groups and demand more pay for less service, if you are one of those who demand government relief without even the early morning disturbance when the money is delivered to you, if you are one of those who believe in trading their votes to politicians in return for the passing of laws which permit the raiding of the public treasury, you may rest securely on your belief, with certain knowledge that no one will disturb you, because this is a free country where every man may think as he pleases, where nearly everybody can live with but little effort, where many may live well without doing any work whatsoever.

However, you should know the full truth concerning this freedom of which so many people boast and so few understand. As great as it is, as far as it reaches, as many privileges as it provides, it does not and cannot bring riches without effort.

There is but one dependable method of accumulating and legally holding riches and that is by rendering useful service. No system has ever been created by which people can legally acquire riches through mere force of numbers or without giving in return an equivalent value of one form or another.

There is a principle known as the law of economics! This is more than a theory. No person can beat this law.

Mark well the name of the principle and remember it, because it is far more powerful than all the politicians and political machines. It is above and beyond the control of all the labour unions. It cannot be swayed nor influenced nor bribed by racketeers or self-appointed leaders of any calling. Moreover, it has an all-seeing eye and a perfect system of bookkeeping, in which it keeps an accurate account of the transactions of every human being engaged in the business of trying to get without giving. Sooner or later its auditors come around, look over the records of individuals both great and small to demand an account.

'Wall Street, Big Business, Capital Predatory Interests,' or whatever name you choose to give the system which has given us American freedom, represents a group of people who understand, respect and adapt themselves to this powerful law of economics! Their financial continuation depends upon their respecting the law.

Most people living in America like this country, its capitalistic system and all. I must confess I know of no better country, where one may find greater opportunities to accumulate riches. Judging by their acts and deeds, there are some in this country who do not like it. That, of course is their privilege; if they do not like this country, its capitalistic system, its boundless opportunities, they have the privilege of clearing out!

America provides all the freedom and all the opportunity to accumulate riches that any honest person may require. When one goes hunting for game, one selects hunting grounds where game is plentiful. When seeking riches, the same rule would naturally obtain.

If it is riches you are seeking, do not overlook the possibilities of a country whose citizens are so rich that women, alone, spend millions of dollars annually for lipsticks, rouge and cosmetics. Think twice, you who are seeking riches, before trying to destroy the capitalistic system of a country whose citizens spend hundreds of million dollars a year for luxury items that people in most nations can only dream about.

Remember, also, that this is but the beginning of the available sources for the accumulation of wealth. Only a few of the luxuries and non-essentials have been mentioned. But, remember that the business of producing, transporting and marketing these few items of merchandise gives regular employment to many millions of men and women, who receive for their services many millions of dollars monthly and spend it freely for both the luxuries and the necessities.

Especially remember, that behind all this exchange of merchandise and personal services may be found an abundance of opportunity to accumulate riches. Here our American freedom comes to one's aid. There is nothing to stop you, or anyone from engaging in any portion of the effort necessary to carry on these businesses. If one has superior talent, training, experience, one may accumulate riches in large amounts. Those not so fortunate may accumulate smaller amounts. Anyone may earn a living in return for a very nominal amount of labour. So – there you are!

Opportunity has spread its wares before you. Step up to the front, select what you want, create your plan, put the plan into action and follow through with persistence. 'Capitalistic' America will do the rest. You can depend upon this much-capitalistic America insures every person the opportunity to render useful service and to collect riches in proportion to the value of the service.

The 'system' denies no one this right, but it does not and cannot promise something for nothing, because the law of economics, itself, irrevocably controls the system, that neither recognises nor tolerates for long, getting without giving.

The law of economics was passed by Nature! There is no Supreme Court to which violators of this law may appeal. The law hands out both penalties for its violation and appropriate rewards for its observance, without interference or the possibility of interference by any human being. The law cannot be repealed. It is as fixed as the stars in the heavens – subject to and a part of the same system that controls the stars.

May one refuse to adapt one's self to the law of economics?

Certainly! This is a free country, where all are born with equal rights, including the privilege of ignoring the law of economics. What happens then?

Well, nothing happens until large numbers of people join forces for the avowed purpose of ignoring the law and taking what they want by force. Then comes the dictator, with well-organised firing squads and machine guns!

We have not yet reached that stage in America! But we have heard all we want to know about how the system works. Perhaps we shall be fortunate enough not to demand personal knowledge of so gruesome a reality. Doubtless we shall prefer to continue with our freedom of speech, freedom of deed and freedom to render useful service in return for riches.

The practice, by government officials of extending to men and women the privilege of raiding the public treasury in return for votes, sometimes results in election, but as night follows day, the final payoff comes; when every penny wrongfully used, must be repaid with compound interest on compound interest. If those who make the grab are not forced to repay, the burden falls on their children and their children's children, 'even unto the third and fourth generations.' There is no way to avoid the debt.

People can and sometimes do, form themselves into groups for the purpose of forcing wages up and working hours down. There is a point beyond which they cannot go. It is the point at which the law of economics steps in and the sheriff gets both the employer and the employees.

These observations are not founded upon short time experience. They are the result of twenty-five years of careful analysis of the methods of both the most successful and the most unsuccessful men America has known.

EIGHT

Decision: The Mastery of Procrastination

Accurate analysis of over 25,000 men and women who had experienced failure, disclosed the fact that lack of decision was near the head of the list of the 30 major causes of failure. This is no mere statement of a theory – it is a fact.

Procrastination, the opposite of decision, is a common enemy that practically everybody must conquer.

You will have an opportunity to test your capacity to reach quick and definite decisions when you finish reading this book and are ready to begin putting into action the principles, which it describes.

Analysis of several hundred people who had accumulated fortunes well beyond the million-dollar mark, disclosed the fact that every one of them had the habit of reaching decisions promptly and of changing these decisions slowly, if and when they were changed. People who fail to accumulate money, without exception, have the habit of reaching decisions, If at all, very slowly and of changing these decisions quickly and often.

The majority of people who fail to accumulate money

sufficient for their needs, are, generally, easily influenced by the 'opinions' of others. They permit the newspapers and the 'gossiping' neighbours to do their 'thinking' for them. 'Opinions' are the cheapest commodities on earth. Everyone has a flock of opinions ready to be wished upon anyone who will accept them. If you are influenced by 'opinions' when you reach decisions, you will not succeed in any undertaking, much less in that of transforming your own desire into money.

If you are influenced by the opinions of others, you will have no desire of your own.

Keep your own counsel, when you begin to put into practice the principles described here, by reaching your own decisions and following them. Take no one into your confidence, except the members of your 'Master Mind' group and be very sure in your selection of this group, that you choose only those who will be in complete sympathy and harmony with your purpose.

Close friends and relatives, while not meaning to do so, often handicap one through 'opinions' and sometimes through ridicule, which is meant to be humorous. Thousands of men and women carry inferiority complexes with them all through life, because some well-meaning, but ignorant person destroyed their confidence through 'opinions' or ridicule.

You have a brain and mind of your own. Use it and reach your own decisions. If you need facts or information from other people, to enable you to reach decisions, as you probably will in many instances; acquire these facts or secure the information you need quietly, without disclosing your purpose.

It is characteristic of people who have but a smattering or a veneer of knowledge to try to give the impression that they have much knowledge. Such people generally do too much talking and too little listening. Keep your eyes and ears wide open and your mouth closed, if you wish to acquire the habit of prompt decision. Those who talk too much do little else. If you talk more than you listen, you not only deprive yourself of many opportunities to accumulate useful knowledge, but you also disclose your plans and purposes to people who will take great delight in defeating you, because they envy you.

Remember, also, that every time you open your mouth in the presence of a person who has an abundance of knowledge, you display to that person, your exact stock of knowledge or your *lack* of it! Genuine wisdom is usually conspicuous through modesty and silence.

Keep in mind the fact that every person with whom you associate is, like yourself, seeking the opportunity to accumulate money. If you talk about your plans too freely, you may be surprised when you learn that some other person has beaten you to your goal by putting into action ahead of you, the plans which you disclosed unwisely. Let one of your first decisions be to keep a closed mouth with open ears and eyes.

As a reminder to yourself to follow this advice, it will be helpful if you copy the following epigram in large letters and place it where you will see it daily. 'Tell the world what you intend to do, but first show it.'

This is the equivalent of saying that 'deeds and not words, are what count most.'

Those who reach decisions promptly and definitely know what they want and generally get it. The leaders in every walk of life decide quickly and firmly. That is the major reason why they are leaders. The world has the habit of making room for people whose words and actions show that they know where they are going.

Indecision is a habit that usually begins in youth. The habit takes on permanency as the youth goes through grade school, high school and even through college, without definiteness of purpose. The major weakness of all educational systems is that they neither teach nor encourage the habit of definite decision.

It would be beneficial if no college would permit the enrollment of any student, unless and until the student declared his or her major purpose in matriculating. It would be of still greater benefit, if every student who enters the grade schools were compelled to accept training in the habit of decision-making and forced to pass a satisfactory examination on this subject before being permitted to advance in the grades.

The habit of indecision acquired because of the deficiencies of our school systems, goes with the students into the occupations they choose, if in fact, they choose their occupations. Generally, young people just out of school seek any job that can find. They take the first place they find, because they have fallen into the habit of indecision. Ninety-eight out of every hundred people working for wages today, are in the positions they hold, because they lacked the definiteness of decision to plan a definite position and the knowledge of how to choose an employer.

Definiteness of decision always requires courage, sometimes very great courage. The fifty-six men who signed the Declaration of Independence staked their lives on the decision to affix their signatures to that document. People who reach a definite decision to procure the particular job and make life pay the price they ask, do not stake their life on that decision; they stake their economic freedom. Financial independence, riches, desirable business and professional positions are not within reach of the person who neglects or refuses to expect, plan and demand these things. The person, who desires riches in the same spirit that Samuel Adams desired freedom for the thirteen original American colonies, is sure to accumulate wealth.

In the chapter on Organised Planning, you will find complete instructions for marketing every type of personal services. You will find also detailed information on how to choose the employer you prefer and the particular job you desire. These instructions will be of no value to you unless you definitely decide to organise them into a plan of action.

NINE

Persistence: The Sustained Effort Necessary to Induce Faith

Persistence is an essential factor in the procedure of transforming desire into its monetary equivalent. The basis of persistence is willpower.

Willpower and desire, when properly combined, make an irresistible pair. People who accumulate great fortunes are generally known as cold-blooded and sometimes ruthless. Often they are misunderstood. What they have is willpower, which they mix with persistence and place their desires to ensure the attainment of their objectives.

The majority of people are ready to throw their aims and purposes overboard and give up at the first sign of opposition or misfortune. A few carry on despite all opposition, until they attain their goal. These few are the Fords, Carnegies, Rockefellers and Edisons.

There may be no heroic connotation to the word 'persistence,' but the quality is to character what carbon is to steel.

The building of a fortune, generally, involves the application of the entire thirteen factors of this philosophy. These principles must be understood, – all who accumulate money must apply them with persistence.

If you are following this book with the intention of applying the knowledge it conveys, your first test as to your persistence will come when you begin to follow the six steps described in Chapter Two. Unless you are one of the two out of every hundred who already have a definite goal at which you are aiming and a definite plan for its attainment, you might read the instructions and then go on with your daily routine and never comply with those instructions.

The author is checking up on you at this point, because lack of persistence is one of the major causes of failure. Moreover, experience with thousands of people has proved that lack of persistence is a weakness common to the majority of people. It is a weakness that may be overcome by effort. The ease with which a lack of persistence may be conquered will depend entirely upon the intensity of one's desire.

The starting point of all achievement is desire. Keep this constantly in mind. Weak desires bring weak results, just as a small amount of fire makes a small amount of heat. If you find yourself lacking in persistence, this weakness may be remedied by building a stronger fire under your desires.

Fortunes gravitate to people whose minds have been prepared to 'attract' them, just as surely as water gravitates to the ocean. In this book you can find all the stimuli necessary to 'attune' any normal mind to the vibrations that will attract the object of one's desires.

If you find you are weak in persistence, centre your attention upon the instructions contained in the chapter on 'Power.' Surround yourself with a 'Master Mind' group and through the cooperative efforts of the members of this group, you can develop persistence. You will find additional instructions for the development of persistence in the chapters on autosuggestion and the subconscious mind. Follow the instructions outlined in these chapters until your nature hands over to your subconscious mind, a clear picture of the object of your desire. You will no longer be handicapped by lack of persistence.

Your subconscious mind works continuously, while you are awake or asleep.

Spasmodic or occasional effort to apply the rules will be of no value to you. To get results, you must apply all of the rules until their application becomes a fixed habit with you. In no other way can you develop the necessary 'money consciousness.' Poverty is attracted to the one whose mind is favourable to it, as money is attracted to one whose mind has been deliberately prepared to attract it through the same laws. Poverty consciousness will voluntarily seize the mind that is not occupied with the money consciousness. A poverty consciousness develops without conscious application of habits favourable to it. The money consciousness must be created in order to attract riches – unless one is born with such a consciousness.

Catch the full significance of the statements in the preceding paragraph and you will understand the importance of persistence in the accumulation of a fortune. Without persistence, you will be defeated, even before you start. With persistence you will win.

If you select your 'Master Mind' group with care, you will have in it, at least one person who will aid you in the development of persistence. Some people who have accumulated great fortunes, did so because of necessity. They developed the habit of persistence, because they were so closely driven by circumstances, that they had to become persistent.

There is no substitute for persistence! It cannot be supplanted by any other quality! Remember this and it will hearten you, in the beginning, when the going may seem difficult and slow.

Those who have cultivated the habit of persistence seem to enjoy insurance against failure. No matter how many times they are defeated, they finally arrive up toward the top of the ladder. Sometimes it appears that there is a hidden guide whose duty is to test people through all sorts of discouraging experiences. Those who pick themselves up after defeat and keep on trying arrive; and the world cries, 'Bravo! I knew you could do it!' The hidden guide lets no one enjoy great achievement without passing the persistence test. Those who can't take it simply do not make the grade.

Those who can 'take it' are bountifully rewarded for their persistence. They receive, as their compensation, whatever goal they are pursuing. That is not all! They receive something infinitely more important than material compensation – the knowledge that 'Every failure brings with it the seed of an equivalent advantage.'

There are exceptions to this rule; a few people know from experience the soundness of persistence. They are the ones who have not accepted defeat as being anything more than temporary. They are the ones whose desires are so persistently applied that defeat is finally changed into victory. We who stand on the sidelines of life see the overwhelmingly large numbers who go down in defeat, never to rise again. We see the few who take the punishment of defeat as an urge to greater effort. These, fortunately, never learn to accept life's reverse gear. Yet what we do not see, what most of us never suspect of existing, is the silent but irresistible power which comes to the rescue of those who fight on in the face of discouragement. If we speak of this power at all we call it persistence and let it go at that. One thing we all know, if one does not possess persistence, one does not achieve noteworthy success in any calling.

Persistence is a state of mind therefore it can be cultivated. Like all states of mind, persistence is based upon definite causes, among them:

a. *Definite purpose* Knowing what one wants is the first and, perhaps, the most important step toward the development of persistence. A strong motive forces one to surmount many difficulties.
b. *Desire* It is comparatively easy to acquire and to maintain persistence in pursuing the object of intense desire.
c. *Self-reliance* Belief in one's ability to carry out a plan encourages one to follow the plan through with persistence. (Self-reliance can be developed through the principle described in the chapter on autosuggestion).
d. *Definite plans* Organised plans, even though they may be weak and entirely impractical, encourage persistence.
e. *Accurate knowledge* Knowing that one's plans are sound, based upon experience or observation, encourages persistence; 'guessing' instead of 'knowing' destroys persistence.
f. *Cooperation* Sympathy, understanding and harmonious cooperation with others tend to develop persistence.
g. *Willpower* The habit of concentrating one's thoughts upon the building of plans for the attainment of a definite purpose, leads to persistence.
h. *Habit* Persistence is the direct result of habit. The mind absorbs and becomes a part of the daily experiences upon which it feeds. Fear, the worst of all enemies, can be effectively cured by forced repetition of acts of courage.

Everyone who has seen active service in war knows this.

Before leaving the subject of persistence, take an inventory of yourself. Determine in what particular way, if any, you are lacking in this essential quality. Measure yourself courageously, point by point. See how many of the eight factors of persistence you lack. The analysis may lead to discoveries that will give you a new grip on yourself.

SYMPTOMS OF LACK OF PERSISTENCE

Here you will find the real enemies that stand between you and noteworthy achievement. Here you will find not only the 'symptoms' indicating weakness of persistence, but also the deeply seated subconscious causes of this weakness. Study the list carefully and face yourself squarely. Only if you really wish to know who you are and what you are capable of doing. These are the weaknesses that must be mastered by all who accumulate riches.

1. Failure to recognise and to clearly define exactly what one wants.
2. Procrastination, with or without cause. (Usually backed up with a formidable array of alibis and excuses).
3. Lack of interest in acquiring specialised knowledge.
4. Indecision, the habit of 'passing the buck' on all occasions, instead of facing issues squarely. (Also backed by alibis).
5. The habit of relying upon alibis instead of creating definite plans for the solution of problems.
6. Self-satisfaction. There is but little remedy for this affliction and no hope for those who suffer from it.
7. Indifference, usually reflected in one's readiness to compromise on all occasions, rather than meet opposition and fight it.
8. The habit of blaming others for one's mistakes and accepting unfavourable circumstances as being unavoidable.

9. Weakness of desire, due to neglect in the choice of motives that impel action.
10. Willingness, even eagerness, to quit at the first sign of defeat. (Based upon one or more of the 6 basic fears).
11. Lack of organised plans, placed in writing where they may be analysed.
12. The habit of neglecting to move on ideas or to grasp opportunity when it presents itself.
13. Wishing instead of willing.
14. The habit of compromising with poverty instead of aiming at riches – a general absence of ambition *to be*, *to do* and *to own*.
15. Searching for all the short-cuts to riches, trying to get without giving a fair equivalent, usually reflected in the habit of gambling, endeavouring to drive 'sharp' bargains.
16 Fear of criticism, failure to create plans and to put them into action, because of what other people will think, do or say. This enemy belongs at the head of the list, because it generally exists in one's subconscious mind, where its presence is not recognised. (See the Six Basic Fears in Chapter 15).

Let us examine some of the symptoms of the fear of criticism. The majority of people permit relatives, friends and the public at large to so influence them that they cannot live their own lives, because they fear criticism.

Huge numbers of people make mistakes in marriage, stand by the bargain and go through life miserable and unhappy, because they fear criticism that may follow if they correct the mistake. (Anyone who has submitted to this form of fear knows the irreparable damage it does, by destroying ambition, self-reliance and the desire to achieve).

Millions of people neglect to acquire belated education, after having left school, because they fear criticism.

Countless numbers of men and women, both young and old, permit relatives to wreck their lives in the name of duty, because they fear criticism. (Duty does not require any person to submit to the destruction of one's personal ambitions and the right to live one's own life in one's own way).

People refuse to take chances in business, because they fear the criticism that may follow if they fail. The fear of criticism, in such cases is stronger than the desire for success.

Too many people refuse to set high goals for themselves or even neglect selecting a career, because they fear the criticism of relatives and 'friends' who may say 'Don't aim so high, people will think you are crazy.'

Many people believe that material success is the result of favourable 'breaks.' There are grounds for the belief, but those depending entirely upon luck, are nearly always disappointed, because they overlook another important factor that must be present before one can be sure of success. It is the knowledge that favourable 'breaks' can be made to order. Examine the first hundred people you meet, ask them what they want most in life and ninety-eight of them will not be able to tell you. If you press them for an answer, some will say – security, many will say – money, a few will say – happiness, others will say – fame and power and still others will say – social recognition, ease in living, ability to sing, dance or write. Yet none of them will be able to define these terms or give the slightest indication of a *plan* by which they hope to attain these vaguely expressed wishes. Riches do not respond to wishes. They respond only to definite plans, backed by definite desires, through constant persistence.

HOW TO DEVELOP PERSISTENCE

There are four simple steps that lead to the habit of persistence. They call for no great amount of intelligence, no particular amount of education and only a little time or effort. The necessary steps are:

1. A definite purpose backed by a burning desire for its fulfilment.
2. A definite plan, expressed in continuous action.
3. A mind closed tightly against all negative and discouraging influences, including negative suggestions of relatives, friends and acquaintances.
4. A friendly alliance with one or more persons who will encourage one to follow through with both plan and purpose.

These four steps are essential for success in all walks of life. The entire purpose of the thirteen principles of this philosophy is to enable one to take these four steps as a matter of *habit*. These are the steps that can control one's economic destiny. They are the steps that lead to freedom and independence of thought. They are the steps that lead to riches, in small or great quantities. They lead the way to power, fame and worldly recognition. They are the four steps which guarantee favourable 'breaks.' They are the steps that convert dreams into physical realities. They lead, also, to the mastery of fear, discouragement, indifference.

There is a magnificent reward for all who learn to take these four steps. It is the privilege of writing one's own ticket and of making life yield whatever price is asked.

TEN

Power of the Master Mind: The Driving Force

Power is essential for success in the accumulation of money. Plans are inert and useless, without sufficient power to translate them into action. This chapter will describe the method for an individual to use to attain and apply power.

Power may be defined as 'organised and intelligently directed knowledge.' Power, as the term is here used, refers to organised effort, sufficient to enable an individual to transmute desire into its monetary equivalent. Organised effort is produced through the coordination of effort of two or more people, who work toward a definite end, in a spirit of harmony.

Power is required for the accumulation of money! Power is necessary for the retention of money after it has been accumulated!

Let us ascertain how power may be acquired. If power is 'organised knowledge,' let us examine the sources of knowledge:

a. *Infinite intelligence* This source of knowledge may be contacted through the procedure described in Chapter 6, with the aid of Creative Imagination.
b. *Accumulated experience* The accumulated experience of

humankind, (or that portion of it which has been organised and recorded), may be found in any well-equipped public library. An important part of this accumulated experience is taught in public schools and colleges, where it has been classified and organised.

c. *Experiment and research* In the field of science and in practically every other walk of life, people are gathering, classifying and organising new facts daily. This is the source to which one must turn when knowledge is not available through 'accumulated experience.' Here, too, creative imagination must often be used.

Knowledge may be acquired from any of the foregoing sources. It may be converted into power by organising it into definite plans and by expressing those plans in terms of action.

Examination of the three major sources of knowledge will readily disclose the difficulty people would have, if they depended upon their efforts alone, in assembling knowledge and expressing it through definite plans in terms of action. If their plans are comprehensive and if they contemplate large proportions, they must, generally, induce others to cooperate with them, before they can inject into them the necessary element of *power*.

GAINING POWER THROUGH THE 'MASTER MIND'

The 'Master Mind' may be defined as: 'Coordination of knowledge and effort, in a spirit of harmony, between two or more people, for the attainment of a definite purpose.'

No individual may have great power without availing himself or herself of the 'Master Mind.' In Chapter 7, instructions were given for the creation of plans for the purpose of translating desire into its monetary equivalent. If you carry out these instructions with persistence and intelligence to use discrimination in the selection of your 'Master Mind' group, your objective will have been halfway reached, even before you begin to recognise it.

You may better understand the 'intangible' potentialities of power available to you, through a properly chosen 'Master Mind' group. We will here explain the two characteristics of the Master Mind principle, one is economic in nature and the other psychic. The economic feature is obvious. Economic advantages may be created by people who surround themselves with the advice, counsel and personal cooperation of a group of people who are willing to lend i.e., wholehearted aid, in a spirit of perfect harmony. This form of cooperative alliance has been the basis of nearly every great fortune. Your understanding of this great truth may definitely determine your financial status.

The psychic phase of the Master Mind principle is much more abstract, much more difficult to comprehend, because it has reference to the spiritual forces with which the human race, as a whole, is not well acquainted. You may catch a significant suggestion from this statement: 'No two minds ever come together without, thereby, creating a third, invisible, intangible force which may be likened to a third mind.'

Keep in mind the fact that there are only two known elements in the whole universe, energy and matter. It is a well-known fact that matter may be broken down into units of molecules, atoms and electrons. There are units of matter that may be isolated, separated and analysed. Likewise, there are units of energy.

The human mind is a form of energy, a part of it being spiritual in nature. When the minds of two people are coordinated in a spirit of harmony, the spiritual units of energy of each mind form an affinity, which constitutes the 'psychic' phase of the Master Mind.

The Master Mind principal or rather Andrew Carnegie, first called the economic feature of it, to my attention, over twenty-five years ago. Discovery of this principle was responsible for the choice of my life's work.

Mr Carnegie's Master Mind group consisted of a staff of approximately fifty men, with whom he surrounded himself, for the definite purpose of manufacturing and marketing steel. He attributed his entire fortune to the power he accumulated through this 'Master Mind.'

Analyse the record of any person who has accumulated a great fortune and many of those who have accumulated modest fortunes and you will find that they have either consciously or unconsciously employed the 'Master Mind' principle.

Great power can be accumulated through no other principle!

Energy is Nature's universal set of building blocks, from which she constructs every material thing in the universe, including humankind and every form of animal and vegetable life. Through a process that only Nature completely understands, she translates energy into matter.

Nature's building blocks are available to us, in the energy involved in thinking! The brain may be compared to an electric battery. It absorbs energy from the ether, which permeates every atom of matter and fills the entire universe.

It is a well-known fact that a group of electric batteries will provide more energy than a single battery. It is also a well-known fact that an individual battery will provide energy in proportion to the number and capacity of the cells it contains.

The brain functions in a similar fashion. This accounts for the fact that some brains are more efficient than others and leads to this significant statement: a group of brains coordinated (or connected) in a spirit of harmony, will provide more thought-energy than a single brain, just as a group of electric batteries will provide more energy than a single battery.

Through this metaphor it becomes immediately obvious that the Master Mind principle holds the secret of the power wielded by people who surround themselves with other people of brains.

There follows, now, another statement which will lead still nearer to an understanding of the psychic phase of the Master Mind principle: when a group of individual brains are coordinated and function in harmony, the increased energy created through that alliance, becomes available to every individual brain in the group. President Franklin Roosevelt brought the best minds of the country to Washington to form a mastermind group he called his 'brain trust.' During and after World War II, mastermind groups called 'think tanks,' were frequently called upon by leaders of government and industry to help deal with critical problems.

We have already mentioned Mahatma Gandhi. Perhaps the majority of those who have heard of Gandhi, look upon him as merely an eccentric little man, who went around without formal clothes and made trouble for the British Government.

In reality, Gandhi was not eccentric, but he was the most powerful man of his generation. (Estimated by the number of his followers and their faith in their leader.) Moreover, he was probably the most powerful man who ever lived. His power was passive, but it was real.

Let us study the method by which he attained his stupendous power. It may be explained in a few words. He came by power through inducing over two hundred million people to coordinate, with mind and body, in a spirit of harmony, for a definite purpose.

In brief, Gandhi accomplished a miracle, for it is a miracle when two hundred million people can be induced – not forced-to cooperate in a spirit of harmony, for a limitless time. If you doubt that this is a miracle, try to induce any two people to cooperate in a spirit of harmony for any length of time.

Every person who manages a business knows what a difficult matter it is to get employees to work together in a spirit even remotely resembling harmony.

The list of the chief sources from which *power* may be attained is, as you have seen, headed by infinite intelligence. When two or more people coordinate in a spirit of harmony and work toward a definite objective, they place themselves in position, through that alliance, to absorb power directly from the great universal storehouse of Infinite Intelligence. This is the greatest of all sources of power. It is the source to which the genius turns. It is, the source to which every great leader turns, (whether conscious of the fact or not).

The other two major sources from which the knowledge, necessary for the accumulation of power, may be obtained are no more reliable than our five senses. The senses are not always reliable. Infinite Intelligence does not err.

In subsequent chapters, the methods by which Infinite Intelligence may be most readily contacted will be adequately described.

This is not a course on religion. No fundamental principle described in this book should be interpreted as being intended to interfere either directly or indirectly, with anyone's religious habits. This book has been confined, exclusively, to instructing the reader how to transform the definite purpose of desire for money, into its monetary equivalent.

Read, think and meditate as you read. Soon, the entire subject will unfold and you will see it in perspective. You are now seeing the detail of the individual chapters.

Money is as shy and elusive as the 'old time' maiden. It

must be wooed and won by methods not unlike those used by a determined lover, in pursuit of a mate. It is a coincidence that, the power used in the 'wooing' of money is not greatly different from that used in wooing a lover. That power, when successfully used in the pursuit of money must be mixed with faith. It must be mixed with desire. It must be mixed with persistence. It must be applied through a plan and that plan must be set into action. When money comes in quantities known as 'the big money,' it flows to the one who accumulates it, as easily as water flows down hill. There exists a great unseen stream of power, which may be compared to a river; except that one side flows in one direction, carrying all who get into that side of the stream, onward and upward to wealth – and the other side flows in the opposite direction, carrying all who are unfortunate enough to get into it (and not able to extricate themselves from it), downward to misery and poverty.

Every person who has accumulated a great fortune has recognised the existence of this stream of life. It consists of one's thinking process. The positive emotions of thought form the side of the stream that carries one to fortune. The negative emotions form the side that carries one down to poverty.

This carries a thought of stupendous importance to the person who is following this book with the object of accumulating a fortune.

If you are in the side of the stream of power that leads to poverty, this may serve as an oar, by which you may propel yourself over into the other side of the stream. It can serve you only through application and use. Merely reading and passing judgement on it, either one way or another, will in no way benefit you.

Some people undergo the experience of alternating between the positive and negative sides of the stream, being at times on the positive side and at times on the negative side. The Wall Street crash of '29 swept millions of people from the positive to the negative side of the stream. These millions struggled – some of them in desperation and fear, to get back to the positive side of the stream. This book was written especially for those millions.

Poverty and riches often change places. Poverty may and generally does, voluntarily take the place of riches. When riches take the place of poverty, the change is usually brought about through well-conceived and carefully executed plans. Poverty needs no plan. It needs no one to aid it, because it is bold and ruthless. Riches are shy and timid. They have to be 'attracted.' Anybody can wish for riches and most people do, but only a few know that a definite plan, plus a burning desire for wealth, is the only dependable means of accumulating wealth. But nobody can assemble and fully execute a plan for wealth alone. You need the help of a Master Mind to get there.

ELEVEN

The Mystery of Sex Transformation

The meaning of the word 'transform' is, in simple language, 'the changing, or transferring of one element, or form of energy, into another.'

The emotion of sex brings into being a state of mind.

Because of ignorance on the subject, this state of mind is generally associated with the physical because most people are subjected of improper influences. In acquiring knowledge of sex, things essentially physical have highly biased the mind.

The emotion of sex has behind it the possibility of three constructive potentialities, they are:

1. The perpetuation of mankind.
2. The maintenance of health, (as a therapeutic agency, it has no equal).
3. The transformation of mediocrity into genius through transformation.

Sex transformation is simple and easily explained. It means the switching of the mind from thoughts of physical expression, to thoughts of some other nature. Sex desire is the most powerful of human desires. When driven by this desire, people develop keenness of imagination, courage, willpower, persistence and creative ability unknown to them at other times. So strong and impelling is the desire for sexual contact that people freely run the risk of life and reputation to indulge it. When harnessed and redirected along other lines, this motivating force maintains all of its attributes of keenness of imagination, courage, etc., to be used as powerful creative forces in literature, art, or in any other profession or calling, including, of course, the accumulation of riches.

The transformation of sex energy calls for the exercise of will power, to be sure, but the reward is worth the effort. The desire for sexual expression is inborn and natural. The desire cannot and should not be submerged or eliminated. Yet it should be given an outlet through forms of expression that enrich the body, mind and spirit. If not given this form of outlet, through transformation, it will seek outlets through purely physical channels.

A river may be dammed – its water controlled for a time, but eventually, it will force an outlet. The same is true of the emotion of sex. It may be submerged and controlled for a time, but its very nature causes it to be ever-seeking a means of expression. If it is not transformed into some creative effort it will find a less worthy outlet.

Fortunate, indeed, are those who have discovered how to give sex emotion an outlet through some form of creative effort, for they have, by that discovery, lifted themselves to the status of genius.

Scientific research on the backgrounds of high achieving men (unfortunately, no similar studies have been made about highly successful women) has disclosed these significant facts:

1. The men of greatest achievement are men with highly developed sex natures; men who have learned the art of sex transformation.
2. The men who have accumulated great fortunes and achieved outstanding recognition in literature, art, industry, architecture and the professions, were motivated by the influence of a woman.

The research, from which these astounding discoveries were made, went back through the pages of biography and history for more than two thousand years. Wherever there was evidence available in connection with the lives of men and women of great achievement, it indicated most convincingly that they possessed highly developed sex natures.

The emotion of sex is an 'irresistible force,' against which there can be no opposition as an 'immovable body.' When driven by this emotion, men become gifted with a super power for action. Understand this truth. You will catch the significance of the statement that sex transformation will lift one to the status of a genius.

The emotion of sex contains the secret of creative ability.

Destroy the sex glands, whether in man or beast – you have removed the major source of action. For proof of this, observe what happens to any animal after it has been castrated. A bull becomes as docile as a cow after it has been altered sexually. Sex alteration takes out of the male, whether man or beast, all the fight that was in him. Sex alteration of the female has the same effect.

THE TEN MIND STIMULI

The human mind responds to stimuli, through which it may

be 'keyed up' to high rates of vibration, known as enthusiasm, creative imagination, intense desire, etc. The stimuli to which the mind responds most freely are:

1. The desire for sex expression
2. Love
3. A burning desire for fame, power, or financial gain, money
4. Music
5. Friendship between either those of the same sex or those of the opposite sex.
6. A Master Mind alliance based upon the harmony of two or more people who ally themselves for spiritual or temporal advancement.
7. Mutual suffering, such as that experienced by people who are persecuted.
8. Auto-suggestion
9. Fear
10. Narcotics and alcohol.

The desire for sex expression comes at the head of the list of stimuli, which most effectively 'step up' the vibrations of the mind and start the 'wheels' of physical action. Eight of these stimuli are natural and constructive. Two are destructive. The list is here presented for the purpose of enabling you to make a comparative study of the major sources of mind stimulation. From this study, it will be readily seen that the emotion of sex is, by great odds, the most intense and powerful of all mind stimuli.

This comparison is necessary as a foundation for proof of the statement that transformation of sex energy may lift one to the status of a genius. Let us find out what constitutes a genius.

A good definition of a genius is, 'a person who has discovered how to increase the vibrations of thought to the point where he or she can freely communicate with sources of knowledge not available through the ordinary rate of vibration of thought.'

The person who thinks will want to ask some questions concerning this definition of genius. The first question will be, 'How may one communicate with sources of knowledge which are not available through the ordinary rate of vibration of thought?'

The next question will be, 'Are there known sources of knowledge which are available only to geniuses and if so, what are these sources and exactly how may they be reached?'

We shall offer proof of the soundness of some of the more important statements made in this book – or at least we shall offer evidence through which you may secure your own proof through experimentation and in doing so, we shall answer both of these questions.

'GENIUS' IS DEVELOPED THROUGH THE SIXTH SENSE

The reality of a 'sixth sense' has been fairly well established. This sixth sense is 'Creative Imagination.' The faculty of creative imagination is one that the majority of people never use during an entire lifetime and if used at all, it usually happens by mere accident. A relatively small number of people use, with deliberation and purpose aforethought, the faculty of creative imagination. Those who use this faculty voluntarily and with understanding of its functions, are geniuses. The faculty of creative imagination is the direct link between the finite mind of humans and Infinite Intelligence. All so-called revelations, referred to in the realm of religion and all discoveries of basic or new principles in the field of invention, take place through the faculty of creative imagination. When ideas or concepts flash into one's mind, through what is popularly called a 'hunch,' they come from one or more of the following sources:

1. Infinite Intelligence
2. One's subconscious mind, that has every sense impression and thought impulse, which ever reached the brain through any of the five senses is stored here.
3. From the mind of some other person who has just released the thought, or picture of the idea or concept, through conscious thought, or
4. From the other person's subconscious storehouse.

There are no other known sources from which 'inspired' ideas or 'hunches' may be received.

The creative imagination functions best when the mind is vibrating (due to some form of mind stimulation) at an exceedingly high rate. That is, when the mind is functioning at a rate of vibration higher than that of ordinary, normal thought.

When brain action has been stimulated, through one or more of the ten mind stimulants, it has the effect of lifting the individual far above the horizon of ordinary thought. This permits one to perceive distance, scope and quality of thoughts not available on the lower plane, such as that occupied while one is engaged in the solution of the problems of business and professional routine.

When lifted to this higher level of thought, through any form of mind stimulation, an individual occupies, relatively, the same position as one who has ascended in an airplane to a height from which one may see over and beyond the horizon line which limits one's vision, while on the ground. Moreover, while on this higher level of thought, the individual is not hampered or bound by any of the stimuli that circumscribe and limit his or her vision while wrestling with the problems of gaining the three basic necessities of food, clothing and shelter. He or she is in a world of thought in which the ordinary, work-a-day thoughts have been as effectively removed as are the hills and valleys and other limitations of physical vision, when rising in an airplane.

While on this exalted plane of thought, the creative faculty of the mind is given freedom for action. The way has been cleared for the sixth sense to function; it becomes receptive to ideas that could not reach the individual under any other circumstances. The 'sixth sense' is the faculty that marks the difference between a genius and an ordinary individual.

The creative faculty becomes more alert and receptive to vibrations, originating outside the individual's subconscious mind, the more this faculty is used and the more the individual relies upon it and makes demands upon it for thought impulses. This faculty can be cultivated and developed only through use.

What is known as one's 'conscience' operates entirely through the faculty of the sixth sense.

The great artists, writers, musicians and poets become great, because they acquire the habit of relying upon the 'still small voice' which speaks from within, through the faculty of creative imagination. It is a fact well-known to people who have 'keen' imaginations that their best ideas come through so-called 'hunches.'

There is a great orator who does not attain to greatness, until he closes his eyes and begins to rely entirely upon the faculty of Creative Imagination. When asked why he closed his eyes just before the climaxes of his oratory, he replied, 'I do it, because, then I speak through ideas which come to me from within.' One of America's most successful and best-known financiers followed the habit of closing his eyes for two or three minutes before making a decision. When asked why he did this, he replied, 'With my eyes closed, I am able to draw upon a source of superior intelligence.'

Dr Elmer R Gates, of Chevy Chase, Maryland, created more than 200 useful patents, many of them basic, through the process of cultivating and using the creative faculty. His method is both significant and interesting to one interested in attaining to the status of genius, in which category Dr Gates, unquestionably belonged. Dr Gates was one of the really great, though less publicised scientists of the world.

In his laboratory, he had what he called his 'personal communication room.' It was practically sound proof and so arranged that all light could be shut out. It was equipped with a small table, on which he kept a pad of writing paper. In front of the table, on the wall, was an electric push button, which controlled the lights. When Dr Gates desired to draw upon the forces available to him through his Creative Imagination, he would go into this room, seat himself at the table, shut off the lights and concentrate upon the known factors of the invention on which he was working, remaining in that position until ideas began to 'flash' into his mind in connection with the unknown factors of the invention.

On one occasion, ideas came through so fast that he was forced to write for almost three hours. When the thoughts stopped flowing and he examined his notes, he found they contained a minute description of principles that had not a parallel among the known data of the scientific world. Moreover, the answer to his problem was intelligently presented in those notes. In this manner Dr Gates completed over 200 patents, which had been begun, but not completed, by 'half-baked' brains. Evidence of the truth of this statement is in the United States Patent Office.

Dr Gates earned his living by 'sitting for ideas' for individuals and corporations. Some of the largest corporations in America paid him substantial fees, by the hour, for 'sitting for ideas.'

The reasoning faculty is often faulty, because it is largely guided by one's accumulated experience. Not all knowledge, which one accumulates through 'experience,' is accurate. Ideas received through the creative faculty are much more reliable, for the reason that they come from sources more reliable than any which are available to the reasoning faculty of the mind.

The major difference between the genius and the ordinary 'crank' inventor may be found in the fact that the genius works through his faculty of creative imagination, while the 'crank' knows nothing of this faculty. The scientific inventor (such as Mr Edison and Dr Gates) makes use of both the synthetic and the creative faculties of imagination.

For example, scientific inventors or 'geniuses,' begin an invention by organising and combining the known ideas, or principles accumulated through experience, through the synthetic faculty (the reasoning faculty). If they find this accumulated knowledge to be insufficient for the completion of the invention, they then draw upon the sources of knowledge available to them through their creative faculty. The method by which this is done varies with the individual, but this is the sum and substance of the procedure:

1. *They stimulate their minds so that they vibrate on a higher than average plane*, using one or more of the ten mind stimulants or some other stimulant of choice.
2. *They concentrate* upon the known factors (the finished part) of the invention and create in their minds a perfect picture of unknown factors (the unfinished part), of the invention. They hold this picture in mind until it has been taken over by the subconscious mind and then relax by clearing their minds of *all* thought and wait for the answer to pop up.

Sometimes the results are both definite and immediate. At other times, the results are negative, depending upon the state of development of the 'sixth sense,' or creative faculty.

Mr Edison tried out more than 10,000 different combinations of ideas through the synthetic faculty of his imagination before he 'tuned in' through the creative faculty and got the answer that perfected the incandescent light. His experience was similar when he produced the talking machine.

There is plenty of reliable evidence that the faculty of creative imagination exists. This evidence is available through accurate analysis of people who have become leaders in their respective callings, without having had any extensive education. Lincoln was a notable example of a great leader who achieved greatness, through the discovery and use of his faculty of creative imagination. He discovered and began to use this faculty as the result of the stimulation of love which he experienced after he met Anne Rutledge, a statement of the highest significance, in connection with the study of the source of genius.

The pages of history are filled with the records of great leaders whose achievements may be traced directly to the influence of women who aroused the creative faculties of their minds, through the stimulation of sex desire. Napoleon Bonaparte was one of these. When inspired by his first wife, Josephine, he was irresistible and invincible. When his 'better judgement' or reasoning faculty prompted him to put Josephine aside, he began to decline. His defeat and St Helena were not far distant.

If good taste would permit, we might easily mention scores of men, well-known to the American people, who climbed to great heights of achievement under the stimulating influence of their wives, only to drop back to destruction after money and power went to their heads. They put aside the old wife for a new one.

Napoleon was not the only man to discover that sex influence, from the right source, is more powerful than any substitute of expediency, which may be created by mere reason. The human mind responds to stimulation! Among the greatest and most powerful of these stimuli is the urge of sex. When harnessed and transmuted, this driving force is capable of lifting one into that higher sphere of thought that enables them to master the sources of worry and petty annoyance that beset their pathway on the lower plane.

Unfortunately, only the geniuses have made the discovery. Others have accepted the experience of sex urge, without discovering one of its major potentialities. This is a fact that accounts for the great number of 'others' as compared to the limited number of geniuses. Sex energy is the creative energy of all geniuses. There never has been and never will be a great leader, builder, or artist lacking in this driving force of sex.

Surely no one will misunderstand these statements to mean that all who are highly sexed are geniuses! One attains to the status of a genius only when and if, one's mind is stimulated so that it draws upon the forces available, through the creative faculty of the imagination. Chief among the stimuli with which this 'stepping up' of the vibrations may be produced is sex energy. The mere possession of this energy is not sufficient to produce a genius. The energy must be transformed from desire for physical contact, into some other form of desire and action, before it will lift one to the status of a genius.

Far from becoming geniuses, because of great sex desires, all too many people lower themselves, through misunderstanding and misuse of this great force, to the status of the lower animals.

WHY MEN SELDOM SUCCEED BEFORE FORTY

I discovered, from the analysis of over 25,000 people, that people who succeed in an outstanding way, seldom do so before the age of forty. More often they do not strike their real pace until they are well beyond the age of fifty. This fact was so astounding that it prompted me to go into the study of its cause most carefully, carrying the investigation over a period of more than twelve years.

This study disclosed the fact that the major reason why the majority of people who succeed do not begin to do so before the age of forty to fifty is their tendency to dissipate their energies through over indulgence in physical expression of the emotion of sex. Most people never learn that the urge of sex has other possibilities, which far transcend in importance, that of mere physical expression. The majority of those who make this discovery do so after having wasted many years at a period when the sex energy is at its height, prior to the age of forty-five to fifty. This usually is followed by noteworthy achievement.

The lives of many people up to and sometimes well past the age of forty, reflect a continued dissipation of energies, which could have been more profitably turned into better channels. Their finer and more powerful emotions are sown wildly to the four winds. Out of this habit grew the term, 'sowing one's wild oats.'

The desire for sexual expression is by far the strongest and most impelling of all the human emotions. For this very reason this desire, when harnessed as also transmuted into action, other than that of physical expression, may raise one to the status of a genius.

One of America's most able businessmen frankly admitted that his attractive secretary was responsible for most of the plans he created. He admitted that her presence lifted him to heights of creative imagination, such as he could experience under no other stimulus.

History has many examples of people who attained the status of geniuses, as the result of the use of artificial mind stimulants in the form of alcohol and narcotics. Edgar Allen Poe wrote the 'Raven' while under the influence of liquor, 'dreaming dreams that mortal never dared to dream before.' Riley did his best writing under the influence of alcohol. Perhaps it was thus he saw 'the ordered intermingling of the real and the dream. The mill above the river and the mist above the stream.' Robert Burns wrote best when intoxicated, 'For auld lang syne, my jo, we'll tak a cup of kindness yet, for auld lang syne.'

Yet let it be remembered that many such people have destroyed themselves in the end. Nature has prepared her own potion which people may safely stimulate their minds so they vibrate on a plane that enables them to tune into fine and rare thoughts, which come from – 'the great unknown!' No satisfactory substitute for Nature's stimulants has ever been found.

It is a fact well known to psychologists that there is a very close relationship between sex desires and spiritual urges – a fact which accounts for the peculiar behaviour of people who participate in the orgies known as religious 'revivals,' common among the primitive types.

The world is ruled and the destiny of civilisation is established, by the human emotions. People are influenced in their actions, not by reason so much as by 'feelings.'

The creative faculty of the mind is set into action entirely by emotions and not by cold reason. The most powerful of all human emotions is that of sex. There are other mind stimulants, some of which have been listed, but no one of them, nor all of them combined, can equal the driving power of sex.

A mind stimulant is any influence that will either temporarily or permanently, increase the vibrations of thought. The ten major stimulants, described, are those resorted to most commonly. Through these sources one may commune with Infinite Intelligence, or enter, at will, the storehouse of the subconscious mind, either one's own, or that of another person. This procedure is all there is of genius.

A teacher, who has trained and directed the efforts of more than 30,000 sales people, made the astounding discovery that highly sexed people are the most efficient sales reps. The explanation is, that the factor of personality known as 'personal magnetism' is nothing more nor less than sex energy. Highly sexed people always have a plentiful supply of magnetism. Through cultivation and understanding, this vital force may be drawn upon and used to great advantage in the relationships between people. This energy may be communicated to others through the following media:

1. *The handshake* The touch of the hand indicates, instantly, the presence of magnetism or the lack of it.
2. *The tone of voice* Magnetism, or sex energy, is the factor with which the voice may be coloured or made musical and charming.
3. *Posture and carriage of the body* Highly sexed people move briskly and with grace and ease.
4. *The vibrations of thought* Highly sexed people mix the emotion of sex with their thoughts or may do so at will and in that way, may influence those around them.
5. *Body adornment* People who are highly sexed are usually very careful about their personal appearance. They usually select clothing of a style becoming to their personality, physique, complexion, etc.

When employing salespeople, the more capable sales manager looks for the quality of personal magnetism as the first requirement for the job. People who lack sex energy will never become enthusiastic nor inspire others. Enthusiasm is one of the most important requisites in salesmanship, no matter what one is selling. The public speaker, orator, preacher, lawyer or salesperson that is lacking in sex energy is a 'flop,' as far as being able to influence others is concerned.

Couple with this the fact, that most people can be influenced only through an appeal to their emotions and you will understand the importance of sex energy as a part of the salesperson's native ability. Master sales reps attain the status of mastery in selling, because they, either consciously or unconsciously, transform the energy of sex into sales enthusiasm! In this statement may be found a very practical suggestion as to the actual meaning of sex transformation.

Salespeople who know how to take their minds off the subject of sex and direct it in sales effort with as much enthusiasm and determination as they would apply to its original purpose, have acquired the art of sex transformation, whether they know it or not. The majority of sales people who transform their sex energy do so without being in the least aware of what they are doing or how they are doing it.

Transformation of sex energy calls for more willpower than the average person cares to use for this purpose. Those who find it difficult to summon will power sufficient for transformation may gradually acquire this ability. Though this requires willpower, the reward for the practice is more than worth the effort.

The entire subject of sex is one that the majority of people appear to be unpardonably ignorant. The urge of sex has been grossly misunderstood, slandered and burlesqued by the ignorant and the evil minded, for so long that the very word sex is seldom used in polite society. Men and women who are known to be blessed – yes, blessed – with highly sexed natures, are usually looked upon as being people who need watching. Instead of being called blessed, they are usually called cursed.

Millions of people, even in this age of enlightenment, have inferiority complexes that they developed because of this false belief that a highly sexed nature is a curse. These statements, of the virtue of sex energy, should not be construed as justification for the libertine. The emotion of sex is a virtue only when used intelligently, with discrimination. It may be misused and often is, to such an extent that it debases, instead of enriches, both body and mind. The better use of this power is the burden of this chapter.

It seemed quite significant to the author, when he made the discovery that practically every great male leader, whom he had the privilege of analysing, was a man whose achievements were largely inspired by a woman. In many instances, the 'woman in the case' was a modest, self-denying wife, of whom the public had heard little or nothing. In a few instances, the source of inspiration has been traced to the 'other woman.' Perhaps such cases may not be entirely unknown to you.

Intemperance in sex habits is just as detrimental as intemperance in habits of drinking and eating. In this age in which we live, an age that began in the 20th century, intemperance in habits of sex is common. This orgy of indulgence may account for the shortage of great leaders. No one can avail the forces of creative imagination, while dissipating them. Humans are the only creatures on earth that violates Nature's purpose in this connection. Every other animal indulges its sex nature in moderation and with purpose that harmonises with the laws of nature. Every other animal responds to the call of sex only in 'season.' The human inclination is to declare 'open season.'

Every intelligent person knows that stimulation in excess, through alcoholic drink and narcotics, is a form of intemperance that destroys the vital organs of the body, including the brain. Not every person knows, however, that over indulgence in sex expression may become a habit as destructive and as detrimental to creative effort as narcotics or liquor.

A sex-mad person is not essentially different than a dope-mad person! Both have lost control over their faculties of reason and will power. Sexual overindulgence may not only destroy reason and willpower, but it may also lead to either temporary, or permanent insanity. Many cases of hypochondria (imaginary illness) grow out of habits developed in ignorance of the true function of sex.

From these brief references to the subject, it may be readily seen that ignorance on the subject of sex transmutation, forces stupendous penalties upon the ignorant on the one hand. It withholds from them equally stupendous benefits, on the other.

Widespread ignorance on the subject of sex is due to the fact that the subject has been surrounded with mystery and clouded by dark silence. The conspiracy of mystery and silence has increased curiosity and desire to acquire more knowledge on this 'verboten' subject. To the shame of all lawmakers and most physicians – by training best qualified to educate youth on that subject – such information has not been easily available.

Seldom does an individual enter upon highly creative effort in any field of endeavour before the age of forty. The greatest capacity to create for the average person is between forty and sixty. These statements are based upon analysis of thousands of men and women who have been carefully observed. They should be encouraging to those who fail to arrive before the age of forty and to those who become frightened at the approach of 'old age,' around the forty-year mark. The years between forty and fifty are, as a rule, the most fruitful. One should approach this age, not with fear and trembling, but with hope and eager anticipation.

If you want evidence that most people do not begin to do their best work before the age of forty, study the records of the most successful people known to the American people and you will find it. Henry Ford had not 'hit his pace' of achievement until he had passed the age of forty. Andrew Carnegie was well past forty before he began to reap the reward of his efforts. James J Hill was still running a telegraph key at the age of forty. His stupendous achievements took place after that age. Biographies of American industrialists and financiers are filled with evidence that the period from forty to sixty is the most productive age.

Between the ages of thirty and forty, one begins to learn (if one ever learns), the art of sex transformation. This discovery is generally accidental and more often than otherwise, the persons who make it are totally unconscious of this discovery. They may observe that their powers of achievement have increased around the age of thirty-five to forty, but in most cases, they are not familiar with the cause of this change; that Nature begins to harmonise the emotions of love and sex in the individual, between the ages of thirty and forty, so that they may draw upon these great forces and apply them jointly as stimuli to action.

Sex, alone, is a mighty urge to action, but its forces are like a cyclone – they are often uncontrollable. When the emotion of love begins to mix itself with the emotion of sex, the result is calmness of purpose, poise, accuracy of judgement and balance. What person, who has attained the age of forty, is so unfortunate as to be unable to analyse these statements and to corroborate them by personal experience?

Love, romance and sex are all emotions capable of driving people to heights of super achievement. Love is the emotion that serves as a safety valve and insures balance, poise and constructive effort. When combined, these three emotions may lift one to an altitude of a genius. There are geniuses, however, which know but little of the emotion of love. Most of them may be found engaged in some form of action which is destructive, or at least, not based upon justice and fairness toward others. If good taste would permit, a dozen geniuses could be named in the field of industry and finance, which ride ruthlessly over the rights of others. They seem totally lacking in conscience. The emotions are states of mind. Nature has provided us with a 'chemistry of the mind' which operates in a manner similar to the principles of chemistry of matter. It is a well-known fact that, through the aid of chemistry of matter, a chemist may create a deadly poison by mixing certain elements, none of which are – in themselves – harmful in the right proportions. The emotions may, likewise, be combined so as to create a deadly poison. The emotions of sex and jealousy, when mixed, may turn a person into an insane beast.

The presence of any one or more of the destructive emotions in the human mind, through the chemistry of the mind, sets up a poison that may destroy one's sense of justice and fairness. In extreme cases, the presence of any combination of these emotions in the mind may destroy one's reason.

The road to genius consists of the development, control and use of sex, love and romance. Briefly, the process may be stated as follows:

Encourage the presence of these emotions as the dominating thoughts in one's mind and discourage the presence of all the destructive emotions. The mind is a creature of habit. It thrives upon the dominating thoughts fed to it. Through the faculty of will power, one may discourage the presence of any emotion and encourage the presence of any other. Control of the mind, through the power of will, is not difficult. Control comes from persistence and habit. The secret of control lies in understanding the process of transformation. When any negative emotion presents itself in one's mind, it can be transformed into a positive or constructive emotion, by the simple procedure of changing one's thoughts.

There is no other road to genius than through voluntary self-effort! People may attain to great heights of financial or business achievement, solely by the driving force of sex energy. History is filled with evidence that they may and usually do, carry with them certain traits of character which rob them of the ability to either hold or enjoy their good fortune. This is worthy of analysis, thought and meditation, for it states a truth, the knowledge of which may be helpful to all people. Ignorance of this has cost thousands of people their privilege of happiness, even though they possessed riches.

The emotions of love and sex leave their unmistakable marks upon the features. Moreover, these signs are so visible, that all who wish may read them. People who are driven by the storm of passion, based upon sex desires alone, plainly advertises that fact to the entire world, by the expression of their eyes and the lines of their faces. The emotion of love, when mixed with the emotion of sex, softens, modifies and beautifies the facial expression. No character analyst is needed to tell you this. You may observe it for yourself.

The emotion of love brings out and develops, the artistic and the aesthetic nature of a person. It leaves its impress upon one's very soul, even after the fire has been subdued by time and circumstance.

Memories of love never pass. They linger, guide and influence us long after the source of stimulation has faded. There is nothing new in this. Every person, who has been moved by genuine love, knows that it leaves enduring traces upon the human heart. The effect of love endures, because love is spiritual in nature. Those who cannot be stimulated to great heights of achievement by love are hopeless – they are dead, though they may seem to live. Even the memories of love are sufficient to lift one to a higher plane of creative effort. The major force of love may spend itself and pass away, like a fire that has burned itself out, but it leaves behind indelible marks as evidence that it passed that way. Its departure often prepares the human heart for a still greater love.

Go back into your yesterdays, at times. Bathe your mind in the beautiful memories of past love. It will soften the influence of the present worries and annoyances. It will give you a source of escape from the unpleasant realities of life. Maybe – who knows? Your mind will yield to you, during this temporary retreat into the world of fantasy, ideas or plans which may change the entire financial or spiritual status of your life.

If you believe yourself unfortunate, because you have 'loved and lost,' perish the thought. One who has loved truly, can never lose entirely. Love is whimsical and temperamental. Its nature is ephemeral and transitory. It comes when it pleases and goes away without warning. Accept and enjoy it while it remains, but spend no time worrying about its departure. Worry will never bring it back.

Dismiss, also, the thought that love never comes but once. Love may come and go, times without number, but there are no two-love experiences that affect one in just the same way. There may be – there usually is, one love experience that leaves a deeper imprint on the heart than all the others Yet all love experiences are beneficial, except to the person who becomes resentful and cynical when love makes its departure.

There should be no disappointment over love. There would be none if people understood the difference between the emotions of love and sex. The major difference is that love is spiritual, while sex is biological. No experience, which touches the human heart with a spiritual force, can possibly be harmful, except through ignorance or jealousy.

Love is, without question, life's greatest experience. It brings one into communion with Infinite Intelligence. When mixed with the emotions of romance and sex, it may lead one far up the ladder of creative effort. The emotions of love, sex and romance, are sides of the eternal triangle of achievement-building genius. Nature creates geniuses through no other force.

Love is an emotion with many sides, shades and colours. The love which one feels for parents or children is quite different from what one feels for one's sweetheart. One is mixed with the emotion of sex, while the other is not.

The love which one feels in true friendship is not the same as that felt for one's sweetheart, parents or children. Yet it, too, is a form of love.

Then, there is the emotion of love for things inanimate, such as the love of Nature's handiwork. However the most intense and burning of all these various kinds of love, is when experienced in the blending of the emotions of love and sex. Marriages, not blessed with the eternal affinity of love, properly balanced and proportioned, with sex, cannot be happy ones and seldom endure. Love, alone, will not bring happiness in marriage nor will sex alone. When these two beautiful emotions are blended, marriage may bring about a state of mind, closest to the spiritual that one may ever know on this earthly plane.

When the emotion of romance is added to those of love and sex, the obstructions between the finite mind of man and Infinite Intelligence are removed. Then a genius has been born!

What a different story is this, than those usually associated with the emotion of sex. Here is an interpretation of the emotion that lifts it out of the commonplace. It becomes potter's clay in the hands of God, from which He fashions all that is beautiful and inspiring. It is an interpretation that would, when properly understood, bring harmony out of the chaos that exists in too many marriages. The disharmonies may usually be traced to lack of knowledge on the subject of sex. Where love, romance and the proper understanding of the emotion and function of sex abide, there is no disharmony between married people.

TWELVE

The Subconscious Mind: The Connecting Link

The subconscious mind consists of a field of consciousness, in which every impulse of thought that reaches the objective mind through any of the five senses, is classified and recorded and from which thoughts may be recalled or withdrawn as letters may be taken from a filing cabinet.

It receives and files, sense impressions or thoughts, regardless of their nature. You may voluntarily plant in your subconscious mind any plan, thought or purpose which you desire to translate into its physical or monetary equivalent. The subconscious acts first on the dominating desires that have been mixed with emotional feeling, such as faith.

Consider this in connection with the instructions given in chapter 2 on desire, for taking the six steps there outlined and the instructions given in the chapter on the building and execution of plans and you will understand the importance of the thought conveyed.

The subconscious mind works day and night to draw upon the forces of Infinite Intelligence. This energy voluntarily transforms one's desires into their physical equivalent, ever ensuring the most practical media for achievement.

You cannot entirely control your subconscious mind, but you can voluntarily hand over to it any plan, desire or purpose that you wish to convert into concrete form. Read again, instructions for using the subconscious mind, in Chapter 4.

There is plenty of evidence to support the belief that the subconscious mind is the connecting link between the finite mind and Infinite Intelligence. It is the intermediary through which one may draw upon the forces of Infinite Intelligence at will. It, alone, contains the secret process by which mental impulses are modified and changed into their spiritual equivalent. It, alone, is the medium through which prayer may be transmitted to the source capable of answering prayer.

The possibilities of creative effort connected with the subconscious mind are stupendous as also infinite. They inspire one with awe.

I never approach the discussion of the subconscious mind without a feeling of smallness and inferiority due, perhaps, to the fact that the entire stock of knowledge on this subject is so pitifully limited. The very fact that the subconscious mind is the medium of communication between the thinking mind and Infinite Intelligence is, of itself, a thought that almost paralyses one's reason.

After you have accepted, as a reality, the existence of the subconscious mind as also form understand its possibilities, as a medium to trans your desires into their physical or monetary equivalent, you will comprehend the full significance of the instructions given in Chapter 2 on desire. You will also understand why you have been repeatedly admonished to make your desires clear and to reduce them to writing. You will also understand the necessity of persistence in carrying out instructions.

The thirteen principles are the stimuli with which you acquire the ability to reach as well as to influence your subconscious mind. Do not become discouraged, if you cannot do this upon the first attempt. Remember that the subconscious mind may be voluntarily directed only through habit, under the directions given in Chapter 3 on faith. You have not yet had time to master faith. Be patient. Be persistent.

A good many statements in the chapters on faith and autosuggestion will be repeated here, for the benefit of your subconscious mind. Remember, your subconscious mind functions voluntarily, whether or not you make any effort to influence it. This, naturally, suggests to you thoughts of fear and poverty.All negative thoughts serve as stimuli to your subconscious mind, unless, you master these impulses to give it more desirable food upon which it may feed.

The subconscious mind will not remain idle! If you fail to plant desires in your subconscious mind, it will feed upon the thoughts that reach it as the result of your neglect. We have already explained that thought impulses, both negative and positive are reaching the subconscious mind continuously, from the four sources that were mentioned in Chapter 11 on Sex Transformation.

For the present, it is sufficient if you remember that you are living daily, in the midst of all manner of thought impulses that are reaching your subconscious mind, without your knowledge. Some of these impulses are negative, some are positive. You are now engaged in trying to help shut off the flow of negative impulses and to aid in voluntarily influencing your subconscious mind, through positive impulses of desire.

When you achieve this, you will possess the key that unlocks the door to your subconscious mind. Moreover, you will control that door so completely, that no undesirable thought may influence your subconscious mind.

Everything that is created begins in the form of a thought impulse. Nothing can be created that is not first conceived in thought. Through the aid of the imagination, thought impulses may be assembled into plans. The imagination, when under control, may be used for the creation of plans or purposes that lead to success in one's chosen occupation.

All thought impulses, intended for transformation form into their physical equivalent, voluntarily planted in the subconscious mind, must pass through the imagination, to be mixed with faith. The 'mixing' of faith with a plan, or purpose, intended for submission to the subconscious mind, may be done only through the imagination.

From these statements, you will readily observe that voluntary use of the subconscious mind calls for coordination and application of all the principles. Thoughts are truly things, for the reason that every material thing begins in the form of thought-energy.

The subconscious mind is more susceptible to influence by impulses of thought mixed with 'feeling' or emotion, than by those originating solely in the reasoning portion of the mind. In fact, there is much evidence to support the theory, that only emotionalised thoughts have any action influence upon the subconscious mind. It is a well-known fact that emotion or feeling, rules the majority of people. If it is true that the subconscious mind responds more quickly to and is influenced more readily by thought impulses that are well mixed with emotion, it is essential to become familiar with the more important of the emotions. There are seven major positive emotions and seven major negative emotions. The negatives voluntarily inject themselves into the thought impulses, which insure passage into the subconscious mind. The positives must be injected, through the principle of autosuggestion, into the thought impulses that an individual wishes to pass on to the subconscious mind. (Instructions have been given on autosuggestion in Chapter 4.)

These emotions or feeling impulses, may be likened to yeast in a loaf of bread, because they constitute the action element, which transforms thought impulses from the passive to the active state. Thus may one understand why thought impulses, which have been well mixed with emotion, are enacted more readily than thought impulses originating in 'cold reason.'

You are preparing yourself to influence and control the 'inner audience' of your subconscious mind, in order to hand over to it the desire for money, which you wish transform into its monetary equivalent. It is essential, therefore, that you understand the method of approach to this 'inner audience.' You must speak its language or it will not heed your call. It understands best the language of emotion or feeling. Let us, therefore describe here the seven major positive emotions and the seven major negative emotions, So you may draw upon the positives and avoid the negatives, when giving instructions to your subconscious mind.

THE SEVEN MAJOR POSITIVE EMOTIONS

The emotion of desire
The emotion of faith
The emotion of love
The emotion of sex
The emotion of enthusiasm
The emotion of romance
The emotion of hope

There are other positive emotions, but these are the seven most powerful and the ones most commonly used in creative effort. Master these seven emotions (they can be mastered only by *use*) and the other positive emotions will be at your command when you need them. Remember, in this connection, that you are studying a book that is intended to help you develop a 'money consciousness' by filling your mind with positive emotions. One does not become money conscious by filling one's mind with negative emotions.

THE SEVEN MAJOR NEGATIVE EMOTIONS (TO BE AVOIDED)

The emotion of fear
The emotion of jealousy
The emotion of hatred
The emotion of revenge
The emotion of greed
The emotion of superstition
The emotion of anger

Positive and negative emotions cannot occupy the mind at the same time. One or the other must dominate. It is your responsibility to make sure that positive emotions constitute the dominating influence of your mind. Here the law of habit will come to your aid. *Form the habit* of applying and using the positive emotions! Eventually, they will dominate your mind so completely, that the negatives *cannot enter it.*

Only by following these instructions literally and continuously, can you gain control over your subconscious mind. The presence of a single negative in your conscious mind is sufficient to destroy all chances of constructive aid from your subconscious mind.

If you are an observant person, you must have noticed that most people resort to prayer only after everything else has failed! Or else they pray by a ritual of meaningless words. And, because it is a fact that most people who pray, do so only after everything else has failed, they go to prayer with their minds filled with fear and doubt, which are the emotions the subconscious mind acts upon and passes on to Infinite Intelligence. Likewise, that is the emotion that Infinite Intelligence receives and acts upon. If you pray for a thing, but have fear as you pray, that you may not receive it or that Infinite Intelligence will not act upon your prayer, your prayer *will have been in vain.*

Prayer does, sometimes, result in the realisation of that for which one prays. If you have ever had the experience of receiving that for which you prayed, go back in your memory and recall your actual state of mind, while you were praying and you will know, for sure, that the theory here described is more than a theory.

The time will come when the schools and educational institutions of the country will teach the 'science of prayer.' Moreover, then prayer may be and will be reduced to a science. When that time comes, (it will come as soon as humankind is ready for it and demands it), no one will approach the Universal Mind in a state of fear, for the very good reason that there will be no such emotion as fear. Ignorance, superstition and false teaching will have disappeared and we will have attained our true status as children of Infinite Intelligence. A few have already attained this blessing.

If you believe this prophesy is far-fetched, take a look at the human race in retrospect. About two hundred years ago, it was commonly believed that lightning was feared as evidence of the wrath of God. Now, thanks to the power of faith, we have harnessed lightning to make it turn the wheels of industry. Until relatively recent times, it was believed that the space between the planets were nothing but a great void, a stretch of dead nothingness. Now, thanks to this same power of faith, we know that far from being either dead or a void, the space between the planets is very much alive, that it is the highest form of vibration known, excepting, perhaps, the vibration of thought. Moreover, we know that this living, pulsating, vibratory energy that permeates every atom of matter and fills every niche of space, connects every human brain with every other human brain. What reason do we have to believe that this same energy does not connect every human brain with Infinite Intelligence?

There are no tollgates between the finite mind of humans and Infinite Intelligence. The communication costs nothing except *patience*, *faith*, *persistence*, *understanding* and a sincere *desire* to communicate. Moreover, the approach can be made only by each of us ourselves. Paid prayers are worthless. Infinite Intelligence does no business by proxy. You either go direct or you do not communicate.

You may buy prayer books and repeat them until the day of your doom, without avail. Thoughts that you wish to communicate to Infinite Intelligence must undergo transformation, such as can be given only through your own subconscious mind.

The method by which you may communicate with Infinite Intelligence is very similar to that through which the vibration of sound is communicated by wireless communication If you understand the working principle of radio, TV and cellular phones, you of course, know that audio and video cannot be communicated through the ether until it has been 'stepped up,' or changed into a rate of vibration which the human ear or eye cannot detect. The sending station picks up the audio and video, 'scrambles,' or modifies it by stepping up the vibration millions of times. Only in this way, can the vibrations be communicated through the ether. After this transformation has taken place, the ether 'picks up' the energy and carries that energy to receiving stations and these receiving sets 'step' that energy back down to its original rate of vibration so it can be seen and heard.

The subconscious mind is the intermediary, which translates one's prayers into terms that Infinite Intelligence can recognise, presents the message and brings back the answer in the form of a definite plan or idea for procuring the object of the prayer. Understand this principle. You will know why mere words read from a prayer book cannot and will never serve as an agency of communication between the human mind and Infinite Intelligence.

Before your prayer will reach Infinite Intelligence (a statement of the author's theory only), it probably is transformed from its original thought vibration into terms of spiritual vibration. Faith is the only known agency that will give your thoughts a spiritual nature. Faith and fear make poor bedfellows. Where one is found, the other cannot exist.

THIRTEEN

The Brain: A Broadcasting and Receiving Station for Thought

In a study by the author with Dr Alexander Graham Bell and Dr Elmer R Gates, it was concluded that every human brain is both a broadcasting and receiving station for the vibration of thought.

Through the medium of the ether, in a fashion similar to that employed by the basic principle of radio and other wireless communication every human brain is capable of picking up vibrations of thought that are being released by other brains.

In connection with the statement in the preceding paragraph, compare and consider the description of the Creative Imagination, as outlined in Chapter 6 on Imagination. The Creative Imagination is the 'receiving set' of the brain, which receives thoughts, released by the brains of others. It is the agency of communication between one's conscious or reasoning mind and the four sources from which one may receive thought stimuli.

When stimulated or 'stepped up' to a high rate of vibration, the mind becomes more receptive to the vibration of thought which reaches it through the ether from outside sources. This 'stepping up' process takes place through the positive emotions or the negative emotions. Through the emotions, the vibrations of thought may be increased. Vibrations of an exceedingly high rate are the only vibrations picked up and carried, by the ether, from one brain to another. Thought is energy travelling at an exceedingly high rate of vibration. Thought, which has been modified or 'stepped up' by any of the major emotions, vibrates at a much higher rate than ordinary thought and it is this type of thought which passes from one brain to another, through the broadcasting machinery of the human brain.

The emotion of sex stands at the head of the list of human emotions, as far as intensity and driving force are concerned. The brain which has been stimulated by the emotion of sex, vibrates at a much more rapid rate than it does when that emotion is inactive or absent.

The result of sex transmutation, is the increase of the rate of vibration of thoughts to such a pitch that the Creative Imagination becomes highly receptive to ideas, which it picks up from the ether. On the other hand, when the brain is vibrating at a rapid rate, it not only attracts thoughts and ideas released by other brains through the medium of the ether, but it gives to one's own thoughts that 'feeling' which is essential before those thoughts will be picked up and acted upon by one's subconscious mind.

Thus, you will see that the broadcasting principle is the factor through which you mix feeling or emotion with your thoughts and pass them on to your subconscious mind.

The subconscious mind is the 'sending station' of the brain, through which vibrations of thought are broadcast. The Creative Imagination is the 'receiving set,' through which the vibrations of thought are picked up from the ether.

Along with the important factors of the subconscious mind

and the faculty of the Creative Imagination, which constitute the sending and receiving sets of your mental broadcasting machinery, consider now the principle of autosuggestion, which is the medium by which you may put into operation your 'broadcasting' station.

Through the instructions described in Chapter 4 on autosuggestion, you were definitely informed of the method by which *desire* may be transformed into its monetary equivalent.

Operation of your mental 'broadcasting' station is a comparatively simple procedure. You have but three principles to bear in mind and to apply, when you wish to use your broadcasting station – the subconscious mind, creative imagination and autosuggestion. The stimuli through which you put these three principles into action have been described – the procedure begins with *desire*.

THE GREATEST FORCES ARE 'INTANGIBLE'

The Great Depression of the 1930s brought the world to the very borderline of understanding of the forces that are intangible and unseen. Through the ages that have passed, man has depended too much upon his physical senses. This has limited his knowledge to physical things, which he could see, touch, weigh and measure. We are now entering the most marvelous of all ages – an age that will teach us something of the intangible forces of the world about us. Perhaps we shall learn, as we pass through this age, that the 'other self' is more powerful than the physical self we see when we look into a mirror.

Sometimes we speak lightly of the intangibles – the things that we cannot perceive through any of our five senses, but we should never forget that all of us are controlled by forces that are unseen and intangible.

The whole of humankind has not the power to cope with nor to control the intangible force wrapped up in the rolling waves of the oceans. The human mind does not have the capacity to understand the intangible force of gravity, which keeps this little Earth suspended in mid-air and keeps us from falling from it, much less the power to control that force. All of us are entirely subservient to the intangible force, which comes with a thunderstorm. We are just as helpless in the presence of the intangible force of electricity. Indeed, many of us do not even know what electricity is, where it comes from or what is its purpose!

Nor is this by any means the end of our ignorance in connection with things unseen and intangible. We do not understand the intangible force (and intelligence) wrapped up in the soil of the Earth – the force that provides us with every morsel of food we eat, every article of clothing we wear, every dollar we carry in our pockets.

THE DRAMATIC STORY OF THE BRAIN

Last, but not least, with all of our boasted culture and education, we understand little or nothing of the intangible force (the greatest of all the intangibles) of thought. We know but little concerning the physical brain and its vast network of intricate machinery through which the power of thought is translated into its material equivalent, but we are now entering an age which shall yield enlightenment on the subject. Already scientists have begun to turn their attention to the study of this stupendous thing called a brain. Even though they are still in the kindergarten stage of their studies, they have uncovered enough knowledge to know that the central switchboard of the human brain, the number of lines which connect the brain cells one with another, equal the figure one, followed by fifteen million ciphers.

'The figure is so stupendous,' said Dr C Judson Herrick, of the University of Chicago, 'that astronomical figures dealing with hundreds of millions of light years, become insignificant by comparison.

It has been determined that there are from 10–14 billion nerve cells in the human cerebral cortex and we know that these are arranged in definite patterns. These arrangements are not haphazard. They are orderly. Recently developed methods of electro-physiology draw off action currents from very precisely located cells, or fibres with micro-electrodes, amplify them and record potential differences to a millionth of a volt.'

It is inconceivable that such a network of intricate machinery should be in existence for the sole purpose of carrying on the physical functions incidental to growth and maintenance of the physical body. Is it not likely that the same system, which gives billions of brain cells the media for communication – one with another, provides, also the means of communication with other intangible forces?

In the late 1930s, *The New York Times* published an editorial showing that at least one great University and one intelligent investigator in the field of mental phenomena, were carrying on an organised research through which conclusions had been reached that parallel many of those described in this and the following chapter. The editorial briefly analysed the work carried on by Dr Rhine and his associates at Duke University.

WHAT IS 'TELEPATHY'?

'A month ago we cited on this page some of the remarkable results achieved by Professor Rhine and his associates in Duke

University from more than a hundred thousand tests to determine the existence of "telepathy" and "clairvoyance." These results were summarised in the first two articles in *Harper's Magazine*. In the second that has now appeared, the author, E H Wright, attempts to summarise what has been learned, or what it seems reasonable to infer, regarding the exact nature of these "extrasensory" modes of perception.

'The actual existence of telepathy and clairvoyance now seems to some scientists enormously probable as the result of Rhine's experiments. Various percipients were asked to name as many cards in a special pack as they could without looking at them and without other sensory access to them. About a score of men and women were discovered who could regularly name so many of the cards correctly that "there was not one chance in many a million million of their having done their feats by luck or accident."

'But how did they do them? These powers, assuming that they exist, do not seem to be sensory. There is no known organ for them. The experiments worked just as well at distances of several hundred miles as they did in the same room. These facts also dispose, in Mr Wright's opinion, of the attempt to explain telepathy or clairvoyance through any physical theory of radiation. All known forms of radiant energy decline inversely as the square of the distance travelled. Telepathy and clairvoyance do not. Yet they do vary through physical causes just as our other mental powers do. Contrary to widespread opinion, they do not improve when the clairvoyant is asleep or half-asleep, but, on the contrary, when he is most wide-awake and alert. Rhine discovered that a narcotic will invariably lower a percipient's score, while a stimulant will always send it higher. The most reliable performer apparently cannot make a good score unless he tries to do his best.

'One conclusion that Wright draws with some confidence is that telepathy and clairvoyance are really one and the same gift. That is, the faculty that 'sees' a card face down on a table seems to be exactly the same one that 'reads' a thought residing only in another mind. There are several grounds for believing this. So far, for example, both gifts have been found in every person who enjoys either one of them. In every one so far the two have been of equal vigour, almost exactly. Screens, walls, distances, have no effect at all on either. Wright advances from this conclusion to express what he puts forward as no more than the mere 'hunch' that other extra-sensory experiences, prophetic dreams, premonitions of disaster and the like, may also prove to be part of the same faculty. The reader is not asked to accept any of these conclusions unless he finds it necessary, but the evidence that Rhine has piled up must remain impressive.'

In view of Dr Rhine's announcement in connection with the conditions under which the mind responds to what he terms 'extra-sensory' modes of perception, I now feel privileged to add to his testimony. My associates and I have discovered what we believe to be the ideal conditions under which the mind can be stimulated so that the sixth sense described in the next chapter, can be made to function in a practical way.

The conditions to which I refer consist of a close working alliance between myself and two members of my staff. Through experimentation and practice, we have discovered how to stimulate our minds (by applying the principle used in connection with the 'Invisible Counsellors' described in the next chapter) so that we can, by a process of blending our three minds into one, find the solution to a great variety of personal problems that are submitted by my clients.

The procedure is very simple. We sit down at a conference

table, clearly state the nature of the problem we have under consideration and then begin discussing it. Each contributes whatever thoughts may occur. The strange thing about this method of mind stimulation is that it places each participant in communication with unknown sources of knowledge definitely outside his own experience.

If you understand the principle described in the chapter on the Master Mind, you of course recognise the round-table procedure here described as being a practical application of the Master Mind.

This method of mind stimulation, through harmonious discussion of definite subjects, between three people, illustrates the simplest as well as most practical use of the Master Mind.

By adopting and following a similar plan any student of this philosophy may come into possession of the famous Carnegie formula briefly described in the Author's Preface. If it means nothing to you at this time, mark this page. Read it again after you have finished the last chapter.

FOURTEEN

The Sixth Sense: The Door to the Temple of Wisdom

The individual knows the 'thirteenth' principle as the sixth sense, through which Infinite Intelligence may and will communicate voluntarily, without any effort from, or demands.

This principle is the apex of the philosophy. It can be assimilated, understood and applied only by first mastering the other twelve principles.

The sixth sense is that portion of the subconscious mind that has been referred to as the Creative Imagination. It has also been referred to as the 'receiving set' through which ideas, plans as also thoughts flash into the mind. The 'flashes' are sometimes called 'hunches' or 'inspirations.'

The sixth sense defies description! It cannot be described to a person who has not mastered the other principles of this philosophy, because such a person has no knowledge and no experience with which the sixth sense may be compared. Understanding of the sixth sense comes only by meditation through mind development from within. The sixth sense probably is the medium of contact between the finite mind individuals and Infinite Intelligence and for this reason, it is a mixture of both the mental and the spiritual. It is believed to be the point where the mind of an individual contacts the Universal Mind.

After you have mastered the principles described in this book, you will be prepared to accept as truth a statement that may, otherwise, be incredible to you, namely: *Through the aid of the sixth sense, you will be warned of impending dangers in time to avoid them and notified of opportunities in time to embrace them.*

There comes to your aid and to do your bidding, with the development of the sixth sense, a 'guardian angel' who will open to you at all times the door to the Temple of Wisdom.

Whether or not this is a statement of truth, you will never know, except by following the instructions described in the pages of this book or some similar method of procedure.

The author is not a believer in nor an advocate of 'miracles,' for the reason that he has enough knowledge of Nature to understand that Nature never deviates from her established laws. Some of her laws are so incomprehensible that they produce what appear to be 'miracles.' The sixth sense comes as near to being a miracle as anything I have ever experienced. It appears so, only because I do not understand how this principle is operated.

This much the author does know – that there is a power or a First Cause, or an Intelligence, which permeates every atom of matter and embraces every unit of perceptible energy that this Infinite Intelligence converts acorns into oak trees, causes water to flow down hill in response to the law of gravity, follows night with day and winter with summer, each maintaining its proper place and relationship to the other. This Intelligence may, through the principles of this philosophy, be induced to aid in transforming desires into concrete or material form. The author has this knowledge, because he has experimented with it and has experienced it.

Step by step, through the preceding chapters, you have been led to this, the last principle. If you have mastered each of the preceding principles, you are now prepared to accept, without being skeptical, the stupendous claims made here. If you have not mastered the other principles, you must do so before you may determine, definitely, whether or not the claims made in this chapter are fact or fiction.

While I was passing through the age of 'hero-worship' I found myself trying to imitate those whom I most admired. Moreover, I discovered that the element of faith, with which I endeavoured to imitate my idols, gave me a great capacity to do so quite successfully.

I have never entirely divested myself of this habit of hero-worship, although I have passed the age commonly given over to such. My experience has taught me that the next best thing to being truly great is to emulate the great, by feeling and action, as nearly as possible.

Long before I had ever written a line for publication or endeavoured to deliver a speech in public. I followed the habit of reshaping my own character, by trying to imitate the nine men whose lives and life-works had been most impressive to me. These nine men were Emerson, Paine, Edison, Darwin, Lincoln, Burbank, Napoleon, Ford and Carnegie. Every night, over many years, I held an imaginary Council meeting with this group whom I called my 'Invisible Counsellors.'

The procedure was this. Just before going to sleep at night, I would shut my eyes, to see in my imagination, this group of men seated with me around my Council Table. Here I had not only an opportunity to sit among those whom I considered to be great, but I actually dominated the group, by serving as the Chairman.

I had a very definite purpose in indulging my imagination through these nightly meetings. My purpose was to rebuild my own character so it would represent a composite of the characters of my imaginary Counsellors. Realising, early in life, that I had to overcome the handicap of birth in an environment of ignorance and superstition, I deliberately assigned myself the task of voluntary rebirth through the method here described.

BUILDING CHARACTER THROUGH AUTOSUGGESTION

Being an earnest student of psychology, I knew, of course, that all people have become what they are, because of their dominating thoughts and desires. I knew that every deeply seated desire has the effect of causing one to seek outward expression through which that desire may be transmuted into reality. I knew that self-suggestion is a powerful factor in building character, that it is, in fact, the sole principle through which character is built. With this knowledge of the principles of mind operation, I was fairly well armed with the equipment needed in rebuilding my character. In these imaginary Council meetings I called on my Cabinet members for the knowledge I wished each to contribute, addressing myself to each member in audible words, as follows:

'Mr Emerson, I desire to acquire from you the marvelous understanding of Nature which distinguished your life. I ask that you make an impression upon my subconscious mind, of whatever qualities you possessed, which enabled you to understand and adapt yourself to the laws of Nature. I ask that you assist me in reaching and drawing upon whatever sources of knowledge are available to this end.

'Mr Burbank, I request that you pass on to me the knowledge

which enabled you to so harmonise the laws of Nature that you caused the cactus to shed its thorns to become an edible food. Give me access to the knowledge which enabled you to make two blades of grass grow where but one grew before that helped you to blend the colouring of the flowers with more splendour and harmony. You, alone, have successfully gilded the lily.

'Napoleon, I desire to acquire from you, by emulation, the marvelous ability you possessed to inspire people – to arouse them to greater and more determined spirit of action. Also to acquire the spirit of enduring faith, which enabled you to turn defeat into victory and to surmount staggering obstacles. Emperor of Fate, King of Chance, Man of Destiny, I salute you!

'Mr Paine, I desire to acquire from you the freedom of thought and the courage and clarity with which to express convictions, which so distinguished you!

'Mr Darwin, I wish to acquire from you the marvelous patience and ability to study cause and effect, without bias or prejudice, so exemplified by you in the field of natural science.

'Mr Lincoln, I desire to build into my own character the keen sense of justice, the untiring spirit of patience, the sense of humor, the human understanding and the tolerance, which were your distinguishing characteristics.

'Mr Carnegie, I am already indebted to you for my choice of a life-work, which has brought me great happiness and peace of mind. I wish to acquire a thorough understanding of the principles of organised effort, which you used so effectively in the building of a great industrial enterprise.

'Mr Ford, you have been among the most helpful of the men who have supplied much of the material essential to my work. I wish to acquire your spirit of persistence, the determination, poise and self-confidence that have enabled you to master poverty, organise, unify and simplify human effort, so I may help others to follow in your footsteps.

'Mr Edison, I have seated you nearest to me, at my right, because of the personal cooperation you have given me, during my research into the causes of success and failure. I wish to acquire from you the marvelous spirit of faith, with which you have uncovered so many of Nature's secrets, the spirit of unremitting toil with which you have so often wrested victory from defeat.'

My method of addressing the members of the imaginary Cabinet would vary, according to the traits of character, which I was, for the moment, most interested in acquiring. I studied the records of their lives with painstaking care. After some months of this nightly procedure, I was astounded by the discovery that these imaginary figures became, apparently real.

Each of these nine men developed individual characteristics, which surprised me. For example Lincoln developed the habit of always being late then walking around in solemn parade. When he came, he walked very slowly, with his hands clasped behind him, Once in a while, he would stop as he passed and rest his hand, momentarily, upon my shoulder. He always wore an expression of seriousness upon his face. Rarely did I see him smile. The cares of a sundered nation made him grave.

That was not true of the others. Burbank and Paine often indulged in witty repartee that seemed, at times, to shock the other members of the cabinet. One night Paine suggested that I prepare a lecture on 'The Age of Reason,' and deliver it from the pulpit of a church that I formerly attended. Many around the table laughed heartily at the suggestion. Not Napoleon! He drew his mouth down at the corners and groaned so loudly that all turned and looked at him with amazement. To him the church was but a pawn of the State not to be reformed, but to be used, as a convenient inciter to mass activity by the people.

On one occasion Burbank was late. When he came, he was excited with enthusiasm and explained that he had been late, because of an experiment he was making, through which he hoped to be able to grow apples on any sort of tree. Paine chided him by reminding him that it was an apple that started all the trouble between man and woman. Darwin chuckled heartily as he suggested that Paine should watch out for little serpents, when he went into the forest to gather apples, as they had the habit of growing into big snakes. Emerson observed – 'No serpents, no apples,' and Napoleon remarked, 'No apples, no state!'

Lincoln developed the habit of always being the last one to leave the table after each meeting. On one occasion, he leaned across the end of the table, his arms folded and remained in that position for many minutes. I made no attempt to disturb him. Finally, he lifted his head slowly, got up and walked to the door, then turned around, came back and laid his hand on my shoulder and said, 'My boy, you will need much courage if you remain steadfast in carrying out your purpose in life. But remember, when difficulties overtake you, the common people have common sense. Adversity will develop it.'

One evening Edison arrived ahead of all the others. He walked over and seated himself at my left, where Emerson was accustomed to sit and said, 'You are destined to witness the discovery of the secret of life. When the time comes, you will observe that life consists of great swarms of energy or entities, each as intelligent as human beings think themselves to be. These units of life group together like hives of bees and remain together until they disintegrate, through lack of harmony.

These units have differences of opinion, the same as human beings and often fight among themselves. These meetings which you are conducting will be very helpful to you. They will bring to your rescue some of the same units of life that served the members of your Cabinet, during their lives.

These units are eternal. They never die! Your own thoughts and desires serve as the magnet that attracts units of life, from the great ocean of life out there. Only the friendly units are attracted – the ones which harmonise with the nature of your desires.'

The other members of the Cabinet began to enter the room. Edison got up and slowly walked around to his own seat. Edison was still living when this happened. It impressed me so greatly that I went to see him and told him about the experience. He smiled broadly and said, 'Your dream was more a reality than you may imagine it to have been.' He added no further explanation to his statement.

These meetings became so realistic that I became fearful of their consequences and discontinued them for several months. The experiences were so uncanny, I was afraid if I continued them I would lose sight of the fact that the meetings were purely experiences of my imagination.

Some six months after I had discontinued the practice I was awakened one night, or thought I was, when I saw Lincoln standing at my bedside. He said, 'The world will soon need your services. It is about to undergo a period of chaos that will cause men and women to lose faith and become panic stricken. Go ahead with your work and complete your philosophy. That is your mission in life. If you neglect it, for any cause whatsoever, you will be reduced to a primal state and be compelled to retrace the cycles through which you have passed during thousands of years.'

I was unable to tell, the following morning, whether I had dreamed this, or had actually been awake and I have never since found out which it was, but I do know that the dream, if it were a dream, was so vivid in my mind the next day that I resumed my meetings the following night.

At our next meeting, the members of my Cabinet all filed into the room together and stood at their accustomed places at the Council Table, while Lincoln raised a glass and said, 'Gentlemen, let us drink a toast to a friend who has returned to the fold.'

After that, I began to add new members to my Cabinet, until now it consists of more than fifty, among them Christ, St Paul, Galileo, Copernicus, Aristotle, Plato, Socrates, Homer, Voltaire, Bruno, Spinoza, Drummond, Kant, Schopenhauer, Newton, Confucius, Elbert Hubbard, Brann, Ingersol, Wilson and William James.

This is the first time that I have had the courage to mention this. Until now, I have remained quiet on the subject, because I knew, from my own attitude in connection with such matters, that I would be misunderstood if I described my unusual experience. I have been emboldened now to reduce my experience to the printed page, because I am now less concerned about what 'they say' than I was in the years that have passed. One of the blessings of maturity is that it sometimes brings greater courage to be truthful, regardless of what those who do not understand, may think or say.

Lest I be misunderstood, I wish here to state most emphatically, that I still regard my Cabinet meetings as being purely imaginary, but I feel entitled to suggest that, while the members of my Cabinet may be purely fictional and the meetings existent only in my own imagination, they have led me into glorious paths of adventure, rekindled an appreciation of true greatness, encouraged creative endeavour and emboldened the expression of honest thought.

Somewhere in the cell-structure of the brain, is located an organ which receives vibrations of thought ordinarily called 'hunches.' So far, science has not discovered where this organ of the sixth sense is located, but this is not important. The fact remains that human beings do receive accurate knowledge, through sources other than the physical senses. Such knowledge, generally, is received when the mind is under the influence of extraordinary stimulation. Any emergency that arouses the emotions and causes the heart to beat more rapidly than normal may generally does, bring the sixth sense into action. Anyone who has experienced a near accident while driving knows that on such occasions, the sixth sense often comes to one's rescue and aids, by split seconds, in avoiding the accident.

These facts are mentioned preliminary to a statement of fact, which I shall now make, namely, that during my meetings with the 'Invisible Counsellors' I find my mind most receptive to ideas, thoughts and knowledge that reach me through the sixth sense. I can truthfully say that I owe entirely to my 'Invisible Counsellors' full credit for such ideas, facts or knowledge as I received through 'inspiration.'

On scores of occasions, when I have faced emergencies, some of them so grave that my life was in jeopardy, I have been miraculously guided past these difficulties through the influence of my 'Invisible Counsellors.'

My original purpose in conducting Council meetings with imaginary beings was solely that of impressing my own subconscious mind, through the principle of autosuggestion, with certain characteristics that I desired to acquire. In more recent years, my experimentation has taken on an entirely different trend. I now go to my imaginary Counsellors with every difficult problem that confronts my clients or me. The results are often astonishing, although I do not depend entirely on this form of Counsel.

You, of course, have recognised that this chapter covers a subject with which a majority of people is not familiar. The Sixth Sense is a subject that will be of great interest and benefit to the person whose aim is to accumulate vast wealth, but it need not claim the attention of those whose desires are more modest.

Henry Ford undoubtedly understood and made practical use of the sixth sense. His vast business and financial operations made it necessary for him to understand and use this principle. Thomas A Edison understood and used the sixth sense in connection with the development of inventions, especially those involving basic patents, in connection with which he had no human experience and no accumulated knowledge to guide him, as was the case while he was working on the talking machine and the moving picture machine.

Nearly all great leaders, such as Napoleon, Joan of Arc, Christ, Buddha, Confucius and Mohammed, understood as well as probably made use of the sixth sense almost continuously. The major portion of their greatness consisted of their knowledge of this principle.

The sixth sense is not something that one can take off and put on at will. Ability to use this great power comes slowly, through application of the other principles outlined in this book. Seldom does any individual come into workable knowledge of the sixth sense before the age of forty. More often the knowledge is not available until one is well past fifty and this, for the reason that the spiritual forces, with which the sixth sense is so closely related, do not mature and become usable except through years of meditation, self-examination and serious thought.

No matter who you are or what may have been your purpose in reading this book, you cannot profit by it without understanding the principle described in this chapter. This is especially true if your major purpose is that of accumulation of money or other material things.

This chapter on the sixth sense was included, because the book is designed for the purpose of presenting a complete philosophy by which individuals may unerringly guide themselves in attaining whatever they ask of life. The starting point of all achievement is desire. The finishing point is that brand of knowledge that leads to understanding – understanding of self, understanding of others, understanding of the laws of Nature, recognition and understanding of happiness.

This sort of understanding comes in its fullness only through familiarity along with the use of the principle of the sixth sense, hence that principle had to be included as a part of this philosophy, for the benefit of those who demand more than money.

Having read the chapter, you must have observed that while reading it, you were lifted to a high level of mental stimulation. Splendid! Come back to this again a month from now, read it once more and observe that your mind will soar to a still higher level of stimulation. Repeat this experience from time to time, giving no concern as to how much or how little you learn at the time and eventually you will find yourself in possession of a power that will enable you to throw off discouragement, master fear, overcome procrastination and draw freely upon your imagination. Then you will have felt the touch of that unknown 'something' which has been the moving spirit of every truly great thinker leader, artist, musician, writer, statesman. Then you will be in position to transform your desires into their physical or financial counterpart as easily as you may lie down and quit at the first sign of opposition.

You have absolute control over but one thing and that is your thoughts. This is the most significant and inspiring of all known facts! It reflects our divine nature. This divine prerogative is the sole means by which you may control your own destiny. If you fail to control your own mind, you may be sure you will control nothing else. If you must be careless with your possessions, let it be in connection with material things. Your mind is your spiritual estate! Protect and use it with the care to which Divine Royalty is entitled. You were given a will power for this purpose.

Mind control is the result of self-discipline and habit. You either control your mind or it controls you. There is no halfway compromise. The most practical of all methods for controlling the mind is the habit of keeping it busy with a definite purpose, backed by a definite plan. Study the record of people who have achieved noteworthy success and you will observe that they have control over their own minds, moreover, that they exercise that control and direct it toward the attainment of definite objectives. Without this control, success is not possible.

In parting, I would remind you that 'Life is a checkerboard and the player opposite you is time. If you hesitate before moving, or neglect to move promptly, your checkers will be wiped off the board by time. You are playing against a partner who will not tolerate indecision!'

Previously you may have had a logical excuse for not having forced life to come through with whatever you asked, but that alibi is now obsolete, because you are in possession of the Master Key that unlocks the door to life's bountiful riches.

The Master Key is intangible, but it is powerful! It is the privilege of creating, in your own mind, a burning desire for a definite form of riches. There is no penalty for the use of the Key, but there is a price you must pay if you do not use it. The price is failure. There is a reward of stupendous proportions if you put the Key to use. It is the satisfaction that comes to all who conquer self and force Life to pay whatever is asked.

The reward is worthy of your effort. Will you make the start and be convinced? 'If we are related,' said the immortal Emerson, we shall meet.' In closing, may I borrow his thought and say, 'If we are related, we have, through these pages, met.'

APPENDIX A

Andrew Carnegie's Formula for Wealth Creation:

Here is the famous wealth creation formula Andrew Carnegie used to go from a poor Scottish immigrant to becoming one of the richest men in the world.

The method, by which desire for riches can be transformed into its financial equivalent, consists of six definite, practical steps. Carnegies 6 Steps To Riches:

First Fix in your mind the exact amount of money you desire. It is not sufficient merely to say, 'I want plenty of money.' Be definite as to the amount. (There is a psychological reason for definiteness, which will be described, in a subsequent chapter).

Second Determine exactly what you intend to give in return for the money you desire. (There is no such reality as 'something for nothing.)

Third Establish a definite date when you intend to possess the money you desire.

Fourth Create a definite plan for carrying out your desire and begin at once, whether you are ready or not, to put this plan into action.

Fifth Write out a clear, concise statement of the amount of money you intend to acquire, name the time limit for its acquisition, state what you intend to give in return for the money and describe clearly the plan through which you intend to accumulate it.

Sixth Read your written statement aloud, twice daily, once just before retiring at night and once after arising in the morning. As you read-see and feel and believe yourself already in possession of the money. It is important that you follow the instructions described in these six steps. It is especially important that you observe and follow the instructions in the sixth paragraph. You may complain that it is impossible for you to 'see yourself in possession of money' before you actually have it. Here is where a burning desire will come to your aid. If you truly *desire* money so keenly that your desire is an obsession, you will have no difficulty in convincing yourself that you will acquire it. The object is to want money and to become so determined to have it that you convince yourself you will have it.

To the uninitiated, who has not been schooled in the working principles of the human mind, these instructions may appear impractical. It may be helpful, to all who fail to recognise the soundness of the six steps, to know that the information they convey was received from Andrew Carnegie, who began as an ordinary labourer in the steel mills, but managed, despite his humble beginning, to make these principles yield him a fortune of considerably more than one hundred million dollars.

Part II

THE POWER OF YOUR SUBCONSCIOUS MIND:

Your Thoughts Can Change Your Life

Joseph Murphy

Introduction

In 1963, Dr Joseph Murphy, a Protestant minister and leader of one of the most broad-based self-help movements of the century, wrote a book called *The Power of Your Subconscious Mind.* While *Think and Grow Rich* showed how the power of our conscious and subconscious mind can help us build wealth, here Dr Murphy focusses on how the subconscious mind in particular can transform every aspect of our lives. The mechanism is simple: our conscious thoughts, whether automatic or disciplined, positive or negative, desired or feared, provide marching orders to our subconscious mind, which proceeds to carry out these marching orders by any means possible. Our subconscious minds are constantly working to turn our hopes and desires into reality. And we can largely control that process by controlling our thoughts – for better or worse. Murphy helps train us to use this power for good in our lives and the lives of others, rather than unwittingly be enslaved to our own automatic, often negative, thoughts.

Again, this concept is not new. Recognition of the power of the subconscious mind long has been at the heart of self-help methods. While experts have freshened up the concept throughout the decades, its practicality and broader framework have been largely lost along the way. Critics of the contemporary 'positive thinking' movement have rightly denounced the notion that thinking positively is the only thing needed for transformation.[2]

[2] '*The Secret* (book),' Wikipedia, http://en.wikipedia.org/wiki/The_Secret_(book).

There would be no danger of such critiques with Murphy's approach. Positive thinking, or 'autosuggestion,' is only one part of a coherent framework. And a major principle of that larger framework is that 'you can't get something for nothing.' Our thoughts never take the place of action; they enable the right action at the right time.

The Power of Your Subconscious Mind is freely available to anyone. Yet most of us have no idea how to use it to best effect. Just as Napoleon Hill did in the realm of business, Murphy explains how our thoughts work much like any other unseen force, such as electricity or the Internet. *The Power of Your Subconscious Mind* is not about religion. It is about practical faith, which anyone can understand and master. If you've ever wondered how faith really works for some and why prayers may be answered, you may be surprised to know how much it has to do with our unspoken mindset, rather than our specific words or even the deity to whom we pray.

The same principles that stem from the power of the mind that we learned about in the previous section – such as desire, self-confidence, positive thinking, setting specific goals, imagining your ideal end result in specific terms, perseverance, generosity, etc. – apply just as powerfully and practically to any aspect of our lives. Applied to making a living, they look like thriving, cutting-edge entrepreneurism that does good and does well. Applied to health, they result in vibrant energy and longevity. Applied to relationships, they result in compassion, humility and the understanding that true love is rooted in sacrifice and service. In any context, they can free you if you're stuck and put you on the path to succeed and thrive.

ONE

The Power of Thought

Infinite riches are all around you if you will open your mental eyes and behold the treasure house of infinity within you. There is a gold mine within you from which you can extract everything you need to live life gloriously, joyously and abundantly.

Many are sound asleep because they do not know about this gold mine of infinite intelligence and boundless love within themselves. Whatever you want, you can draw forth. A magnetised piece of steel will lift about twelve times its own weight and if you demagnetise this same piece of steel, it will not even lift a feather. Similarly, there are two types of people. There is the magnetised person who is full of confidence and faith. He knows that he is born to win and to succeed. Then, there is the type of person who is demagnetised. He is full of fears and doubts. Opportunities come and he says, 'I might fail; I might lose my money; people will laugh at me.' This type of person will not get very far in life because, if he is afraid to go forward, he will simply stay where he is. Become a magnetised person and discover the master secret of the ages.

THE MASTER SECRET OF THE AGES

What, in your opinion, is the master secret of the ages? The secret of atomic energy? Thermonuclear energy? The neutron bomb? Interplanetary travel? No – not any of these. Then, what is this master secret? Where can one find it and how can it be contacted and brought into action? The answer is extraordinarily simple. This secret is the marvellous, miracle-working power found in your own subconscious mind, the last place that most people would seek it.

THE MARVELOUS POWER OF YOUR SUBCONSCIOUS

You can bring into your life more power, more wealth, more health, more happiness and more joy by learning to contact and release the hidden power of your subconscious mind. You need not acquire this power; you already possess it. But, you want to learn how to use it; you want to understand it so that you can apply it in all departments of your life.

As you follow the simple techniques and processes set forth here, you can gain the necessary knowledge and understanding. You can be inspired by a new light. You can generate a new force enabling you to realise your hopes and make all your dreams come true. Decide now to make your life grander, greater, richer and nobler than ever before. The infinite intelligence within your subconscious mind can reveal to you everything you need to know at every moment of time and point of space provided you are open-minded and receptive. You can receive new thoughts and ideas enabling you to bring forth new inventions, make new discoveries or write books and plays. Moreover, the infinite intelligence in your subconscious can impart to you wonderful kinds of knowledge of an original nature. It can reveal to you and open the way for perfect expression and true place in your life. Through the wisdom of your subconscious mind you can attract the ideal companion, as well as the right business associate or partner. It can find the right buyer for your home and provide you with all the money you need and the financial freedom to be, to do and to go as your heart desires. It is your right to discover this inner world of thought, feeling and power, of light, love and beauty. Though invisible, its forces are mighty. Within your subconscious mind you will find the solution for every problem and the cause for every effect. Because you can draw out the hidden powers, you come into actual possession of the power and wisdom necessary to move forward in abundance, security, joy and dominion. I have seen the power of the subconscious lift people up out of crippled states, making them whole, vital and strong once more and free to go out into the world to experience happiness, health and joyous expression. There is a miraculous healing power in your subconscious that can heal the troubled mind and the broken heart. It can open the prison door of the mind and liberate you. It can free you from all kinds of material and physical bondage.

NECESSITY OF A WORKING BASIS

Substantial progress in any field of endeavour is impossible in the absence of a working basis which is universal in its application. You can become skilled in the operation of your subconscious mind. You can practice its powers with a certainty of results in exact proportion to your knowledge of its principles and to your application of them for definite specific purposes and goals you wish to achieve. Being a former chemist, I would like to point out that if you combine hydrogen and oxygen in the proportions of two atoms of the former to one of the latter, water will be the result. You are very familiar with the fact that one atom of oxygen and one atom of carbon will produce carbon monoxide, a poisonous gas. However, if you add another atom of oxygen, you will get carbon dioxide, a harmless gas and so on throughout the vast realm of chemical compounds. You must not think that the principles of chemistry, physics and mathematics differ from the principles of your subconscious mind. Let us consider a generally accepted principle: 'Water seeks its own level.' This is a universal principle which is applicable to water everywhere. Consider another principle: 'Matter expands when heated.'

This is true anywhere, at any time and under all circumstances. You can heat a piece of steel and it will expand regardless whether the steel is found in China, England or India. It is a universal truth that matter expands when heated. It is also a universal truth that whatever you impress on your subconscious mind is expressed on the screen of space as condition, experience and event.

Your prayer is answered because your subconscious mind is a principle. By principle I mean the way a thing works. For example, the principle of electricity is that it works from a higher to a lower potential. You do not change the principle of electricity when you use it, but by cooperating with nature, you can bring forth marvelous inventions and discoveries which bless humanity in countless ways.

Your subconscious mind is principle and works according to the law of belief. You must know what belief is, why it works and how it works. The law of your mind is the law of belief. This means to believe in the way your mind works, to believe in belief itself. The belief of your mind is the thought of your mind – that is simple – just that and nothing else.

All your experiences, events, conditions and acts are the reactions of your subconscious mind to your thoughts. Remember, it is not the thing believed in, but the belief in your own mind which brings about the result. Cease believing in the false beliefs, opinions, superstitions and fears of mankind. Begin to believe in the eternal verities and truths of life which never change. Then, you will move onward, upward and Godward. Whoever reads this book and applies the principles of the subconscious mind herein set forth, will be able to pray scientifically and effectively for himself and for others. Your prayer is answered according to the universal law of action and reaction. Thought is incipient action. The reaction is the response from your subconscious mind which corresponds with the nature of your thought. Busy your mind with the concepts of harmony, health, peace and goodwill and wonders will happen in your life.

THE DUALITY OF MIND

You have only one mind, but your mind possesses two distinctive characteristics. The line of demarcation between the two is well known to all thinking men and women today. The two functions of your mind are essentially dissimilar. Each is endowed with separate and distinct attributes and powers. The nomenclature generally used to distinguish the two functions of your mind is as follows: The objective and subjective mind, the conscious and subconscious mind, the waking and sleeping mind, the surface self and the deep self, the voluntary mind and the involuntary mind and many other terms. You will find here the terms 'conscious' and 'subconscious' used to represent the dual nature of your mind.

THE CONSCIOUS AND SUBCONSCIOUS MINDS

An excellent way to get acquainted with the two functions of your mind is to look upon your own mind as a garden. You are a gardener and you are planting seeds (thoughts) in your subconscious mind all day long, based on your habitual thinking. As you sow in your subconscious mind, so shall you reap in your body and environment.

Begin now to sow thoughts of peace, happiness, right action, goodwill and prosperity. Think quietly and with interest on these qualities and accept them fully in your conscious reasoning mind. Continue to plant these wonderful seeds (thoughts) in the garden of your mind and you will reap a glorious harvest. Your subconscious mind may be likened to the soil which will grow all kinds of seeds, good or bad. *Do men gather grapes of thorns, or figs of thistles?* Every thought is, therefore, a cause and every condition is an effect. For this reason, it is essential that you take charge of your thoughts so as to bring forth only desirable conditions. When your mind thinks correctly, when you understand the truth, when the thoughts deposited in your subconscious mind are constructive, harmonious and peaceful, the magic working power of your subconscious will respond and bring about harmonious conditions, agreeable surroundings and the best of everything. When you begin to control your thought processes, you can apply the powers of your subconscious to any problem or difficulty. In other words, you will actually be consciously co-operating with the infinite power and omnipotent law which governs all things.

Look around you wherever you live and you will notice that the vast majority of mankind lives in the world without; the more enlightened men are intensely interested in the world within. Remember, it is the world within, namely, your thoughts, feelings and imagery that makes your world without. It is, therefore, the only creative power and everything which you find in your world of expression has been created by you in the inner world of your mind consciously or unconsciously.

A knowledge of the interaction of your conscious and subconscious minds will enable you to transform your whole life. In order to change external conditions, you must change the cause. Most men try to change conditions and circumstances by working with conditions and circumstances. To remove discord, confusion, lack and limitation, you must remove the cause and the cause is the way you are using your conscious mind. In other words, the way you are thinking and picturing in your mind.

You are living in a fathomless sea of infinite riches. Your subconscious is very sensitive to your thoughts. Your thoughts form the mold or matrix through which the infinite intelligence, wisdom, vital forces and energies of your subconscious flow. The practical application of the laws of your mind as illustrated in each chapter of this book will cause you to experience abundance for poverty, wisdom for superstition and ignorance, peace for pain, joy for sadness, light for darkness, harmony for discord, faith and confidence for fear, success for failure and freedom from the law of averages. Certainly, there can be no more wonderful blessing than these from a mental, emotional and material standpoint.

Your subconscious mind is reactive and responds to the nature of your thoughts. When your conscious mind is full of fear, worry and anxiety, the negative emotions engendered in your subconscious mind are released and flood the conscious mind with a sense of panic, foreboding and despair. When this happens, you can speak affirmatively and with a deep sense of authority to the irrational emotions generated in your deeper mind as follows: 'Be still, be quiet, I am in control, you must obey me, you are subject to my command, you cannot intrude where you do not belong.'

It is fascinating and intensely interesting to observe how you can speak authoritatively and with conviction to the irrational movement of your deeper self bringing silence, harmony and peace to your mind. The subconscious is subject to the conscious mind and that is why it is called subconscious or subjective.

OUTSTANDING DIFFERENCES AND MODES OF OPERATION

You will perceive the main differences by the following illustrations: The conscious mind is like the navigator or captain at the bridge of a ship. He directs the ship and signals orders to men in the engine room, who in turn control all the boilers, instruments, gauges, etc. The men in the engine room do not know where they are going; they follow orders. They would go on the rocks if the man on the bridge issued faulty or wrong instructions based on his findings with the compass, sextant or other instruments. The men in the engine room obey him because he is in charge and issues orders which are automatically obeyed. Members of the crew do not talk back to the captain; they simply carry out orders.

The captain is the master of his ship and his decrees are carried out. Likewise, your conscious mind is the captain and the master of your ship, which represents your body, environment and all your affairs. Your subconscious mind takes the orders you give it based upon what your conscious mind believes and accepts as true.

When you repeatedly say to people, 'I can't afford it,' then your subconscious mind takes you at your word and sees to it that you will not be in a position to purchase what you want. As long as you persist in saying, 'I can't afford that car, that trip to Europe, that home, that fur coat or ermine wrap,' you can rest assured that your subconscious mind will follow your orders and you will go through life experiencing the lack of all these things.

TWO

How Your Own Mind Works: The Miracle-Working Power of Your Subconscious Mind

You have a mind and you should learn how to use it. There are two levels of your mind – the conscious or rational level. The subconscious or irrational level. You think with your conscious mind. Whatever you habitually think sinks down into your subconscious mind, which functions according to the nature of your thoughts. Your subconscious mind is the seat of your emotions and is the creative mind. If you think good, good will follow; if you think evil, evil will follow. This is the way your mind works.

The main point to remember is once the subconscious mind accepts an idea, it begins to execute it. It is an interesting, subtle truth – the law of the subconscious mind works for good and bad ideas alike. This law, when applied in a negative way, is the cause of failure, frustration and unhappiness. However, when your habitual thinking is harmonious and constructive, you experience perfect health, success and prosperity.

Peace of mind and a healthy body are inevitable when you

begin to think and feel in the right way. Whatever you claim mentally and feel as true, your subconscious mind will accept and bring forth into your experience. The only thing necessary for you to do is to get your subconscious mind to accept your idea and the law of your own subconscious mind will bring forth the health, peace, or the position you desire. You give the command or decree. Your subconscious will faithfully reproduce the idea impressed upon it. The law of your mind is this: You will get a reaction or response from your subconscious mind according to the nature of the thought or idea you hold in your conscious mind.

Psychologists and psychiatrists point out that when thoughts are conveyed to your subconscious mind, impressions are made in the brain cells. As soon as your subconscious accepts any idea, it proceeds to put it into effect immediately. It works by association of ideas and uses every bit of knowledge that you have gathered in your lifetime to bring about its purpose. It draws on the infinite power, energy and wisdom within you. It lines up all the laws of nature to get its way. Sometimes it seems to bring about an immediate solution to your difficulties, but at other times it may take days, weeks or longer.

CONSCIOUS AND SUBCONSCIOUS TERMS DIFFERENTIATED

You must remember that these are not two minds. They are merely two spheres of activity within one mind. Your conscious mind is the reasoning mind. It is that phase of mind which chooses. For example, you choose your books, your home and your partner in life. You make all your decisions with your conscious mind. On the other hand, without any conscious choice on your part, your heart is kept functioning automatically. The process of digestion, circulation and breathing are carried on by your subconscious mind through processes independent of your conscious control.

Your subconscious mind accepts what is impressed upon it or what you consciously believe. It does not reason things out like your conscious mind and it does not argue with you controversially. Your subconscious mind is like the soil which accepts any kind of seed, good or bad. Your thoughts are active and might be likened unto seeds. Negative, destructive thoughts continue to work negatively in your subconscious mind. In due time they will come forth into the outer experience which corresponds with them.

Remember, your subconscious mind does not engage in proving whether your thoughts are good or bad, true or false. Yet it responds according to the nature of your thoughts or suggestions. For example, if you consciously assume something as true, even though it may be false, your subconscious mind will accept it as true and proceed to bring about results which must necessarily follow, because you consciously assumed it to be true.

THE TERMS OBJECTIVE AND SUBJECTIVE MIND CLARIFIED

Your conscious mind is sometimes referred to as your objective mind because it deals with outward objects. The objective mind takes cognizance of the objective world. Its media of observation are your five physical senses. Your objective mind is your guide and director in your contact with your environment. You gain knowledge through your five senses. Your objective mind learns through observation, experience and education. As previously pointed out, the greatest function of the objective mind is that of reasoning.

Suppose you are one of the thousands of tourists who comes

to Los Angeles annually. You would come to the conclusion that it is a beautiful city based upon your observation of the parks, pretty gardens, majestic buildings and lovely homes. This is the working of your objective mind.

Your subconscious mind is oftentimes referred to as your subjective mind. Your subjective mind takes cognisance of its environment by means independent of the five senses. Your subjective mind perceives by intuition. It is the seat of your emotion and the storehouse of memory.

Your subjective mind performs its highest functions when your objective senses are in abeyance. In a word, it is that intelligence, which performs when the objective mind is suspended or in a sleepy, drowsy state. Your subjective mind sees without the use of the natural organs of vision. It has the capacity of clairvoyance and clairaudience. Your subjective mind can leave your body, travel to distant lands and bring back information often of the most exact and truthful character.

Through your subjective mind you can read the thoughts of others, read the contents of sealed envelopes and closed safes. Your subjective mind has the ability to apprehend the thoughts of others without the use of the ordinary objective means of communication. It is of the greatest importance that we understand the interaction of the objective and subjective mind in order to learn the true art of prayer.

YOUR SUBCONSCIOUS CANNOT REASON LIKE YOUR CONSCIOUS MIND

Your subconscious mind cannot argue controversially. Hence, if you give it wrong suggestions, it will accept them as true and will proceed to bring them to pass as conditions, experiences and events. All things that have happened to you are based on thoughts impressed on your subconscious mind through belief. If you have conveyed erroneous concepts to your subconscious mind, the sure method of overcoming them is by the repetition of constructive, harmonious thoughts frequently repeated which your subconscious mind accepts, thus forming new and healthy habits of thought and life, for your subconscious mind is the seat of habit. The habitual thinking of your conscious mind establishes deep grooves in your subconscious mind. This is very favourable for you if your habitual thoughts are harmonious, peaceful and constructive. If you have indulged in fear, worry and other destructive forms of thinking, the remedy is to recognise the omnipotence of your subconscious mind and decree freedom, happiness and perfect health. Your subconscious mind, being creative and one with your divine source, will proceed to create the freedom and happiness which you have earnestly decreed.

THE TREMENDOUS POWER OF SUGGESTION

You must realise by now that your conscious mind is the 'watchman at the gate.' Its chief function is to protect your subconscious mind from false impressions. You are now aware of one of the basic laws of mind: Your subconscious mind is amenable to suggestion. As you know, your subconscious mind does not make comparisons or contrasts, neither does it reason and think things out for itself. This latter function belongs to your conscious mind. It simply reacts to the impressions given to it by your conscious mind. It does not show a preference for one course of action over another. It is true that different people will react in different ways to the same suggestion because of their subconscious conditioning or belief. For example, if you go to a sailor on the ship and say to him sympathetically, 'My dear fellow, you're looking very ill. Aren't you feeling sick? You look to me as if you were going to be seasick.' According to his temperament he either laughs at your 'joke,' or expresses a mild irritation. Your suggestion fell on deaf ears in this instance because your suggestion of seasickness was associated in his mind with his own immunity from it. Therefore, it called up not fear or worry, but self-confidence. The dictionary says that a suggestion is the act or instance of putting something into one's mind, the mental process by which the thought or idea suggested is entertained accepted, or put into effect. You must remember that a suggestion cannot impose something on the subconscious mind against the will of the conscious mind. In other words, your conscious mind has the power to reject the suggestion given. In the case of the sailor, he had no fear of seasickness. He had convinced himself of his immunity and the negative suggestion had absolutely no power to evoke fear.

Each of us has our own inner fears, beliefs, opinion. These inner assumptions rule and govern our lives. A suggestion has no power in and of itself except it is accepted mentally by you. This causes your subconscious powers to flow in a limited and restricted way according to the nature of the suggestion.

HOW HE LOST HIS ARM

Every two or three years I give a series of lectures at the London Truth Forum in Caxton Hall. This is a forum I founded a number of years ago. Dr Evelyn Fleet, the director, told me about an article which appeared in the English newspapers dealing with the power of suggestion. This is the suggestion a man gave to his subconscious mind over a period of about two years: 'I would give my right arm to see my daughter cured.' It appeared that his daughter had a crippling form of arthritis together with a so-called incurable form of skin disease. Medical treatment had failed to alleviate the condition and the father had an intense longing for his daughter's healing and expressed his desire in the words just quoted. Dr Evelyn Fleet said that the newspaper article pointed out that one day the family was out riding when their car collided with another. The father's right arm was torn off at the shoulder and immediately the daughter's arthritis and skin condition vanished. You must make certain to give your subconscious only suggestions which heal, bless, elevate and inspire you in all your ways. Remember that your subconscious mind cannot take a joke. It takes you at your word.

HOW AUTOSUGGESTION BANISHES FEAR

Illustrations of autosuggestion: Autosuggestion means suggesting something definite and specific to oneself. Herbert Parkyn, in his excellent manual of autosuggestion,[3] records the following incident. It has its amusing side, so that one remembers it. 'A New York visitor in Chicago looks at his watch, which is set an hour ahead of Chicago time and tells a Chicago friend that it is twelve o'clock. The Chicago friend, not considering the difference in time between Chicago and New York, tells the New Yorker that he is hungry and that he must go to lunch.'

Autosuggestion may be used to banish various fears and other negative conditions. A young singer was invited to give an audition. She had been looking forward to the interview, but on three previous occasions she had failed miserably due to fear of

[3]Herbert Parkyn, *Autosuggestion* (London: Fowler, 1916).

failure. This young lady had a very good voice, but she had been saying to herself, 'When the time comes for me to sing, maybe they won't like me. I will try, but I'm full of fear and anxiety.' Her subconscious mind accepted these negative autosuggestions as a request and proceeded to manifest them and bring them into her experience. The cause was an involuntary autosuggestion, i.e., silent fear thoughts emotionalised and subjectified. She overcame it by the following technique: Three times a day she isolated herself in a room.

She sat down comfortably in an armchair, relaxed her body and closed her eyes. She stilled her mind and body as best she could. Physical inertia favours mental passivity and renders the mind more receptive to suggestion. She counteracted the fear suggestion by saying to herself, 'I sing beautifully. I am poised, serene, confident and calm.' She repeated this statement slowly, quietly and with feeling from five to ten times at each sitting. She had three such 'sittings' every day and one immediately prior to sleep. At the end of a week she was completely poised and confident. When the invitation to audition came, she gave a remarkable, wonderful audition.

HOW SHE RESTORED HER MEMORY

A woman, aged seventy-five, was in the habit of saying to herself, 'I am losing my memory.' She reversed the procedure and practiced induced autosuggestion several times a day as follows: 'My memory from today on – is improving in every department. I shall always remember whatever I need to know at every moment of time and point of space. The impressions received will be clearer and more definite. I shall retain them automatically and with ease. Whatever I wish to recall will immediately present itself in the correct form in my mind. I am improving rapidly every day and very soon my memory will be better than it has ever been before.' At the end of three weeks, her memory was back to normal and she was delighted.

HOW HE OVERCAME A NASTY TEMPER

Many men who complained of irritability and bad temper proved to be very susceptible to autosuggestion and obtained marvelous results by using the following statements three or four times a day – morning, noon and at night prior to sleep for about a month. 'Henceforth, I shall grow more good-humoured. Joy, happiness and cheerfulness are now becoming my normal states of mind. Every day I am becoming more and more lovable and understanding. I am now becoming the centre of cheer and goodwill to all those about me, infecting them with good humour. This happy, joyous and cheerful mood is now becoming my normal, natural state of mind. I am grateful.'

THE CONSTRUCTIVE AND DESTRUCTIVE POWER OF SUGGESTION

Heterosuggestion means suggestions from another person. In all ages the power of suggestion has played a part in the life and thought of man in every period of time, in each country of the earth. In many parts of the world it is the controlling power in religion. Suggestion may be used to discipline and control ourselves, but it can also be used to take control and command over others who do not know the laws of mind. In its constructive form it is wonderful and magnificent. In its negative aspects, it is one of the most destructive of all the response patterns of the mind, resulting in patterns of misery, failure, suffering, sickness and disaster.

HAVE YOU ACCEPTED ANY OF THESE?

From infancy on the majority of us have been given many negative suggestions. Not knowing how to thwart them, we unconsciously accepted them. Here are some of the negative suggestions:

'You can't.'
'You'll never amount to anything.'
'You mustn't.' 'You'll fail.'
'You haven't got a chance.'
'You're all wrong.'
'It's no use.'
'It's not what you know, but who you know.'
'The world is going to the dogs.'
'What's the use, nobody cares.'
'It's no use trying so hard.'
'You're too old now.'
'Things are getting worse and worse.'
'Life is an endless grind.'
'Love is for the birds.'
'You just can't win.'
'Pretty soon you'll be bankrupt.'
'Watch out, you'll get the virus.'
'You can't trust a soul,' etc.

Unless, as an adult, you use constructive autosuggestion, which is a reconditioning therapy, the impressions made on you in the past can cause behaviour patterns that cause failure in your personal and social life. Autosuggestion is a means releasing you from the mass of negative verbal conditioning that might otherwise distort your life pattern, making the development of good habits difficult.

YOU CAN COUNTERACT NEGATIVE SUGGESTIONS

Pick up the paper any day and you can read dozens of items that could sow the seeds of futility, fear, worry, anxiety and impending doom. If accepted, these thoughts of fear could cause you to lose the will for life. Knowing that you can reject all these negative suggestions by giving your subconscious mind constructive autosuggestions, you counteract all these destructive ideas.

Check regularly on the negative suggestions that people make to you. You do not have to be influenced by destructive heterosuggestion. All of us have suffered from it in our childhood and in our teens. If you look back, you can easily recall how parents, friends, relatives, teachers and associates contributed in a campaign of negative suggestions. Study the things said to you and you will discover much of it was in the form of propaganda. The purpose of much of what was said was to control you or instil fear into you.

This heterosuggestion process goes on in every home, office, factory and club. You will find that many of these suggestions are for the purpose of making you think, feel and act as others want you to and in ways that are to their advantage.

How suggestion killed a man

Here is an illustration of heterosuggestion: A relative of mine went to a crystal gazer in India who told him that he had a bad heart and predicted that he would die at the next new moon. He began to tell all members of his family about this prediction and he arranged his will. This powerful suggestion entered into his subconscious mind because he accepted it completely. My relative also told me that this crystal gazer was believed to have some strange occult powers – he could do harm or good to a person. He died as predicted not knowing that he was the cause of his own death. I suppose many of us have heard similar stupid, ridiculous, superstitious stories.

Let us look at what happened in the light of our knowledge of the way the subconscious mind works. Whatever the conscious, reasoning mind of man believes, the subconscious mind will accept and act upon. My relative was happy, healthy, vigorous and robust when he went to see the fortuneteller. She gave him a very negative suggestion which he accepted. He became terrified and constantly dwelt upon the fact that he was going to die at the next new moon. He proceeded to tell everyone about it and he prepared for the end. The activity took place in his own mind and his own thought was the cause. He brought about his own so-called death or rather destruction of the physical body, by his fear and expectation of the end. The woman who predicted his death had no more power than the stones and sticks in the field. Her suggestion had no power to create or bring about the end she suggested. If he had known the laws of his mind, he would have completely rejected the negative suggestion and refused to give her words any attention, knowing in his heart that he was governed and controlled by his own thought and feeling. Like tin arrows aimed at a battleship, her prophecy could have been completely neutralised and dissipated without hurting him.

The suggestions of others in themselves have absolutely no power whatever over you except the power that you give them through your own thoughts. You have to give your mental consent; you have to entertain the thought. Then, it becomes your thought and you do the thinking. Remember, you have the capacity to choose. Choose life! Choose love! Choose health!

THE POWER OF AN ASSUMED MAJOR PREMISE

Your mind works like a syllogism. This means that whatever major premise your conscious mind assumes to be true determines the conclusion your subconscious mind comes to in regard to any particular question or problem in your mind. If your premise is true, the conclusion must be true as in the following example:

Every virtue is laudable; Kindness is a virtue;

Therefore, kindness is laudable.

Another example:

All formed things change and pass away. The Pyramids of Egypt are formed, things; Therefore, some day the Pyramids will pass away. The first statement is referred to as the major premise and the right conclusion must necessarily follow the right premise. A college professor, who attended some of my science of mind lectures in May, 1962, at Town Hall, New York, said to me, 'Everything in my life is topsy-turvy and I have lost health, wealth and friends. Everything I touch turns out wrong.'

I explained to him that he should establish a major premise in his thinking, that the infinite intelligence of his subconscious mind was guiding, directing and making him prosper spiritually, mentally and materially. Then, his subconscious mind would automatically direct him wisely in his investments, decisions and also heal his body and restore his mind to peace and tranquillity.

This professor formulated an over-all picture of the way he wanted his life to be and this was his major premise: 'Infinite intelligence leads and guides me in all my ways. Perfect health is mine and the Law of Harmony operates in my mind and body.

Beauty, love, peace and abundance are mine. The principle of right action and divine order govern my entire life. I know my major premise is based on the eternal truths of life and I know, feel and believe that my subconscious mind responds according to the nature of my conscious mind thinking.

He wrote me as follows: 'I repeated the above statements slowly, quietly and lovingly several times a day knowing that they were sinking deep down into my subconscious mind and that results must follow. I am deeply grateful for the interview you gave me and I would like to add that all departments of my life are changing for the better. It works!'

YOUR SUBCONSCIOUS DOES NOT ARGUE CONTROVERSIALLY

Your subconscious mind is all-wise and knows the answers to all questions. It does not argue with you or talk back to you. It does not say, 'You must not impress me with that.' For example, when you say, 'I can't do this.' 'I am too old now.' 'I can't meet this obligation.' 'I was born on the wrong side of the tracks.' 'I don't know the right politician,' you are impregnating your subconscious with these negative thoughts and it responds accordingly. You are actually blocking your own good, thereby bringing lack, limitation and frustration into your life.

When you set up obstacles, impediments and delays in your conscious mind, you are denying the wisdom and intelligence resident in your subconscious mind. You are actually saying in effect that your subconscious mind cannot solve your problem. This leads to mental and emotional congestion, followed by sickness and neurotic tendencies.

To realise your desire and overcome your frustration, affirm boldly several times a day: 'The infinite intelligence, which gave me this desire leads, guides and reveals to me the perfect plan for the unfolding of my desire. I know the deeper wisdom of my subconscious is now responding and what I feel and claim within is expressed in my outward life. There is a balance, equilibrium and equanimity.'

If you say, 'There is no way out; I am lost; I am stymied and blocked,' you will get no answer or response from your subconscious mind. If you want the subconscious to work for you, give it the right request and attain its cooperation. It is always working for you. It is controlling your heartbeat this minute and also your breathing. It heals a cut on your finger and its tendency is life ward, forever seeking to take care of you and preserve you. Your subconscious has a mind of its own, but it accepts your patterns of thought and imagery. When you are seeking an answer to a problem, your subconscious will respond, but it expects you to come to a decision and to a true judgement in your conscious mind. You must acknowledge the answer is in your subconscious mind. However, if you say, 'I don't think there is any way out; I am all mixed up and confused; why don't I get an answer?' you are neutralising your prayer. Like the soldier marking time, you do not get anywhere. Still the wheels of your mind, relax, let go and quietly affirm: 'My subconscious knows the answer. It is responding to me now. I give thanks because I know the infinite intelligence of my subconscious knows all things and is revealing the perfect answer to me now. My real conviction is now setting free the majesty and glory of my subconscious mind. I rejoice that it is so.'

THE MIRACLE-WORKING POWER OF YOUR SUBCONSCIOUS

The power of your subconscious is enormous. It inspires you it guides you and it reveals to you names, facts and scenes from the storehouse of memory. Your subconscious started your heartbeat, controls the circulation of your blood, regulates your digestion, assimilation and elimination. When you eat a piece of bread, your subconscious mind transforms it into tissue, muscle, bone and blood. This process is beyond the ken of the wisest man who walks the earth. Your subconscious mind controls all the vital processes and functions of your body and knows the answer to all problems.

Your subconscious mind never sleeps, never rests. It is always on the job. You can discover the miracle-working power of your subconscious by plainly stating to your subconscious prior to sleep that you wish a certain specific thing accomplished. You will be delighted to discover that forces within you will be released, leading to the desired result. Here, then, is a source of power and wisdom, which places you in touch with omnipotence or the power that moves the world, guides the planets in their course and causes the sun to shine.

Your subconscious mind is the source of your ideals, aspirations and altruistic urges. It was through the subconscious mind that Shakespeare perceived great truths hidden from the average man of his day. Undoubtedly, it was the response of his subconscious mind that caused the Greek sculptor, Phidias, to portray beauty, order, symmetry and proportion in marble and bronze. It enabled the Italian artist, Raphael, to paint Madonnas and Ludwig van Beethoven to compose symphonies.

In 1955 I lectured at the Yoga Forest University, Rishikesh, India and there I chatted with a visiting surgeon from Bombay. He told me about Dr James Esdaille, a Scottish surgeon, who worked in Bengal before ether or other modern methods of anesthesia were discovered. Between 1843 and 1846, Dr Esdaille performed about four hundred major operations of all kinds, such as amputations, removal of tumours and cancerous growths, as well as operations on the eye, ear and throat. All operations were conducted under mental anesthesia only. This Indian doctor at Rishikesh informed me that the postoperative mortality rate of patients operated on by Dr Esdaille was extremely low, probably two or three percent. Patients felt no pain and there were no deaths during the operations.

Dr Esdaille suggested to the subconscious minds of all his patients, who were in a hypnotic state, that no infection or septic condition would develop. You must remember that this was before Louis Pasteur, Joseph Lister and others who pointed out the bacterial origin of disease and causes of infection due to unsterilised instruments and virulent organisms. This Indian surgeon said that the reason for the low mortality rate and the general absence of infection, which was reduced to a minimum, was undoubtedly due to the suggestions of Dr Esdaille to the subconscious minds of his patients. They responded according to the nature of his suggestion.

It is simply wonderful, when you conceive how a surgeon, over one hundred twenty years ago, discovered the miraculous wonder-working powers of the subconscious mind. Doesn't it cause you to be seized with a sort of mystic awe when you stop and think of the transcendental powers of your subconscious mind? Consider its extrasensory perceptions, such as its capacity for clairvoyance and clairaudience, its independence of time and space, its capacity to render you free from all pain and suffering and its capacity to get the answer to all problems, be they what they may. All these and many more reveal to you that there is a power and an intelligence within you that far transcends your intellect, causing you to marvel at the wonders of it all. All these experiences cause you to rejoice and believe in the miracle-working powers of your own subconscious mind.

WHAT IS IMPRESSED IN YOUR SUBCONSCIOUS IS EXPRESSED

William James, the father of American psychology, said that the power to move the world is in your subconscious mind. Your subconscious mind is one with infinite intelligence and boundless wisdom. It is fed by hidden springs and is called the law of life. Whatever you impress upon your subconscious mind, the latter will move heaven and earth to bring it to pass. You must, therefore, impress it with right ideas and constructive thoughts. The reason there is so much chaos and misery in the world is because people do not understand the interaction of their conscious and subconscious minds. When these two principles work in accord, in concord, in peace and synchronously together, you will have health, happiness, peace and joy. There is no sickness or discord when the conscious and subconscious work together harmoniously and peacefully.

The tomb of Hermes was opened with great expectancy and a sense of wonder because people believed that the greatest secret of the ages was contained therein. The secret was *as within, so without; as above, so below.*

In other words, whatever is impressed in your subconscious mind is expressed on the screen of space. Moses, Isaiah, Jesus, Buddha, Zoroaster, Laotze and all the illumined seers of the ages proclaimed this same truth. Whatever you feel as true subjectively is expressed as conditions, experiences and events. Motion and emotion must balance. *As in heaven* [your own mind], *so on earth* [in your body and environment]. This is the great law of life. You will find throughout all nature the law of action and reaction, of rest and motion. These two must balance, then there will be harmony and equilibrium. You are here to let the life principle flow through you rhythmically and harmoniously. The intake and the outgo must be equal. The impression and the expression must be equal. All your frustration is due to unfulfilled desire.

If you think negatively, destructively and viciously, these thoughts generate destructive emotions which must be expressed and find an outlet. These emotions, being of a negative nature, are frequently expressed as ulcers, heart trouble, tension and anxieties. What is your idea or feeling about yourself now? Every part of your being expresses that idea. Your vitality, body, financial status, friends and social status represent a perfect reflection of the idea you have of yourself. This is the real meaning of what is impressed in your subconscious mind and which is expressed in all phases of your life.

We injure ourselves by the negative ideas which we entertain. How often have you wounded yourself by getting angry, fearful, jealous, or vengeful? These are the poisons that enter your subconscious mind. You were not born with these negative attitudes. Feed your subconscious mind life-giving thoughts and you will wipe out all the negative patterns lodged therein. As you continue to do this, all the past will be wiped out and remembered no more.

The subconscious heals a malignancy of the skin

A personal healing will ever be the most convincing evidence of the healing power of the subconscious mind. Over forty years ago I resolved a malignancy of the skin through prayer. Medical therapy had failed to check the growth and it was getting progressively worse. A clergyman, with a deep psychological knowledge, explained to me the inner meaning of the 139th Psalm wherein it says, *In thy book all my members were written, which in continuance were fashioned, when as yet there was none of them.* He explained that the term *book* meant my subconscious mind which fashioned and molded all my organs from an invisible cell. He also pointed out that inasmuch as my subconscious mind made my body, it could also recreate it and heal it according to the perfect pattern within it.

This clergyman showed me his watch and said, 'This had a maker and the watchmaker had to have the idea first in mind before the watch became an objective reality and if the watch was out of order, the watchmaker could fix it.' My friend reminded me that the subconscious intelligence which created my body was like a watchmaker and it also knew exactly how to heal, restore and direct all the vital functions and processes of my body, but that I had to give it the perfect idea of health. This would act as the cause while the effect would be a healing.

I prayed in a very simple way as follows: 'My body and all its organs were created by the infinite intelligence in my subconscious mind. It knows how to heal me. Its wisdom fashioned all my organs, tissues, muscles and bones. This infinite healing presence within me is now transforming every atom of my being making me whole and perfect now. I give thanks for the healing I know is taking place now. Wonderful are the works of the creative intelligence within me.'

I prayed aloud for about five minutes two or three times a day repeating the above simple prayer. In about three months my skin was whole and perfect. As you can see, all I did was give life-giving patterns of wholeness, beauty and perfection to my subconscious mind, thereby obliterating the negative images and patterns of thought lodged in my subconscious mind which were the cause of all my trouble. Nothing appears on your body except when the mental equivalent is first in your mind and as you change your mind by drenching it with incessant affirmatives, you change your body. This is the basis of all healing.... *Marvelous are thy works; and that my soul* [subconscious mind] *knoweth right well.* – Psalm 139:14.

HOW YOUR SUBCONSCIOUS CONTROLS ALL FUNCTIONS OF THE BODY

While you are awake or sound asleep in your bed, the ceaseless, tireless action of your subconscious mind controls all the vital functions of your body without the help of your conscious mind. For example, while you are asleep your heart continues to beat rhythmically, your lungs do not rest. The process of inhalation and exhalation, your blood absorbs fresh air, goes on just the same as when you are awake. Your subconscious controls your digestive processes and glandular secretions, as well as all the other mysterious operations of your body. The hair on your face continues to grow whether you are asleep or awake. Scientists tell us that the skin secretes much more perspiration during sleep than during the waking hours. Your eyes, ears and other senses are active during sleep. For instance, many of our great scientists have received answers to perplexing problems while they were asleep. They saw the answers in a dream.

Often your conscious mind interferes with the normal rhythm of the heart, lungs and functioning of the stomach and intestines by worry, anxiety, fear and depression. These patterns of thought interfere with the harmonious functioning of your subconscious mind. When mentally disturbed, the best procedure is to let go, relax and still the wheels of your thought processes. Speak to your subconscious mind, telling it to take over in peace, harmony and divine order. You will find that all the functions of your body will become normal again. Be sure to speak to your subconscious mind with authority and conviction. It will then conform to your command.

Your subconscious seeks to preserve your life and restore you to health at all costs. It causes you to love your children which also illustrates an instinctive desire to preserve all life. Let us suppose you accidentally ate some bad food.

Your subconscious mind would cause you to regurgitate it. If you inadvertently took some poison, your subconscious powers would proceed to neutralise it. If you completely entrusted yourself to its wonder-working power, you would be entirely restored to health.

HOW TO GET YOUR SUBCONSCIOUS TO WORK FOR YOU

The first thing to realise is that your subconscious mind is always working. It is active night and day, whether you act upon it or not. Your subconscious is the builder of your body but you cannot consciously perceive or hear that inner silent process. Your business is with your conscious mind and not your subconscious mind. Just keep your conscious mind busy with the expectation of the best. Make sure the thoughts you habitually think are based on things lovely, true, just and all. Begin now to take care of your conscious mind, knowing in your heart and soul that your subconscious mind is always expressing, reproducing and manifesting according to your habitual thinking. Remember, just as water takes the shape of the pipe it flows through, the life principle in you flows through you according to the nature of your thoughts. Claim that the healing presence in your subconscious is flowing through you as harmony, health, peace, joy republic and abundance. Think of it as a living intelligence, a lovely companion on the way. Firmly believe it is continually flowing through you to enliven and inspire: make a more prosperous you. It will respond exactly this way. It is done unto you as you believe.

THREE

Using the Power of Your Subconscious Mind for Health

MENTAL HEALINGS IN ANCIENT TIMES

Down through the ages men of all nations have somehow instinctively believed that somewhere there resided a healing power which could restore to normal the functions and sensations of man's body. They believed that this strange power could be invoked under certain conditions and that the alleviation of human suffering would follow. The history of all nations presents testimony in support of this belief.

In the early history of the world the power of secretly influencing men for good or evil, including the healing of the sick, was said to be possessed by the priests and holy men of all nations. Healing of the sick was supposed to be a power derived directly by them from God and the procedures and processes of healing varied throughout the world. The healing processes took the form of supplications to God attended by various ceremonies, such as the laying on of hands, incantations, the application of amulets, talismans, rings, relics and images.

For example, in the religions of antiquity priests in the ancient temples gave drugs to the patient and practiced hypnotic suggestions prior to the patient's sleep, telling him that the Gods would visit him in his sleep and heal him. Many healings followed. Obviously, all this was the work of potent suggestions to the subconscious mind.

After the performance of certain mysterious rites, the devotees of Hecate would see the goddess while asleep, provided that before going to sleep they had prayed to her according to weird and fantastic instructions, They were told to mix lizards with resin, frankincense and myrrh then pound all this together in the open air under the crescent moon. Healings were reported in many cases following this grotesque procedure.

It is obvious that these strange procedures, as mentioned in the illustrations given, favoured suggestion and acceptance by the subconscious mind of these people. It made a powerful appeal to their imagination. Actually, in all these healings, the subconscious mind of the subject was the healer.

In all ages unofficial healers have obtained remarkable results in cases where authorised medical skill has failed. This gives cause for thought. How do these healers in all parts of the world effect their cures? The answer to all these healings is due to the blind belief of the sick person which released the healing power resident in his subconscious mind. Many of the remedies and methods employed were rather strange and fantastic, which fired the imagination of the patients, causing an aroused emotional state. This state of mind facilitated the suggestion of health and was accepted both by the conscious and subconscious mind of the sick. This will be elaborated on further in the next chapter.

Biblical accounts on the use of the subconscious powers

> *What things soever ye desire, when ye pray believe that ye receive them and ye shall have them.* – Mark 11:24.

Note the difference in tenses. The inspired writer tells us to believe and accept as true the fact that our desire has already been accomplished and fulfilled, that it is already completed as also that its realisation will follow as a thing in the future.

The success of this technique depends on the confident conviction that the thought, the idea, the picture is already a fact in mind. In order for anything to have substance in the realm of mind, it must be thought of as actually existing there.

Here in a few cryptic words is a concise and specific direction for making use of the creative power of thought by impressing upon the subconscious the particular thing which you desire. Your thought, idea, plans or purpose is as real on its own plane as your hand or your heart. In following the Biblical technique, you completely eliminate from your mind all consideration of conditions, circumstances or anything, which might imply adverse contingencies. You are planting a seed (concept) in the mind even if you leave it undisturbed, will infallibly germinate into external fruition.

The prime condition, which Jesus insisted upon, was faith. Over and over again you read in the Bible, *According to your faith is it done unto you.* If you plant certain types of seeds in the ground, you have faith they will grow after their kind. This is the way of seeds and trusting the laws of growth and agriculture, you know that the seeds will come forth after their kind. Faith as mentioned in the Bible is a way of thinking, an attitude of mind, an inner certitude, knowing that the idea you fully accept in your conscious mind will be embodied in your subconscious mind and made manifest. Faith is, in a sense, accepting as true what your reason and senses deny, i.e., a shutting out of the little, rational, analytical, conscious mind and embracing an attitude of complete reliance on the inner power of your subconscious mind. A classical instance of Bible technique is recorded in Matthew 9:28–30:

> *And when he was come into the house; the blind men came to him: and Jesus saith unto them, Believe ye that I am able to do this? They said unto him, Yea, Lord. Then touched he their eyes, saying, according to your faith be it unto you. And their eyes were opened; and Jesus straitly charged them, saying, see that no man know it.*

In the words *according to your faith be it unto you, you* can see that Jesus was actually appealing to the cooperation of the subconscious mind of the blind men. Here faith was their great expectancy, their inner feeling, their inner conviction that something miraculous would happen. Their prayer would be answered and it was. This is the time-honoured technique of healing, utilised alike by all healing groups throughout the world regardless of religious affiliation.

In the words *see that no man know it,* Jesus enjoins the newly healed patients not to discuss their healing because they might be subjected to the skeptical and derogatory criticisms of the unbelieving. This might tend to undo the benefits they had received at the hand of Jesus by depositing thoughts of fear, doubt and anxiety in the subconscious mind.

> *...for with authority and power he commandeth the unclean spirits and they came out.* – Luke 4:36.

When the sick came to Jesus to be healed, they were healed by their faith together with his faith and understanding of the healing power of the subconscious mind. Whatever he decreed, he felt inwardly to be true. He and the people needing help were in the one universal subjective mind and his silent inner knowing and conviction of the healing power changed the negative destructive patterns in the patients' subconscious. The resultant healings were the automatic response to the internal mental change. His command was his appeal to the subconscious mind of the patients plus his awareness, feeling and absolute trust in the response of the subconscious mind to the words, which he spoke with authority.

Miracles at various shrines throughout the world

It is an established fact that cures have taken place at various shrines throughout the world, such as in Japan, India, Europe and America. I have visited several of the famous shrines in Japan. At the world famous shrine called Diabutsu is a gigantic divinity of bronze where Buddha is seated with folded hands and the head is inclined in an attitude of profound contemplative ecstasy. It is 42 feet in height and is called the great Buddha. Here I saw young and old making offerings at its feet. Money, fruit, rice and oranges were offered. Candles were lit, incense was burned and prayers of petition recited.

The guide explained the chant of a young girl as she murmured a prayer, bowed low and placed two oranges as an offering. She also lit a candle. He said she had lost her voice and it was restored at the shrine. She was thanking Buddha for restoring her voice. She had the simple faith that Buddha would give her back her singing voice if she followed a certain ritual, fasted and made certain offerings. All this helped to kindle faith and expectancy, resulting in a conditioning of her mind to the point of belief. Her subconscious mind responded to her belief.

To illustrate further the power of imagination and blind belief I will relate the case of a relative of mine who had tuberculosis. His lungs were badly diseased. His son decided to heal his father. He came home to Perth, Western Australia, where his father lived and said to him that he had met a monk who had returned from one of the healing shrines in Europe. This monk sold him a piece of the true cross. He said that he gave the monk the equivalent of $500 for it.

This young man had actually picked up a splinter of wood from the sidewalk, went to the jeweller and had it set in a ring so that it looked real. He told his father that just touching the ring or the cross healed many. He inflamed and fired his father's imagination to the point that the old gentleman snatched the ring from him, placed it over his chest, prayed silently and went to sleep. In the morning he was healed. All the clinic's tests proved negative. You know, of course, it was not the splinter of wood from the sidewalk that healed him. It was his imagination aroused to an intense degree, plus the confident expectancy of a perfect healing. Imagination was joined to faith or subjective feeling and the union of the two brought about a healing. The father never learned of the trick that had been played upon him. If he had, he probably would have had a relapse. He remained completely cured and passed away fifteen years later at the age of 89.

One universal healing principle

It is a well-known fact that all of the various schools of healing enable cures of the most wonderful character. The most obvious conclusion, which strikes your mind, is that there must be some underlying principle, which is common to them all, namely, the subconscious mind. The one common process of healing is faith. It will now be in order to recall to your mind once more the following fundamental truths: First, that you possess mental functions, which have been distinguished by designating one, the conscious mind and the other the subconscious mind. Secondly, your subconscious mind is constantly amenable to the power of suggestion. Furthermore, your subconscious mind has complete control of the functions, conditions and sensations of your body.

Notice how it heals a cut on your face caused by shaving. It knows exactly how to do it. The doctor dresses the wound and says, 'Nature heals it!' Nature refers to natural law, the law of the subconscious mind or self-preservation. This is the function of the subconscious mind. The instinct of self-preservation is the first law of nature. Your strongest instinct is the most potent of all autosuggestions. Widely different theories

It would be tedious and unprofitable to discuss to any great extent the numerous theories advanced by different religious sects and prayer therapy groups. There are a great number who claim that because their theory produces results it is, therefore, the correct one. This, as explained in this chapter, cannot be true. You are aware that there are all types of healing. Franz Anton Mesmer, an Austrian physician (1734–1815) who practised in Paris, discovered that by applying magnets to the diseased body, he could cure that disease miraculously. He also performed cures with various other pieces of glass and metals. He discontinued this form of healing and claimed that his cures were due to 'animal magnetism,' theorising that this substance was projected from the healer to the patient.

His method of treating disease from then on was by hypnotism, which was called mesmerism in his day. Other physicians said that all his healings were due to suggestion and nothing else. All of these groups, such as psychiatrists, psychologists, osteopaths, chiropractors, physicians and all the churches are using the one universal power resident in the subconscious mind. Each may proclaim the healings are due to their theory. The process of all healing is a definite, positive, mental attitude, an inner attitude or a way of thinking called faith. Healing is due to a confident expectancy. This acts as a powerful suggestion to the subconscious mind releasing its healing potency.

One man does not heal by a different power than another. It is true he may have his own theory or method. There is only one process of healing and that is faith. There is only one healing power, namely, your subconscious mind. Select the theory and method you prefer. You can rest assured, if you have faith, you shall get results.

Healing today: faith and the power of prayer

Everyone is definitely concerned with the healing of bodily conditions and human affairs. What is it that heals? Where is this healing power? These are questions asked by everyone. The answer is that this healing power is in the subconscious mind of each person and a changed mental attitude on the part of the sick person releases this healing power. No mental or religious science practitioner, psychologist, psychiatrist or medical doctor ever healed a patient. There is an old saying, 'The doctor dresses the wound, but God heals it.' The psychologist or psychiatrist proceeds to remove the mental blocks in the patient so that the healing principle may be released, restoring the patient to health. Likewise, the surgeon removes the physical block enabling the healing currents to function normally. No physician, surgeon, or mental science practitioner claims, 'he healed the patient.' The one healing power is called by many names – Nature, Life, God, Creative Intelligence and Subconscious Power. As previously outlined, there are many different methods used to remove the mental, emotional and physical blocks which inhibit the flow of the healing life principle animating all of us. The healing principle resident in your subconscious mind can and will, if properly directed by you or some other person, heal your mind and body of all disease. This healing principle is operative in all men regardless of creed, colour or race. You do not have to belong to some particular church in order to use and participate in this healing process. Your subconscious will heal the burn or cut on your hand even though you profess to be an atheist or agnostic.

The modern mental therapeutic procedure is based on the truth that the infinite intelligence and power of your subconscious mind responds according to your faith. The mental science practitioner or minister follows the injunction of the Bible, i.e., he goes into his closet and shuts the door, which means he stills his mind, relaxes, lets go and thinks of the infinite healing presence within him. He closes the door of his mind to all outside distractions as well as appearances. Then he quietly and knowingly turns over his request or desire to his subconscious mind, realising that the intelligence of his mind will answer him according to his specific needs.

The most wonderful thing to know is this: Imagine the end desired and feel its reality; then the infinite life principle will respond to your conscious choice and your conscious request. This is the meaning of *believe you have received and you shall receive.* This is what the modern mental scientist does when he practises prayer therapy.

One process of healing

There is only one universal healing principle operating through everything – the cat, the dog, the tree, the grass, the wind, the earth – for everything is alive. This life principle operates through the animal, vegetable and mineral kingdoms as instinct and the law of growth. Man is consciously aware of this life principle and he can consciously direct it to bless himself in countless ways. There are many different approaches, techniques and methods in using the universal power, but there is only one process of healing, which is faith, for *according to your faith is it done unto you.*

The law of belief

All religions of the world represent forms of belief and these beliefs are explained in many ways. The law of life is belief. What do you believe about yourself, life and the universe? *It is done unto you as you believe.*

Belief is a thought in your mind, which causes the power of your subconscious to be distributed into all phases of your life according to your thinking habits. You must realise the Bible is not talking about your belief in some ritual, ceremony, form, institution, man, or formula. It is talking about belief itself. The belief of your mind is simply the thought of your mind. *If thou canst believe, all things are possible to him that believeth* – Mark 9:23. It is foolish to believe in something to hurt or harm you. Remember, it is not the thing believed in that hurts or harms you, but the belief or thought in your mind, which creates the result. All your experiences, all your actions and all the events and circumstances of your life are but the reflections and reactions to your own thought.

Prayer therapy is the combined function of the conscious and subconscious mind scientifically directed

Prayer therapy is the synchronised, harmonious and intelligent function of the conscious and subconscious levels of mind specifically directed for a definite purpose. In scientific prayer or prayer therapy, you must know what you are doing and why you are doing it. You trust the law of healing. Prayer therapy is sometimes referred to as mental treatment and another term is scientific prayer. In prayer therapy you consciously choose a certain idea, mental picture or plan which you desire to experience. You realise your capacity to convey this idea or mental image to your subconscious by feeling the reality of the state assumed. As you remain faithful in your mental attitude, your prayer will be answered. Prayer therapy is a definite mental action for a definite specific purpose.

Let us suppose that you decide to heal a certain difficulty by prayer therapy. You are aware that your problem or sickness, whatever it may be, must be caused by negative thoughts charged with fear and lodged in your subconscious mind. If you can succeed in cleansing your mind of these thoughts, you will get healing. You, therefore, turn to the healing power within your own subconscious mind as also remind yourself of its *infinite* power and intelligence and its capacity to heal all conditions. As you dwell on these truths, your fear will begin to dissolve. The recollection of these truths also corrects the erroneous beliefs.

You give thanks for the healing that you know will come. Then you keep your mind off the difficulty until you feel guided, after an interval, to pray again. While you are praying, you absolutely refuse to give any power to the negative conditions or to admit for a second that the healing will not come. This attitude of mind brings about the harmonious union of the conscious and subconscious mind, which releases the healing power.

Faith healing, what it means and how blind faith works

What is popularly termed faith healing is not the faith mentioned in the Bible, which means knowledge of the interaction of the conscious and subconscious mind. A faith healer is one who heals without any real scientific understanding of the powers and forces involved. He may claim that he has a special gift of healing. The sick person's blind belief in him or his powers may bring results. The voodoo doctor in South Africa and other parts of the world may heal by incantations or a person may be healed by touching the so-called bones of saints or anything else which cause the patients to honestly believe in the method or process.

Any method, which causes you to move from fear and worry to faith and expectancy, will heal. There are many persons, each of whom claims that because his personal theory produces results, it is, therefore, the correct one. This, as already explained in this chapter, cannot be true.

Subjective faith and what it means

You will recall the proposition, which need not be repeated at length, that the subjective or subconscious mind of an individual is as amenable to the control of his own conscious or objective mind as it is by the suggestions of another. It follows that whatever may be your objective belief, if you will assume to have faith actively or passively, your subconscious mind will be controlled by the suggestion and your desire will be fulfilled.

The faith required in mental healings is a purely subjective faith and it is attainable upon the cessation of active opposition on the part of the objective or conscious mind. In the healing of the body it is, of course, desirable to secure the concurrent faith of both the conscious and subconscious mind. However, it is not always essential if you will enter into a state of passivity and receptivity by relaxing the mind and the body and getting into a sleepy state. In this drowsy state your passivity becomes receptive to subjective impression.

Recently, I was asked by a man, 'How is it that I got a healing through a minister? I did not believe what he said when he told me that there is no such thing as disease and that matter does not exist.' This man at first thought his intelligence was being insulted and he protested against such a palpable absurdity. The explanation is simple. He was quieted by soothing words and told to get into a perfectly passive condition, to say nothing and think of nothing for the time being. His minister also became passive and affirmed quietly, peacefully and constantly for about one half hour that this man would have perfect health, peace, harmony and wholeness. He felt immense relief and was restored to health. It is easy to see that his subjective faith had been made manifest by his passivity under treatment and the suggestions of perfect healthfulness by the minister were conveyed to his subconscious mind. The two subjective minds were then synchronised. The minister was not handicapped by antagonistic autosuggestions of the patient arising from objective doubt of the power of the healer or the correctness of the theory. In this sleepy, drowsy state when the conscious mind resistance is reduced to a minimum – results followed. The subconscious mind of the patient being necessarily controlled by such suggestion exercised its function, accordingly a healing followed.

The meaning of absent treatment

Suppose you learned that your mother was sick in New York

City and you lived in Los Angeles. Your mother would not be physically present where you are but you could pray for her. *It is the Father within which doeth the work.*

The creative law of mind (subconscious mind) serves you and will do the work. Its response to you is automatic. Your treatment is for the purpose of inducing an inner realisation of health and harmony in your mentality. This inner realisation, acting through the subconscious mind, operates through your mother's subconscious mind as there is but one creative mind. Your thoughts of health, vitality and perfection operate through the one universal subjective mind. This sets a law in motion on the subjective side of life, to *manifest* through her body as a healing.

In the mind principle there is no time or space. It is the same mind that operates through your mother no matter where she may be. In reality there is no absent treatment as opposed to present treatment for the universal mind is omnipresent. You do not try to send out thoughts or hold a thought. Your treatment is a conscious movement of thought and as you become conscious of the qualities of health, well-being and relaxation, these qualities will be resurrected in the experience of your mother and results will follow. The following is a perfect example of what is called absent treatment. Recently, a listener of our radio program in Los Angeles prayed as follows for her mother in New York who had a coronary thrombosis: 'The healing presence is right where my mother is. Her bodily condition is but a reflection of her thought-life like shadows cast on the screen. I know that in order to change the images on the screen I must change the projection reel. My mind is the projection reel and I now project in my own mind the image of wholeness, harmony and perfect health for my mother. The infinite healing presence, which created my mother's body and all her organs is now saturating every atom of her being and a river of peace, flows through every cell of her body. The doctors are divinely guided and directed and whoever touches my mother is guided to do the right thing. I know that disease has no ultimate reality; if it had, no one could be healed. I now align myself with the infinite principle of love and life and I know and decree that harmony, health and peace are now being expressed in my mother's body.'

She prayed in the above manner several times daily and her mother had a most remarkable recovery after a few days, much to the amazement of her specialist. He complimented her on her great faith in the power of God.

The conclusion arrived at in the daughter's mind set the creative law of mind in motion on the subjective side of life, which manifested itself through her mother's body as perfect health and harmony. What the daughter felt as true about her mother was simultaneously resurrected in the experience of her mother.

Releasing the kinetic action of the subconscious mind

A psychologist friend of mine told me that one of his lungs was infected. X-rays and analysis showed the presence of tuberculosis. At night before going to sleep he would quietly affirm, 'Every cell, nerve, tissue and muscle of my lungs are now being made whole, pure and perfect. My whole body is being restored to health and harmony.'

These are not his exact words, but they represent the essence of what he affirmed. A complete healing followed in about a month's time. Subsequent X-rays showed a perfect healing. I wanted to know his method, so I asked him why he repeated the words prior to sleep. Here is his reply, 'The kinetic action of the subconscious mind continues throughout your sleep-time period. Hence, give the subconscious mind something good to work on as you drop off into slumber.' This was a very wise answer. In thinking of harmony and perfect health, he never mentioned his trouble by name.

I strongly suggest that you cease talking about your ailments or giving them a name. The only sap from which they draw life is your attention and fear of them. Like the above mentioned psychologist, become a mental surgeon. Then your troubles will be cut off like dead branches are pruned from a tree. If you are constantly naming your aches and symptoms, you inhibit the kinetic action, which means the release of the healing power and energy of your subconscious mind. Further more, by the law of your own mind, these imaginings tend to take shape. *As the thing I greatly feared.* Fill your mind with the great truths of life and walk forward in the light of love.

PRACTICAL TECHNIQUES IN MENTAL HEALINGS

An engineer has a technique and a process for building a bridge or an engine. Like the engineer, your mind also has a technique for governing, controlling and directing your life. You must realise that methods and techniques are primary.

In building the Golden Gate bridge, the chief engineer understood mathematical principles, stresses and strains. Secondly, he had a picture of the ideal bridge across the bay. The third step was his application of tried and proven methods by which the principles were implemented until the bridge took form and we drive on it. There also are techniques and methods by which your prayers are answered. If your prayer is answered, there is a way in which it is answered and this is a scientific way. Nothing happens by chance. This is a world of law and order. In this chapter you will find practical techniques for the unfolding and nurture of your spiritual life. Your prayers must not remain up in the air like a balloon. They must go somewhere and accomplish something in your life.

When we come to analyse prayer we discover there are many different approaches and methods. We will not consider in this book the formal, ritual prayers used in religious services. These have an important place in group worship. We are immediately concerned with the methods of personal prayer as it is applied in your daily life and as it is used to help others.

Prayer is the formulation of an idea concerning something we wish to accomplish. Prayer is the soul's sincere desire. Your desire is your prayer. It comes out of your deepest needs while it reveals the things you want in life. *Blessed are they that hunger and thirst after righteousness: for they shall be filled. That is* really prayer, life's hunger and thirst for peace, harmony, health, joy and all the other blessings of life.

The passing-over technique for impregnating the subconscious

This consists essentially in inducing the subconscious mind to take over your request as handed it by the conscious mind. This passing-over is best accomplished in the reverie-like state. Know that in your deeper mind is Infinite Intelligence and Infinite Power. Just calmly think over what you want; see it coming into fuller fruition from this moment forward. Be like the little girl who had a very bad cough and a sore throat. She declared firmly and repeatedly, 'It is passing away now. It is passing away now.' It passed away in about an hour. Use this technique with complete simplicity and naivety.

Your subconscious will accept your blueprint

If you were building a new home for yourself and family, you know that you would be intensely interested in regard to the blueprint for your home; you would see to it that the builders conformed to the blueprint. You would watch the material and select only the best wood, steel, in fact, the best of everything. What about your mental home and your mental blueprint for happiness and abundance? All your experiences and everything that enters into your life depend upon the nature of the mental building blocks, which you use in the construction of your mental home.

If your blueprint is full of mental patterns of fear, worry, anxiety or lack and if you are despondent, doubtful and cynical, then the texture of the mental material you are weaving into your mind will come forth as more toil, care, tension, anxiety and limitation of all kinds. The most fundamental and the most far-reaching activity in life is that which you build into your mentality every waking hour. Your word is silent and invisible; nevertheless, it is real. You are building your mental home all the time and your thought and mental imagery represent your blueprint. Hour by hour, moment by moment, you can build radiant health, success and happiness by the thoughts you think, the ideas which you harbour, the beliefs that you accept and the scenes that you rehearse in the hidden studio of your mind. This stately mansion, upon the construction of which you are perpetually engaged, is your personality, your identity in this plane, your whole life story on this earth.

Get a new blueprint; build silently by realising peace, harmony, joy and goodwill in the present moment. By dwelling upon these things and claiming them, your subconscious will accept your blueprint and bring all these things to pass. *By their fruits ye shall know them.*

The science and art of true prayer

The term 'science' means knowledge, which is coordinated, arranged and systematised. Let us think of the science and art of true prayer as it deals with the fundamental principles of life and the techniques and processes by which they can be demonstrated in your life, as well as in the life of every human being when he applies them faithfully. The art is your technique or process and the science behind it is the definite response of creative mind to your mental picture or thought.

> *Ask and it shall be given you; seek and ye shall find; knock and it shall be opened unto you.* – Matthew 7:7.

Here you are told you shall receive what you ask. It shall be opened to you when you knock and you shall find what you are searching. This teaching implies the definiteness of mental and spiritual laws. There is always a direct response from the Infinite Intelligence of your subconscious mind to your conscious thinking. If you ask for bread, you will not receive a stone. You must ask *believing*, if you are to receive. Your mind moves from the thought to the thing. Unless there is first an image in the mind, it cannot move, for there would be nothing for it to move toward. Your prayer, which is your mental act, must be accepted as an image in your mind before the power from your subconscious will play upon it and make it productive. You must reach a point of acceptance in your mind, an unqualified and undisputed state of agreement.

This contemplation should be accompanied by a feeling of joy and restfulness in foreseeing the certain accomplishment of your desire. The sound basis for the art and science of true prayer is your knowledge and complete confidence that the movement of your conscious mind will gain a definite response from your subconscious mind which is one with boundless wisdom and infinite power. By following this procedure, your prayers will be answered.

The visualisation technique

The easiest and most obvious way to formulate an idea is to visualise it, to see it in your mind's eye as vividly as if it were alive. You can see with the naked eye only what already exists in the external world; in a similar way, that which you can visualise in your mind's eye already exists in the invisible realms of your mind. Any picture which you have in your mind is *the substance of things hoped for and the evidence of things not seen.* What you form in your imagination is as real as any part of your body. The idea and the thought are real and will one day appear **in** your objective world if you are faithful to your mental image. This process of thinking forms impressions in your mind; these impressions in turn become manifested as facts and experiences in your life. The builder visualises the type of building he wants; he sees it as he desires it to be completed. His imagery and thought processes become a plastic mold from which the building will emerge – a beautiful or an ugly one, a skyscraper or a very low one. His mental imagery is projected as it is drawn on paper. Eventually, the contractor and his workers gather the essential materials and the building progresses until it stands finished, conforming perfectly to the mental patterns of the architect.

I use the visualisation technique prior to speaking from the platform. I quiet the wheels of my mind in order that I may present to the subconscious mind my images of thought. Then, I picture the entire auditorium and the seats filled with men and women. Each one of them is illumined and inspired by the infinite healing presence within each of them. I see them as radiant, happy and free.

Having first built up the idea in my imagination, I quietly sustain it there as a mental picture while I imagine I hear men and women saying, 'I am healed,' 'I feel wonderful,' 'I've had an instantaneous healing,' 'I'm transformed.' I keep this up for about ten minutes or more, knowing and feeling that each person's mind and body are saturated with love, wholeness, beauty and perfection. My awareness grows to the point where in my mind I can actually hear the voices of the multitude proclaiming their health and happiness; then I release the whole picture and go onto the platform. Almost every Sunday some people stop and say that their prayers were answered.

Mental movie method

The Chinese say, 'A picture is worth a thousand words.' William James, the father of American psychology, stressed the fact that the subconscious mind will bring to pass any picture held in the mind and backed by faith. *Act as though I am and I will be.*

A number of years ago I was in the Midwest United States lecturing in several states and I desired to have a permanent location in the general area from which I could serve those who desired help. I travelled far, but the desire did not leave my mind. One evening, while in a hotel in Spokane, Washington, I relaxed completely on a couch, immobilised my attention and in a quiet, passive manner imagined that I was talking to a large audience, saying in effect, 'I am glad to be here; I have prayed for the ideal opportunity.' I saw in my mind's eye the imaginary audience and I felt the reality of it all. I played the role of the actor, dramatised this mental movie and felt satisfied that this picture was being conveyed to my subconscious mind, which would bring it to pass in its own way. The next morning, on awakening, I felt a great sense of peace and satisfaction. In a few days' time I received a telegram asking me to take over an organisation in the Midwest, which I did. I enjoyed it immensely for several years.

The method outlined here appeals to many who have described it as 'the mental movie method.' I have received numerous letters from people who listen to my radio talks and weekly public lectures. They tell me of the wonderful results they get using this technique in the sale of their property. I suggest to those who have homes or property for sale that they satisfy themselves in their own mind that their price is right. Then, I claim that the Infinite Intelligence is attracting to them the buyer who really wants to have the property and who will love it and prosper in it. After having done this I suggest that they quiet their mind, relax, let go and get into a drowsy, sleepy state. This reduces all mental effort to a minimum. Then, they are to picture the check in their hands, rejoice in the check, give thanks for the check. After that go off to sleep feeling the naturalness of the whole mental movie created in their own mind. They must act as though it were an objective reality. The subconscious mind will take it as an impression and through the deeper currents of the mind the buyer and the seller are brought together. A mental picture held in the mind – backed by faith – will come to pass.

The sleeping technique

By entering into a sleepy, drowsy state, effort is reduced to a minimum. The conscious mind is submerged to a great extent when in a sleepy state. The reason for this is that the highest degree of outcropping of the subconscious occurs prior to sleep and just after we awaken. In this state the negative thoughts, which tend to neutralise your desire and so prevent acceptance by your subconscious mind, are no longer present.

Suppose you want to get rid of a destructive habit. Assume a comfortable posture, relax your body and be still. Get into a sleepy state and in that sleepy state, say quietly, over and over again as a lullaby, 'I am completely free from this habit; harmony and peace of mind reign supreme.' Repeat the above slowly, quietly and lovingly for five or ten minutes night and morning. Each time you repeat the words the emotional value becomes greater. When the urge comes to repeat the negative habit, repeat the above formula out loud by yourself. By this means you induce the subconscious to accept the idea and a healing follows.

The 'thank-you' technique

In the Bible, Paul recommends that we make known our requests with praise and thanksgiving. Some extraordinary results follow this simple method of prayer. The thankful heart is always close to the creative forces of the universe, causing countless blessings to flow toward it by the law of reciprocal relationship, based on a cosmic law of action and reaction.

For instance, a father promises his son a car for graduation; the boy has not yet received the car, but he is very thankful and happy. It is as joyous as though he had actually received the car. He knows his father will fulfill his promise. He is full of gratitude and joy even though he has not yet received the car, objectively speaking. He has, however, received it with joy and thankfulness in his mind.

I shall illustrate how Mr Broke applied this technique with excellent results. He said, 'Bills are piling up, I am out of work, I have three children and no money. What shall I do?' Regularly every night and morning, for a period of about three weeks, he repeated the words, 'Thank you, Father, for my wealth,' in a relaxed, peaceful manner until the feeling or mood of thankfulness dominated his mind. He imagined he was addressing the infinite power and intelligence within him knowing, of course, that he could not see the creative intelligence or infinite mind. He was seeing with the inner eye of spiritual perception, realising that his thought-image of wealth was the *first cause,* relative to the money, position and food he needed. His thought feeling was the substance of wealth untrammeled by antecedent conditions of any kind. By, repeating, 'Thank you, Father,' over and over again, his mind and heart were lifted up to the point of acceptance and when fear, thoughts of, poverty and distress came into his mind, he would say, 'Thank you, Father,' as often as necessary. He knew that as he kept up the thankful attitude he would recondition his mind to the idea of wealth, which is what happened.

The sequel to his prayer is very interesting. After praying as described, he met a former employer of his on the street whom he had not seen for twenty years. The man offered him a very lucrative position and advanced him $500 as a temporary loan. Today, Mr Broke is vice-president of the company for which he works. His recent remark to me was, 'I shall never forget the wonders of "Thank you, Father." It has worked wonders for me.'

The affirmative method

The effectiveness of an affirmation is determined largely by your understanding of the truth and the meaning back of the words, '*In praying use not vain repetition.*' Therefore, the power of your affirmation lies in the intelligent application of definite and specific positives. For example, a boy adds three and three and puts down seven on the blackboard. The teacher affirms with mathematical certainty that three and three are six; therefore, the boy changes his figures accordingly. The teacher's statement did not make three and three equal six because the latter was already a mathematical truth. The mathematical truth caused the boy to rearrange the figures on the blackboard. It is abnormal to be sick; it is normal to be healthy. Health is the truth of your being. When you affirm health, harmony and peace for yourself or another as also when you realise these are universal principles of your own being, you will rearrange the negative patterns of your subconscious mind based on your faith and understanding of that which you affirm.

The result of the affirmative process of prayer depends on your conforming to the principles of life, regardless of appearances. Consider for a moment that there is a principle of mathematics and none of error; there is a principle of truth but none of dishonesty. There is a principle of intelligence but none of ignorance; there is a principle of harmony and none of discord. There is a principle of health but none of disease and there is a principle of abundance but none of poverty.

The affirmative method was chosen by the author for use on his sister who was to be operated for the removal of gallstones in a hospital in England. The condition described was based on the diagnosis of hospital tests with the usual X-ray procedures. She asked me to pray for her. We were separated geographically about 6,500 miles, but there is no time or space in the mind principle. Infinite mind or intelligence is present in its entirety at every point simultaneously. I withdrew all thought from the contemplation of symptoms and from the corporeal personality altogether. I affirmed as follows: 'This prayer is for my sister Catherine. She is relaxed and at peace, poised, balanced, serene and calm. The healing intelligence of her subconscious mind, which created her body, is now transforming every cell, nerve, tissue, muscle and bone of her being according to the perfect pattern of all organs lodged in her subconscious mind. Silently, quietly, all distorted thought patterns in her subconscious mind are removed and dissolved. The vitality, wholeness and beauty of the life principle are made manifest in every atom of her being. She is now open and receptive to the healing currents, which are flowing through her like a river, restoring her to perfect health, harmony and peace. All distortions and ugly images are now washed away by the infinite ocean of love and peace flowing through her and it is so.'

I affirmed the above several times a day and at the end of two weeks my sister had an examination, which showed a remarkable healing and the X-ray, proved negative. *To affirm* is to state that it is so. As you maintain this attitude of mind as true, regardless of all evidence to the contrary, you will receive an answer to your prayer. Your thought can only affirm, for even if you deny something, you are actually affirming the presence of what you deny, Repeating an affirmation, knowing what you are saying and why you are saying it, leads the mind to that state of consciousness where it accepts that which you state as true. Keep on affirming the truths of life until you get the subconscious reaction which satisfies.

The argumentative method

This method is just what the word implies. It stems from the procedure of Dr Phineas Parkhurst Quimby of Maine. Dr Quimby, a pioneer in mental and spiritual healing, lived and practiced in Belfast, Maine, about one hundred years ago. *The Quimby Manuscripts,* was edited by Horatio Dresser and published in 1921 by Thomas Y Crowell Company, New York City. This book gives newspaper accounts of this man's remarkable results in prayer treatment of the sick. Quimby duplicated many of the healing miracles recorded in the Bible. In brief, the argumentative method employed according to Quimby consists of spiritual reasoning where you convince the patient and yourself that his sickness is due to his false belief, groundless fears and negative patterns lodged in his subconscious mind. You reason it out clearly in your mind and convince your patient that the disease or ailment is due only to a distorted, twisted pattern of thought which has taken form in his body. This wrong belief in some external power and external causes has now externalised itself as sickness and can be changed by changing the thought patterns.

You explain to the sick person that the basis of all healing is a change of belief. You also point out that the subconscious mind created the body and all its organs; therefore, it knows how to heal it, can heal it and is doing so now as you speak. You argue in the courtroom of your mind that the disease is a shadow of the mind based on disease-soaked, morbid thought-imagery. You continue to build up all the evidence you can muster on behalf of the healing power within, which created all the organs in the first place and which has a perfect pattern of every cell, nerve and tissue within it. Then, you render a verdict in the courthouse of your mind in favour of yourself or your patient. You liberate the sick one by faith and spiritual understanding. Your mental and spiritual evidence is overwhelming; there being but one mind, what you feel as true will be resurrected in the experience of the patient. This procedure is essentially the argumentative method used by Dr Quimby of Maine from 1849 to 1869.

The absolute method is like modern sound wave therapy

Many people throughout the world practise this form of prayer treatment with wonderful results. The person using the absolute method mentions the name of the patient, such as John Jones, then quietly and silently thinks of God and His qualities and attributes, such as, God is all bliss, boundless love, infinite intelligence, all-powerful, boundless wisdom, absolute harmony, indescribable beauty and perfection. As he quietly thinks along these lines he is lifted up in consciousness into a new spiritual wave length, at which times he feels the infinite ocean of God's love is now dissolving everything unlike itself in the mind and body of John Jones for whom he is praying. He feels all the power and love of God are now focused on John Jones and whatever is bothering or vexing him is now completely neutralised in the presence of the infinite ocean of life and love.

The absolute method of prayer might be likened to the sound wave or sonic therapy recently shown to me by a distinguished physician in Los Angeles. He has an ultrasound wave machine which oscillates at a tremendous speed and sends sound waves to any area of the body to which it is directed. These sound waves can be controlled. He told me of achieving remarkable results in dissolving arthritic calcareous deposits, as well as the healing and removal of other disturbing conditions.

To the degree that we rise in consciousness by contemplating qualities and attributes of God, do we generate spiritual electronic waves of harmony, health and peace? Many remarkable healings follow this technique of prayer.

The decree method

Power goes into our word according to the feeling and faith behind it. When we realise the power that moves the world is moving on our behalf and is backing up our word, our confidence and assurance grow. You do not try to add power to power; therefore, there must be no mental striving, coercion, force or mental wrestling.

A young girl used the decree method on a young man who was constantly phoning her, pressing her for dates and meeting her at her place of business. She found it very difficult to get rid of him. She decreed as follows: 'I release unto God. He is in his true place at all times. I am free and he is free. I now decree that my words go forth into infinite mind and it brings it to pass. It is so.' She said he vanished and she has never seen him since, adding, 'It was as though the ground swallowed him up.'

> *Thou shalt decree a thing and it shall be established unto thee: and the light shall shine upon thy ways.* – Job 22:28.

HOW TO GET THE RESULTS YOU WANT

The principle reasons for failure are: lack of confidence and too much effort. Many people block answers to their prayers by failing to fully comprehend the workings of their subconscious mind. When you know how your mind functions, you gain a measure of confidence. You must remember whenever your subconscious mind accepts an idea, it immediately begins to execute it. It uses all its mighty resources to that end and mobilises all the mental and spiritual laws of your deeper mind. This law is true for good or bad ideas. Consequently, if you use it negatively, it brings trouble, failure and confusion. When you use it constructively, it brings guidance, freedom as also peace of mind.

The right answer is inevitable when your thoughts are positive, constructive and loving. From this it is perfectly obvious that the only thing you have to do in order to overcome failure is to get your subconscious to accept your idea or request by feeling its reality now then the law of your mind will do the rest. Turn over your request with faith and confidence. Your subconscious will take over and answer for you.

You will always fail to get results by trying to use mental coercion – your subconscious mind does not respond to coercion, it responds to your faith or conscious mind acceptance. Your failure to get results may also arise from such statements as: 'Things are getting worse.' 'I will never get an answer.' 'I see no way out.' 'It is hopeless.' 'I don't know what to do.' 'I'm all mixed up.' When you use such statements, you get no response or cooperation from your subconscious mind. Like a soldier marking time, you neither go forward nor backward; in other words, you don't get anywhere.

If you get into a taxi and give a half dozen different directions to the driver in five minutes, he would become hopelessly confused. He, then probably would refuse to take you anywhere. It is the same when working with your subconscious mind. There must be a clear-cut idea in your mind. You must arrive at the definite decision that there is a way out, a solution to the vexing problem in sickness. Only the infinite intelligence within your subconscious knows the answer. When you come to that clear-cut conclusion in your conscious mind, your mind is then made up and according to your belief it is done for you.

Easy does it

A house owner once remonstrated a furnace repairman for charging two hundred dollars for fixing the boiler. The mechanic said, 'I charged five cents for the missing bolt and one hundred ninety-nine dollars and ninety-five cents for knowing what was wrong.' Similarly, your subconscious mind is the master mechanic, the all-wise one, who knows ways and means of healing any organ of your body, as well as your affairs. Decree health and your subconscious will establish it, but relaxation is the key. 'Easy does it.' Do not be concerned with details and means, but know the end result. Get the *feel* of the happy solution to your problem whether it is health, finances or employment. Remember how you felt after you had recovered from a severe state of illness. Bear in mind that your feeling is the touchstone of all subconscious demonstration. Your new idea must be felt subjectively in a finished state, not the future, but as coming about now.

Infer no opponent, use imagination and not will power

In using your subconscious mind you infer no opponent, you use no will power. You imagine the end and the freedom state. You will find your intellect trying to get in the way but persist in maintaining a simple, childlike, miracle-making faith. Picture yourself without the ailment or problem. Imagine the emotional accompaniment of the freedom state you crave. Cut out all red tape from the process. The simple way is the best.

How disciplined imagination works wonders

A wonderful way to get a response from your subconscious mind is through disciplined or scientific imagination. As previously pointed out, your subconscious mind is the builder of the body and controls all its vital functions.

The Bible says, *Whatsoever ye shall ask in prayer, believing, ye shall receive.* To believe is to accept something as true or to live in the state of being it. As you sustain this mood, you shall experience the joy of the answered prayer!

The three steps to success in prayer

The usual procedure is as follows:

Take a look at the problem.

Turn to the solution or way out known only to the subconscious mind.

Rest in a sense of deep conviction that it is done.

Do not weaken your prayer by saying, 'I wish I might be healed.' 'I hope so.' Your feeling about the work to be done is 'the boss.' Harmony is yours. Know that health is yours. Become intelligent by becoming a vehicle for the infinite healing power of the subconscious mind. Pass on the idea of health to your subconscious mind to the point of conviction; then relax. Get yourself off your hands. Say to the condition and circumstance, 'This, too, shall pass.' Through relaxation you impress your subconscious mind enabling the kinetic energy behind the idea to take over and bring it into concrete realisation.

The law of reversed effort and why you get the opposite of what you pray for. Coue, the famous psychologist from France who visited America about forty years ago, defined the law of reversed effort as follows: 'When your desires and imagination are in conflict your imagination invariably gains the day.' If, for example, you were asked to walk a plank on the floor, you would do so without question. Now suppose the same plank were placed twenty feet up in the air between two walls, would you walk it? Your desire to walk it would be counteracted by your imagination or fear of falling. Your dominant idea, which would be the picture of falling, would conquer. Your desire, will or effort to walk on the plank would be reversed and the dominant idea of failure would be reinforced. Mental effort is invariably self-defeated, eventuating always in the opposite of what is desired. The suggestions of powerlessness to overcome the condition dominate the mind; your subconscious is always controlled by the dominant idea. Your subconscious will accept the stronger of two contradictory propositions. The effortless way is the better.

If you say, 'I want a healing, but I can't get it;' 'I try so hard;' 'I force myself to pray;' 'I use all the will power I have,' you must realise that your error lies in your effort. Never try to compel the subconscious mind to accept your idea by exercising will power. Such attempts are doomed to failure and you get the opposite of what you prayed for.

The following is a rather common experience. Students, when taking examinations and reading through their papers, find that all their knowledge has suddenly deserted them. Their minds become appalling blank. They are unable to recall one relevant thought. The more they grit their teeth and summon the powers of the will, the further the answers seem to flee. But, when they have left the examination room and the mental pressure relaxes, the answers they were seeking flow tantalisingly back into their minds. Trying to force themselves to remember was the cause of their failure. This is an example of the law of reversed effort whereby you get the opposite of what you asked or prayed for.

The conflict of desire and imagination must be reconciled

To use mental *force is to* presuppose that there is opposition. When your mind is concentrated on the means to overcome a problem, it is no longer concerned with the obstacle.

> *If two of you shall agree on earth as touching anything that they shall ask, it shall be done for them of my Father which is in heaven.* – Mattew 18:19.

Who are these two? It means the harmonious union or agreement between your conscious and subconscious on any idea, desire or mental image. When there is no longer any quarrel in either part of your mind, your prayer will be answered. The two agreeing may also be represented as you and your desire, your thought and feeling, your idea and emotion, your desire and imagination.

You avoid all conflict between your desires and imagination by entering into a drowsy, sleepy state which brings all effort to a minimum. The conscious mind is submerged to a great extent when in a sleepy state. The best time to impregnate your subconscious is prior to sleep. The reason for this is that the highest degree of outcropping of the subconscious occurs prior to sleep and just after we awaken. In this state the negative thoughts and imagery which tend to neutralise your desire and so prevent acceptance by your subconscious mind no longer present themselves. When you imagine the reality of the fulfilled desire and feel the thrill of accomplishment, your subconscious brings about the realisation of your desire.

A great many people solve all their dilemmas and problems by the play of their controlled, directed and disciplined imagination. They know that whatever they imagine and feel as true *will* and *must* come to pass.

The following will clearly illustrate how a young woman overcame the conflict between her desire and her imagination. She desired a harmonious solution to her legal problem, yet her mental imagery was constantly on failure, loss, bankruptcy and poverty. It was a complicated lawsuit and there was one postponement after another with no solution in sight. At my suggestion, she got into a sleepy, drowsy state each night prior to sleep and she began to imagine the happy ending, feeling it to the best of her ability. She knew that the image in her mind had to agree with her heart's desire. Prior to sleep she began to dramatise as vividly as possible her lawyer having an animated discussion with her regarding the outcome. She would ask him questions and he would answer her appropriately. He would say to her over and over again, 'There has been a perfect, harmonious solution. The case has been settled out of court.' During the day when fear thoughts came into her mind, she would run her mental movie with gestures, voice and sound equipment. She could easily imagine the sound of his voice, smile and mannerism. She ran this mental picture so often, it became a subjective pattern, a regular train track. At the end of a few weeks her attorney called her and confirmed objectively what she had been imagining and feeling as true subjectively.

This is really what the Psalmist meant when he wrote,

> *Let the words of my mouth and the meditations of my heart be acceptable in thy sight, O Lord my strength and my redeemer.* – Psalm 19:14.

> This is really what the Psalmist meant: Your good thoughts, mental images, your feeling, nature, emotion the law of your subconscious mind, the power and wisdom of your subconscious mind can redeem you from sickness, bondage and misery.

FOUR

Using the Power of Your Subconscious Mind for Wealth

If you are having financial difficulties, if you are trying to make ends meet, it means you have not convinced your subconscious mind that you will always have plenty and some to spare. You know men and women who work a few hours a week and make fabulous sums of money. They do not strive or slave hard. Do not believe the story that the only way you can become wealthy is by the sweat of your brow and hard labour. It is not so; the effortless way of life is the best. Do the thing you love to do and do it for the joy and thrill of it. I know an executive in Los Angeles who receives a huge yearly salary. Last year he went on a nine-month cruise to see the world and its beauty spots. He said to me that he had succeeded in convincing his subconscious mind that he is worth that much money. He told me that many men in his organisation getting about one hundred dollars a week knew more about the business than he did and could manage it better, but they had no ambition, no creative ideas and were not interested in the wonders of their subconscious mind.

BUILDING A WEALTH CONSCIOUSNESS

Wealth is simply a subconscious conviction on the part of the individual. You will not become a millionaire by saying, 'I am a millionaire, I am a millionaire.' You will grow into a wealth consciousness by building into your mentality the idea of wealth and abundance.

Your invisible means of support

The trouble with most people is that they have no invisible means of support. When business falls away, the stock market drops or they lose their investments, they seem helpless. The reason for such insecurity is that they do not know how to tap the subconscious mind. They are unacquainted with the inexhaustible storehouse within.

A man with a poverty type mind finds himself in poverty-stricken conditions. Another man with a mind filled with ideas of wealth is surrounded with everything he needs. It was never intended that man should lead a life of poverty. You can have wealth, everything you need and plenty to spare. Your words have power to cleanse your mind of wrong ideas and to instill right ideas in their place.

The ideal method for building a wealth consciousness

Perhaps you are saying as you read this chapter, 'I need wealth and success.' This is what you do: Repeat for about five minutes to yourself three or four times a day, 'Wealth – Success.' These words have tremendous power. They represent the inner power of the subconscious mind. Anchor your mind on this substantial power within you; then conditions and circumstances corresponding to their nature and quality will be manifested in your life. You are not saying, 'I am wealthy,' you are dwelling on real powers within you. There is no conflict in the mind when you say, 'Wealth.' Furthermore, the feeling of wealth will well up within you as you dwell on the idea of wealth. The feeling of wealth produces wealth; keep this in mind at all times. Your subconscious mind is like a bank, a sort of universal financial institution. It magnifies whatever you deposit or impress upon it whether it is the idea of wealth or of poverty. Choose wealth.

Why your affirmations for wealth fail

I have talked to many people during the past thirty-five years whose usual complaint is, 'I have said for weeks and months, "I am wealthy, I am prosperous," and nothing has happened.' I discovered that when they said, 'I am prosperous, I am wealthy,' they felt within that they were lying to themselves.

One man told me, 'I have affirmed that I am prosperous until I am tired. Things are now worse. I knew when I made the statement that it was obviously not true.' His statements were rejected by the conscious mind and the very opposite of what he outwardly affirmed and claimed was manifest.

Your affirmation succeeds best when it is specific and when it does not produce a mental conflict or argument; hence the statements made by this man made matters worse because they suggested his lack. Your subconscious accepts what you really feel to be true, not just idle words or statements. The dominant idea or belief is always accepted by the subconscious mind.

How to avoid mental conflict

The following is the ideal way to overcome this conflict for those who have this difficulty. Make this practical statement frequently, particularly prior to sleep: 'By day and by night I am being prospered in all of my interests.' This affirmation will not arouse any argument because it does not contradict your subconscious mind's impression of financial lack. I suggested to one businessman whose sales and finances were very low and who was greatly worried, that he sit down in his office, become quiet and repeat this statement over and over again: 'My sales are improving every day.' This statement engaged the cooperation of the conscious and subconscious mind; results followed.

Don't sign blank checks

You sign blank checks when you make such statements as, 'There is not enough to go around.' 'There is a shortage.' 'I will lose the house because of the mortgage,' etc. If you are full of fear about the future, you are also writing a blank check and attracting negative conditions to you. Your subconscious mind takes your fear and negative statement as your request and proceeds in its own way to bring obstacles, delays, lack and limitation into your life.

Your subconscious gives you compound interest

To him that hath the feeling of wealth, more wealth shall be added; to him that hath the feeling of lack, more lack shall be added. Your subconscious multiplies and magnifies whatever you deposit in it. Every morning as you awaken deposit thoughts of prosperity, success, wealth and peace. Dwell upon these concepts. Busy your mind with them as often as possible. These constructive thoughts will find their way as deposits in your subconscious mind and bring forth abundance and prosperity.

Why nothing happened

I can hear you saying, 'Oh, I did that and nothing happened.' You did not get results because you indulged in fear thoughts perhaps ten minutes later and neutralised the good you had affirmed. When you place a seed in the ground, you do not dig it up. You let it take root and grow.

Suppose, for example, you are going to say, 'I shall not be able to make that payment.' Before you get further than, 'I shall –' stop the sentence and dwell on a constructive statement, such as, 'By day and by night I am prospered in all my ways.'

True source of wealth

Your subconscious mind is never short of ideas. There are within it an infinite number of ideas ready to flow into your conscious mind and appear as cash in your pocketbook in countless ways. This process will continue to go on in your mind regardless of whether the stock market goes up or down or whether the pound sterling or dollar drops in value. Your wealth is never truly dependent on bonds, stocks or money in the bank; these are really only symbols necessary and useful, of course, but only symbols.

The point I wish to emphasise is that if you convince your subconscious mind that wealth is yours and that it is always circulating in your life, you will always and inevitably have it, regardless of the form it takes.

Trying to make ends meet and the real cause

There are people who claim that they are always trying to make ends meet. They seem to have a great struggle to meet their obligations. Have you listened to their conversation? In many instances their conversation runs along this vein. They are constantly condemning those who have succeeded in life, these who have raised their heads above the crowd. Perhaps they are saying, 'Oh, that fellow has a racket; he is ruthless; he is a crook.' This is why they lack; they are condemning the thing they desire and want. The reason they speak critically of their more prosperous associates is because they are envious and covetous of the others' prosperity. The quickest way to cause wealth to take wings and fly away is to criticise and condemn others who have more wealth than you.

A common stumbling block to wealth

There is one emotion, which is the cause of the lack of wealth in the lives of many. Most people learn this the hard way. It is envy. For example, if you see a competitor depositing large sums of money in the bank and you have only a meager amount to deposit, does it make you envious? The way to overcome this emotion is to say to yourself, 'Isn't it wonderful! I rejoice in that man's prosperity. I wish for him greater and greater wealth.' To entertain envious thoughts is devastating because it places you in a very negative position; therefore, wealth flows *from* you instead of *to* you. If you are ever annoyed or irritated by the prosperity or great wealth of another, claim immediately that you truly wish for him greater wealth in every possible way. This will neutralise the negative thoughts in your mind and cause an ever greater measure of wealth to flow to you by the law of your own subconscious mind.

Rubbing out a great mental block to wealth

If you are worried and critical about someone whom you claim is making money dishonestly, cease worrying about him. You know such a person is using the law of mind negatively; the law of mind takes care of him. Be careful not to criticise him for the reasons previously indicated. Remember! The block or obstacle to wealth is in your own mind. You can now destroy that mental block. This you may do by getting on mental good terms with everyone.

Sleep and grow rich

As you go to sleep at night, practice the following technique. Repeat the word, 'Wealth,' quietly, easily and feelingly. Do this over and over again, just like a lullaby. Lull yourself to sleep with the one word, 'Wealth.' You should be amazed at the result. Wealth should flow to you in avalanches of abundance. This is another example of the magic power of your subconscious mind.

YOUR RIGHT TO BE RICH

It is your right to be rich. You are here to lead the abundant life and be happy, radiant and free. You should, therefore, have all the money you need to lead a full, happy and prosperous life.

You are here to grow, expand and unfold spiritually, mentally and materially. You have the inalienable right to fully develop and express yourself along all lines. You should surround yourself with beauty and luxury.

Why be satisfied with just enough to go around when you can enjoy the riches of your subconscious mind? In this chapter you can learn to make friends with money and you should always have a surplus. Your desire to be rich is a desire for a fuller, happier, more wonderful life. It is a cosmic urge. It is not only good, but very good.

Money is a symbol

Money is a symbol of exchange. It means to you not only freedom from want, but beauty, luxury, abundance and refinement. It is merely a symbol of the economic health of the nation. When your blood is circulating freely in your body, you are healthy. When money is circulating freely in your life, you are economically healthy. When people begin to hoard money, to put it away in tin boxes and become charged with fear, there is economic illness. Money has taken many forms as a medium of exchange down through the centuries, such as, salt, beads and trinkets of various kinds. In early times a man's wealth was determined by the number of sheep and oxen he had. Now we use currency and other negotiable instruments, as it is much more convenient to write a check than carry some sheep around with you to pay bills.

How to walk the royal road to riches

Knowledge of the powers of your subconscious mind is the means to the royal road to riches of all kinds – spiritual, mental, or financial. The student of the laws of mind believes and knows definitely that regardless of economic situations, stock market fluctuation, depression, strikes, war, other conditions or circumstances, he will always be amply supplied, regardless of what form money takes. The reason for this is that he has conveyed the idea of wealth to his subconscious mind. It keeps him supplied wherever he may be. He has convinced himself in his mind that money is forever flowing freely in his life also that there is always a wonderful surplus. Should there be a financial collapse of government tomorrow and all the man's present holdings become valueless, as the German marks did after the first World War, he would still attract wealth and be cared for, regardless of the form the new currency took.

Why you do not have more money

As you read this chapter, you are probably saying, 'I am worthy of a higher salary than I am receiving.' I believe most people are inadequately compensated. One of the causes many people do not have more money is that they are silently or openly condemning it. They refer to money as 'filthy lucre' or 'the love of money is the root of all evil.' Another reason they do not prosper is that they have a sneaky subconscious feeling there is some virtue in poverty. This subconscious pattern may be due to early childhood training, superstition or it could be based on a false interpretation of scriptures.

Money and a balanced life

One time a man said to me, 'I am broke. I do not like money. It is the root of all evil.' These statements represent a confused neurotic mind. Love of money to the exclusion of everything else will cause you to become lopsided and unbalanced. You are here to use your power or authority wisely. Some men crave power, others crave money. If you set your heart on money exclusively and say, 'Money is all I want; I am going to give all my attention to amassing money; nothing else matters,' you can get money and attain a fortune, but you have forgotten that you are here to lead a balanced life. You must also satisfy the hunger for peace of mind, harmony, love, joy and perfect health.

By making money your sole aim, you simply made a wrong choice. You thought that was all you wanted, but you found after all your efforts that it was not only money you needed. You also desired true expression of your hidden talents, true place in life, beauty and the joy of contributing to the welfare and success of others. By learning the laws of your subconscious mind, you could have a million dollars or many millions, if you wanted them and still have peace of mind, harmony, perfect health and perfect expression.

Poverty is a mental disease

There is no virtue in poverty; it is a disease like any other mental disease. If you were physically ill, you would think there was something wrong with you. You would seek help and do something about the condition at once. Likewise, if you do not have money constantly circulating in your life, there is something radically wrong with you. The urge of the life principle in you is toward growth, expansion and the life more abundant. You are not here to live in a hovel, dress in rags and go hungry. You should be happy, prosperous and successful.

Why you must never criticise money

Cleanse your mind of all weird and superstitious beliefs about money. Do not ever regard money as evil or filthy. If you do, you cause it to take wings and fly away from you. Remember that you lose what you condemn. You cannot attract what you criticise.

Getting the right attitude toward money

Here is a simple technique you may use to multiply money in your experience. Use the following statements several times a day, 'I like money, I love it, I use it wisely, constructively and judiciously. Money is constantly circulating in my life. I release it with joy and it returns to me multiplied in a wonderful way. It is good and very good. Money flows to me in avalanches of abundance. I use it for good only and I am grateful for my good and for the riches of my mind.'

How to attract the money you need

Many years ago I met a young boy in Australia who wanted to become a physician and surgeon, but he had no money. I explained to him how a seed deposited in the soil attracts to itself everything necessary for its unfolding and that all he had to do was to take a lesson from the seed and deposit the required idea in his subconscious mind. For expenses this young, brilliant boy used to clean out doctors' offices, wash windows and do odd repair jobs. He told me that every night, as he went to sleep, he used to picture in his mind's eye a medical diploma on a wall with his name on it in big, bold letters. He used to clean and shine the framed diplomas in the medical building where he worked. It was not hard for him to engrave the image of a diploma in his mind and develop it there. Definite results followed as he persisted with his mental picture every night for about four months.

The sequel of this story was very interesting. One of the doctors took a great liking to this young boy and after training him in the art of sterilising instruments, giving hypodermic injections and other miscellaneous first-aid work, he employed him as a technical assistant in his office. The doctor later sent him to medical school at his own expense. Today, this young man is a prominent medical doctor in Montreal, Canada. He discovered the law of attraction by using his subconscious mind the right way. He operated an age-old law which says, 'Having seen the end, you have willed the means to the realisation of the end.' The end in this case was to become a medical doctor.

This young man was able to imagine, see and feel the reality of being a doctor. He lived with that idea, sustained it nourished it and loved it until through his imagination it penetrated the layers of his subconscious mind and became a conviction, thereby attracting to him everything necessary for the fulfillment of his dream.

Why some men do not get a raise in pay

If you are working in a large organisation and you are silently thinking of and resenting the fact you are underpaid, that you are not appreciated and that you deserve more money and greater recognition, you are subconsciously severing your ties with that organisation. You are setting a law in motion and the superintendent or manager will say to you, 'We have to let you go.' Actually, you dismissed yourself. The manager was simply the instrument through which your own negative mental state was confirmed. It was an example of the law of action and reaction. The action was your thought. The reaction was the response of your subconscious mind.

Obstacles and impediments on the pathway to riches

I am sure you have heard men say, 'That fellow has a racket.' 'He is a racketeer.' 'He is getting money dishonestly.' 'He is a faker.' 'I knew him when he had nothing.' 'He is **a** crook, a thief and a swindler.'

If you analyse the man who talks like that, you discover he is usually in want or suffering from some financial or physical illness. Perhaps his former college friends went up the ladder of success and excelled him. Now he is bitter and envious of their progress. In many instances this is the cause of his downfall. Thinking negatively of these classmates and condemning their wealth causes the wealth and prosperity he is praying for to vanish and flee away. He is condemning the thing he is praying for.

He is praying two ways. On the one hand he is saying, 'Wealth is flowing to me now,' and in the next breath, silently or audibly, he is saying, 'I resent that fellow's wealth.' Always make it a special point to rejoice in the wealth of the other person.

Protect your investments

If you are seeking wisdom regarding investments or if you are worried about your stocks or bonds, quietly claim, 'Infinite intelligence governs and watches over all my financial transactions and whatsoever I do shall prosper.' Do this frequently and you will find that your investments will be wise; moreover, you will be protected from loss, as you will be prompted to sell your securities or holdings before you accrue any loss.

You cannot get something for nothing

In large stores the management employs store detectives to prevent people from stealing. They catch a number of people everyday trying to get something for nothing. All such people are living in the mental atmosphere of lack and limitation. They are stealing from themselves peace, harmony, faith, honesty, integrity, goodwill and confidence. Furthermore, they are attracting to themselves all manner of loss, such as, loss of character, prestige, social status and peace of mind. These people lack faith in the source of supply as also the understanding of how their minds work. If they would mentally call on the powers of their subconscious mind and claim that they are guided to their true expression, they would find work and constant supply. Then by honesty, integrity and perseverance, they would become a credit to themselves and to society at large.

Your constant supply of money

Recognising the powers of your subconscious mind and the creative power of your thought or mental image is the way to opulence, freedom and constant supply. Accept the abundant life in your own mind. Your mental acceptance and expectancy of wealth has its own mathematics and mechanics of expression. As you enter into the mood of opulence, all things necessary for the abundant life will come to pass.

Let this be your daily affirmation; write it in your heart, 'I am one with the infinite riches of my subconscious mind. It is my right to be rich, happy and successful. Money flows to me freely, copiously and endlessly. I am forever conscious of my true worth. I give of my talents freely and I am wonderfully blessed financially. It is wonderful!'

YOUR SUBCONSCIOUS MIND AS A PARTNER IN SUCCESS

Success means successful *living*. A long period of peace, joy and happiness on this plane may be *termed* success. The eternal experience of these qualities is the everlasting life spoken of by Jesus. The real things of life, such as peace, harmony, integrity, security and happiness are intangible. They come from the Deep Self of man. Meditating on these qualities builds these treasures of heaven in our subconscious. It is where *moth and rust do not consume and where thieves do not break through and steal.* – Matthew 6:20.

The three steps to success

Let us discuss three steps to success. The first step to success is to find out the thing you love to do, then do it. Success is in loving your work. Although, if a man is a psychiatrist, it is not adequate for him to get a diploma and place it on the wall; he must keep up with the times, attend conventions and continue studying the mind and its workings. The successful psychiatrist visits clinics and reads the latest scientific articles. In other words, he is informed in the most advanced methods of alleviating human suffering. The successful psychiatrist or doctor must have the interest of his patients at heart. Someone may say, 'How can I put the first step into operation? I do not know what I should do.' In such a case, pray for guidance as follows: 'The infinite intelligence of my subconscious mind reveals to me my true place in life.' Repeat this prayer quietly, positively and lovingly to your deeper mind. As you persist with faith and confidence, the answer will come to you as a feeling, a hunch or a tendency in a certain direction. It will come to you clearly and in peace and as an inner silent awareness.

The second step to success is to specialise in some particular branch of work and know more about it than anyone else. For example, if a young man chooses chemistry as his profession, he should concentrate on one of the many branches in this field. He should give all of his time and attention to his chosen specialty. He should become sufficiently enthusiastic to try to know all there is available about his field; if possible, he should know more than anyone else. The young man should become ardently interested in his work and should desire to serve the world.

He that is greatest among you, let him become your servant. There is a great contrast in this attitude of mind in comparison to that of the man who only wants to makes a living or just 'get by'. 'Getting by' is not true success. Man's motive must be greater, nobler and more altruistic. He must serve others, thereby casting his bread upon the waters.

The third step is the most important one. You must be sure that the thing you want to do, does not reflect your success only. Your desire must not be selfish; it must benefit humanity. The path of a complete circuit must be formed. In other words, your idea must go forth with the purpose of blessing or serving the world. It will then come back to you pressed down, shaken together and running over. If it is to benefit yourself exclusively, the circle or complete circuit is not formed and you may experience a short circuit in your life which may consist of limitation or sickness.

The measure of true success

Some people may say, 'But, Mr James made a fortune in selling fraudulent oil stock.' A man may seem to succeed for a while, but the money he obtained by fraud usually takes wings and flies away. When we rob from another we rob from ourselves, because we are in a mood of lack and limitation which may manifest itself in our body, home life and affairs. What we think and feel, we create. We create what we believe. Even though a man may have accumulated a fortune fraudulently, he is not successful. There is no success without peace of mind. What good is man's accumulated wealth if he cannot sleep nights, is sick or has a guilt complex?

I knew a man in London who told me of his exploits. He had been a professional pickpocket and had amassed a large amount of money. He had a summer home in France and lived in a royal fashion in England. His story was that he was in constant dread of being arrested by Scotland Yard. He had many inner disorders, which were undoubtedly caused by his constant fear and deep-seated guilt complex. He knew he had done wrong. This deep sense of guilt attracted all kinds of trouble to him. Subsequently, he voluntarily surrendered to the police and served a prison sentence. After his release from prison, he sought psychological and spiritual counsel and became transformed. He went to work and became an honest, law-abiding citizen. He found what he loved to do and was happy.

A successful person loves his work and expresses himself fully. Success is contingent upon a higher ideal than the mere accumulation of riches. The man of success is the man who possesses great psychological and spiritual understanding. Many of the great industrialists today depend upon the correct use of their subconscious minds for their success.

There was an article published some years ago about Flagler, an oil magnate. He admitted that the secret of his success was his ability to see a project in its completion. For instance, in his case, he closed his eyes, imagined a big oil industry, saw trains running on tracks, heard whistles blowing and saw smoke. Having seen and felt the fulfillment of his prayer, his subconscious mind brought about its realisation. If you imagine an objective clearly, you will be provided with the necessities, in ways you know not of, through the wonder-working power of your subconscious mind.

In considering the three steps to success you must never forget the underlying power of the creative forces of your subconscious mind. This is the energy in back of all steps in *any* plan of success. Your thought is creative. Thought fused with feeling becomes a subjective faith or belief...*and according to your belief is it done unto you.* Matt. 9:29.

A knowledge of a mighty force in you, which is capable of bringing to pass all your desires gives you confidence and a sense of peace. Whatever your field of action may be, you should learn the laws of your subconscious mind. When you know how to apply the powers of your mind and when you are expressing yourself fully and giving of your talents to others, you are on the sure path to true success. If you are about God's business or any part of it, God, by His very nature, is for you, so who can be against you? With this understanding there is no power in heaven or on earth to withhold success from you.

How he made his dream come true

A movie actor told me that he had very little education, but he had a dream as a boy of becoming a successful movie actor. Out in the field mowing hay, driving the cows home or even when milking them he said, 'I would constantly imagine I saw my name in big lights at a large theatre. I kept this up for years until finally I ran away from home. I got extra jobs in the motion-picture field. The day finally came when I saw my name in great, big lights as I did when I was a boy!' Then he added, 'I know the power of sustained imagination to bring success.'

His dream pharmacy became a reality

Thirty years ago I knew a young pharmacist who was receiving forty dollars a week plus commission on sales. 'After twenty-five years,' he said to me, 'I will get a pension and retire.'

I said to this young man, 'Why don't you own your own store? Get out of this place. Raise your sights! Have a dream for your children. Maybe your son wants to be a doctor; perhaps your daughter desires to be a great musician.'

His answer was that he had no money! He began to awaken to the fact that whatever he could conceive as true, he could give conception.

The first step toward his goal was his awakening to the powers of his subconscious mind, which I briefly elaborated on for his benefit. His second step was his realisation that if he could succeed in conveying an idea to his subconscious mind, the latter would somehow bring it to pass.

He began to imagine that he was in his own store. He mentally arranged the bottles, dispensed prescriptions and imagined several clerks in the store waiting on customers. He also visualised a big bank balance. Mentally he worked in that imaginary store. Like a good actor he lived the role. *Act as though I am and I will be.* This pharmacist put himself wholeheartedly into the act, living, moving and acting on the assumption that he owned the store. The sequel was interesting. He was discharged from his position. He found new employment with a large chain store, became manager and later on, district manager. He saved enough money in four years to provide a down payment on a drugstore of his own. He called it his 'Dream Pharmacy.'

'It was,' he said, 'exactly the store I saw in my imagination.' He became a recognised success in his chosen field and was happy doing what he loved to do.

Using the subconscious mind in business

Some years ago I gave a lecture to a group of businessmen on the powers of imagination and the subconscious mind. In this lecture I pointed out how Goethe used his imagination wisely when confronted with difficulties and predicaments.

His biographers point out that he was accustomed to fill many hours quietly holding imaginary conversations. It is well known that his custom was to imagine one of his friends before him in a chair answering him in the right way. In other words, if he were concerned over any problems, he imagined his friend giving him the right or appropriate answer, accompanied with the usual gestures and tonal qualities of the voice. He made the entire imaginary scene as real and as vivid as possible.

One of the men present at this lecture was a young stockbroker. He proceeded to adopt the technique of Goethe. He began to have mental, imaginary conversations with a multimillionaire banker friend of his who used to congratulate him on his wise and sound judgement and compliment him on his purchase of the right stocks. He used to dramatise this imaginary conversation until he had psychologically fixed it as a form of belief in his mind. This broker's inner talking and controlled imagination certainly agreed with his aim which was to make sound investments for his clients. His main purpose in life was to make money for his clients and to see them prosper financially by his wise counsel. He is still using his subconscious mind in his business and he is a brilliant success in his field of endeavour.

Boy of sixteen years turns failure into success

A young boy who was attending high school said to me, 'I am getting very poor grades. My memory is failing. I do not know what is the matter.' I discovered that the only thing wrong with this boy was his attitude. It was one of indifference and resentment toward some of his teachers and fellow students. I taught him how to use his subconscious mind and how to succeed in his studies.

He began to affirm certain truths several times a day particularly at night prior to sleep and also in the morning after awakening. These are the best times to impregnate the subconscious mind.

He affirmed as follows: 'I realise that my subconscious mind is a storehouse of memory. It retains everything I read and hear from my teachers. I have a perfect memory and the infinite intelligence in my subconscious mind constantly reveals to me everything I need to know at all my examinations, whether written or oral. I radiate love and goodwill to all my teachers and fellow students. I sincerely wish for them success and all good things.'

This young man is now enjoying a greater freedom than he has ever known. He is now receiving all 'A-s.' He constantly imagines the teachers and his mother congratulating him on his success in his studies.

How to become successful in buying and selling

In buying and selling, remember that your conscious mind is the starter and your subconscious mind is the motor. You must start the motor to enable it to perform its work. Your conscious mind is the dynamo that awakens the power of your subconscious mind. The first step in conveying your clarified desire, idea or image to the deeper mind is to relax, immobilise the attention, get still and be quiet. This quiet, relaxed and peaceful attitude of mind prevents extraneous matter and false ideas from interfering with your mental absorption of your ideal. Furthermore, in the quiet, passive and receptive attitude of mind, effort is reduced to a minimum.

The second step is to begin to imagine the reality of whatever you desire. For example, you may wish to buy a home. In your relaxed state of mind affirm as follows: 'The infinite intelligence of my subconscious mind is all wise. It reveals to me now the ideal home, which is central, ideal, is in a lovely environment, meets with all my requirements and is commensurate with my income. I am now turning this request over to my subconscious mind and I know it responds according to the nature of my request. I release this request with absolute faith and confidence in the same way that a farmer deposits a seed in the ground, trusting implicitly in the laws of growth.'

The answer to your prayer may come through an advertisement in the paper, through a friend or you may be guided directly to a particular home, which is exactly what you are seeking. There are many ways that your prayer may be answered. The principal knowledge, in which you may place your confidence, is that the answer always comes, provided you trust the working of your deeper mind.

You may wish to sell a home, land or any kind of property. In private consultation with real estate brokers – I have told them of the way I sold my own home on Orlando Avenue in Los Angeles. Many of them have applied the technique I used with remarkable and speedy results. I placed a sign which read, 'For sale by owner' in the garden in front of my home. The day after I said to myself as I was going to sleep, 'Supposing you sold your house, what would you do?'

I answered my own question and I said, 'I would take that sign down and throw it into the garage.' In my imagination I took hold of the sign, pulled it up from the ground, placed it on my shoulder, went to the garage, threw it on the floor and said jokingly to the sign, 'I don't need you any more!' I felt the inner satisfaction of it all, realising it was finished. The next day a man gave me a deposit of $1,000 and said to me, 'Take your sign down.'

Immediately I pulled the sign up and took it to the garage. The outer action conformed to the inner. There is nothing new about this. *As within, so without*, meaning according to the image impressed on your subconscious mind, so it is on the objective screen of your life. The outside mirrors the inside. External action follows internal action.

Here is another very popular method used in selling homes, land or any kind of property. Affirm slowly, quietly and feelingly as follows: 'Infinite intelligence attracts to me the buyer for this home who wants it and who prospers in it. This buyer is being sent to me by the creative intelligence of my subconscious mind which makes no mistakes. This buyer may look at many other homes, but mine is the only one he wants and will buy, because he is guided by the infinite intelligence within him. I know the buyer is right, the time is right and the price is right. Everything about it is right. The deeper currents of my subconscious mind are now in operation bringing both of us together in divine order. I know that it is so.'

Remember always, that what you are seeking is also seeking

you and whenever you want to sell a home or property of any kind, there is always someone who wants what you have to offer. By using the powers of your subconscious mind correctly, you free your mind of all sense of competition and anxiety in buying and selling.

How she succeeded in getting what she wanted

There is a young lady who regularly comes to my lectures and classes. She had to change buses three times; it took her one and a half hours each time to come to the lectures. In one lecture I explained how a young man who needed a car in his work received one. She went home and experimented as outlined in my lecture. Here is her letter in part, narrating her application of my method and published by her permission:

> Dear Dr Murphy:
>
> This is how I received a Cadillac car – I wanted one to come to the lectures regularly. In my imagination I went through the identical process I would go through if I were actually driving a car. I went to the showroom and the salesman took me for a ride in one. I also drove it several blocks. I claimed the Cadillac car as my own over and over again.
>
> I kept the mental picture of getting into the car, driving it, feeling the upholstery, etc., consistently for over two weeks. Last week I drove to your lectures in a Cadillac. My uncle in Inglewood passed away and left me his Cadillac and his entire estate.

A success technique employed by many outstanding executives and businessmen

There are many prominent businessmen who quietly use the abstract term, 'success,' over and over many times a day until they reach a conviction that *success* is theirs. They know that the *idea of success* contains all the essential elements of success. Likewise, you can begin now to repeat the word, 'success,' to yourself with faith and conviction. Your subconscious mind will accept it as true of you and you will be under a subconscious compulsion to succeed.

You are compelled to express your subjective beliefs, impressions and convictions. What does success imply to you? You want, undoubtedly, to be successful in your home life and in your relationship with others. You wish to be outstanding in your chosen work or profession. You wish to possess a beautiful home and all the money you need to live comfortably and happily. You want to be successful in your prayers and spirituel life as also in your contact with the powers of your subconscious mind.

You are a businessman also because you are in the business of living. Become a successful businessman by imagining yourself doing what you long to do and possessing the things you long to possess. Become imaginative; mentally participate in the reality of the successful state. Make a habit of it. Go to sleep feeling successful every night and perfectly satisfied. You will eventually succeed in implanting the idea of success in your subconscious mind. Believe you were born to succeed and wonders will happen as you pray!

FIVE

Finding Guidance from Your Subconscious Mind

HOW INVENTIONS AND DISCOVERIES WERE MADE USING THE SUBCONSCIOUS

Many scientists realise the true importance of the subconscious mind. Edison, Marconi, Kettering, Poincare, Einstein and many others have used the subconscious mind. It has given them the insight and the 'know-how' for all their great achievements in modern science and industry. Research has shown that the ability to bring into action the subconscious power has determined the success of all the great scientific and research workers. An instance of how a famous chemist, Friedrich von Stradonitz, used his subconscious mind to solve his problem is as follows: He had been working laboriously for a long time trying to rearrange the six carbon and the six hydrogen atoms of the benzene formula and he was constantly perplexed and unable to solve the matter. Tired and exhausted, he turned the request over completely to his subconscious mind. Shortly afterward, as he was about to board a London bus, his subconscious presented his conscious mind with a sudden flash of a snake biting its own tail and turning around like a pinwheel. This answer, from his subconscious mind, gave him the long-sought answer of the circular rearrangement of the atoms that is known as the benzene ring.

How a distinguished scientist brought forth his inventions

Nikola Tesla was a brilliant electrical scientist who brought forth the most amazing innovations. When an idea for a new invention came into his mind, he would build it up in his imagination. He knew his subconscious mind would reconstruct and reveal to his conscious mind all the parts needed for its manufacture in concrete form. Through quietly contemplating every possible improvement, he spent no time in correcting defects and was able to give the technicians the perfect product of his mind. He said, 'Invariably, my device works as I imagined it should. In twenty years there has not been a single exception.'

How a famous naturalist solved his problem

Professor Agassiz, a distinguished American naturalist, discovered the indefatigable activities of his subconscious mind while he slept. His widow in her biography of her famous husband has reported the following.

'He had been for two weeks striving to decipher the somewhat obscure impression of a fossil fish on the stone slab in which it was preserved. Weary and perplexed, he put his work aside at last and tried to dismiss it from his mind. Shortly after, he awoke one night persuaded that while asleep he had seen his fish with all the missing features perfectly restored. But when he tried to hold and make fast the image it escaped him. Nevertheless, he went early to the Jardin des Plantes, thinking that on looking anew at the impression he should see something which would put him on the track of his vision. In vain – the blurred record was as black as ever. The next night he saw the fish again, but with no more satisfactory result. When he awoke it disappeared from his memory as before. Hoping that the same experience might be repeated, on the third night he placed a pencil and paper beside his bed before going to sleep. 'Accordingly, toward morning the fish reappeared in his dream, confusedly at first, but at last with such distinctness that he had no longer any doubt as to its zoological characters. Still half dreaming, in perfect darkness, he traced these characters on the sheet of paper at the bedside. In the morning he was surprised to see in his nocturnal sketch features, which he thought it impossible the fossil itself should reveal. He hastened to the Jardin des Plantes and with his drawing as a guide, succeeded in chiseling away the surface of the stone under which portions of the fish proved to be hidden. When wholly exposed it corresponded with his dream and his drawing and he succeeded in classifying it with ease.'

An outstanding physician solved the problem of diabetes

Some years ago I received a clipping from a magazine describing the origin of the discovery of insulin. This is the essence of the article as I recall it.

About forty years ago or more, Dr Frederick Banting, a brilliant Canadian physician and surgeon, was concentrating his attention on the ravages of diabetes. At that time medical science offered no effective method of arresting the disease. Dr Banting spent considerable time experimenting and studying the international literature on the subject. One night he was exhausted and fell asleep. While asleep, his subconscious mind instructed him to extract the residue from the degenerated pancreatic duct of dogs. This was the origin of insulin which has helped millions of people.

You will note that Dr Banting had been consciously dwelling on the problem for some time seeking a solution, a way out and his subconscious responded accordingly.

It does not follow that you will always get an answer overnight. The answer may not come for some time. Do not be discouraged. Keep on turning the problem over every night to the subconscious mind prior to sleep, as if you had never done it before.

One of the reasons for the delay may be that you look upon it as a major problem. You may believe it will take a long time to solve it.

Your subconscious mind is timeless and spaceless. Go to sleep believing you have the answer now. Do not postulate the answer in the future. Have an abiding faith in the outcome. Become convinced now as you read this book that there is an answer and a perfect solution for you.

How a famous scientist and physicist escaped from a Russian concentration camp

Dr Lothar von Blenk-Schmidt, a member of the Rocket Society and an outstanding research electronic engineer, gives the following condensed summary of how he used his subconscious mind to free himself from certain death at the hands of brutal guards in a Russian prison camp coal mine. He states as follows:

'I was a prisoner of war in a coal mine in Russia and I saw men dying all around me in that prison compound. We were watched over by brutal guards, arrogant officers and sharp, fast-thinking commissars. After a short medical checkup, a quota of coal was assigned to each person. My quota was three hundred pounds per day. In case any man did not fill his quota, his small food ration was cut down and in a short time he was resting in the cemetery.

'I started concentrating on my escape. I knew that my subconscious mind would somehow find a way. My home in Germany was destroyed, my family wiped out; all my friends and former associates were either killed in the war or were in concentration camps.

'I said to my subconscious mind, "I want to go to Los Angeles and you will find the way." I had seen pictures of Los Angeles and I remembered some of the boulevards very well as well as some of the buildings.

'Every day and night I would imagine I was walking down Wilshire Boulevard with an American girl whom I met in Berlin prior to the war (she is now my wife). In my imagination we would visit the stores, ride buses and eat in the restaurants. Every night I made it a special point to drive my imaginary American automobile up and down the boulevards of Los Angeles. I made all this vivid and real. These pictures in my mind were as real and as natural to me as one of the trees out-side the prison camp.

'Every morning the chief guard would count the prisoners as they were lined up. He would call out "one, two, three," etc. When seventeen was called out, which was my number in sequence, I stepped aside. In the meantime, the guard was called away for a minute or so and on his return he started by mistake on the next man as number seventeen. When the crew returned in the evening, the number of men was the same and I was not missed. The discovery would take a long time.

'I walked out of the camp undetected and kept walking for twenty-four hours, resting in a deserted town the next day. I was able to live by fishing and killing some wildlife. I found coal trains going to Poland and travelled on them by night, until finally I reached Poland. With the help of friends, I made my way to Lucerne, Switzerland.

'One evening at the Palace Hotel, Lucerne, I had a talk with a man and his wife from the United States of America. This man asked me if I would care to be a guest at his home in Santa Monica, California. I accepted and when I arrived in Los Angeles, I found that their chauffeur drove me along Wilshire Boulevard and many other boulevards which I had imagined so vividly in the long months in the Russian coal mines. I recognised the buildings, which I had seen in my mind so often. It actually seemed as if I had been in Los Angeles before. I had reached my goal.

'I will never cease to marvel at the wonders of the subconscious mind. Truly, it has ways we know not of.'

HOW TO RECEIVE GUIDANCE FROM YOUR SUBCONSCIOUS

When you have what you term 'a difficult decision' to make or when you fail to see the solution to your problem, begin at once to think constructively about it. If you are fearful and worried, you are not really thinking. True thinking is free from fear.

Here is a simple technique you can use to receive guidance on any subject: Quiet the mind and still the body. Tell the body to relax; it has to obey you. It has no volition, initiative or self-conscious intelligence. Your body is an emotional disk which records your beliefs and impressions. Mobilise your attention; focus your thought on the solution to your problem. Try to solve it with your conscious mind. Think how happy you would be about the perfect solution. Sense the feeling you would have if the perfect answer were yours now. Let your mind play with this mood in a relaxed way; then drop off to sleep. When you awaken and you do not have the answer, get busy about something else.

Probably, when you are preoccupied with something else, the answer will come into your mind like toast pops out of a toaster.

In receiving guidance from the subconscious mind, the simple way is the best. This is an illustration: I once lost a valuable ring, which was an heirloom. I looked everywhere for it and could not locate it. At night I talked to the subconscious in the same manner that I would talk to anyone. I said to it prior to dropping off to sleep, 'You know all things; you know where that ring is and you now reveal to me where it is.'

In the morning I awoke suddenly with the words ringing in my ear, 'Ask Robert!' I thought it very strange that I should ask Robert, a young boy about nine years of age; however, I followed the inner voice of intuition.

Robert said, 'Oh, yes, I picked it up in the yard while I was playing with the boys. I placed it on the desk in my room. I did not think it worth anything, so I did not say anything about it.' The subconscious mind will always answer you if you trust it.

His subconscious revealed the location of his father's will

A young man who attends my lectures had this experience. His father died and apparently left no will. However, this man's sister told him that their father had confided to her that a will had been executed, which was fair to all. Every attempt to locate the will failed. Prior to sleep he talked to his deeper mind as follows: 'I now turn this request over to the subconscious mind. It knows just where that will is and reveals it to me.' Then he condensed his request down to one word, 'Answer,' repeating it over and over again as a lullaby. He lulled himself to sleep with the word, 'Answer.'

The next morning this young man had an overpowering hunch to go to a certain bank in Los Angeles where he found a safe deposit vault registered in the name of his father, the contents of which solved all his problems.

Your thought, as you go to sleep, arouses the powerful latency, which is within you. For example, let us suppose you are wondering whether to sell your home, buy a certain stock, sever a partnership, move to New York or stay in Los Angeles, dissolve the present contract or take a new one. Do this: Sit quietly in your armchair or at the desk in your office. Remember that there is a universal law of action and reaction. The action is your thought. The reaction is the response from your subconscious mind. The subconscious mind is reactive and reflexive; this is its nature. It rebounds, rewards and repays. It is the law of correspondence. It responds by corresponding. As you contemplate right action, you will automatically experience a reaction or response in yourself which represents the guidance or answer of your subconscious mind.

In seeking guidance, you simply think quietly about right action which means that you are using the infinite intelligence resident in the subconscious mind to the point where it begins to use you. From there on, your course of action is directed and controlled by the subjective wisdom within you, which is all wise and omnipotent. Your decision will be right. There will only be right action because you are under a subjective compulsion to do the right thing. I use the word *compulsion* because the law of the subconscious is compulsion.

The secret of guidance

The secret of guidance or right action is to mentally devote yourself to the right answer, until you find its response in you. The response is a feeling, an inner awareness, an overpowering hunch whereby you know that you know. You have used the power to the point where it begins to use you. You cannot possibly fail or make one false step while operating under the subjective wisdom within you., You will find that all your ways are pleasantness and all your paths are peace.

YOUR SUBCONSCIOUS AND THE WONDERS OF SLEEP

You spend about eight out of every twenty-four hours or one-third of your entire life, in sleep. This is an inexorable law of life. This also applies to the animal and vegetable kingdoms. Sleep is a divine law and many answers to our problems come to us when we are sound asleep.

Many people have advocated the theory that you get tired during the day, that you go to sleep to rest the body and that a reparative process takes place while you sleep. Nothing rests in sleep. Your heart, lungs and all your vital organs function while you are asleep. If you eat prior to sleep, the food is digested and assimilated; also, your skin secretes perspiration and your nails and hair continue to grow.

Your subconscious mind never rests or sleeps. It is always active, controlling all your vital forces. The healing process takes place more rapidly while you are asleep as there is no interference from your conscious mind. Remarkable answers are given to you while you are asleep.

WHY WE SLEEP

Dr John Bigelow, a famous research authority, on sleep,[4] demonstrated that at night while asleep you receive impressions

---

[4]Dr John Bigelow, *The Mystery of Sleep* (New York and London: Harper Brothers, 1903).

showing that the nerves of the eyes, ears, nose and taste buds are active during sleep and also that the nerves of your brain are quite active. He says that the main reason we sleep is because 'the nobler part of the soul is united by abstraction to our higher nature and becomes a participant in the wisdom and foreknowledge of the gods.'

Dr Bigelow states also, 'The results of my studies have not only strengthened my convictions that the supposed exemption from customary toils and activities was not the final purpose of sleep, but have also made clearer to my mind the conviction that no part of a man's life deserves to be considered more indispensable to its symmetrical and perfect spiritual development than the while he is separated from the phenomenal world in sleep.'

Prayer, a form of sleep

Your conscious mind gets involved with vexations, strife and contentions of the day and it is very necessary to withdraw periodically from sense evidence and the objective world and commune silently with the inner wisdom of your subconscious mind. By claiming guidance, strength and greater intelligence in all phases of your life, you will be enabled to overcome all difficulties and solve your daily problems.

This regular withdrawal from sense evidence and the noise and confusion of everyday living is also a form of sleep, i.e., you become asleep to the world of the senses and alive to the wisdom and power of your subconscious mind.

Startling effects of sleep deprivation

Lack of sleep can cause you to become irritable, moody and depressed. Dr George Stevenson of the National Association for Mental Health says, 'I believe it can safely be said that all human beings need a minimum of six hours' sleep to be healthy. Most people need more. Those who think they can get along on less are fooling themselves.' Medical research scholars, investigating sleep processes and deprivation of sleep, point out that severe insomnia has preceded psychotic breakdown in some instances. Remember, you are spiritually recharged during sleep and adequate sleep is essential to produce joy and vitality in life.

Sleep brings counsel

A young lady in Los Angeles who listens to my morning radio talks told me that she had been offered a lucrative position in New York City at twice her present salary. She was wondering whether to accept or not and prayed prior to sleep as follows: 'The creative intelligence of my subconscious mind knows what is best for me. Its tendency is always lifeward and it reveals to me the right decision which blesses me and all concerned. I give thanks for the answer, which I know will come to me.'

She repeated this simple prayer over and over again as a lullaby prior to sleep and in the morning she had a persistent feeling that she should not accept the offer. She rejected the offer and subsequent events verified her inward sense of knowing, because the company went bankrupt in a few months following their offer of employment to her.

The conscious mind may be correct on the facts objectively known, but the intuitive faculty of her subconscious mind saw the failure of the concern in question and prompted her accordingly.

Saved from certain disaster

I will illustrate how the wisdom of your subconscious mind can instruct you and protect you – relative to your request for right action as you go to sleep. Many years ago, before the

Second World War, I was offered a very lucrative assignment in the Orient and I prayed for guidance and the right decision as follows: 'Infinite intelligence within me knows all things and the right decision is revealed to me in divine order. I will recognise the answer when it comes.'

I repeated this simple prayer over and over again as a lullaby prior to sleep and in a dream came the vivid realisation of things to come three years later. An old friend appeared in the dream and said, 'Read these headlines – do not go!' The headlines of the newspaper which appeared in the dream related to war and the attack on Pearl Harbor.

Occasionally, the writer dreams literally. The aforementioned dream was undoubtedly a dramatisation of the subconscious mind, which projected a person whom I trusted and respected. To some a warning may come in the form of a mother who appears in a dream. She tells the person not to go here or there and the reason for the warning. Your subconscious mind is all-wise. It knows all things. Often it will speak to you only in a voice that your conscious mind will immediately accept as true. Sometimes your subconscious will warn you in a voice which sounds like that of your mother or some loved one which may cause you to stop on the street and you find, if you had gone another step, a falling object from a window might have struck you on the head.

My subconscious mind is one with the universal subconscious and it knew the Japanese were planning a war and it also knew when the war would start. Dr Rhine, director of the Department of Psychology at Duke University, has gathered together a vast amount of evidence showing that a great number of people all over the world see events before they happen and in many instances are, therefore, able to avoid the tragic event, which was foreseen vividly in a dream.

The dream which I had showed clearly the headlines in *The New York Times* about three years prior to the tragedy of Pearl Harbour. In consequence of this dream, I immediately cancelled the trip as I felt a subconscious compulsion to do so. Three years later the Second World War proved the truth of the inner voice of intuition.

Your future is in your subconscious mind

Remember that the future, the result of your habitual thinking, is already in your mind except when you change it through prayer. The future of a country, likewise, is in the collective subconscious of the people of that nation. There is nothing strange in the dream I had wherein I saw the headlines of the New York newspapers long before the war began. The war had already taken place in the mind and all the plans of attack were already engraved on that great recording instrument, the subconscious mind or collective unconscious of the universal mind. Tomorrow's events are in your subconscious mind, so are next week's and next month's and they may be seen by a highly psychic or clairvoyant person.

No disaster or tragedy can happen to you if you decide to pray. Nothing is predetermined or foreordained. Your mental attitude, i.e., the way you think, feel and believe determines your destiny. You can, through scientific prayer, which is explained in a previous chapter, mold, fashion and create your own future. *Whatsoever a man soweth, that shall he also reap.*

Sleep in peace and wake in joy

To those who suffer from insomnia, you will find the following prayer very effective. Repeat it slowly, quietly and lovingly prior to sleep: 'My toes are relaxed, my ankles are relaxed, my abdominal muscles are relaxed, my heart and lungs are relaxed, my hands and arms are relaxed, my neck is relaxed, my brain is relaxed, my face is relaxed, my eyes are relaxed, my whole mind and body are relaxed. I fully and freely forgive everyone and I sincerely wish for them harmony, health, peace and all the blessings of life. I am at peace, I am poised, serene and calm. I rest in security and in peace. A great stillness steals over me and a great calm quiets my whole being as I realise the Divine Presence within me. I know that the realisation of life and love heals me. I wrap myself in the mantle of love and fall asleep filled with goodwill for all. Throughout the night peace remains with me and in the morning I shall be filled with life and love. A circle of love is drawn around me. *I will fear no evil, for Thou art with me. I sleep in peace, I wake in joy and in Him I live, move and have my being.*'

SIX

Using the Power of Your Subconscious Mind for Fulfilling Relationships

SOLVING MARITAL PROBLEMS

Ignorance of the functions and powers of the mind is the cause of all marital trouble. Friction between husband and wife can be solved by each using the law of mind correctly. By praying together they stay together. The contemplation of divine ideals, the study of the laws of life, the mutual agreement on a common purpose and plan and the enjoyment of personal freedom bring about that harmonious marriage, that wedded bliss, that sense of oneness where the two become one.

The best time to prevent divorce is before marriage. It is not wrong to try to get out of a very bad situation. But, why get into the bad situation in the first place? Would it not be better to give attention to the real cause of marital problems, in other words, to really get at the root of the matter involved?

As with all other problems of men and women, the problems

of divorce, separation, annulment and endless litigation are directly traceable to lack of knowledge of the working and interrelationship of the conscious and subconscious mind.

The meaning of marriage

Marriage to be real must first be on a spiritual basis. It must be of the heart and the heart is the chalice of love. Honesty, sincerity, kindness and integrity are also forms of love. Each partner should be perfectly honest and sincere with the other. It is not a true marriage when a man marries a woman for her money, social position, or to lift his ego, because this indicates a lack of sincerity, honesty and true love. Such a marriage is a farce, a sham and a masquerade.

When a woman says, 'I am tired working; I want to get married because I want security,' her premise is false. She is not using the laws of mind correctly. Her security depends upon her knowledge of the interaction of the conscious and subconscious mind and its application. For example, a woman will never lack for wealth or health if she applies the techniques outlined in the respective chapters of this book. Her wealth can come to her independent of her husband, father or anyone else. A woman is not dependent on her husband for health, peace, joy, inspiration, guidance, love, wealth, security, happiness or anything in the world.

Her security and peace of mind come from her knowledge of the inner powers within her and from the constant use of the laws of her own mind in a constructive fashion.

How to attract the ideal husband

You are now acquainted with the way your subconscious mind works. You know that whatever you impress upon it will be experienced in your world. Begin now to impress your subconscious mind with the qualities and characteristics you desire in a man.

The following is an excellent technique: Sit down at night in your armchair, close your eyes, let go, relax the body, become very quiet, passive and receptive. Talk to your subconscious mind and say to it, 'I am now attracting a man into my experience who is honest, sincere, loyal, faithful, peaceful, happy and prosperous. These qualities which I admire are sinking down into my subconscious mind now. As I dwell upon these characteristics, they become a part of me and are embodied subconsciously.

'I know there is an irresistible law of attraction and that I attract to me a man according to my subconscious belief. I at-tract that which I feel to be true in my subconscious mind.

'I know I can contribute to his peace and happiness. He loves my ideals and I love his ideals. He does not want to make me over; neither do I want to make him over. There is mutual love, freedom and respect.'

Practice this process of impregnating your subconscious mind. Then, you will have the joy of attracting to you a man possessing the qualities and characteristics you mentally dwelt upon. Your subconscious intelligence will open up a pathway, whereby both of you will meet, according to the irresistible and changeless flow of your own subconscious mind. Have a keen desire to give the best that is in you of love, devotion and cooperation. Be receptive to this gift of love which you have given to your subconscious mind.

How to attract the ideal wife

Affirm as follows: 'I now attract the right woman who is in complete accord with me. This is a spiritual union because it is divine love functioning through the personality of someone with whom I blend perfectly. I know I can give to this woman love, light, peace and joy. I feel and believe I can make this woman's life full, complete and wonderful. I now decree that she possesses the following qualities and attributes: She is spiritual, loyal, faithful and true. She is harmonious, peaceful and happy. We are irresistibly attracted to each other. Only what belongs to love, truth and beauty can enter my experience. I accept my ideal companion now.' As you think quietly and with interest on the qualities and attributes which you admire in the companion you seek, you will build the mental equivalent into your mentality. Then, the deeper currents of your subconscious mind will bring both of you together in divine order.

No need for third mistake

Recently a teacher said to me, 'I have had three husbands and all three have been passive, submissive and dependent on me to make all decisions and govern everything. Why do I attract such type men?'

I asked her whether she had known that her second husband was the effeminate type and she replied, 'Of course not. Had I known, I would not have married him.' Apparently she had not learned anything from the first mistake. The trouble was with her own personality make-up. She was very masculine, domineering and unconsciously wanted someone who would be submissive and passive so that she could play the dominant role. All this was unconscious motivation and her subconscious picture attracted to her what she subjectively wanted. She had to learn to *break the pattern by adopting the right prayer process.*

How she broke the negative pattern

The above-mentioned woman learned a simple truth. When you believe you can have the type of man you idealise, it is done unto you as you believe. The following is the specific prayer she used to break the old subconscious pattern and attract to her the ideal mate: 'I am building into my mentality the type of man I deeply desire. The man I attract for a husband is strong, powerful, loving, very masculine, successful, honest, loyal and faithful. He finds love and happiness with me.

'I know he wants me and I want him. I am honest, sincere, loving and kind. I have wonderful gifts to offer him. They are goodwill, a joyous heart and a healthy body. He offers me the same. It is mutual. I give and I receive. Divine intelligence knows where this man is and the deeper wisdom of my subconscious mind is now bringing both of us together in its own way and we recognise each other immediately. I release this request to my subconscious mind, which knows how to bring my request to pass. I give thanks for the perfect answer.' She prayed in the above manner night and morning, affirming these truths and knowing that through frequent occupation of the mind she would reach the mental equivalent of that which she sought.

The answer to her prayer

Several months went by. She had a great number of dates and social engagements, none of which was agreeable to her. When she was about to question, waiver, doubt and vacillate, she reminded herself that the infinite intelligence was bringing it to pass in its own way and that there was nothing to be concerned about. Her final decree in her divorce proceedings was granted which brought her a great sense of release and mental freedom.

Shortly afterward she went to work as a receptionist in a doctor's office. She told me that the minute she saw the physician she knew he was the man she was praying about. Apparently he knew it, too, because he proposed to her the first week she was in the office and their subsequent marriage was ideally happy. This physician was not the passive or submissive type, but was a real man, a former football player, an outstanding athlete and was a deeply spiritual man though he was completely devoid of any sectarian or denominational affiliation. She got what she prayed for because she claimed it mentally until she reached the point of saturation. In other words, she mentally and emotionally united with her idea and it became a part of her in the same way that an apple becomes a part of her blood stream.

Should one get a divorce?

Divorce is an individual problem. It cannot be generalised. In some cases, of course, there never should have been a marriage. In some cases, divorce is not the solution, no more so than marriage is the solution for a lonely man. Divorce may be right for one person and wrong for another. A divorced woman may be far more sincere and noble than many of her married sisters who perhaps are living a lie.

For example, I once talked with a woman whose husband was a dope fiend, an ex-convict, a wife-beater and a non-provider. She had been told it was wrong to get a divorce. I explained to her that marriage is of the heart. If two hearts blend harmoniously, lovingly and sincerely, that is the ideal marriage. The pure action of the heart is love.

Following this explanation she knew what to do. She knew in her heart that there is no divine law which compelled her to be browbeaten, intimidated and beaten because someone said, 'I pronounce you man and wife.'

If you are in doubt as to what to do, ask for guidance, knowing that there is always an answer and you will receive it.

Follow the *lead* that comes to you in the silence of your soul. It speaks to you in peace.

Drifting into divorce

Recently a young couple, married for only a few months, were seeking a divorce. I discovered that the young man had a constant fear that his wife would leave him. He expected rejection and he believed that she would be unfaithful. These thoughts haunted his mind and became an obsession with him. His mental attitude was one of separation and suspicion. She felt unresponsive to him; it was his own feeling or atmosphere of loss and separation operating through them. This brought about a condition or action in accordance with the mental pattern behind it. There is a law of action and reaction or cause and effect. The thought is the action and the response of the subconscious mind is the reaction.

His wife left home and asked for a divorce, which is what he feared and believed she would do.

Divorce begins in the mind

Divorce takes place first in the mind; the legal proceedings follow after. These two young people were full of resentment, fear, suspicion and anger. These attitudes weaken, exhaust and debilitate the whole being. They learned that hate divides and that love unites. They began to realise what they had been doing with their minds. Neither one of them knew the law of mental action and they were misusing their minds and bringing on chaos and misery. These two people went back together at my suggestion and experimented with prayer therapy. They began to radiate love, peace and goodwill to each other. Each one practiced radiating harmony, health, peace and love to the other. They alternated in the reading of the Psalms every night. Their marriage is growing more beautiful every day.

The nagging wife

Many times the reason the wife nags is because she gets no attention. Frequently it is a craving for love and affection. Give your wife attention, show your appreciation. Praise and exalt all her many good points. There is also the nagging type of woman who wants to make the man conform to her particular pattern. This is about the quickest way in the world to get rid of a man.

The wife and the husband must cease being scavengers – always looking at the petty faults or errors in each other. Let each give attention and praise for the constructive and wonderful qualities in the other.

The brooding husband

If a man begins to brood, grows morbid against his wife because of the things she said or did, he is, psychologically speaking, committing adultery. One of the meanings of adultery is idolatry, i.e., giving attention to or uniting mentally with what is negative and destructive. When a man is silently resenting his wife and is full of hostility toward her, he is unfaithful. He is not faithful to his marriage vows, which are to love, cherish and honour her all the days of his life.

The man who is brooding, bitter and resentful can swallow his sharp remarks, abate his anger. He can go to great lengths to be considerate, kind and courteous. He can deftly skirt the differences. Through praise and mental effort, he can get out of the habit of antagonism. Then, he will be able to get along better, not only with his wife, but with business associates also. Assume the harmonious state and eventually you will find peace and harmony.

The great mistake

A great mistake is to discuss your marital problems or difficulties with neighbours and relatives. Suppose, for example, a wife says to a neighbour, 'John never gives me any money. He treats my mother abominably, drinks to excess and is constantly abusive and insulting.'

Now, this wife is degrading and belittling her husband in the eyes of all the neighbours and relatives. He no longer appears as the ideal husband to them. Never discuss your marital problems with anyone except a trained counselor. Why cause numerous people to think negatively of your marriage? Moreover, as you discuss and dwell upon these shortcomings of your husband, you are actually creating these states within yourself. Who is thinking and feeling it? You are! As you think and feel, so are you.

Relatives will usually give you the wrong advice. It is usually biased and prejudiced because it is not given in an impersonal way. Any advice you receive which violates the golden rule, which is a cosmic law, is not good or sound.

It is well to remember that no two human beings ever lived beneath the same roof without clashes of temperament, periods of hurts and strain. Never display the unhappy side of your marriage to your friends. Keep your quarrels to yourself. Refrain from criticism and condemnation of your partner.

Don't try to make your wife over

A husband must not try to make his wife over into a second edition of himself. The tactless attempt to change her in many ways is foreign to her nature. These attempts are always foolish and many times result in a dissolution of the marriage. These attempts to alter her destroy her pride and self-esteem and arouse a spirit of contrariness and resentment that proves fatal to the marriage bond.

Adjustments are needed, of course, but if you have a good look inside your own mind and study your character and behaviour, you will find so many shortcomings, they will keep you busy the rest of your life. If you say, 'I will make him over into what I want,' you are looking for trouble and the divorce court. You are asking for misery. You will have to learn the hard way that there is no one to change but yourself.

Pray together and stay together through steps in prayer

The first step: Never carry over from one day to another accumulated irritations arising from little disappointments. Be sure to forgive each other for any sharpness before you retire at night. The moment you awaken in the morning, claim infinite intelligence is guiding you in all your ways. Send out loving thoughts of peace, harmony and love to your marriage partner, to all members of the family and to the whole world.

The second step: Say grace at breakfast. Give thanks for the wonderful food, for your abundance and for all your blessings. Make sure that no problems, worries or arguments shall enter into the table conversation; the same applies at dinner time. Say to your wife or husband, 'I appreciate all you are doing and I radiate love and goodwill to you all day long.'

The third step: The husband and wife should alternate in praying each night. Do not take your marriage partner for granted. Show your appreciation and love. Think appreciation and goodwill, rather than condemnation, criticism and nagging. The way to build a peaceful home and a happy marriage is to use a foundation of love, beauty, harmony, mutual respect, faith in God and all things good. Read the 23rd, 27th and 91st Psalms, the 11th chapter of Hebrews, the 13th chapter of I Corinthians and other great texts of the Bible before going to sleep. As you practice these truths, your marriage will grow more and more blessed through the years.

Creating Harmonious Human Relations

In studying this book, you learn that your subconscious mind is a recording machine which faithfully reproduces what-ever you impress upon it. This is one of the reasons for the application of the Golden Rule in human relations. Mattew 7:12 says, *All things whatsoever ye would that men should do unto you, do ye even so to them.* This quotation has outer and inner meanings. You are interested in its inner meaning from the standpoint of your subconscious mind which is: As you would that men should *think* about you, think you about them in the same manner. As you would that men should *feel* about you, feel you also about them in the same manner. As you would want men to *act* toward you, act you toward them in the same manner.

For example, you may be polite and courteous to someone in your office, but when his back is turned, you are very critical and resentful toward him in your mind. Such negative thoughts are highly destructive to you. It is like taking poison. You are actually taking mental poisons which rob you of vitality, enthusiasm, strength, guidance and goodwill. These negative thoughts and emotions sink down into your subconscious and cause all kinds of difficulties and maladies in your life.

The master key to happy relationships with others

> *Judge not, that ye be not judged. For with what judgement ye judge, ye shall be judged: and with what measure ye mete, it shall be measured to you again.* – Matthew 7:1–2.

A study of these verses and the application of the inner truths contained there represent the real key to harmonious relations. To judge is to think, to arrive at a mental verdict or conclusion in your mind. The thought you have about the other person is your thought, because you are thinking it. Your thoughts are creative, therefore, you actually create in your own experience what you think and feel about the other person. It is also true that the suggestion you give to another, you give to yourself because your mind is the creative medium.

This is why it is said, *For with what judgement ye judge, ye shall be judged.* When you know this law and the way your subconscious mind works, you are careful to think, feel and act right, toward the other. These verses teach you about the emancipation of man and reveal to you the solution to your individual problems.

And with what measure ye mete, it shall be measured to you again

The good you do for others comes back to you in the same measure; and the evil you do returns to you by the law of your own mind. If a man cheats and deceives another, he is actually cheating and deceiving himself. His sense of guilt and mood of loss inevitably will attract loss to him in some way, at some time. His subconscious records his mental act and reacts according to the mental intention or motivation.

Your subconscious mind is impersonal and unchanging, neither considering persons nor respecting religious affiliations or institutions of any kind. It is neither compassionate nor vindictive. The way you think, feel and act toward others returns at last upon yourself.

The daily headlines made him sick

Begin now to observe yourself. Observe your reactions to people, conditions and circumstances. How do you respond to the events and news of the day? It makes no difference if all the other people were wrong and you alone were right. If the news disturbs you, it is your evil because your negative emotions robbed you of peace and harmony.

A woman wrote me about her husband, saying that he goes into a rage when he reads what certain newspaper columnists write in the newspaper. She added that this constant reaction of anger and suppressed rage on his part brought on bleeding ulcers and his physician recommended an emotional reconditioning.

I invited this man to see me and I explained to him the way his mind functions indicating how emotionally immature it was to get angry when others write articles with which he disapproves or disagrees.

He began to realise that he should give the newspaperman freedom to express himself even though the latter disagreed with him politically, religiously or in any other way. In the same manner, the newspaperman would give him freedom to write a letter to the newspaper disagreeing with his published statements. He learned that he could disagree without being disagreeable. He awakened to the simple truth that it is never what a person says or does that affects him, it is his reaction to what is said or done that matters.

This explanation was the cure for this man and he realised that with a little practice he could master his morning tantrums. His wife told me, subsequently, that he laughed at himself and also at what the columnists say. They no longer have power to disturb, annoy and irritate him. His ulcers have disappeared due to his emotional poise and serenity.

I hate women, but I like men

A private secretary was very bitter toward some of the girls in her office because they were gossiping about her and as she said, spreading vicious lies about her. She admitted that she did not like women. She said, 'I hate women, but I like men.' I discovered also that she spoke to the girls who were under her in the office in a very haughty, imperious and irritable tone of voice. She pointed out that they took a delight in making things difficult for her. There was a certain pomposity in her way of speaking and I could see how her tone of voice would affect some people unpleasantly.

If all the people in the office or factory annoy you, isn't it a possibility that the vibration, annoyance and turmoil may be due to some subconscious pattern or mental projection from you? We know that a dog will react ferociously if you hate or fear dogs. Animals pick up your subconscious vibrations and react accordingly. Many undisciplined human beings are just as sensitive as dogs, cats and other animals.

I suggested a process of prayer to this private secretary who hated women, explaining to her that when she began to identify herself with spiritual values and commenced to affirm the truths of life, her voice, mannerisms and hatred of women would completely disappear. She was surprised to know that the emotion of hatred shows up in a person's speech, actions, in his writings and in all phases of his life. She ceased reacting in the typical, resentful and angry way. She established a pattern of prayer which she practiced regularly, systematically and conscientiously in the office.

The prayer was as follows: 'I think, speak and act lovingly, quietly and peacefully. I now radiate love, peace, tolerance and kindliness to all the girls who criticised me and gossiped about me. I anchor my thoughts on peace, harmony and goodwill to all. Whenever I am about to react negatively, I say firmly to myself, "I am going to think, speak and act from the standpoint of the principle of harmony, health and peace within myself." Creative intelligence leads, rules and guides me in all my ways.'

The practice of this prayer transformed her life and she found that all criticism and annoyance ceased. The girls became co-workers and friends along life's journey. She discovered that *there is no one to change but myself.*

His inner speech held back his promotion

One day a salesman came to see me and described his difficulties in working with the sales manager of his organisation. He had been with the company ten years and had received no promotion or recognition of any kind. He showed me his sales figures which were greater proportionately than the other men in the territory. He said that the sales manager did not like him, that he was unjustly treated and that at conferences the manager was rude to him and at times ridiculed his suggestions.

I explained that undoubtedly the cause was to a great degree within himself and that his concept and belief about his superior bore witness to the reaction of this man. *The measure we mete,* [give] *shall be measured to us again.* His mental measure or concept of the sales manager was that he was mean and cantankerous. He was filled with bitterness and hostility toward the executive. On his way to work he conducted a vigorous conversation with himself filled with criticism, mental arguments, recriminations and denunciations of his sales manager. What he gave out mentally, he was inevitably bound to get back. This salesman realised that his inner speech was highly destructive because the intensity and force of his silent thoughts and emotions and personally conducted mental condemnation and vilification of the sales manager entered into his own subconscious mind. This brought about the negative response from his boss as well as creating many other personal, physical and emotional disorders. He began to pray frequently as follows: 'I am the only thinker in my universe. I am responsible for what I think about my boss. My sales manager is not responsible for the way I think about him. I refuse to give power to any person, place or thing to annoy me or disturb me. I wish health, success, peace of mind and happiness for my boss. I sincerely wish him well and I know – he is divinely guided in all his ways.'

He repeated this prayer out loud slowly, quietly and feelingly, knowing that his mind is like a garden and that whatever he plants in the garden will come forth like seeds after their kind I also taught him to practice mental imagery prior to sleep in this way: He imagined that his sales manager was congratulating him on his fine work, on his zeal and enthusiasm as also on his wonderful response from customers. He felt the reality of all this, felt his handshake, heard the tone of his voice and saw him smile. He made a real mental movie, dramatising it to the best of his ability. Night after night he conducted this mental movie, knowing that his subconscious mind was the receptive plate on which his conscious imagery would be impressed.

Gradually by a process of what may be termed mental and spiritual osmosis, the impression was made on his subconscious mind and the expression automatically came forth. The sales manager subsequently called him up to San Francisco, congratulated him and gave him a new assignment as Division Sales Manager over one hundred men with a big increase in salary. He changed his concept and estimate of his boss and the latter responded accordingly.

Becoming emotionally mature

What the other person says or does cannot really annoy or irritate you except when you permit him to disturb you. The only way he can annoy you is through your own thought. For example, if you get angry, you have to go through four stages in your mind: You begin to think about what he said. You decide to get angry and generate an emotion of rage. Then, you decide to act. Perhaps, you talk back and react in kind. You see that the thought, emotion, reaction and action all take place in your mind.

When you become emotionally mature, you do not respond negatively to the criticism and resentment of others. To do so would mean that you had descended to that state of low mental vibration and become one with the negative atmosphere of the other. Identify yourself with your aim in life. Do not permit any person, place or thing to deflect you from your inner sense of peace, tranquility and radiant health.

The meaning of love in harmonious human relations

Sigmund Freud, the Austrian founder of psychoanalysis, said that unless the personality has love, it sickens and dies. Love includes understanding, goodwill and respect for the divinity in the other person. The more love and goodwill you emanate and exude, the more comes back to you.

If you puncture the other fellow's *ego* and wound his estimate of himself, you cannot gain his goodwill. Recognise that every man wants to be loved and appreciated and made to feel important in the world. Realise that the other man is conscious of his true worth and that, like yourself, he feels the dignity of being an expression of the One Life-Principle animating all men. As you do this consciously and knowingly, you build the other person up and he returns your love and goodwill.

He hated audiences

An actor told me that the audience booed and hissed him on his first appearance on the stage. He added that the play was badly written and that undoubtedly he did not play a good role. He admitted openly to me that for months afterward he hated audiences. He called them dopes, dummies, stupid, ignorant, gullible, etc. He quit the stage in disgust and went to work in a drugstore for a year.

One day a friend invited him to hear a lecture in Town Hall, New York City, on 'How to Get Along With Ourselves.' This lecture changed his life. He went back to the stage and began to pray sincerely for the audience and himself. He poured out love and goodwill every night before appearing on the stage. He made it a habit to claim that the peace of God filled the hearts of all present and that all present were lifted up and inspired. During each performance he sent out love vibrations to the audience. Today, he is a great actor and he loves and respects people. His goodwill and esteem are transmitted to others and are felt by them.

Handling difficult people

There are difficult people in the world who are twisted and distorted mentally. They are malconditioned. Many are mental 'delinquents, argumentative, uncooperative, cantankerous, cynical and sour on life. They are sick psychologically. Many people have deformed and distorted minds, probably warped during childhood. Many have congenital deformities. You would not condemn a person who had tuberculosis, nor should you condemn a person who is mentally ill. No one, for example, hates or resents a hunchback;

there are many mental hunchbacks. You should have compassion and understanding. *To understand all is to forgive all.*

Misery Loves company

The person with a hateful, frustrated, distorted and twisted personality is out of tune with the Infinite. He resents those who are peaceful, happy and joyous. Usually he criticises, condemns and vilifies those who have been very good and kind to him. His attitude is this: Why should others be so happy when he is so miserable? He wants to drag them down to his own level. Misery loves company. When you understand this you remain unmoved, calm and dispassionate.

The practice of empathy in human relations

A woman visited me recently stating that she hated another woman in her office. She gave as her reason that the other woman was prettier, happier and wealthier than she. In addition, was engaged to the boss of the company where they worked. One day after the marriage had taken place, the crippled daughter (by a former marriage) of the woman whom she hated came into the office. The child put her arms around her mother and said, 'Mommy, Mommy, I love my new Daddy! Look what he gave me!' She showed her mother a wonderful new toy.

She said to me, 'My heart went out to that little girl and I knew how happy she must feel. I got a vision of how happy this woman was. All of a sudden I felt love for her and I went into the office and wished her all the happiness in the world and I meant it.'

In psychological circles today, this is called empathy, which simply means the imaginative projection of your mental attitude into that of another. She projected her mental mood or the feeling of her heart into that of the other woman and began to think and look out through the other woman's brain. She was actually thinking and feeling as the other woman and also as the child, because she likewise had projected herself into the mind of the child. She was looking out from that vantage point on the child's mother.

If tempted to injure or think ill of another, project yourself mentally into the mind of Moses and think from the standpoint of the Ten Commandments. If you are prone to be envious, jealous or angry, project yourself into the mind of Jesus and think from that standpoint and you will feel the truth of the words *Love ye one another.*

Appeasement never wins

Do not permit people to take advantage of you and gain their point by temper tantrums, crying jags or so-called heart attacks. These people are dictators who try to enslave you and make you do their bidding. Be firm but kind and refuse to yield. Appeasement never wins. Refuse to contribute to their delinquency, selfishness and possessiveness. Remember, do what is right. You are here to fulfill your ideal and remain true to the eternal verities and spiritual values of life which are eternal.

Give no one in all the world the power to deflect you from your goal, your aim in life, which is to express your hidden talents to the world, to serve humanity and to reveal more and more of God's wisdom, truth and beauty to all people in the world. Remain true to your ideal. Know definitely and absolutely that whatever contributes to your peace, happiness and fulfillment must of necessity bless all men who walk the Earth. The harmony of the part is the harmony of the whole, for the whole is in the part and the part is in the whole. All you owe the other, as Paul says, is love and love is the fulfilling of the law of health, happiness and peace of mind.

HOW TO USE YOUR SUBCONSCIOUS MIND TO FORGIVE

Life plays no favourites. God is Life and this Life-Principle is flowing through you this moment. God loves to express Himself as harmony, peace, beauty, joy and abundance through you. This is called the will of God or the tendency of Life.

If you set up resistance in your mind to the flow of Life through you, this emotional congestion will get snarled up in your subconscious mind and cause all kinds of negative conditions. God has nothing to do with unhappy or chaotic conditions in the world. All these conditions are brought about by man's negative and destructive thinking. Therefore, it is silly to blame God for your trouble or sickness.

Many persons habitually set up mental resistance to the flow of Life by accusing and reproaching God for the sin, sickness and suffering of mankind. Others cast the blame on God for their pains, aches, loss of loved ones, personal tragedies and accidents. They are angry at God and they believe He is responsible for their misery.

As long as people entertain such negative concepts about God, they will experience the automatic negative reactions from their subconscious minds. Actually, such people do not know that they are punishing themselves. They must see the truth, find release and give up all condemnation, resentment and anger against anyone or any power outside themselves. Otherwise, they cannot go forward into a healthy, happy or creative activity. The minute these people entertain a God of love in their minds and hearts and when they believe that God is their Loving Father who watches over them, cares for them, guides them, sustains and strengthens them, this concept and belief about God or the Life-Principle will be accepted by their subconscious mind and they will find themselves blessed in countless ways.

Life always forgives you

Life forgives you when you cut your finger. The subconscious intelligence within you sets about immediately to repair it. New cells build bridges over the cut. Should you take some tainted food by error, Life forgives you and causes you to regurgitate it in order to preserve you. If you burn your hand, the Life-Principle reduces the edema and congestion and gives you new skin, tissue and cells. Life holds no grudges against you and it is always forgiving you. Life brings you back to health, vitality, harmony and peace, if you cooperate by thinking in harmony with nature. Negative, hurtful memories, bitterness and ill will clutter up and impede the free flow of the Life-Principle in you.

How he banished that feeling of guilt

I knew a man who worked every night until about one o'clock in the morning. He paid no attention to his two boys or his wife. He was always too busy working hard. He thought people should pat him on the back because he was working so arduously and persistently past midnight every night. He had a blood pressure of over two hundred and was full of guilt. Unconsciously, he proceeded to punish himself by hard work and he completely ignored his children. A normal man does not do that. He is interested in his boys and in their development. He does not shut his wife out of his world.

I explained to him why he was working so arduously, 'There is something eating you inside, otherwise, you would not act this way. You are punishing yourself and you have to learn to forgive yourself.' He did have a deep sense of guilt. It was towards a brother. I explained to him that God was not punishing him, but *that he was* punishing himself. For example, if you misuse the laws of life, you will suffer accordingly. If you put your hand on a naked charged wire, you will get burned. The forces of nature are not evil; it is your use of them that determines whether they have a good or evil effect. Electricity is not evil; it depends on how you use it, whether to burn down a structure or light up a home. The only sin is ignorance of the law and the only punishment is the automatic reaction of man's misuse of the law.

If you misuse the principle of chemistry, you may blow up the office or the factory. If you strike your hand on a board, you may cause your hand to bleed. The board is not for that purpose. Its purpose may be to lean upon or to support your feet. This man realised that God does not condemn or punish anyone and that all his suffering was due to the reaction of his subconscious mind to his own negative and destructive thinking. He had cheated his brother at one time and the brother had now passed on. Still, he was full of remorse and guilt.

I asked him, 'Would you cheat your brother now?'

He said, 'No.'

'Did you feel you were justified at the time?'

His reply was, 'Yes.'

'But, you would not do it now?'

He added, 'No, I am helping others to know how to live.'

I added the following comment, 'You have a greater reason and understanding now. Forgiveness is first to forgive yourself. Forgiveness is getting your thoughts in line with the divine law of harmony. Self-condemnation is called hell (bondage and restriction); forgiveness is called heaven (harmony and peace).'

The burden of guilt and self-condemnation was lifted from his mind and he had a complete healing. The doctor tested his blood pressure and it had become normal. The explanation was the cure.

Criticism cannot hurt you without your consent

A schoolteacher told me that one of her associates criticised a speech she had given, saying to her that she spoke too fast, she swallowed some of her words, she couldn't be heard, her diction was poor and her speech ineffective. This teacher was furious and full of resentment toward her critic.

She admitted to me that the criticisms were just. Her first reaction was really childish and she agreed that the letter was really a blessing and a marvelous corrective. She proceeded immediately to supplement her deficiencies in her speech by enrolling in a course in public speaking at City College. She wrote and thanked the writer of the note for her interest, expressing appreciation for her conclusions and findings which enabled the teacher to correct the matter at once.

How to be compassionate

Suppose none of the things mentioned in the letter had been true of the teacher. The latter would have realised that her class material had upset the prejudices, superstitions or narrow sectarian beliefs of the writer of the note and that a psychologically ill person was simply pouring forth her resentment because a psychological boil had been hurt.

To understand this fact is to be compassionate. The next logical step would be to pray for the other person's peace, harmony and understanding. You cannot be hurt when you know that you are the master of your thoughts, reactions and emotions. Emotions follow thoughts and you have the power to reject all thoughts which may disturb or upset you.

Left at the altar

Some years ago I visited a church to perform a marriage ceremony. The young man did not appear and at the end of two hours, the bride-to-be shed a few tears and then said to me, 'I prayed for divine guidance. This might be the answer for He never faileth.'

That was her reaction – faith in God and all things good. She had no bitterness in her heart because as she said, 'It must not have been right action because my prayer was for right action for both of us.' Someone else having a similar experience would have gone into a tantrum, have had an emotional fit, required sedation and perhaps needed hospitalisation. Tune in with the infinite intelligence within your subconscious depths, trusting the answer in the same way that you trusted your mother when she held you in her arms. This is how you can acquire poise and mental and emotional health.

It is wrong to marry. Sex is evil and I am evil

Some time ago I talked to a young lady aged twenty-two. She was taught that it was a sin to dance, to play cards, to swim and to go out with men. She was threatened by her mother who told her she would burn eternally in hell-fire if she disobeyed her will and her religious teachings. This girl wore a black dress and black stockings. She wore no rouge, lipstick or any form of make-up because her mother said that these things were sinful. Her mother told her that all men were evil and that sex was of the devil and simply diabolic debauchery. This girl had to learn how to forgive herself as she was full of guilt. She had to give up all these false beliefs for the truths of life and a new estimate of herself. When she went out with young men in the office where she worked, she had a deep sense of guilt and thought that God would punish her. Several eligible young men proposed to her, but she said to me, 'It is wrong to marry. Sex is evil and I am evil.' This was her conscience or early conditioning speaking.

She came to me once weekly for about ten weeks and I taught her the workings of the conscious and subconscious mind as set forth in this book. This young girl gradually came to see that she had been completely brainwashed, mesmerised and conditioned by an ignorant, superstitious, bigoted and frustrated mother. She broke away completely from her family and started to live a wonderful life.

At my suggestion she dressed up and attended to her hair. She took lessons in dancing from *a man a*nd she also took driving lessons. She learned to swim, play cards and had a number of dates. She began to love life. She prayed for a divine companion by claiming that Infinite Spirit would attract to her a man who harmonised with her thoroughly. Eventually this came to pass. As she left my office one evening, there was a man waiting to see me and I casually introduced them. They are now married and harmonise with each other perfectly.

Forgiveness is necessary for healing

And when ye stand praying, forgive, if ye have ought against any. – Mark 11:25. Forgiveness of others is essential for mental peace and radiant health. You must forgive everyone who has ever hurt you if you want perfect health and happiness. Forgive yourself by getting your thoughts in harmony with divine law and order. You cannot really forgive yourself completely until you have forgiven others first. To refuse to forgive yourself is nothing more or less than spiritual pride or ignorance.

In the psychosomatic field of medicine today, it is being constantly stressed that resentment, condemnation of others, remorse and hostility are behind a host of maladies ranging from arthritis to cardiac disease. They point out that these sick people, who were hurt, mistreated, deceived or injured, were full of resentment and hatred for those who hurt them. This caused inflamed and festering wounds in their subconscious minds. There is only one remedy. They have to cut out and discard the hurts. The one and only sure way is by forgiveness.

Forgiveness is love in action

The essential ingredient in the art of forgiveness is the willingness to forgive. If you sincerely desire to forgive the other, you are fifty-one percent over the hurdle. I feel sure you know that to forgive the other does not necessarily mean that you like him or want to associate with him. You cannot be compelled to like someone, neither can a government legislate goodwill, love, peace or tolerance. It is quite impossible to like people because someone in Washington issues an edict to that effect. We can, however, love people without liking them.

The Bible says, *Love ye one another.* This, anyone can do who really wants to do it. Love means that you wish for the other health, happiness, peace, joy and all the blessings of life. There is only one prerequisite and that is sincerity. You are not being magnanimous when you forgive, you are really being selfish, because what you wish for the other, you are actually wishing for yourself. The reason is that you are thinking it and you are feeling it. As you think and feel, so are you. Could anything be simpler than that?

Technique of forgiveness

The following is a simple method which works wonders in your life as you practice it: Quiet your mind, relax and let go. Think of God and His love for you and then affirm, 'I fully and freely forgive (mention the name of the offender); I release him mentally and spiritually. I completely forgive everything connected with the matter in question. I am free and he/she is free. It is a marvelous feeling. It is my day of general amnesty. I release anybody and everybody who has ever hurt me and I wish for each and everyone – health, happiness, peace and all the blessings of life. I do this freely, joyously and lovingly and whenever I think of the person or persons who hurt me, I say, "I have released you and all the blessings of life are yours." I am free and you are free. It is wonderful!'

The great secret of true forgiveness is that once you have forgiven the person, it is unnecessary to repeat the prayer. Whenever the person comes to your mind or the particular hurt happens to enter your mind, wish the delinquent well and say, 'Peace be to you.' Do this as often as the thought enters your mind. You will find that after a few days the thought of the person or experience will return less and less often, until it fades into nothingness.

The acid test for forgiveness

There is an acid test for gold. There is also an acid test for forgiveness. If I should tell you something wonderful about someone who has wronged you, cheated you or defrauded you and you sizzled at hearing the good news about this person, the roots of hatred would still be in your subconscious mind, playing havoc with you.

Let us suppose you had a painful abscess on your jaw a year

ago and you told me about it. I would casually ask you if you had any pain now. You would automatically say, 'Of course not, I have a memory of it but no pain.' That is the whole story. You may have a memory of the incident but no sting or hurt any more. This is the acid test and you must meet it psychologically and spiritually, otherwise, you are simply deceiving yourself and not practicing the true art of forgiveness.

To understand all is to forgive all

When man understands the creative law of his own mind, he ceases to blame other people and conditions for making or marring his life. He knows that his own thoughts and feelings create his destiny. Furthermore, he is aware that externals are not the causes and conditioners of his life and his experiences. To think that others can mar your happiness, that you are the football of a cruel fate, that you must oppose and fight others for a living – all these and others like them are untenable when you understand that thoughts are things. The Bible says the same thing.

For as a man thinketh in his heart, so is he.

– Proverbs 23:7.

SEVEN

Building Positive Habits with Your Subconscious Mind

William James, father of American psychology, said that the greatest discovery of the nineteenth century was not in the realm of physical science. The greatest discovery was the power of the subconscious touched by faith. In every human being is that limitless reservoir of power which can overcome any problem in the world.

True and lasting happiness will come into your life the day you get the clear realisation that you can overcome any weakness – the day you realise that your subconscious can solve your problems, heal your body and make you prosper beyond your fondest dream.

You might have felt very happy when your child was born, when you got married, when you graduated from college or when you won a great victory or a prize. You might have been very happy when you became engaged to the loveliest girl or the most handsome man. You could go on and list innumerable experiences, which have made you happy. However, no matter how marvelous these experiences are, they do not give real lasting happiness – they are transitory.

The Book of Proverbs gives the answer: *Whosoever trusteth in the Lord, happy is he.* When you trust in the Lord (the power and wisdom of your subconscious mind) to lead, guide, govern and direct all your ways, you will become poised, serene and relaxed. As you radiate love, peace and goodwill to all, you are really building a superstructure of happiness for all the days of your life.

CHOOSING HAPPINESS

Happiness is a state of mind. There is a phrase in the Bible which says, *Choose ye this day whom ye will serve. You* have the freedom to choose happiness. This may seem extraordinarily simple and it is. Perhaps this is why people stumble over the way to happiness; they do not see the simplicity of the key to happiness. The great things of life are simple, dynamic and creative. They produce well-being and happiness. St Paul reveals to you how you can think your way into a life of dynamic power and happiness in these words: *Finally, brethren, whatsoever things are true, whatsoever things are honest, whatsoever things are just, whatsoever things are pure, whatsoever things are lovely, whatsoever things are of good report; if there be any virtue and if there be any praise, think on these things.* Philippians. 4:8.

How to choose happiness

Begin now to choose happiness. This is how you do it: When you open your eyes in the morning, say to yourself, 'Divine order takes charge of my life today and every day. All things work together for good for me today. This is a new and wonderful day for me. There will never be another day like this one. I am divinely guided all day long and whatever I do will prosper. Divine love surrounds me, enfolds me and enwraps me and I go forth in peace. Whenever my attention wanders away from that which is good and constructive, I will immediately bring it back to the contemplation of that which is lovely and of good report. I am a spiritual and mental magnet attracting to myself all things which bless and prosper me. I am going to be a wonderful success in all my undertakings today. I am definitely going to be happy all day long.'

Start each day in this manner; then you will be choosing happiness and you will be a radiant joyous person.

He made it a habit to be happy

A number of years ago, I stayed for about a week in a farmer's house in Connemarra on the west coast of Ireland. He seemed to be always singing and whistling and was full of humour. I asked him the secret of his happiness and his reply was: 'It is a habit of mine to be happy. Every morning when I awaken and every night before I go to sleep, I bless my family, the crops, the cattle and I thank God for the wonderful harvest.'

This farmer had made a practice of this for over forty years. As you know, thoughts repeated regularly and systematically sink into the subconscious mind and become habitual. He discovered that happiness is a habit.

You must desire to be happy

There is one very important point about being happy. You must sincerely *desire* to be happy. There are people who have been depressed, dejected and unhappy so long that were they suddenly made happy by some wonderful, good, joyous news, they would actually be like the woman who said to me, 'It is wrong to be so happy!' They have been so accustomed to the old mental patterns that they do not feel at home being happy! They long for the former, depressed, unhappy state.

I knew a woman in England who had rheumatism for many years. She would pat herself on the knee and say, 'My rheumatism is bad today. I cannot go out. My rheumatism keeps me miserable.'

This dear elderly lady got a lot of attention from her son, daughter and the neighbours. She really wanted her rheumatism. She enjoyed her 'misery' as she called it. This woman did not really want to be happy.

I suggested a curative procedure to her. I wrote down some biblical verses and told her that if she gave attention to these truths, her mental attitude would undoubtedly change and would result in her faith and confidence in being restored to health. She was not interested. There seems to be a peculiar, mental, morbid streak in many people, whereby they seem to enjoy being miserable and sad.

Why choose unhappiness?

Many people choose unhappiness by entertaining these ideas: 'Today is a black day; everything is going to go wrong.' 'I am not going to succeed.' 'Everyone is against me.' 'Business is bad and it is going to get worse.' 'I'm always late.' 'I never get the breaks.' 'He can, but I can't.' If you have this attitude of mind the first thing in the morning, you will attract all these experiences to you and you will be very unhappy.

Begin to realise that the world you live in is determined largely by what goes on in your mind. Marcus Aurelius, the great Roman philosopher and sage, said, 'A man's life is what his thoughts make of it.' Emerson, America's foremost philosopher, said, 'A man is what he thinks all day long.' The thoughts you habitually entertain in your mind have the tendency to actualise themselves in physical conditions.

Make certain you do not indulge in negative thoughts, defeatist thoughts, or unkind, depressing thoughts. Recall frequently to your mind that you can experience nothing outside your own mentality.

If I had a million dollars, I would be happy

I have visited many men in mental institutions who were millionaires, but they insisted they were penniless and destitute. They were incarcerated because of psychotic, paranoiac and manic-depressive tendencies. Wealth in and of itself will not make you happy. On the other hand, it is not a deterrent to happiness. Today, there are many people trying to buy happiness through the purchase of radios, television sets, automobiles, a home in the country, a private yacht and a swimming pool, but happiness cannot be purchased or procured in that way. The kingdom of happiness is in your thought and feeling. Too many people have the idea that it takes something artificial to produce happiness. Some say, 'If I were elected mayor, made president of the organisation, promoted to general manager of the corporation, I would be happy.'

The truth is that happiness is a mental and spiritual state. None of these positions mentioned will necessarily bequeath happiness. Your strength, joy and happiness consist in finding out the law of divine order and right action lodged in your subconscious mind and by applying these principles in all phases of your life.

He found happiness to be the harvest of a quiet mind

Lecturing in San Francisco some years ago, I interviewed a man who was very unhappy and dejected over the way his business was going. He was the general manager. His heart was filled with resentment toward the vice president and the president of the organisation. He claimed that they opposed him. Because of this internal strife, business was declining; he was receiving no dividends or stock bonuses.

This is how he solved his business problem: The first thing in the morning he affirmed quietly as follows, 'All those working in our corporation are honest, sincere, cooperative, faithful and full of goodwill to all. They are mental and spiritual links in the chain of this corporation's growth, welfare and prosperity. I radiate love, peace and goodwill in my thoughts, words and deeds to my two associates and to all those in the company. The president and the vice-president of our company are divinely guided in all their undertakings.

The infinite intelligence of my subconscious mind makes all decisions through me. There is only right action in all our business transactions and in our relationship with each other. I send the messengers of peace. love and goodwill before me to the office. Peace and harmony reign supreme in the minds and hearts of all those in the company including myself. I now go forth into a new day, full of faith, confidence and trust.'

This business executive repeated the above meditation slowly three times in the morning, feeling the truth of what he affirmed. When fearful or angry thoughts came into his mind during the day, he would say to himself, 'Peace, harmony and poise govern my mind at all times.'

As he continued disciplining his mind in this manner, all the harmful thoughts ceased to come and peace came into his mind. He reaped the harvest. Subsequently, he wrote me to the effect that at the end of about two weeks of reordering his mind, the president and the vice-president called him into the office, praised his operations and his new constructive ideas and remarked how fortunate they were in having him as general manager. He was very happy in discovering that man finds happiness within himself.

The block or stump is not really there

I read a newspaper article some years ago about a horse who had shied when he came to a stump on the road. Subsequently, every time the horse came to that same stump, he shied. The farmer dug the stump out, burned it and leveled the old road. Yet, for twenty-five years, every time the horse passed the place where the former stump was, he shied. The horse was shying at the memory of a stump.

There is no block to your happiness save in your own thought life and mental imagery. Are fear or worry holding you back? Fear is a thought in your mind. You can dig it up this very moment by supplanting it with faith in success, achievement and victory over all problems. I knew a man who failed in business. He said to me, 'I made mistakes. I've learned a lot. I am going back into business and I will be a tremendous success.' He faced up to that stump in his mind. He did not whine or complain, but he tore up the stump of failure and through believing in his inner powers to back him up, he banished all fear thoughts and old depressions. Believe in yourself – you will succeed and be happy.

The happiest people

The happiest man is he who constantly brings forth and practises what is best in him. Happiness and virtue complement each other. The best are not only the happiest but the happiest are usually the best in the art of living life successfully. God is the highest and best in you. Express more of God's love, light, truth and beauty. You will become one of the happiest persons in the world today.

Epictetus, the Greek stoic philosopher, said, 'There is but one way to tranquility of mind and happiness; let this, therefore, be always ready at hand with thee, both when thou wakest early in the morning and all the day long and when thou goest late to sleep, to account no external things thine own, but commit all these to God.'

HOW YOUR SUBCONSCIOUS REMOVES MENTAL BLOCKS

The solution lies within the problem. The answer is in every question. If you are presented with a difficult situation and you cannot see your way clear, the best procedure is to assume that infinite intelligence within your subconscious mind knows all and sees all, has the answer and is revealing it to you now. Your new mental attitude that the creative intelligence is bringing about a happy solution will enable you to find the answer. Rest assured that such an attitude of mind will bring order, peace and meaning to all your undertakings.

How to break or build a habit

You are a creature of habit. Habit is the function of your subconscious mind. You learned to swim, ride a bicycle, dance and drive a car by consciously doing these things over and over again until they established tracks in your subconscious mind. Then, the automatic habit action of your subconscious mind took over. This is sometimes called second nature, which is a reaction of your subconscious mind to your thinking and acting. You are free to choose a good habit or a bad habit. If you repeat a negative thought or act over a period of time, you will be under the compulsion of a habit. The law of your subconscious is compulsion.

How he broke a bad habit

Mr Jones said to me, 'An uncontrollable urge to drink seizes me and I remain drunk for two weeks at a time. I can't give up this terrible habit.'

Time and time again these experiences had occurred to this unfortunate man. He had grown into the habit of drinking to excess. Although he had started drinking of his own initiative, he also began to realise that he could change the habit and establish a new one. He said that while through his willpower he was able to suppress his desires temporarily, his continued efforts to suppress the many urges only made matters worse. His repeated failures convinced him that he was hopeless and powerless to control his urge or obsession. This idea of being powerless operated as a powerful suggestion to his subconscious mind and aggravated his weakness, making his life a succession of failures.

I taught him to harmonise the functions of the conscious and subconscious mind. When these two cooperate, the idea or desire implanted in the subconscious mind is realised. His reasoning mind agreed that if the old habit path or track had carried him into trouble, he could consciously form a new path to freedom, sobriety and peace of mind. He knew that his destructive habit was automatic, but since it was acquired through his conscious choice, he realised that if he had been conditioned negatively, he also could be conditioned positively. As a result, he ceased thinking of the fact that he was powerless to overcome the habit. Moreover, he understood clearly that there was no obstacle to his healing other than his own thought. Therefore, there was no occasion for great mental effort or mental coercion.

The power of his mental picture

This man acquired a practice of relaxing his body and getting into a relaxed, drowsy, msnowing his subconscious mind could bring it about the easiest way. He imagined his daughter congratulating him on his freedom and saying to him, 'Daddy, it's wonderful to have you home!' He had lost his family through drink. He was not allowed to visit them and his wife would not speak to him.

Regularly, systematically, he used to sit down and meditate in the way outlined. When his attention wandered, he made it a habit to immediately recall the mental picture of his daughter with her smile and the scene of his home enlivened by her cheerful voice. All this brought about a reconditioning of his mind. It was a gradual process. He kept it up. He persevered knowing that sooner or later he would establish a new habit pattern in his subconscious mind. I told him that he could liken his conscious mind to a camera, that his subconscious mind was the sensitive plate on which he registered and impressed the picture. This made a profound impression on him and his whole aim was to firmly impress the picture on his mind and develop it there. Films are developed in the dark; likewise, mental pictures are developed in the darkroom of the subconscious mind.

Focussed attention

Realising that his conscious mind was simply a camera, he used no effort. There was no mental struggle. He quietly adjusted his thoughts and focused his attention on the scene before him until he gradually became identified with the picture. He became absorbed in the mental atmosphere, repeating the mental movie frequently. There was no room for doubt that a healing would follow. When there was any temptation to drink, he would switch his imagination from any reveries of drinking bouts to the feeling of being at home with his family. He was successful because he confidently expected to experience the picture he was developing in his mind. Today he is the president of a multimillion-dollar concern and is radiantly happy.

How much do you want what you want?

A young man asked Socrates how he could get wisdom. Socrates replied, 'Come with me.' He took the lad to a river, pushed the boy's head under the water, held it there until the boy was gasping for air, then relaxed and released his head. When the boy regained his composure, he asked him, 'What did you desire most when you were under water?'

'I wanted air,' said the boy.

Socrates said to him, 'When you want wisdom as much as you wanted air when you were immersed in the water, you will receive it.'

Likewise, when you really have an intense desire to overcome any block in your life and you come to a clear-cut decision that there is a way out and that is the course you wish to follow, then victory and triumph are assured.

If you really want peace of mind and inner calm, you will get it. Regardless of how unjustly you have been treated, or how unfair the boss has been, or what a mean scoundrel someone has proved to be, all this makes no difference to you when you awaken to your mental and spiritual powers. You know what you want and you will definitely refuse to let the thieves (thoughts) of hatred, anger, hostility and ill will rob you of peace, harmony, health and happiness. You cease to become upset by people, conditions, news and events by identifying your thoughts immediately with your aim in life. Your aim is peace, health, inspiration, harmony and abundance. Feel a river of peace flowing through you now. Your thought is the immaterial and invisible power and you choose to let it bless, inspire and give you peace.

Why he could not be healed

This is a case history of a married man with four children who was supporting and secretly living with another woman during his business trips. He was ill, nervous, irritable and cantankerous and he could not sleep without drugs. The doctor's medicine failed to bring down his high blood pressure of over two hundred. He had pains in numerous organs of his body which doctors could not diagnose or relieve. To make matters worse, he was drinking heavily.

The cause of all this was a deep unconscious sense of guilt. He had violated the marriage vows and this troubled him. The religious creed he was brought up on was deeply lodged in his subconscious mind and he drank excessively to heal the wound of guilt. Some invalids take morphine and codeine for severe pains; he was taking alcohol for the pain or wound in his mind. It was the old story of adding fuel to the fire.

The explanation and the cure

He listened to the explanation of how his mind worked. He faced his problem, looked at it and gave up his dual role. He knew that his drinking was an unconscious attempt to escape. The hidden cause lodged in his subconscious mind had to be eradicated; then the healing would follow.

He began to impress his subconscious mind three or four times a day by using the following prayer: 'My mind is full of peace, poise, balance and equilibrium. The infinite lies stretched in smiling repose within me. I am not afraid of anything in the past, the present or the future. The infinite intelligence of my subconscious mind leads, guides and directs me in all ways. I now meet every situation with faith, poise, calmness and confidence. I am now completely free from the habit. My mind is full of inner peace, freedom and joy. I forgive myself; then I am forgiven. Peace, sobriety and confidence reign supreme in my mind.'

He repeated this prayer frequently as outlined, being fully aware of what he was doing and why he was doing it. Knowing what he was doing gave him the necessary faith and confidence. I explained to him that as he spoke these statements out loud, slowly, lovingly and meaningfully, they would gradually sink down into his subconscious mind. Like seeds, they would grow after their kind. These truths, on which he concentrated, went in through his eyes, his ears heard the sound and the healing vibrations of these words reached his subconscious mind. This obliterated all the negative mental patterns, which caused all the trouble. Light dispels darkness. The constructive thought destroys the negative thought. He became a transformed man within a month.

Refusing to admit it

If you are an alcoholic or drug addict, admit it. Do not dodge the issue. Many people remain alcoholics because they refuse to admit it.

Your disease is an instability, an inner fear. You are refusing to face life and so you try to escape your responsibilities through the bottle. As an alcoholic you have no free will, although you think you have and you may even boast about your will power. If you are a habitual drunkard and say bravely, 'I will not touch it any more,' you have no power to make this assertion come true, because you do not know where to locate the power.

You are living in a psychological prison of your own making.

You are bound by your beliefs, opinions, training and environmental influences. Like most people, you are a creature of habit. You are conditioned to react the way you do.

Building in the idea of freedom

You can build the idea of freedom and peace of mind into your mentality so that it reaches your subconscious depths. The latter, being all-powerful, will free you from all desire for alcohol. Then, you will have the new understanding of how your mind works and you can truly back up your statement and prove the truth to yourself.

Fifty-one percent healed

If you have a keen desire to free yourself from any destructive habit, you are fifty-one percent healed already. When you have a greater desire to give up the bad habit than to continue it, you will not experience too much difficulty in gaining complete freedom.

Whatever thought you anchor the mind upon, the latter magnifies. You need to engage the mind on the concept of freedom (freedom from the habit) and peace of mind. If you keep it focused on this new direction of attention, you generate feelings and emotions which gradually emotionalise the concept of freedom and peace. Whatever idea you emotionalise is accepted by your subconscious and brought to pass.

The law of substitution

Realise that something good can come out of your suffering. You have not suffered in vain. However, it is foolish to continue to suffer.

If you continue as an alcoholic, it will bring about mental and physical deterioration and decay. Realise that the power in your subconscious is backing you up. Even though you may be seized with melancholia, you should begin to imagine the joy of freedom that is in store for you. This is the law of substitution. Your imagination took you to the bottle; let it take you now to freedom and peace of mind. You will suffer a little bit, but it is for a constructive purpose. You will bear it like a mother in the pangs of childbirth. You will, likewise, bring forth a child of the mind. Your subconscious will give birth to sobriety.

Cause of alcoholism

The real cause of alcoholism is negative and destructive thinking; for as a man thinketh, so is he. The alcoholic has a deep sense of inferiority, inadequacy, defeat and frustration. This is usually accompanied by a deep inner hostility. He has countless alibis as to his reason for drinking, but the sole reason is in his *thought life.*

Three magic steps

The first step: Get still; quiet the wheels of the mind. Enter into a sleepy, drowsy state. In this relaxed, peaceful, receptive state, you are preparing for the second step.

The second step: Take a brief phrase, which can readily be graven on the memory and repeat it over and over as a lullaby. Use the phrase, 'Sobriety and peace of mind are mine now and I give thanks.' To prevent the mind from wandering, repeat it aloud or sketch its pronunciation with the lips and tongue as you say it mentally. This helps its entry into the subconscious mind. Do this for five minutes or more. You will find a deep emotional response.

The third step: Just before going to sleep, practice what Johann von Goethe, German author, used to do. Imagine a friend, a loved one in front of you. Your eyes are closed, you are relaxed and at peace. The loved one or friend is subjectively present and is saying to you, 'Congratulations!' You see the smile; you hear the voice. You mentally touch the hand; it is all real and vivid. The word *congratulations* implies complete freedom. Hear it over and over again until you get the subconscious reaction which satisfies.

Keep on keeping on

When fear knocks at the door of your mind or when worry, anxiety and doubt cross your mind, hold on to your vision, your goal. Think of the infinite power within your subconscious mind, which you can generate by your thinking and imagining and this will give you confidence, power and courage. Keep on, persevere, *until the day breaks and the shadows flee away.*

OVERCOMING FEARS

One of our students told me that he was invited to speak at a banquet. He said he was panic-stricken at the thought of speaking before a thousand people. He overcame his fear this way: For several nights he sat down in an armchair for about five minutes and said to himself slowly, quietly and positively, 'I am going to master this fear. I am overcoming it now. I speak with poise and confidence. I am relaxed and at ease.' He operated a definite law of mind and overcame his fear.

The subconscious mind is amenable to suggestion and is controlled by suggestion. When you still your mind and relax, the thoughts of your conscious mind sink down into the subconscious through a process similar to osmosis, whereby fluids separated by a porous membrane intermingle. As these positive seeds or thoughts, sink into the subconscious area, they grow after their kind. You become poised, serene and calm.

Man's greatest enemy

It is said that fear is man's greatest enemy. Fear is behind failure, sickness and poor human relations. Millions of people are afraid of the past, the future, old age, insanity and death. Fear is a thought in your mind and you are afraid of your own thoughts.

A little boy can be paralysed with fear when he is told there is a boogieman under his bed who is going to take him away. When his father turns on the light and shows him there is no boogieman, he is freed from fear. The fear in the mind of the boy was as real as if there really was a boogie man there. He was healed of a false thought in his mind. The thing he feared did not exist. Likewise, most of your fears have no reality. They are merely a conglomeration of sinister shadows. Shadows have no reality.

Do the thing you fear

Ralph Waldo Emerson, philosopher and poet, said, 'Do the thing you are afraid to do and the death of fear is certain.'

There was a time when the writer of this chapter was filled with unutterable fear when standing before an audience. The way I overcame it was to stand before the audience, do the thing I was afraid to do and the death of fear was certain.

When you affirm positively that you are going to master your fears and you come to a definite decision in your conscious mind, you release the power of the subconscious, which flows in response to the nature of your thought.

Banishing stage fright

A young lady was invited to an audition. She had been looking forward to the interview. However, on three previous occasions, she had failed miserably due to stage fright. She possessed a very good voice, but she was certain that when the time came for her to sing, she would be seized with stage fright. The subconscious mind takes your fears as a request, proceeds to manifest them and brings them into your experience. On three previous auditions she sang wrong notes and she finally broke down and cried. The cause, as previously outlined, was an involuntary autosuggestion, i.e., a silent fear thought emotionalised and subjectified.

She overcame it by the following technique: Three times a day she isolated herself in a room. She sat down comfortably in an armchair, relaxed her body and closed her eyes. She stilled her mind and body to the best of her ability. Physical inertia favour s passivity and renders the mind more receptive to suggestion. She counteracted the fear suggestion by its converse, saying to herself, 'I sing beautifully. I am poised, serene, confident and calm.'

She repeated the words slowly, quietly and with feeling from five to ten times at each sitting. She had three such 'sittings' every day and one immediately prior to sleep at night. At the end of a week she was completely poised and confident. She gave a definitely outstanding audition. Carry out the above procedure and the death of fear is certain.

Fear of failure

Occasionally young men from the local university come to see me, as well as schoolteachers, who often seem to suffer from suggestive amnesia at examinations. The complaint is always the same: 'I know the answers after the examination is over, but I can't remember the answers during the examination.'

The idea, which realises itself, is the one to which we invariably give concentrated attention. I find that each one is obsessed with the idea of failure. Fear is behind the temporary amnesia. It is the cause of the whole experience.

One young medical student was the most brilliant person in his class, yet he found himself failing to answer simple questions at the time of written or oral examinations. I explained to him that the reason was he had been worrying. He was fearful for several days previous to the examination. These negative thoughts became charged with fear.

Thoughts enveloped in the powerful emotion of fear are realised in the subconscious mind. In other words, this young man was requesting his subconscious mind to see to it that he failed and that is exactly what it did. On the day of the examination he found himself stricken with what is called, in psychological circles, suggestive amnesia.

How he overcame the fear

He learned that his subconscious mind was the storehouse of memory and that it had a perfect record of all he had heard and read during his medical training. Moreover, he learned that the subconscious mind was responsive and reciprocal. The way to be *en rapport* with it was to be relaxed, peaceful and confident.

Every night and morning he began to imagine his mother congratulating him on his wonderful record. He would hold an imaginary letter from her in his hand. As he began to contemplate the happy result, he called forth a corresponding or reciprocal response or reaction in himself. The all-wise and omnipotent power of the subconscious took over, dictated and directed his conscious mind accordingly. He imagined the end, thereby willing the means to the realisation of the end. Following this procedure, he had no trouble passing subsequent examinations. In other words, the subjective wisdom took over, compelling him to give an excellent account of himself.

Fear of water, mountains, closed places, etc.

There are many people who are afraid to go into an elevator, climb mountains or even swim in the water. It may well be that the individual had unpleasant experiences in the water in his youth, such as having been thrown forcibly into the water without being able to swim. He might have been forcibly detained in an elevator, which failed to function properly, causing resultant fear of closed places.

I had an experience when I was about ten years of age. I accidentally fell into a pool and went down three times. I can still remember the dark water engulfing my head my gasping for air until another boy pulled me out at the last moment. This experience sank into my subconscious mind for years I feared the water.

An elderly psychologist said to me, 'Go down to the swimming pool, look at the water and say out loud in strong tones, "I am going to master you. I can dominate you." Then go into the water, take lessons and overcome it.' This I did and I mastered the water. Do not permit water to master you. Remember, you are the master of the water. When I assumed a new attitude of mind, the omnipotent power of the subconscious responded, giving me strength, faith and confidence. This enabled me to overcome my fear.

Master technique for overcoming any particular fear

The following is a process and technique for overcoming fear, which I teach from the platform. It works like a charm. Try it!

Suppose you are afraid of the water, a mountain, an interview, an audition, or you fear closed places. If you are afraid of swimming, begin now to sit still for five or ten minutes three or four times a day and imagine you are swimming. Actually, you are swimming in your mind. It is a subjective experience. Mentally you have projected yourself into the water. You feel the chill of the water and the movement of your arms and legs. It is all real, vivid and a joyous activity of the mind. It is not idle daydreaming, for you know that what you are experiencing in your imagination will be developed in your subconscious mind. Then you will be compelled to express the image and likeness of the picture you impressed on your deeper mind. This is the law of the subconscious.

You could apply the same technique if you are afraid of mountains or high places. Imagine you are climbing the mountain, feel the reality of it all, enjoy the scenery, knowing that as you continue to do this mentally, you will do it physically with ease and comfort.

He blessed the elevator

I knew an executive of a large corporation who was terrified to ride in an elevator. He would walk up five flights of stairs to his office every morning. He said that he began to bless the elevator every night and several times a day. He finally overcame his fear. This was how he blessed the elevator: 'The elevator in our building is a wonderful idea. It came out of the universal mind. It is a boon and a blessing to all our employees. It gives wonderful service. It operates in divine order. I ride in it in peace and joy. I remain silent now while the currents of life, love and understanding flow through the patterns of my thought. In my imagination I am now in the elevator and I step out into my office. The elevator is full of our employees. I talk to them and they are friendly, joyous and free. It is a wonderful experience of freedom, faith and confidence. I give thanks.'

He continued this prayer for about ten days and on the eleventh day, he walked into the elevator with other members of the organisation and felt completely free.

Normal and abnormal fear

Man is born only with two fears, the fear of falling and the fear of noise. These are a sort of alarm system given to you by nature as a means of self-preservation. Normal fear is good. You hear an automobile coming down the road and you step aside to survive. The momentary fear of being run over is overcome by your action. All other fears were given to you by parents, relatives, teachers and all those who influenced your early years.

Abnormal fear

Abnormal fear takes place when man lets his imagination run riot. I knew a woman who was invited to go on a trip around the world by plane. She began to cut out of the newspapers all reports of airplane catastrophes. She pictured herself going down in the ocean, being drowned, etc. This is abnormal fear. Had she persisted in this, she would undoubtedly have attracted what she feared most.

Another example of abnormal fear is that of a businessman in New York, who was very prosperous and successful. He had his own private mental motion picture of which he was the director. He would run this mental movie of failure, bankruptcy, empty shelves and no bank balance until he sank into a deep depression. He refused to stop this morbid imagery and kept reminding his wife that 'this can't last,' 'there will be a recession,' 'I feel sure we will go bankrupt,' etc.

His wife told me that he finally did go into bankruptcy and all the things he imagined and feared came to pass. The things he feared did not exist, but he brought them to pass by constantly fearing, believing and expecting financial disaster. *Job said, the thing I feared has come upon me.*

There are people who are afraid that something terrible will happen to their children and that some dread catastrophe will befall them. When they read about an epidemic or rare disease, they live in fear that they will catch it and some imagine they have the disease already. All this is abnormal fear.

The answer to abnormal fear

Move mentally to the opposite. To stay at the extreme of fear is stagnation plus mental and physical deterioration. When fear arises, there immediately comes with it a desire for something opposite to the thing feared. Place your attention on the thing immediately desired. Get absorbed and engrossed in your desire, knowing that the subjective always overturns the objective. This attitude will give you confidence and lift your spirits. The infinite power of your subconscious mind is moving on your behalf and it cannot fail. Peace and assurance are yours.

Examine your fears

The president of a large organisation told me that when he was a salesman he used to walk around the block five or six times before he called on a customer. The sales manager came along one day and said to him, 'Don't be afraid of the boogieman behind the door. There is no boogieman. It is a false belief.'

The manager told him that whenever he looked at his own fears he stared them in the face and stood up to them, looking them straight in the eye. Then they faded and shrank into insignificance.

He landed in the jungle

A chaplain told me of his experiences in the Second World War. He had to parachute from a damaged plane and land in the jungle. He said he was frightened, but he knew there were two kinds of fear, normal and abnormal, which we have previously pointed out. He decided to do something about the fear immediately and began to talk to himself saying, 'John, you can't surrender to your fear. Your fear is a desire for safety and security and a way out.'

He began to claim, 'Infinite intelligence which guides the planets in their courses is now leading and guiding me out of this jungle.' He kept saying this out loud to himself for ten minutes or more. 'Then,' he added, 'something began to stir inside me. A mood of confidence began to seize me and I began to walk. After a few days, I miraculously came out of the jungle and was picked up by a rescue plane.' His changed mental attitude saved him. His confidence and trust in the subjective wisdom and power within him was the solution to his problem.

He said, 'Had I begun to bemoan my fate and indulge my fears, I would have succumbed to the monster fear and probably would have died of fear and starvation.'

He dismissed himself

The general manager of an organisation told me that for three years he feared he would lose his position. He was always imagining failure. The thing he feared did not exist, save as a morbid anxious thought in his own mind. His vivid imagination dramatised the loss of his job until he became nervous and neurotic. Finally he was asked to resign.

Actually, he dismissed himself. His constant negative imagery and fear suggestions to his subconscious mind caused the latter to respond and react accordingly. It caused him to make mistakes and foolish decisions, which resulted in his failure as a general manager. His dismissal would never have happened, if he had immediately moved to the opposite in his mind.

They plotted against him

During a recent world lecture tour, I had a two-hour conversation with a prominent government official. He had a deep sense of inner peace and serenity. He said that all the abuse he receives politically from newspapers and the opposition party never disturb him. His practice is to sit still for fifteen minutes in the morning and realise that in the centre of himself is a deep still ocean of peace. Meditating in this way, he generates tremendous power which overcomes all manner of difficulties and fears.

Some time previously, a colleague called him at midnight and told him a group of people were plotting against him. This is what he said to his colleague, 'I am going to sleep now in perfect peace. You can discuss it with me at 10:00AM tomorrow.'

He said to me, 'I know that no negative thought can ever manifest except I emotionalise the thought and accept it mentally. I refuse to entertain their suggestion of fear. Therefore, no harm can come to me.'

Notice how calm he was, how cool how peaceful! He did not start getting excited, tearing his hair, or wringing his hands. At his centre he found the still water, an inner peace and there was a great calm.

Deliver yourself from all your fears

Use this perfect formula for casting out fear.

> *I sought the Lord and He heard me and delivered me from all my fears.* – Psalm 34:4.

The *Lord* is an ancient word meaning *law – the* power of your subconscious mind. Learn the wonders of your subconscious and how it works and functions. Master the techniques given to you in this chapter. Put them into practice now, today! Your subconscious will respond and you will be free of all fears. *I sought the Lord and He heard me and delivered me from all my fears.*

EIGHT

How to Stay Young in Spirit Forever

Your subconscious mind never grows old. It is timeless, ageless and endless. It is a part of the universal mind of God which was never born and it will never die.

Fatigue or old age cannot be predicated on any spiritual quality or power. Patience, kindness, veracity, humility, goodwill, peace, harmony and brotherly love are attributes and qualities which never grow old. If you continue to generate these qualities here on this plane of life, you will always remain young in spirit.

I remember reading an article in one of our magazines some years ago which stated that a group of eminent medical men at the De Courcy Clinic, in Cincinnati, Ohio, reported that years alone are not responsible for bringing about degenerative disorders. These same physicians stated that it is the fear of time, not time itself, that has a harmful aging effect on our minds and bodies. The neurotic fear of the effects of time may well be the cause of premature aging.

During the many years of my public life, I have had occasion to study the biographies of the famous men and women who have continued their productive activities into the years well beyond the normal span of life. Some of them achieve their greatness in old age. At the same time, it has been my privilege to meet and to know countless individuals of no prominence who, in their lesser sphere, belonged to those hardy mortals who have proved that old age itself does not destroy the creative powers of the mind and body.

He had grown old in his thought life

A few years ago I called on an old friend in London, England. He was over 80 years of age, very ill and obviously was yielding to his advancing years. Our conversation revealed his physical weakness, his sense of frustration and a general deterioration almost approaching lifelessness. His cry was that he was useless and that no one wanted him. With an expression of hopelessness he betrayed his false philosophy, 'We are born, grow up, become old, good for nothing and that's the end.'

This mental attitude of futility and worthlessness was the chief reason for his sickness. He was looking forward only to senescence and after that – nothing. Indeed, he had grown old in his thought life. His subconscious mind brought about all the evidence of his habitual thinking.

Age is the dawn of wisdom

Unfortunately, many people have the same attitude as this unhappy man. They are afraid of what they term 'old age,' the end and extinction, which really means that they are afraid of life. Yet, life is endless. Age is not the flight of years, but the dawn of wisdom.

Wisdom is an awareness of the tremendous spiritual powers in your subconscious mind and the knowledge of how to apply these powers to lead a full and happy life. Get it out of your head once and for all that 65, 75 or 85 years of age is synonymous with the end for you or anybody else. It can be the beginning of a glorious, fruitful, active and most productive life pattern, better than you have ever experienced. Believe this, expect it and your subconscious will bring it to pass.

Welcome the change

Old age is not a tragic occurrence. What we call the aging process is really change. It is to be welcomed joyfully and gladly as each phase of human life is a step forward on the path which has no end. Man has powers which transcend his bodily powers. He has senses which transcend his five physical senses.

Scientists today are finding positive indisputable evidence that something conscious in man can leave his present body and travel thousands of miles to see, hear, touch and speak to people even though his physical body never leaves the couch on which it reclines. Man's life is spiritual and eternal. He need never grow old for Life or God, cannot grow old. The Bible says that God is Life. Life is self-renewing, eternal, indestructible and is the reality of all men.

Evidence for survival

The evidence gathered by the psychical research societies both in Great Britain and America is overwhelming. You may go into any large metropolitan library and get volumes on *The Proceedings of the Psychical Research Society* based on findings of distinguished scientists on survival following so-called death. You will find a startling report on scientific experiments establishing the reality of life after death in *The Case for Psychic Survival* by Hereward Carrington, Director of the American Psychical Institute.

Life is

A woman asked Thomas Edison, the electrical wizard, 'Mr Edison, what is electricity?' He replied, 'Madame, electricity is. Use it.' Electricity is a name we give an invisible power which we do not fully comprehend, but we learn all we can about the principle of electricity and its uses. We use it in countless ways.

The scientist cannot see an electron with his eyes, yet he accepts it as a scientific fact, because it is the only valid conclusion which coincides with his other experimental evidence. We cannot see life. However, we know we are alive. Life is and we are here to express it in all its beauty and glory.

Mind and spirit do not grow old

> The Bible says...*and this is life eternal, that they might know thee the only true God.* – John 17:3.

The man who thinks or believes that the earthly cycle of birth, adolescence, youth, maturity and old age is all there is to life, is indeed to be pitied. Such a man has no anchor, no hope, no vision and to him life has no meaning.

This type of belief brings frustration, stagnation, cynicism and a sense of hopelessness resulting in neurosis and mental aberrations of all kinds. If you cannot play a fast game of tennis, or swim as fast as your son, or if your body has slowed down, or you walk with a slow step, remember life is always clothing itself anew. What men call death is but a journey to a new city in another dimension of Life.

I say to men and women in my lectures that they should accept what we call old age gracefully. Age has its own glory, beauty and wisdom, which belong to it. Peace, love, joy, beauty, happiness, wisdom, goodwill and understanding are qualities, which never grow old or die.

Ralph Waldo Emerson, poet and philosopher, said, 'We do not count a man's years until he has nothing else to count.' Your character, the quality of your mind, your faith and your convictions are not subject to decay.

You are as young as you think you are

I give public lectures in Caxton Hall, London, England, every few years. Following one of these lectures, a surgeon said to me, 'I am 84 years of age. I operate every morning, visit patients in the afternoons and I write for medical and other scientific journals in the evening.' His attitude was that he was as useful as he believed himself to be. He was as young as his thoughts. He said to me, 'It's true what you said, "Man is as strong as he thinks he is and as valuable as he thinks he is."'

This surgeon has not surrendered to advancing years. He knows that he is immortal. His final comment to me was, 'If I should pass on tomorrow, I would be operating on people in the next dimension, not with a surgeon's scalpel, but with mental and spiritual surgery.'

Your gray hair is an asset

Don't ever quit a job and say, 'I am retired; I am old; I am finished.' That would be stagnation, death – you would be finished. Some men are old at 30, while others are young at 80. The mind is the master weaver, the architect, the designer and the sculptor. George Bernard Shaw was active at 90. The artistic quality of his mind had not relaxed from active duty.

I meet men and women who tell me that some employers almost slam the door in their faces when they say they are over

40. This attitude on the part of the employers is to be considered cold, callous, evil and completely void of compassion and understanding. The total emphasis seems to be on youth, i.e., you must be under 35 years of age to receive consideration. The reasoning behind this is certainly very shallow. If the employer would stop and think, he would realise that the man or woman was not selling his age or gray hair, rather, he was willing to give of his talents, his experience and his wisdom gathered through years of experience in the market place of life.

Age is an asset

Your age should be a distinct asset to any organisation, because of your practice and application through the years of the principles of the Golden Rule and the law of love and goodwill. Your gray hair, if you have any, should stand for greater wisdom, skill and understanding. Your emotional and spiritual maturity should be a tremendous blessing to any organisation.

A man should not be asked to resign when he is 65 years of age. That is the time of life when he could be most useful in handling personnel problems, making plans for the future, making decisions and guiding others in the realm of creative ideas based on his experience and insight into the nature of the business.

Be your age

A motion-picture writer in Hollywood told me that he had to write scripts which would cater to the twelve-year-old mind. This is a tragic state of affairs if the great masses of people are expected to become emotionally and spiritually mature. It means that the emphasis is placed on youth in spite of the fact that youth stands for inexperience, lack of discernment and hasty judgement.

I can keep up with the best of them

I am now thinking of a man 65 years of age who is trying frantically to keep young. He swims with young men every Sunday, goes on long hikes, plays tennis and boasts of his prowess and physical powers, saying, 'Look, I can keep up with the best of them!' He should remember the great truth:

> *As a man thinketh in his heart, so is he.* – Proverbs 23:7.

Diets, exercises and games of all kinds will not keep this man young. It is necessary for him to observe that he grows old or remains young in accordance with his processes of thinking. Your subconscious mind is conditioned by your thoughts. If your thoughts are constantly on the beautiful, the noble and the good, you will remain young regardless of the chronological years.

Fear of old age

Job said, *The thing which 1 greatly feared is come upon me.* There are many people who fear old age and are uncertain about the future, because they anticipate mental and physical deterioration as the years advance. What they think and feel comes to pass. You grow old when you lose interest in life, when you cease to dream, to hunger after new truths and to search for new worlds to conquer. When your mind is open to new ideas, new interests and when you raise the curtain and let in the sunshine and inspiration of new truths of life and the universe, you will be young and vital.

You have much to give

If you are 65 or 95 years of age, realise you have much to give. You can help stabilise, advise and direct the younger generation.

You can give the benefit of your knowledge, your experience and your wisdom. You can always look ahead for at all times you are gazing into infinite life. You will find that you can never cease to unveil the glories and wonders of life. Try to learn something new every moment of the day and you will find your mind will always be young.

One hundred and ten years old

Some years ago while lecturing in Bombay, India, I was introduced to a man who said he was 110 years old. He had the most beautiful face I have ever seen. He seemed transfigured by the radiance of an inner light. There was a rare beauty in his eyes indicating he had grown old in years with gladness and with no indication that his mind had dimmed its lights.

Retirement – a new venture

Be sure that your mind never retires. It must be like a parachute which is no good unless it opens up. Be open and receptive to new ideas. I have seen men of 65 and 70 retire. They seemed to rot away and in a few months passed on. They obviously felt that life was at an end.

Retirement can be a new venture, a new challenge, a new path, the beginning of the fulfillment of a long dream. It is inexpressibly depressing to hear a man say, 'What shall I do now that I am retired?' He is saying in effect, 'I am mentally and physically dead. My mind is bankrupt of ideas.'

All this is a false picture. The real truth is that you can accomplish more at 90 than you did at 60, because each day you are growing in wisdom and understanding of life as also the universe through your new studies and interest.

He graduated to a better job

An executive, who lives near me, was forced to retire a few months ago because he had reached the age of 65. He said to me, 'I look upon my retirement as promotion from kindergarten to the first grade.' He philosophised in this manner: He said that when he left high school, he went up the ladder by going to college. He realised this was a step forward in his education and understanding of life in general. Likewise, he added, now he could do the things he had always wanted to do and therefore, his retirement was still another step forward on the ladder of life and wisdom.

He came to the wise conclusion that he was no longer going to concentrate on making a living. Now he was going to give all his attention to living life. He is an amateur photographer and he took additional courses on the subject. He took a trip around the world and took movies of famous places. He now lectures before various groups, lodges and clubs and is in popular demand.

There are countless ways of taking an interest in something worthwhile outside yourself. Become enthusiastic over new creative ideas, make spiritual progress and continue to learn and to grow. In this manner you remain young in heart, because you are hungering and thirsting after new truths and your body will reflect your thinking at all times.

You must be a producer and not a prisoner of society

The newspapers are taking cognizance of the fact that the voting population of the elderly in California elections is increasing by leaps and bounds. This means that their voices will be heard in the legislature of the state and also in the halls of Congress. I believe there will be enacted a federal law prohibiting employers from discrimination against men and women because of age.

A man of 65 years may be younger mentally, physically and physiologically than many men at 30. It is stupid and ridiculous to tell a man he cannot be hired because he is over 40. It is like saying to him that he is ready for the scrap heap or the junk pile.

What is a man of 40 or over to do? Must he bury his talents and hide his light under a bushel? Men, who are deprived and prevented from working because of age must be sustained by government treasuries at county, state and federal levels. The many organisations who refuse to hire them and benefit from their wisdom and experience will be taxed to support them. This is a form of financial suicide.

Man is here to enjoy the fruit of his labour and he is here to be a producer and not a prisoner of society which compels him to idleness.

Man's body slows down gradually as he advances through the years, but his conscious mind can be made much more active, alert, alive and quickened by the inspiration from his subconscious mind. His mind, in reality, never grows old.

> *Oh that I were as in months past, as in the days when God preserved me; When his candle shined upon my head and when by his light I walked through darkness; As I was in the days of my youth, when the secret of God was upon my tabernacle.* – Job 29:2–4.

Secret of youth

To recapture the days of your youth, feel the miraculous, healing, self-renewing power of your subconscious mind moving through your whole being. Know and feel that you are inspired, lifted up, rejuvenated, revitalised and recharged spiritually. You can bubble over with enthusiasm and joy, as in the days of your youth, for the simple reason that you can always mentally and emotionally recapture the joyous state.

The candle which shines upon your head is divine intelligence and reveals to you everything you need to know; it enables you to affirm the presence of your good, regardless of appearances. You walk by the guidance of your subconscious mind, because you know that the dawn appears and the shadows flee away.

Get a vision

Instead of saying, 'I am old,' say, 'I am wise in the way of the Divine Life.' Don't let the corporation, newspapers or statistics hold a picture before you of old age, declining years, decrepitude, senility and uselessness. Reject it, for it is a lie. Refuse to be hypnotised by such propaganda. Affirm life – not death. Get a vision of yourself as happy, radiant, successful, serene and powerful.

His mind active at ninety-nine

My father learned the French language at 65 years of age and became an authority on it at 70. He made a study of Gaelic when he was over 60 and became an acknowledged and famous teacher of the subject. He assisted my sister in a school of higher learning and continued to do so until he passed away at 99. His mind was as clear at 99 as it was when he was 20. Moreover, his handwriting and his reasoning powers had improved with age. Truly, you are as old as you think and feel.

We need our senior citizens

Marcus Porcius Cato, the Roman patriot, learned Greek at 80. Madame Ernestine Schumann-Heink, the great German-American contralto, reached the pinnacle of her musical success after she became a grandmother. It is wonderful to behold the accomplishments of the oldsters. General Douglas MacArthur, Harry S Truman, General Dwight David Eisenhower and American financier Bernard Baruch are interesting, active and contributing their talents and wisdom to the world.

The Greek philosopher, Socrates, learned to play musical instruments when he was 80 years old. Michelangelo was painting his greatest canvases at 80. At 80, Cios Simonides won the prize for poetry, Johann von Goethe finished *Faust a*nd Leopold von Ranke commenced his *History of the World*, which he finished at 92.

Alfred Tennyson wrote a magnificent poem, 'Crossing the Bar,' at 83. Isaac Newton was hard at work close to 85. At 88 John Wesley was directing, preaching and guiding Methodism. We have several men of 95 years who come to my lectures and they tell me they are in better health now than they were at 20. Let us place our senior citizens in high places and give them every opportunity to bring forth the flowers of Paradise. If you are retired, get interested in the laws of life and the wonders of your subconscious mind. Do something you have always wanted to do. Study new subjects and investigate new ideas. Pray as follows:

> *As the hart panteth after the water brooks, so panteth my soul after thee, O God.* – Psalm 42:1.

The fruits of old age

> *His flesh shall be fresher than a child's: he shall return to the days of his youth.* – Job 33:25.

Old age really means the contemplation of the truths of God from the highest standpoint. Realise that you are on an endless journey, a series of important steps in the ceaseless, tireless, endless ocean of life. Then, with the Psalmist you will say,

> *They shall still bring forth fruit in old age; they shall be fat and flourishing.* Psalm 92:14. *But the fruit of the Spirit is love, joy, peace, patience, gentleness, goodness, faith, meekness, temperance: against such there is no law.* – Galatians 5:22–23.

You are a child of Infinite Life which knows no end and you are a child of Eternity.

Part III

PUBLIC SPEAKING AND INFLUENCING PEOPLE

Build the Skills of
Mutual Friendship and Public Speaking

Dale Carnegie

Introduction

At this point, you've learned about two key life skills crucial to breakthrough success: *how to establish a wealth mindset* to direct your life toward success (life skill 1) and *how to leverage the power of your subconscious mind* to make those thoughts into realities (life skill 2). Yet if you stop here, you may still find yourself stuck. You may have the best ideas that seem to have so much promise, but they never take off. The third practical life skill you need to truly achieve breakthrough success is to learn *how to influence others* – by building mutual friendships that naturally seek the other's best and learning the practical skills of public speaking. With a powerful network of friends and partners around you, seeking to pursue your best and help you become profitable (just as you are doing for them) and the ability to powerfully articulate your ideas to that network and beyond, your success will truly have no limit. There's no one more suited to teach us about how to influence others than Dale Carnegie.

Dale Carnegie has been better known for helping business professionals master the practical skills of influence – particularly friendship and public speaking – than anyone else in the last century.

In 1936, Carnegie wrote the classic book *How to Win Friends and Influence People*. Ironically, despite the fact that we're more connected socially than ever before, we need his practical insights on interpersonal relationships more than ever. As many rely more on social media than face-to-face contact to build relationships, whole generations have lost the simple, commonsense skills of friendship. You'll find his practical insights about building quality relationships here, as well as a special section for young people new to the workforce (adapted from the 1938 booklet, *How to Get Ahead in the World Today*), who may not have learned these commonsense skills most older generations take for granted.

Yet even before he wrote *How to Win Friends and Influence People,* Carnegie taught public speaking, training over seven thousand business professionals in his courses at the YMCA throughout the eastern seaboard. His course was so popular that he published it in book form in 1920 as *Public Speaking*, which was revised and reprinted four times over the next forty years. Just like the skill of building authentic relationships, public speaking is a crucial skill for success in today's marketplace in virtually every field. During a time when thought leaders need to earn their keep in presentations and speaking gigs, when Internet marketing includes video and podcasts as a matter of course and when the Internet broadcasts our amateur videos across the globe instantly, mastering this skill may be even more relevant now than ever before. If you keep up with current trends in public speaking and marketing, you'll know that the power of telling a story effectively is still the rage.

So in this section, we'll learn how to influence the world around us with an authentic message that is truly our own, truly profitable and truly helpful for our audiences. But just like developing a wealth mindset in Part I and mastering the power of the subconscious mind in Part II, learning to influence others doesn't come instantly through five easy lessons, but by using and building upon many of the principles you've already learned.

You won't be surprised to discover that the secret to speaking effectively starts with desire. Or requires the combination of thought and feeling. Or depends upon the disciplines of practice and perseverance.

Dale Carnegie, like Napoleon Hill and Joseph Murphy, knew that successful people were integrated people of character who understand the cause-and-effect ways the world works. They invest the time needed to master the skills that will take them to the top level of achievement. Not just to benefit themselves, but to benefit others. Once you master this final skill of influencing others through authentic friendship and public speaking, you too will be ready to soar.

ONE

Dale Carnegie's Golden Rules for Success

BECOME A FRIENDLIER PERSON

1. Don't criticise, condemn or complain.
2. Give honest, sincere appreciation.
3. Arouse in the other person an eager desire.
4. Become genuinely interested in other people.
5. Smile.
6. Remember that a person's name is to that person the sweetest and most important sound in any language.
7. Be a good listener. Encourage others to talk about themselves.
8. Talk in terms of the other person's interests.
9. Make the other person feel important – and do it sincerely.

WIN PEOPLE TO YOUR WAY OF THINKING

1. The only way to get the best of an argument is to avoid it.
2. Show respect for the other person's opinion. Never say, 'You're wrong.'

3. If you are wrong, admit it quickly and emphatically.
4. Begin in a friendly way.
5. Get the other person to say 'yes, yes' immediately.
6. Let the other person do a great deal of the talking.
7. Let the other person feel that the idea is his or hers.
8. Try honestly to see things from the other person's point of view.
9. Be sympathetic with the other person's ideas and desires.
10. Appeal to the nobler motives.
11. Dramatise your ideas.
12. Throw up a challenge.

BE A LEADER

1. Begin with praise and honest appreciation.
2. Call attention to people's mistakes indirectly.
3. Talk about your own mistakes before criticising the other person.
4. Ask questions instead of giving direct orders.
5. Let the other person save face.
6. Praise the slightest improvement and praise every improvement. Be 'hearty in your approbation and lavish in your praise.'
7. Give the other person a chance to live up to a fine reputation.
8. Use encouragement. Make the fault seem easy to correct.
9. Make the other person happy about doing the thing you suggest.

FUNDAMENTAL PRINCIPLES FOR OVERCOMING WORRY

1. Live in 'day tight compartments.'
2. How to face trouble:

  a. Ask yourself, 'What is the worst that can possibly happen?'
  b. Prepare to accept the worst.
  c. Try to improve on the worst.
3. Remind yourself of the exorbitant price you can pay for worry in terms of your health.

BASIC TECHNIQUES IN ANALYSING WORRY

1. Get all the facts.
2. Weigh all the facts – then come to a decision.
3. Once a decision is reached, act!
4. Write out and answer the following questions:
   a. What is the problem?
   b. What are the causes of the problem?
   c. What are the possible solutions?
   d. What is the best possible solution?

BREAK THE WORRY HABIT BEFORE IT BREAKS YOU

1. Keep busy.
2. Don't fuss about trifles.
3. Use the law of averages to outlaw your worries.
4. Cooperate with the inevitable.
5. Decide just how much anxiety a thing may be worth and refuse to give it more.
6. Don't worry about the past.

CULTIVATE A MENTAL ATTITUDE THAT WILL BRING YOU PEACE AND HAPPINESS

1. Fill your mind with thoughts of peace, courage, health and hope.

2. Never try to get even with your enemies.
3. Expect ingratitude.
4. Count your blessings – not your troubles.
5. Do not imitate others.
6. Try to profit from your losses.
7. Create happiness for others.

THE PERFECT WAY TO CONQUER WORRY

1. Pray.

DON'T WORRY ABOUT CRITICISM

1. Remember that unjust criticism is often a disguised compliment.
2. Do the very best you can.
3. Analyse your own mistakes and criticise yourself.

PREVENT FATIGUE AND WORRY TO KEEP YOUR ENERGY AND SPIRITS HIGH

1. Rest before you get tired.
2. Learn to relax at your work.
3. Protect your health and appearance by relaxing at home.
4. Apply these four good working habits:
    a. Clear your desk of all papers except those relating to the immediate work at hand.
    b. Do things in the order of their importance.
    c. When you face a problem, solve it then and there if you have the facts necessary to make a decision.
    d. Learn to organise, deputise and supervise.

5. Put enthusiasm into your work.
6. Don't worry about insomnia.

FRIENDSHIP IS THE FOUNDATION OF ROMANTIC RELATIONSHIPS

Friendship is the first and most important element of the foundation for joyful relationships. For a relationship to survive and have a chance to thrive, this foundational element must be established early in the dating stage of the relationship.

Here are a few tips on building friendship using Dale Carnegie's principles of how to win friends and influence people:

- *Do not criticise, condemn, or complain.* In normal everyday life, these three C-s can ruin relationships between folks. Their negative impact is more pronounced in the affairs of the heart. Dating, courtship and marriage relationships are periods to build up. Criticism, condemnation and complaining only tear people, institutions and ideologies down. Avoid this three C-s like a plague and you have great opportunity to build friendship in your relationship.
- *Give honest and sincere appreciation.* Everyone, no matter his or her height in life, blushes when flattered. Think about what would happen in a person's heart if he or she is genuinely appreciated for little or great efforts made to give or be worthy. That person would be happy and anticipate more opportunities to be with you.
- *Arouse in the other person an eager want.* This is a powerful seductive tool used even by leaders. Look for creative ways to keep your partner increasingly interested in the project of finding out if both of you could hit off a marriage relationship together. Avoiding the first

principle and accentuating the second principle above would help here. If you are fun to be with, your partner would eagerly want to be with you.

- *Become genuinely interested in other people.* In all forms of relationship, attention is key. Interest in other people gives you the power to connect with them. It helps you to break the barriers to communication. Genuine interest would present you as an unselfish person seeking for the other person's welfare. The law of reciprocity is real. If you are genuinely interested in other people, they would gravitate towards you.
- *Smile.* A smile, they say, is the most infectious disease in the world. If you smile, even at the opportunity to meet someone, he or she would smile back at you. Nobody likes to be where there is strife and turmoil. The best place to be is where there are happy people. A smile is evidence of peace and confidence. It is magnetic. If you have not yet noticed how effective this gift of life is, try experimenting with your siblings or close associates. The toughest and most worried person you would ever meet would succumb to a smile.
- *Remember people's names.* A person's name is the sweetest sound in any language. Even in a strange land, if you meet someone you had known before or just got his or her name by any means, it quickly creates a sense of familiarity. This breaks barriers and allows communication to flow and understanding to take place.
- *Be a good listener and encourage others to talk about themselves.* One art that would help grow a relationship is the art of listening. People like to talk about themselves. You would gain power over people who talk if you listen

because, then you would be able to know much about them. Knowledge is power. If you know about my desires and aspirations, you can have a chance to meet or help to meet them. This can sustain our relationship and even control it to your advantage.

- *Talk in terms of the other person's interests.* If you are attentive to the needs of the other person, that person would pay attention to your needs. Remember the golden rule; do unto others, as you would have them do to you. Your attention to the needs of the other person would produce a reciprocal action.
- *Make the other person feel important and do so sincerely.* The true relationship religion is to give. Is not it what all religions preach? Genuine praise, sincere appreciation and responsibility would make the other person feel important. Give and accept responsibility from the person you are in a relationship with. Both acts given with sincerity engender a feeling of self-worth and importance.

TWO

How to Get Ahead in the World Today

A SPECIAL MESSAGE FOR YOUNG PEOPLE

INTRODUCTION

In this chapter, I have attempted to outline some of the things you must know, if you are going to get along in our ever-changing global economy. This knowledge is not the sort of knowledge you have been taught in school – but it is just as true and just as vital to you as a multiplication table or your ABCs.

There is one thing you must remember. While others can tell you how to do these things, only one person in the world can ever really make you do them – and that person is *you*. When you finished your formal education, your education had only begun. As you unlearn many of the things you believed you knew and learn many things that were not taught in your classrooms, it is inevitable that you will make mistakes. By those very mistakes you will learn, too. So do not let them discourage you. Say to yourself, instead: 'It is not a mistake the first time. It is not a mistake until I commit the same blunder twice.'

One other thing. Your success in life will depend to an overwhelming degree on your ability to get along with other people. It is from your study and observation of them that you will complete your education. For as Emerson said: 'Every man I meet is my superior in some way. In that, I learn of [for] him.' I shall be extremely happy if this chapter proves of practical assistance in helping you to seize the great opportunities that time holds in store for you.

THE IMPORTANCE OF A COLLEGE DEGREE

Many people have asked me if a college education is necessary for success. The question is utterly ridiculous, as many people who are not college graduates have nonetheless gone right to the top of the business world. Both Mark Zuckerberg and Bill Gates are college dropouts. Don't be discouraged if you are unable to go to college – it is not necessary for success.

However, it is to your benefit to get all you can in the way of a formal education in your youth for it will make it easier for you to attain success – provided you don't rely too much on it. A college education ought to train your mind, broaden your life and develop your confidence; all of which should help you make more money in later life.

You will get a good start through attending high school or college, but don't sit back and depend on your diploma to take you through life. A college education is like getting a head start in a foot race. However if you don't run as fast as you can, those who have started from scratch behind you will catch up and pass you.

HOW TO DEVELOP GREAT HABITS

If you really want to successfully participate in today's business world, you will need to have a strong character. Your character, in a nutshell, is just a sum total of your daily habits.

Here are five specific rules that you can start using today to help you form new and desirable habits that will help you to get ahead.

Rule No. 1. Take inventory of yourself. Look yourself over calmly and honestly. It's often advisable to ask the candid opinion of a friend or adult whose advice you value. Find out what good habits you should try to acquire and what bad habits you should get rid of.

Rule No. 2. Start yourself off with all your enthusiasm at your command. Early in life Benjamin Franklin drew up for himself a list of thirteen virtues he wanted to cultivate. He concentrated on one virtue each week until he had covered all thirteen. Then he went back to the beginning and began all over again. He kept repeating them until he had mastered all thirteen. Franklin realised that habit is nothing but repetition. Make the formation of your new habits seem like the most important achievement in the world to you.

Rule No. 3. Grasp every opportunity for practicing your new resolutions. For example, if you have decided that you do not smile enough (and you might consider this a sort of silly resolution, but studies show that smiling actually makes the smiler happier!), start in right now. Smile at yourself in the mirror as you wash your face in the morning. Smile at everybody you meet during the day. If somebody steps on your feet in the elevator or shoves you in the subway, smile at him or her, too. If you do this and keep it up, it won't be long before you'll be known as one of the most congenial persons in your town.

Rule No. 4. Don't make excuses for yourself. William James said: 'Every lapse is like the letting fall of a ball of string, which one is carefully winding up; a single slip undoes more than a great many turns will wind again.' Edna Ferber told me that she forced herself to work at least six hours writing every day. There were many days, she confessed, when she had nothing to write about and she longed to do other things. But she kept faith with herself. If you want to form a new habit, don't permit yourself to fail in the application of that habit. Should you stray, immediately return to your program. You need not berate yourself, but don't listen to your excuses either.

Rule No. 5. Make definitive commitments. Any truly successful athlete provides an example of someone who makes definitive commitments. Young athletes – from figure skaters to boxers – practice every day, all year 'round, in addition to attending to their academic requirements. They don't let the desire for leisure activities impact on their devotion to becoming the best in their field. If you decide to do something difficult, keep your goal front and centre in your mind as well in your actions every single day. Reinforce your commitment by making it public – tell all your friends about it and post it on your facebook page – so that if you should fail to follow through, all your friends will be sure to hold you accountable. This will ensure your going through with your resolution to the end.

ENTHUSIASM

To me it is a great tragedy if people do not find early in life the kind of work they like to do so that they may apply in full force all the enthusiasm of youth. If I had children, I would, almost from the day of their birth, try to steer them toward the work they like and instil in them the enthusiasm for their tasks. Enthusiasm will make up for the lack of many things. Ralph Waldo Emerson said, 'Every good movement in the annals of history is the triumph of enthusiasm.'

The word enthusiasm comes from two Greek words – *en* and *theos* – meaning 'the God within.' Those people who are fired with enthusiasm do have a God within them – a God that will help them get ahead – a God that will help them perform miracles. In addition to physical exercise, we need spiritual and mental exercise everyday. One of the best ways of developing your enthusiasm is to give yourself a good pep talk at the start of every day. Follow this up at any time during the day whenever you feel discouragement creeping up on you.

DETERMINATION

On the question of realising one's dream, businessman Bill Rancic has said, '...hard work will get you there. You don't necessarily need to have an Ivy League education or millions of dollars startup money. It can be done with an idea, hard work and determination.'

That's plain common sense, isn't it? Yes it is, but most of us need to be reminded of it now and then. For example, I know a bright, college-educated man who I once thought would be quite successful. Over 50 now he has fallen far short of his expectations. He would start any new thing with enthusiasm only to then cool off and drop it in a little while to run after something else. In 30 years he started a score of jobs, but never finished any one of them. Everything he had ever undertaken in life had failed. Why? Because he lacked persistence to see a thing through to the finish. He never stuck at anything long enough to give it a chance to succeed.

The philosopher William James once said, 'What we do compared to what we could do is like comparing the waves on the surface of the sea to the ocean's great depth.' Many years ago a writer known as Vash Young was a popular inspirational figure and the author of several successful motivational books. However, his early years were full of struggle and hardship. Mr Young blamed his early failures upon himself; his own thoughts were his own worst enemy. He suddenly realised that by changing his thoughts he could change his life. He drew up a list of good qualities he wanted to possess and determined to think these qualities, live these qualities and be these qualities. The nine qualities he decided would turn failure into success were: love, courage, cheerfulness, activity, compassion, friendliness, generosity, tolerance and justice. Mr Young admitted that it was a hard battle to change his life over so completely. But he was determined and he finally succeeded in this and at the same time he succeeded as a businessman.

More recently, we've seen the basketball player Michael Jordan effectively redefine his sport. Jordan did not start off as a superstar – in high school, he was actually dropped from his school's basketball team. Obviously, Jordan did not let that setback keep him from following his dream. Jordan has said, 'I have missed more than nine thousand shots in my career. I have lost almost three hundred games. On twenty-six occasions I have been entrusted to take the game winning shot and I missed. I have failed over and over and over again in my life. That is why I succeed.' I won't argue that Mr Jordan is not exceptionally talented. But his determination kept him going at a time when his talent wasn't enough. It is this singlemindedness that we all want to emulate.

Determination and application are two of the first requisites of success in any undertaking. When you make up your mind to achieve something and really go after it with hard work and perseverance, you'll find you're getting ahead almost before you know it.

FEAR AND COURAGE

Fear doesn't exist anywhere except in the mind. But even if fear is only an idea, it can be utterly defeating. Many leaders have recognised the power of fear to dispirit a people and lead to their demise. As a warrior, Napoleon held that there are four elements that go to make an army: size, training, equipment and morale. He said that morale was more important than the other three all put together. In other words, an army's confidence, courage and willpower had more to do with its success than its size, its training and the number of its guns. Confidence and courage are just as important in the battles of business as they are in the battles of bullets.

How can you develop courage? Exercise it. Just as you would develop a strong arm or a strong body by exercise, so must you develop your courage by using it. Do the thing you are afraid to do. Ralph Waldo Emerson advised: 'Do the thing you fear to do and the death of fear is absolutely certain.'

If you know someone you are afraid to call on, call on that person tomorrow. You may be so scared that you have to walk up and down in front of his home or his office half a dozen times before you enter. If you do, tell him about it. Tell him something like this: 'You know, I have always been intimidated by you; I had to walk up and down the hallway out there a half dozen times before I could get up enough courage to come in and see you. I am trembling right now. I'm so scared I can hardly talk.' This will not make the other person laugh at you. He will feel that he must be very important in your eyes or you wouldn't be afraid of him. Moreover, he'll understand your experience – there's no doubt that he has been afraid of someone during the course of his life and he'll respect your courage in facing him.

HOW TO GET A JOB

When you are looking for a job, remember that employers are buyers – and they are in the market to buy, provided you have something to sell. Therefore, visualise yourself as a product. Find out why someone should invest in you and present yourself in the best package possible.

Interviewers are not interested in your problems; they're interested in their own problems. First, find out what their needs are and how you can fulfill those needs. Then you really have something to talk about.

I recall a time when a man came to me during my slow season, when I really wanted to cut down overheads. I didn't want to increase my staff at that time. Yet this man had made a special study of my problems and came to me with concrete suggestions as to how he could save me money. The thing that impressed me most about him was that he did not ask for a salary. He merely said, 'I'm so sure that I can save you money, that I'll be glad to work for my gas and meals until I can prove what I can do for you. After I've demonstrated my worth, we'll talk about my salary.' That man is now working for me, yet I did not want to hire him. He sold himself to me. If he had come to me and merely asked me for a job, I would have answered truthfully that there was no opening.

Here are three rules for getting a job: First, find out what you like to do, because that is probably what you can do best. Second, devote plenty of time to discovering who needs the services you have to offer. Third, study the specific needs of the firm. When you arrive at the interview, show the interviewer how you can help him or her solve the firm's problems. While the economy has changed in many ways over the past few decades, good interviewing principles have remained a constant. Here's the advice of Mr Ernest Lawton, who at one time was the personnel director for Macy's. Mr Lawton and his assistants interviewed about 150,000 applicants a year. Of this number, about 15,000 won the jobs they were seeking. Most people fell down on the very first requirement, which was personality. That's the first thing Macy's staff looked for and two applicants out of three lacked it. If potential employees can sell Macy's their personality in a few minutes, the staff members are pretty sure they can sell to the customer, too. Getting a job is really a selling proposition. The individuals looking for a job have something to sell just as definitely as Macy's has. The store sells merchandise and what the individuals have to sell are themselves, their personality, their services and their capacity for work.

In evaluating potential employee's personalities, here are the things that Mr Lawton would look for: Do they speak sincerely and convincingly? Do they talk in a natural, well-modulated voice? Do they smile in a friendly way? Do they dress well? (By that he meant: are the clothes neat, clean and well pressed? Mr Lawton considered personality more important in hiring a person than his or her experience. Macy's was mainly interested in the material that their employees were made of and how they presented it. Staff members knew that they could teach the tricks of the trade in their training course. After personality, Mr Lawton would look for ambition. In the follow-up interviews a lot of questions were asked to determine whether the potential staff members would be content merely to hold a job and collect their pay, or whether they were definitely on their way up.

A third requirement was the ability to get along with other people. Macy's employed more than 25,000 people and it was (and is!) important that they be congenial. It takes self-control to get along with all sorts of people. Keeping a job is as much a matter of salesmanship as getting a job.

Two high school boys once called me up and asked me for an interview. They craved knowledge on how to get hired. I told them that dozens of books had been written about the subject and ten thousand lectures had been delivered on it and that it would take me two days to cover the subject fully. But they wanted to see me nevertheless. Before they arrived, I wrote down six rules that I consider helpful in an interview with a prospective boss. Here they are:

1. Memorise (no more than ten lines), a vest pocket history of yourself – think of what you would say if someone were to ask you 'Tell me about yourself.' Include only the items that would affect your work – your education, your general background, your experience and your aims.
2. Have three references ready to offer to the interviewer. Of course, include cellphone numbers and email IDs.
3. Be confident, but don't brag. You want to be perceived as eager and poised, but not full of yourself.
4. Avoid familiarity. Sit up straight and don't place your elbows or hands on the interviewer's desk. This may seem inconsequential, but the idea is to avoid having him think you consider his office a lounging room. Remember that this is a time to devote solely to the interviewer. Do not bring

food with you or chew gum. Turn your cellphone off and under no circumstances should you look at it.

5. Look the interviewer in the eye with confidence; be convinced of what you are saying and say it in a few words. When you sense that the interview is over, don't linger. Most interviews are decided in the first two minutes, anyway.
6. Make the interviewer for whom you want to work know that you are interested in working for him or her, not for yourself.

HOW TO KEEP A JOB

Staying employed is just as important as getting employed. The most important factor in keeping a job is your personal value. You must constantly maintain your employer's consciousness of your value to the firm and you must get along with the rest of the people. Do not listen to office gossip and be careful of what you say.

Don't be a clock-watcher – be more interested in finishing your job than in finishing the workday.

Don't shrink from responsibilities for fear of making a mistake. Immediately admit your errors and learn from them. Never offer excuses for your mistakes. One survey that considered the common causes for firing people, found that most people were fired because they lacked plain everyday virtues. It also found that 14 percent were fired for carelessness; nearly 11 percent were uncooperative; over 10 percent were under performers. Others lose their jobs because they stay away from work, or they're dishonest, or they have no initiative, or they spend their time on personal matters during office hours. In seeking advancement, do not overlook the importance of your relations with other people.

If you find that you dislike people that you work with and they in turn dislike you, your mission is not to change the people you dislike, but to change yourself. Perhaps you wouldn't dislike them if you knew more about them. Instead of thinking about the things you dislike in these people, why not concentrate on their good points? The sure way for you to make these people like you is for you to first learn to like them. You know yourself it's difficult to dislike a person who likes you.

HOW TO MAKE A GOOD IMPRESSION

There are three things about you that make a lasting impression on those you meet.

1. Your personal appearance; whether you are well groomed.
2. Your manner; the poise with which you hold yourself.
3. Your speech; not only the correctness of your grammar, but your tone of voice.

Remember, it isn't important that you be handsome or beautiful. What do you want, however, is to be warm and affable. Went you enter a room, be sure to smile. When you meet someone for the first time, make a point of finding a topic that he or she would like to talk about and talk about that. If you don't have much expertise in that area, ask the other person questions. People enjoy sharing information about topics that interest them. If you're at a complete loss for words, offer a compliment. You can always tell someone that you like her necklace or his shoes. It's a way to break the ice and the recipient of the compliment will feel good about herself or himself. Lastly, always be positive. Negative comments may make you feel smart, but they don't make you look smart.

HOW TO DEVELOP YOUR PERSONALITY

We always want to work with people who do a good job and make our business thrive. And because we spend so much time at work, we also want to be surrounded by people who are pleasant to spend that time with. A study by the Carnegie Foundation revealed that in business, about 15 percent of one's success depends upon superior knowledge and about 85 percent is due to superior personality.

Dr Henry C Link, was an eminent psychologist who pioneered the idea of 'Employment Psychology.' Link also devised the Personality Quotient, a measurement of one's acquisition, through practice, of the skills that serve others. Link said, 'Personality is the extent to which a person has developed habits which interest and serve other people. Personality can be developed just as we develop the habits of writing the ABCs or eating with a knife and fork. No one is born with the natural ability to eat with a knife and fork or with the ABCs in his head. No one is born with a good personality. It develops by practice.'

Here are some of the ways that Dr Link advises us to develop and practice our personality. First, at least once a week, play games that require physical exertion and other games that just revolve around a matching of wits, such as bridge, chess or competitive video games. Competitive contacts (either physical or mental) with other people can further your sense of good sportsmanship and will help you to develop unselfish habits. They will teach you to obey the rules of good social behavior, will add great deal to the charm of your personality and will win many friends.

The second is to do something for other people. Teach a Sunday school class. Solicit funds for the Red Cross or another charitable organisation. Become active in the Boy Scouts or Girl

Scouts. The main thing is to go out and do something for other people.

Third, stay interested in your job. Learn to do your job especially well. Put your heart and soul into your work. Focussing on the excellence of your work will keep you from thinking about yourself. As your selflessness grows, you will find that others are increasingly attracted to you. Your success at work will grow as well.

POISE

Today, we don't talk much about being well poised. In fact, from the behaviour you see on reality shows, you'd almost think that lack of poise is an asset. Yet in the business world and certainly the international business world, having poise is critical to gaining the respect of others.

Think about your friends and the people you work with. How many people do you know who are well poised? Are you? It is surprising how many people lack poise. Poise is not difficult to acquire, but it never will be acquired through thinking of yourself or how you appear to others or what impression you are making.

Years ago, President Woodrow Wilson admitted that he had despaired in his early youth of ever overcoming his self-consciousness and lack of poise. So he sat down one day and thought it out with himself. Then he formed the habit of remaining quietly observant of those around him for a few seconds when in a social or political gathering. This gave him an opportunity to collect himself and he realised that the important thing was to think about other people and not himself. There is nothing old-fashioned about taking the time to be quiet and listen to others. His Holiness the Dalai Lama has observed that, 'sometimes one creates a dynamic impression by saying something and sometimes one creates as significant an impression by remaining silent.'

There are certain nervous affectations that may readily grow into common habits, hindering from acquiring poise and robbing you of attractiveness. Among them are:

1. Fumbling with a string of beads or other jewellery.
2. Pulling your tie.
3. Smoothing your clothing.
4. Checking your makeup in your pocket mirror or putting on lipstick.
5. Biting your lips or your nails.
6. Drumming with your fingers.
7. Tapping your feet as you sit.
8. Pacing up and down the room.
9. Looking at your smartphone when in a meeting or in a conversation with others.

When you are in the presence of other people, forget about your appearance and what the others might be thinking of you – concentrate all your thoughts on the others.

HOW TO KEEP FIT

While we're constantly being told to exercise and take better care of our bodies, the number of us who are out of shape is alarming. If you work out regularly, you know how good you feel as a result of your efforts. If you don't work out regularly, now is the time to start.

In addition to consistent physical exercise, here are a few other commonsense rules for good health offered by Dr Walter B. Pitkin, a psychologist and philosopher:

Rule 1 Relax at least once an hour. If you stand at your work, sit down, stretch out your legs and relax. If you sit at your work, get up, stretch and walk around. Remove the strain from the part of your body that you have been using.

Rule 2 Get enough sleep. Sleep is the greatest medicine in the world. Find out how much sleep you need and see that you get it. Go to bed at a regular hour every night.

Rule 3 Eat properly. Different kinds of work require different kinds of food. A man who does heavy manual labour needs plenty of nourishment, but office workers generally overeat. There are enough calories in a single salted peanut to take care of a man for two hours of intellectual work.

Rule 4 Take care of your teeth and gums. Go to your dentist regularly. Floss every day. Gum health is considered by many to be directly related to heart health.

Rule 5 Organise your work. Your mental health will remain strong if you deliberately avoid constant distractions. At the beginning of each day, outline the tasks you have to do and approach them methodically. You will be much more effective if you focus on one thing at a time, regardless of how tempting it is to check your email or Twitter feed every few minutes.

Rule 6 Allow yourself to heal. When you do get sick, stay home from work. You wouldn't expect a clock to run when it's out of order, so why should you expect this from your body? If you're sick, visit the doctor and follow his or her advice until you're well.

TIME – WHAT IT CAN DO FOR YOU

Time is something that everybody has, but few of us make the most of it. Years ago I was in Paris shopping for dinner and trying to buy some produce at the market. The vendor became impatient because I took so much time examining the different vegetables and he began talking to me at a furious rate. He was speaking French and I couldn't understand a word until finally he said in English, 'Time is money.' That expression is so well known that the French don't even try to translate it. Yes, time is money in every language as well as in every country. Time is even more than money, time is life itself. Bill Gates may possess more money than you, Hillary Clinton may have more power and George Clooney may have more fame, but no one has more time than you. You will never have more time than you have now. You must spend every last second of it every day. How you spend your spare time will very largely determine where you will be five years from now.

A few years ago, a man in one of my public speaking classes held up his hand and said, 'I don't know how I'll be a success in business. I never finished college.' I told him that he didn't need to necessarily go back to school – all he had to give was his leisure time. I reminded him that by devoting his leisure time to study he could, within a few years, have the equivalent of a college education.

The average college student does not spend every waking moment studying and attending classes. For the average person to better himself or herself, he or she has nearly as much time for study as the usual student does to devote to improving his mind. Today, on average, people have many hours left outside of the time that they take for work, sleeping and eating, that they can devote to any of their leisure occupations. The trouble is not that people don't have time. The trouble is that they do not do anything useful with it.

For example, social networking now consumes a great deal of our leisure time of many of us. There are all sorts of benefits from spending time on social media sites, but there is no reason not to balance that time with more productive pursuits. We can devote a few hours to study and self-improvement and then give ourselves thirty minutes on facebook. Similarly, we don't actually need to watch three hours of television on any given night. If this is your habit, ask yourself, 'Do I feel accomplished as I go to bed at night?' Chances are you feel as though the evening just passed you by. But in reality, you passed the evening fruitlessly, the evening didn't leave you behind somehow.

As a young man many years ago, George Eastman, of Eastman Kodak fame, worked all day in an insurance office and then worked most of the night developing his idea for making photographic films. And, as is often the case, George Eastman didn't have to do this all his life. His business expanded until he finally became the greatest camera manufacturer in the world. He then had leisure for travel and music and the things that he loved. He looked after his time. His time looked after him. The example Eastman provides is as valid today as it was in his era. Successful individuals will certainly devote some time to relaxation and rejuvenation, but they do not spend time in idle pursuits.

Your time is without a doubt the most valuable thing you possess. Make it work for you.

THREE

Developing Courage and Self-Confidence Through Public Speaking

'The ability to speak effectively is an acquirement rather than a gift.' – William Jennings Bryan

More than seven thousand business professionals, since 1912, have been members of the various public speaking courses conducted by the author. Most of them have, at his request, written stating why they had enrolled for this training and what they hoped to obtain from it. Naturally, the phraseology varied; but the central desire in these letters, the basic want in the vast majority, remained surprisingly the same: 'When I am called upon to stand up and speak,' man after man wrote, 'I become so self-conscious, so frightened, that I can't think clearly, can't concentrate, can't remember what I had intended to say. I want to gain self-confidence, poise and the ability to think on my feet. I want to get my thoughts together in logical order and

I want to be able to say my say clearly and convincingly before a business group or audience.' Gaining self-confidence and courage and the ability to think calmly and clearly while talking to a group is not one-tenth as difficult as most people imagine. It is not a gift bestowed by providence on only a few rarely endowed individuals. It is like the ability to play golf. Anyone can develop his own latent capacity if they have sufficient desire to do so.

Is there the faintest shadow of a reason why you should not be able to think as well in a perpendicular position before an audience as you can when sitting down? Surely, you know there is not. In fact, you ought to think better when facing a group of men. Their presence ought to stir you and lift you. A great many speakers will tell you that the presence of an audience is a stimulus, an inspiration, that drives their brains to function more clearly, more keenly. At such times, thoughts, facts, ideas, that they did not know they possessed, drift smoking by, as Henry Ward Beecher said; and they have but to reach out and lay their hands hot upon them, That ought to be your experience. It probably will be if you practice and persevere.

Of this much, however, you may be absolutely sure: Training and practice will wear away your audience-fright and give you self-confidence and an abiding courage.

After watching the careers and aiding somewhat in the development of so many speakers, the author is always glad when a student has, at the outset, a certain amount of flutter and nervous agitation.

There is a certain responsibility in making a talk, even if it is to only two dozen men in a business conference – certain strain, a certain shock, a certain excitement. The speaker ought to be keyed up like a thoroughbred straining at the bit. The immortal Cicero said, two thousand years ago, that all public speaking of real merit was characterised by nervousness.

Some men, no matter how often they speak, always experience this self-consciousness just before they commence but, in a few seconds after they have gotten on their feet, it disappears.

In order to learn the vital skill of public speaking, four things are essential:

First: Start with a Strong and Persistent Desire

This is of far more importance than you probably realise. If your instructor could look into your mind and heart now and ascertain the depth of your desires, he could foretell, almost with certainty, the swiftness of the progress you will make. If your desire is pale and flabby, your achievements will also take on that hue and consistency. But, if you go after this subject with persistence and with the energy of a bulldog after a cat, nothing underneath the Milky Way will defeat you.

Therefore, arouse your enthusiasm for this study. Enumerate its benefits. Think of what additional self-confidence and the ability to talk more convincingly in business will mean to you. Think of what it may mean and what it ought to mean, in dollars and cents. Think of what it may mean to you socially; of the friends it will bring, of the increase of your personal influence, of the leadership it will give you. And it will give you leadership more rapidly than almost any other activity you can think of or imagine.

Think of the glow of satisfaction and pleasure that will accrue from the exercise of this new power. The author has travelled around over no small part of this terrestrial ball; and has had many and varied experiences; but for downright and lasting inward satisfaction, he knows of few things that will compare to standing before an audience and making men think your thoughts after you. It will give you a sense of strength, a feeling of power. It will appeal to your pride of personal accomplishment. It will set you off from and raise you above your fellow-men. There is magic in it and a never-to-be-forgotten thrill. 'Two minutes before I begin,' a speaker confessed, 'I would rather be whipped than start; but two minutes before I finish, I would rather be shot than stop.'

In every endeavour, some men grow faint-hearted and fall by the wayside; so you should keep thinking of what this skill will mean to you until your desire is white-hot.

Second: Know Thoroughly What You Are Going To Talk About

Unless a man has thought out and planned his talk and knows what he is going to say, he can't feel very comfortable when he faces his auditors. He is like the blind leading the blind. Under such circumstances, your speaker ought to be self-conscious, ought to feel repentant, ought to be ashamed of his negligence.

'I was elected to the Legislature in the fall of 1881,' Roosevelt records in his *Autobiography*, 'and found myself the youngest man in that body. Like all young men and inexperienced members, I had considerable difficulty in teaching myself to speak. I profited much by the advice of a hard-headed old countryman – who was unconsciously paraphrasing the Duke of Wellington, who was himself doubtless paraphrasing somebody else. The advice ran: 'Don't speak until you are sure you have something to say and know just what it is; then say it and sit down.'

This 'hard-headed old countryman' ought to have told Roosevelt of another aid in overcoming nervousness. He ought to have added: 'It will help you to throw off your embarrassment if you can find something to do before an audience – if you can exhibit something, write a word on the blackboard or point out a spot on the map or move a table or throw open a window or shift some books and papers – any physical action with a purpose behind it may help you to feel more at home.'

True, it is not always easy to find an excuse for doing such things; but there is the suggestion. Use it if you can; but use it the first few times only. A baby does not cling to chairs after it once learns to walk.

Third: Act Confident

Professor William James, wrote as follows:

'Action seems to follow feeling, but really action and feeling go together; and by regulating the action, which is under the more direct control of the will, we can indirectly regulate the feeling, which is not.

'Thus the sovereign voluntary path to cheerfulness, if our spontaneous cheerfulness be lost, is to sit up cheerfully and to act and speak as if cheerfulness were already there. If such conduct does not make you feel cheerful, nothing else on that occasion can.

'So, to feel brave, act as if we were brave, use all of our will to that end and a courage-fit will very likely replace the fit of fear.'

Apply Professor James' advice. To develop courage when you are facing an audience, act as if you already had it. Of course, unless you are prepared, all the acting in the world will be of little value. But granted that you know what you are going to talk about, step out briskly and take a deep breath. In fact, breathe deeply for thirty seconds before you ever face your audience. The increased supply of oxygen will buoy you up and give you courage. The great tenor, Jean de Reszke, used to say that, when you held your breath so you 'could sit on it,' nervousness vanished.

Draw yourself up to your full height and look your audience straight in the eyes and begin to talk as confidently as if every one of them owed you money. Imagine that they do. Imagine that they have assembled there to beg you for an extension of credit. The psychological effect on you will be beneficial.

Do not nervously button and unbutton your coat and fumble with your hands. If you must make nervous movements, place your hands behind your back and twist your fingers there where no one can see the performance – or wiggle your toes.

As a general rule, it is bad for a speaker to hide behind furniture; but it may give you a little courage the first few times to stand behind a table or chair and to grip them tightly or hold a coin firmly in the palm of your hand.

Have a message and then think of yourself as a Western Union boy instructed to deliver it. We pay slight attention to the boy. It is the telegram that we want. The message – that is the thing. Keep your mind on it. Keep your heart in it. Know it like the back of your hand. Believe it feelingly. Then talk as if you were determined to say it. Do that and the chances are ten to one that you will soon be master of the occasion and master of yourself.

Fourth: Practice! Practice! Practice!

The last point we have to make here is emphatically the most important. Even though you forget everything you have read so far, do remember this: the first way, the last way, the never-failing way to develop self-confidence in speaking is – to speak. Really the whole matter finally simmers down to but one essential; practice, practice, practice. That is the *sine qua non* of it all, 'the without which not.'

'Any beginner,' warned Roosevelt, 'is apt to have "buck fever." "Buck fever" means a state of intense nervous excitement, which may be entirely divorced from timidity. It may affect a man the first time he has to speak to a large audience just as it may affect him the first time he sees a buck or goes into battle. What such a man needs is not courage, but nerve control, cool headedness. *This he can get only by actual practice. He must, by custom and repeated exercise of self-mastery, get his nerves thoroughly under control. This is largely a matter of habit; in the sense of repeated effort and repeated exercise of will power. If the man has the right stuff in him, he will grow stronger and stronger with each exercise of it.*'

You want to get rid of your audience fear? You must first know what causes it.

To put it simply: it is the result of a lack of confidence.

And what causes that? It is the result of not knowing what you can really do. And not knowing what you can do is caused by a lack of experience. When you get a record of successful experience behind you, your fears will vanish; they will melt like night mists under the glare of a July sun.

FOUR

Preparing Your Talk

SELF-CONFIDENCE THROUGH PREPARATION

It has been the author's professional duty as well as his pleasure to listen to and criticise approximately six thousand speeches a year each season since 1912. These were made, not by college students, but by mature business professionals. If that experience has engraved on his mind any one thing more deeply than another, surely it is this: the urgent necessity of preparing a talk before one starts to make it and of having something clear and definite to say, something that has impressed one, something that won't stay unsaid. Aren't you unconsciously drawn to the speaker who, you feel, has a real message in his head and heart that he zealously desires to communicate to your head and heart? That is half the secret of speaking.

When a speaker is in that kind of mental and emotional state he will discover a significant fact. Namely, that his talk will almost make itself. Its yoke will be easy, its burden will be light. A well-prepared speech is already nine-tenths delivered.

Why don't some speakers prepare their talks more carefully?

Why? Some don't clearly understand what preparation is or how to go about it wisely; others plead a lack of time.

The Right Way to Prepare

What is preparation? Reading a book? That is one kind, but not the best. Reading may help; but if one attempts to lift many 'canned' thoughts out of a book and to give them out immediately as his own, the whole performance will be lacking in something. The audience may not know precisely what is lacking, but they will not warm to the speaker.

What Preparation Really Is

Does the preparation of a speech mean the getting together of some faultless phrases written down or memorised? No. Does it mean the assembling of a few casual thoughts that really convey very little to you personally? Not at all. It means the assembling of *your* thoughts, *your* ideas, *your* convictions and *your* urges. And you have such thoughts, such urges. You have them every day of your waking life. They even swarm through your dreams. Your whole existence has been filled with feelings and experiences. These things are lying deep in your subconscious mind as thick as pebbles on the seashore. Preparation means thinking, brooding, recalling, selecting the ones that appeal to you most, polishing them, working them into a pattern, a mosaic of your own. That doesn't sound like such a difficult program, does it? It isn't. Just requires a little concentration and thinking to a purpose.

HOW TO PREPARE YOUR TALK

Don't make the almost universal mistake of trying to cover too much ground in a brief talk. Just take one or two angles of a subject and attempt to cover them adequately. You will be fortunate if you can do that in the short speeches that are necessitated by the time schedule of this course.

Determine your subject a week in advance, so that you will have time to think it over in odd moments. Think over it for seven days; dream over it for seven nights. Think of it the last thing when you retire. Think of it the next morning while you are shaving, while you are bathing, while you are riding downtown, while you are waiting for elevators, for lunch, for appointments. Discuss it with your friends. Make it a topic of conversation.

Ask yourself all possible questions concerning it. If, for example, you are to speak on divorce, ask yourself what causes divorce, what are the effects economically, socially? How can the evil be remedied? Should we have uniform divorce laws? Why? Or should we have any divorce laws? Should divorce be made impossible? More difficult? Easier?

Above all else, don't make your talk an abstract preachment. That will bore us. Make your talk a regular layer cake of illustrations and general statements. Think of concrete cases you have observed and of the fundamental truths, which you believe those specific instances, illustrate. You will also discover that these concrete cases are far easier to remember than abstractions; are far easier to talk about. They will also aid and brighten your delivery.

Some men, in speaking of their businesses, commit the unforgivable error of talking only of the features that interest them. Shouldn't the speaker try to ascertain what will entertain not himself but the members his audience? Shouldn't he try to appeal to their selfish interests? If, for example, he sells fire insurance, shouldn't he tell them how to prevent fires on their own property? If he is a banker, shouldn't he give them advice on finance or investments? While preparing, study your audience.

Think of their wants, their wishes. That is sometimes half the battle.

In preparing some topics, it is very advisable – if time permits – to do some reading, to discover what others have thought, what others have said on the same subject. But don't read until you have first thought yourself dry.

The Secret of Reserve Power

Luther Burbank said, shortly before his death: 'I have often produced a million plant specimens to find but one or two superlatively good ones and have then destroyed all the inferior specimens.' A speech ought to be prepared somewhat in that lavish and discriminating spirit. Assemble a hundred thoughts and discard ninety.

Collect more material, more information, than there is any possibility of employing. Get it for the additional confidence it will give you, for the sureness of touch. Get it for the effect it will have on your mind and heart and whole manner of speaking. This is a basic, important factor of preparation; yet speakers, both in public and private, constantly ignore it.

'What!' you object. 'Does this author imagine that I can find time for all this? I would like him to know that I have a business to conduct and a wife and two children and a couple of Airedale dogs to support. I can't be running to museums and reading books and sitting up in bed at daylight mumbling my speeches.'

If you procrastinate until you have leisure to prepare and plan your talk, the leisure will probably never be found. However, it is easy to do the habitual, the accustomed thing, isn't it? So why not set aside one specific evening a week, from eight to ten o'clock, to be devoted to nothing but this task? That is the sure way, the systematic way. Why not try it?

No sane man would start to build a house without some sort of plan; but why will he begin to deliver a speech without the vaguest kind of outline or program?

A speech is a voyage with a purpose and it must be charted. The man who starts nowhere, generally gets there.

I wish that I could paint this saying of Napoleon's in flaming letters of red a foot high over every doorway on the globe where students of public speaking foregather: 'The art of war is a science in which nothing succeeds which has not been calculated and thought out.'

That is just as true of speaking as of shooting. But do speakers realise it – or; if they do – do they always act on it? They do not. Most emphatically they do not. Many a talk has just a trifle more plan and arrangement than a bowl of Irish stew.

What is the best and most effective arrangement for a given set of ideas? No one can say until he has studied them. It is always a new problem, an eternal question that every speaker must ask and answer himself again and again.

There are no designs or schemes or charts that will fit all or even a majority of speeches; yet here are a few speech plans that will prove usable in some instances. State your facts.

1. Argue from them.
2. Appeal for action.

Many students of my public speaking course have found this plan very helpful and stimulating.

1. Show something that is wrong.
2. Show how to remedy it.
3. Ask for cooperation.

Or, to put it in another way:

1. Here is a situation that ought to be remedied.
2. We ought to do so and so about the matter.
3. You ought to help for these reasons.

The section How To Get Action below outlines still another speech plan. Briefly it is this:

1. Secure interested attention.
2. Win confidence.
3. State your facts; educate people regarding the merits of your proposition.
4. Appeal to the motives that make men act. If interested, turn now to that section and study this plan in detail.

Play Solitaire With Your Notes

You were advised to research your topic thoroughly and to make notes. Having gotten your various ideas and illustrations down on scraps of paper, play solitaire with them – toss them into series of related piles. These main piles ought to represent, approximately, the main points of your talk. Subdivide them into smaller lots. Throw out the chaff until there is nothing but number one wheat left-and even some of the wheat will probably have to be put aside and not used. No man, if he works right, is ever able to use but a percentage of the material he gathers.

One ought never to cease this process of revision until the speech has been made-even then he is very likely to think of points and improvements and refinements that ought to have been made.

A good speaker usually finds when he finishes that there have been four versions of his speech. The one that he prepared, the one that he delivered, the one that the newspapers said that he delivered and the one that he wishes, on his way home, that he had delivered.

'Shall I Use Notes While Speaking?'

Although he was an excellent impromptu speaker, Lincoln, after he reached the White House, never made any address, not even an informal talk to his cabinet, until he had carefully put it all down in writing beforehand. Of course, he was obliged to read his inaugural addresses. The exact phraseology of historical state papers of that character is too important to be left to extemporising. Yet, back in Illinois, Lincoln never used even notes in his speaking. 'They always tend to tire and confuse the listener,' he said.

And who of us, pray, would contradict him? Don't notes destroy about fifty per cent of your interest in a talk? Don't they prevent, or at least render difficult, a very precious contact and intimacy that ought to exist between the speaker and the audience? Don't they create an air of artificiality? Don't they restrain an audience from feeling that the speaker has the confidence and reserve power that he ought to have?

Make notes, I repeat, during the preparation – elabourate ones, profuse ones. You may wish to refer to them when you are practicing your talk alone. You may possibly feel more comfortable if you have them stored away in your pocket when you are facing an audience. Hoever, like the hammer and saw and axe in a Pullman coach, they should be emergency tools, only for use in the case of a smash-up, a total wreck and threatening death and disaster.

If you must use notes, make them extremely brief and write them in large letters on an ample sheet of paper. Then arrive early at the place where you are to speak and hide your notes behind some books on a table. Glance at them when you must, but endeavour to screen your weakness from the audience. John Bright used to secret his notes in his big hat lying on the table before him.

However in spite of all that has been said there may be times when it is the part of wisdom to use notes. For example, some men during their first few talks, are so nervous and self-conscious that they are utterly unable to remember their prepared speeches. The result? They shoot off at a tangent; they forget the material they had so carefully rehearsed; they drift off the high road and flounder about in a morass. Why should not such men hold a few very condensed notes in their hands during their maiden efforts? A child clutches the furniture when it is first attempting to walk; but it does not continue it very long.

Do Not Memorise Word For Word

Don't read and don't attempt to memorise your talk word for word. That consumes time and courts disaster. Yet, in spite of this warning, some of the men reading these lines will try it; if they do, when they stand up to speak what will they be thinking? Of their messages? No, they will be attempting to recall their exact phraseology. They will be thinking backwards, not forwards, reversing the usual processes of the human mind. The whole exhibition will be stiff, cold and colourless inhuman. Do not, I beg of you, waste hours and energy in such futility.

When you have an important business interview, do you sit down and memorise, verbatim, what you are going to say? Do you? Of course not. You reflect until you get your main ideas clearly in mind. You may make a few notes and consult some records. You say to yourself: 'I shall bring out this point and that. I am going to say that a certain thing ought to be done for these reasons. Then you enumerate the reasons to yourself and illustrate them with concrete cases. Isn't that the way you prepare for a business interview? Why not use the same common sense method in preparing a talk?

After you have your ideas firmly in mind, then rehearse your talk from beginning to end. Do it silently, mentally, as you walk the street, as you wait for cars and elevators. Get off in a room by yourself and go over it aloud, gesturing, saying it with life and energy. As you practice, imagine there is a real audience before you. Imagine it so strongly that when there is one, it will seem like an old experience. That is the reason why so many criminals are able to go to the scaffold with such bravado; they have already done it so many thousand times in their imagination that they have lost fear of it. When the actual execution does take place, it seems like something that they have gone through very often before.

Study the careers of famous speakers and you will find one fact that is true of them all: *they practiced*. THEY PRACTISED. And the men who make the most rapid progress in this course are those who practice most.

No time for all this? We all have three hours a day that we can do with as we please. That was all Darwin had to work with as he had poor health. Three hours out of twenty-four, wisely used, made him famous.

You must have relaxation and a change from your regular work. That is what the practising of your talks ought to be.

THE IMPROVEMENT OF MEMORY

> *The man whose acquisitions stick is the man who is always achieving and advancing whilst his neighbours, spending*

most of their time in relearning what they once knew, but have forgotten, simply hold their own.

– Professor William James

'The average man,' says the noted psychologist, Professor Carl Seashore, 'does not use above ten per cent of his actual inherited capacity for memory. He wastes the ninety per cent by violating the natural laws of remembering.'

Are you one of these average men? If so, you are struggling under a handicap socially and commercially; consequently, you will be interested in and profit by, reading and rereading this section. It describes and explains these natural laws of remembering and shows how to use them in business as well as in speaking.

These 'natural laws of remembering' are very simple. There are only three. Every so-called 'memory system' has been founded upon them. Briefly, they are impression, repetition and association.

The first mandate of memory is: get a deep, vivid and lasting *impression* of the thing you wish to retain. And to do that, you must concentrate. Five minutes of vivid, energetic concentration will produce greater results than days of mooning about in a mental haze.

This is one of the secrets of power, especially memory power.

Introduce the average man to two or three of your friends and, the chances are, that two minutes afterwards he cannot recall the name of a single one of them. And why? Because he never paid sufficient attention to them in the first place, he never accurately observed them. He will likely tell you he has a poor memory. No, he has a poor observation. He would not condemn a camera because it failed to take pictures in a fog, but he expects his mind to retain impressions that are hazy and foggy to a degree. Of course, it can't be done.

Accuracy is what we want. Hear the man's name precisely. Insist on it. Ask him to repeat it. Inquire how it is spelled. He will be flattered by your interest and you will be able to remember his name because you have concentrated on it. You have got a clear accurate impression.

The ideal thing would be not only to see and hear the thing to be remembered, but to touch it and smell it and taste it.

But, above all else, see it. We are visual minded. Eye impressions stick. We can often remember a man's face, even though we cannot recall his name. The nerves that lead from the eye to the brain are twenty times as large as those leading from the car to the brain. The Chinese have a proverb that says 'one time seeing is worth a thousand times hearing.'

Write down the name, the telephone number and the speech outline you want to remember. Look at it. Close your eyes. Visualise it in flaming letters of fire.

By *repetition*, the second 'natural law of remembering.'

You can memorise an almost endless amount of material if you will repeat it often enough. Go over the knowledge you want to remember. Use it. Apply it. Employ the new word in your conversation. Call the stranger by his name if you want to remember it. Talk over in conversation the points you want to make in your public address. The knowledge that is used tends to stick.

The Kind of Repetition That Counts

Yet the mere blind, mechanical going over a thing by rote is not enough. Intelligent repetition, repetition done in accordance with certain well-established traits of the mind – that is what we must have. We know now that the man who sits down and repeats a thing over and over until he finally fastens it in his memory, is using twice as much time and energy as is necessary to achieve the same results when the repeating process is done at judicious intervals.

This peculiarity of the mind – if we can call it such – can be explained by two factors.

First, during the intervals between repetitions, our subconscious minds are busy making the associations more secure. Second, the mind, coming to the task at intervals, is not fatigued by the strain of an unbroken application. Surely, now, in the face of these facts, no man who prides himself on his common sense will delay the preparation of a talk until the night before it is to be given. If he does, his memory will, of necessity, be working at only one-half its possible efficiency.

Here is a very helpful discovery about the way in which we forget. Psychological experiments have repeatedly shown that of the new material we have learned, we forget more during the first eight hours than during the next thirty days. An amazing ratio! So, immediately before you go into a business conference, immediately before you make a speech, look over your data, think over your facts and refresh your memory.

Association: How to Link Your Facts Together. So much for the first two laws of remembering. The third one, *association*, however, is the indispensable element in recalling. In fact, it is the explanation of memory itself. So how are we to set about weaving our facts into systematic relations with each other? The answer is: by finding their meaning, by thinking them over. For example, if you will ask and answer these questions about any new fact, that process will help to weave it into a systematic relation with other facts.

a. Why is this so?

b. How is this so?
c. When is it so?
d. Where is it so?
e. Who said it is so?

If it is a stranger's name, for example and it is a common one, we can perhaps tie it to some business friend who bears the same name. On the other hand, if it is unusual, we can take occasion to say so. This often leads the stranger to talk about his name. For example: while writing this chapter, I was introduced to a Mrs Soter. I requested her to spell the name and remarked upon its unusualness. 'Yes,' she replied, 'it is very uncommon. It is a Greek word meaning 'the saviour'.' Then she told me about her husband's people who had come from Athens and of the high positions they had held in the government there. I have found it quite easy to get people to talk about their names and it always helps me to remember them.

Observe the stranger's look sharply. Note the colour of his eyes and his hair and look closely at his features. Note how he is dressed. Listen to his manner of talking. Get a clear, keen, vivid impression of his looks and personality and associate these with his name. The next time these sharp impressions return to your mind, they will help bring the name with them.

Haven't you had the experience, when meeting a man for the second or third time, to discover that although you could remember his business or profession, you could not recall his name? The reason is this: a man's business is something definite and concrete. It has a meaning. It will adhere like a court plaster while his meaningless name will roll away like hail failing on a steep roof. Consequently, to make sure of your ability to recall a man's name, fashion a phrase about it that will tie it up to his business. There can be no doubt whatever about the efficacy of this method. For example, twenty men, strangers to one another, recently met in the Penn Athletic Club of Philadelphia to study this course. Each man was asked to rise, announce his name and business. A phrase was then manufactured to connect the two; and, within a few minutes, each person present could repeat the name of every other individual in the room. Even to the end of the course, neither the names nor businesses were forgotten, for they were linked together. They adhered.

How to Remember Dates

Connecting them with important dates already firmly established in the mind can best retain dates. Isn't it far more difficult, for example, for an American to remember that the Suéz Canal was opened in 1869 than to remember that the first ship passed through it four years after the close of the Civil War? If an American tried to remember that the first settlement in Australia was made in 1788, the date is likely to drop out of his mind like a loose bolt out of a car; it is far more likely to stick if he thinks of it in connection with 1776 and remembers that it occurred years after the Declaration of Independence. That is like screwing a nut on the loose bolt it holds.

It is well to bear this principle in mind when you are selecting a telephone number. For example, the writer's phone number, during the war, was 1776. No one had difficulty in remembering it. If you can secure from the phone company some such number as 1492, 1861, 1865, 1914, 1918, your friends will not have to consult the directory. They might forget that your phone number was 1492, if YOU gave them the information in a colourless fashion; but would it slip their minds if you said, 'You can easily remember my phone number; 1492, the year Columbus discovered America.'

The Australians, New Zealanders and Canadians who are reading these lines would, of course, substitute 1776, 1861, 1865 with significant dates in their own history.

How to Remember the Points of Your Talk

There are only two ways by which we can possibly think of a thing: first, by means of an outside stimulus; second, by association with something already in the mind. Applied to speeches, that means just this: first, you can recall your points by the aid of some outside stimulus such as notes – but who likes to see a speaker use notes? Second, you can remember your points by associating them with something already in the mind. They should be arranged in such a logical order that the first one leads inevitably to the second and the second to the third as naturally as the door of one room leads into another.

That sounds simple, but it may not prove so for the beginner whose thinking powers are rendered *hors de combat* with fear. There is, however, a method of tying your points together that is easy, rapid and all but foolproof. I refer to the use of a nonsense sentence. To illustrate: suppose you wish to discuss a veritable jumble of ideas, unassociated and hence hard to remember, such as, for example, *cow, cigar, Napoleon, house, religion*. Let us see if we cannot weld those ideas like the links of a chain by means of this absurd sentence: 'The cow smoked a cigar and hooked Napoleon and the house burned down with religion.'

Now, will you please cover the above sentence with your hand while you answer these questions? What is the third point in that talk; the fifth; fourth; second; first?

Does the method work? It does! And the members of this course are urged to use it.

Any group of ideas can be linked together in some such fashion. The more ridiculous the sentence used for the linking, the easier it will be to recall.

What To Do in Case of a Complete Breakdown

Let us suppose that, in spite of all the preparation and precaution, a speaker, in the middle of the talk, suddenly finds the mind a blank – suddenly staring at the audience completely balked, unable to go on – a terrifying situation. Pride rebels at sitting down in confusion and defeat. He feels that he might be able to think of his next point, of some point, if he had only ten, fifteen seconds of grace; but even fifteen seconds of frantic silence before an audience would be little less than disastrous. What is to be done? When a certain well known US Senator recently found himself in this situation he asked his audience if he were speaking loudly enough, if he could be heard distinctly in the back of the room. He knew that he was. He was not seeking information. He was seeking time. In that momentary pause, he grasped his thought and proceeded.

Perhaps the best lifesaver in such a mental hurricane is this: use the last word, or phrase, or idea in your last sentence for the beginning of a new sentence. This will make an endless chain that, like Tennyson's brook and, I regret to say, with as little purpose as Tennyson's brook, will run on forever. While the speaker is saying these platitudes off the top of his mind, he should, at the same time, be thinking hard of the next point in his planned speech, of the thing he had originally intended to say.

This endless chain method of talking will, if continued very long, trap the speaker into discussing plum pudding or the price of canary birds. However, it is a splendid first aid to the injured mind broken down temporarily through forgetfulness.

It has been the means of resuscitating many a gasping and dying speech.

We Cannot Improve Our Memories For All Classes Of Things

I have pointed out in this chapter how we may improve our *methods* of getting vivid impressions, of repeating and of tying our facts together. Yet memory is so essentially a matter of association that 'there can be,' as Professor James points out, 'no improvement of the general or elementary faculty of memory; there can only be improvement of our memory for special systems of associated things.'

By memorising, for instance, a quotation a day from Shakespeare, we may improve our memory for literary quotations to a surprising degree. Each additional quotation will find many friends in the mind to tie to. But the memorising of everything from Hamlet to Romeo will not necessarily aid one in retaining facts about the cotton market or the Bessemer process for desiliconising pig iron.

Let us repeat: if we apply and use the principles discussed in this chapter, we will improve our *manner* and *efficiency* for memorising anything; but, if we do not apply these principles, then the memorising of ten million facts about baseball will not help us in the slightest in memorising facts about the stock market. Such unrelated data cannot be tied together. 'Our mind is essentially an associating machine.'

DEVELOPING ENTHUSIASM: THE SECRET TO KEEPING YOUR AUDIENCE AWAKE

'Every great movement in the annals of history,' said Emerson, 'is the triumph of enthusiasm.'

It is derived, that magic name, from two Greek words: *en*, meaning in; and *theos*, meaning God. Enthusiasm is literally *God in* us. The enthusiastic man is one who speaks as if God possessed him.

This quality is the most effective, the most important factor in advertising and selling goods and getting things done. The largest advertiser of any single product in the world came to Chicago thirty years ago with less than fifty dollars in his pocket. Wrigley now sells thirty million dollars worth of his chewing gum every year and on the wall of his private office hang these framed words of Emerson: 'Nothing great was ever achieved without enthusiasm.'

There was a time when I put considerable reliance in the *rules* of public speaking; but with the passing of the years I have come to put more and more faith in the *spirit* of speaking.

This is a most important fact to remember: every time we speak we determine the attitude of our hearers. We hold them in the hollow of our hands. If we are lackadaisical, they will be lackadaisical. If we are reserved, they will be reserved. If we are only mildly concerned, they will be only mildly concerned. But if we are deadly in earnest about what we say and if we say it with feeling and spontaneity and force and contagious conviction, they cannot keep from catching our spirit to a degree.

Given heat and earnestness and enthusiasm, a speaker's influence expands like steam. Passion...Feeling...Spirit...Emotional Sincerity – get these qualities in your talk. Your auditors will condone-yes, will hardly be conscious of – minor shortcomings. You must have something that you very much want to say

'Ah, very good,' you say, 'but how am I to develop this earnestness and spirit and enthusiasm that you praise so highly?' This much is sure: you will never develop it by talking from the surface. Any discerning listener can detect whether a speaker is talking from skin-deep impressions or whether his expression is welling up from deep within him. So shake yourself out of your inertia. Put your heart in your work. Dig. Seek for the hidden resources that lie buried away inside you. Get the facts and the causes behind the facts. Concentrate. Dwell on them, brood over them until they matter to you. In the last analysis, you see it is all conditioned back upon thorough preparation and the right kind of preparation. Heart preparation is as essential as head preparation. 'I must live,' cried a young man to Voltaire; and the philosopher replied. 'I do not perceive the necessity.'

That, in many instances, will be the attitude of the world towards what you have to say: it won't perceive the necessity of its being said. But you, if you would succeed, must *feel* the necessity – if there is one. The thing ought to grip you. It ought, for the time being, to seem to you like the most important thing on *terra firma*.

Generating heart-felt earnestness is a fundamental part of preparation. As we learned earlier, the preparation of a speech, a real speech, does not consist in merely getting some mechanical words down on paper, nor of memorising phrases. Neither does it consist in lifting a few thoughts second hand from some book or newspaper article. No, no. However it does consist in digging away down deep into your own mind and heart and life to bring forth some enthusiasms and convictions that are essentially yours. Yours! YOURS! Dig. Dig. Dig. It is there. Never doubt it. Mines of it, quantities of it, of whose existence you have never even dreamed. Do you, yourself, realise the strength of your own potentialities? I doubt it. The late Professor James said that the average man does not develop more than ten per cent of his possible mental powers. Worse than an eight-cylinder machine with only one cylinder sparking!

Yes, the great thing in a speech is not the cold phraseology, but the man, the spirit, the convictions behind that phraseology. Always remember that *you* are the most important factor in your talk. Hear these golden words from Emerson! They contain a world of wisdom: '*Use what language you will, you can never say anything but what you are.*' That is one of the most significant statements I ever heard about the art of self-expression; and, for the sake of emphasis, I am going to repeat it: '*Use what language you will, you can never say anything but what you are.*'

I hope that I have made plain that the first requisite in generating your warmth and enthusiasm is to prepare until you have a real message you want to share. Now to continue this process to the next step.

Act in Earnest

To feel earnest and enthusiastic, stand up and *act* in earnest and *be* enthusiastic. Stop leaning against the table. Stand tall. Stand still. Don't rock back and forth. Don't bob up and down. Don't shift your weight from one foot to the other and back again like a tired horse. In short, don't make a lot of nervous movements, which will proclaim your lack of ease and self-possession to the housetops. Control yourself physically. It will convey a sense of poise and power. Stand up and stand out 'like a strong man rejoicing to run a race.' I repeat: fill your lungs with oxygen. Fill them to the full. Look straight at your audience. Look at them as if you had something urgent to say and as if you knew it was urgent. Look at them with the confidence and courage of a teacher viewing his pupils, for you *are* a teacher and they are there to hear you and to be taught. So speak out confidently and with energy. And use emphatic gestures. Never mind, just now, whether they are beautiful or graceful. Think only of making them forceful and spontaneous. Make them now, not for the sense they will convey to others, but for what they will do for you. And they will do wonders. Even if you are speaking to a radio audience, gesture, gesture. Your gestures won't, of course, be visible to the unseen hearers, but the result of your gestures will be audible to them. They will give increased aliveness and energy to your tones and to your whole manner.

Above all else, open your mouth and speak out. I recently listened to a public address by the head of a great university. I sat in the fourth row and could hardly hear more than half he said. The ambassador of an important European nation recently delivered the commencement address before Union College; his delivery was so flabby that his words were almost inaudible twenty feet from the platform.

If experienced speakers commit such errors, what is to be expected of the beginner? He is not used to having his voice enlarged so that it will carry over an audience; so, when he speaks with sufficient vitality, he will imagine that he is fairly shouting and that people are ready to laugh at him.

Use conversational tones; but enlarge them. Intensify them. We can read fine print a foot from the eye; but it takes bold headlines to be seen across a hall.

'Weasel Words' and Onions

Put energy behind what you say and say it positively. Yet don't be too positive. Only an ignoramus is positive about everything; but only a weakling prefaces every remark with an *it seems to me*, or *perhaps* or *in my opinion*.

The almost universal trouble with beginning speakers is not that they are too positive, but that they vitiate their talks with these timid phrases. I remember listening to a New York business man describe a motor trip through Connecticut. 'On the left side of the road,' he said, 'there *seemed* to be a field of onions.' Now, there is no *seeming* about onions. They either are or are not. And it does not require extraordinary powers to recognise an onion field when one sees it. Yet this shows to what absurd lengths a speaker will sometimes go.

'Weasel words' is what Roosevelt called such expressions, for a weasel sucks the heart out of an egg and leaves nothing but the empty shell. That is what these phrases do to your talk.

Shrinking, apologetic tones and eggshell phrases will riot display much confidence and conviction. Imagine business houses using such slogans as these: 'It seems to us the Underwood is the machine you will eventually buy.' 'In our opinion, the Prudential has the strength of Gibraltar.' 'We think you'll use our flour eventually – why not now?'

But do not, as I have said, be too positive on all occasions. There are times, there are places, there are subjects, there are audiences, where too much positive ness will hinder rather than help. In general, the higher the level of intelligence of one's hearers, the less successful mere forceful assertions will be. Thinking people want to be led, not driven. They want to have the facts presented and to draw their own conclusions. They like to be asked questions, not to have a ceaseless stream of direct statements poured at them.

Love Your Audience

A few years ago I had to employ and train a number of public lecturers in England. After painful and costly trials, three of them had to be dismissed and one had to be sent back three thousand miles to America. Their main trouble was that they were not genuinely interested in serving their audiences. They were chiefly concerned, not about others, but about themselves and their pay envelops. Everyone could feel it. They were cold to their audiences; and their audiences, in return, were cold to them.

The well-known human race is very quick to detect whether a talk is coming from above the eyebrows or back of the breastbone. Even a dog can sense that.

The finest thing in speaking is neither physical nor mental. It is spiritual. The Book that Daniel Webster had on his pillow while dying is a book that every speaker should have on his desk while living.

Jesus loved men and their hearts burned within them as He talked with them by the way. If you want a splendid text on public speaking, why not read your New Testament?

The Importance of Persistence

Years ago, when I first engaged in educational work, I was astounded to learn how large a percentage of students who enrolled in night schools of all sorts grew weary and fainted by the wayside before their goals were attained. The number is both lamentable and amazing. It is a sad commentary on human nature.

When we start to learn any new thing, like French, or golf or public speaking, we never advance steadily. We do not improve gradually. We do it by sudden jerks, by abrupt starts. Then we remain stationary a time, or we may even slip back and lose some of the ground we have previously gained. These periods of stagnation or retrogression, are well known by all psychologists; and they have been named 'plateaus in the curve of learning.' Students of public speaking will sometimes be stalled for weeks on one of these plateaus. Work as hard as they may, they cannot get off it. The weak ones give up in despair. Those with grit persist and they find that suddenly, overnight, without their knowing how or why it has happened, they have made great progress. They have lifted from the plateau like an aeroplane. Abruptly they have gotten the knack of the thing. Abruptly they have acquired naturalness and force and confidence in their speaking.

You may always, as we have noted elsewhere in these pages, experience some fleeting fear, some shock, some nervous anxiety the first few moments you face an audience. If only you persevere, you will soon eradicate everything but this initial fear. That will be initial fear and nothing more. After the first few sentences, you will have control of yourself. You will be speaking with positive pleasure.

I shall go so far as to say that if you pursue this course faithfully and with enthusiasm and keep right on practicing intelligently, you may confidently hope to wake up one fine morning and find yourself one of the competent speakers of your city or community.

Regardless of how fantastic that may sound to you now, *it is true as a general principle*. Exceptions, of course, there are. A man with an inferior mentality and personality and with nothing to talk about, is not going to develop into a local Daniel Webster. Yet, within reason, the assertion is correct.

The entire question of your success as a speaker hinges upon only two things – your native ability and the depth and strength of your desires.

'In almost any subject,' said Professor James, 'your passion for the subject will save you. If you only care enough for a result, you will most certainly attain it. If you wish to be rich, you will be rich; if you wish to be learned, you will be learned; if you wish to be good, you will be good. Only you must, then, really wish these things and wish them with exclusiveness and not wish at the same time a hundred other incompatible things just as strongly.'

And Professor James might have added, with equal truth, 'If you want to be a confident public speaker, you will be a confident public speaker. But you must *really* wish it.'

I have known and carefully watched literally thousands of men trying to gain self-confidence and the ability to talk in public. Those that succeeded were, in only a few instances, men of unusual brilliancy. For the most part, they were the ordinary run of businessmen that you will find in your own hometown. But they kept on. Smarter men sometimes got discouraged or too deeply immersed in moneymaking and they did not get very far; but the ordinary individuals with grit and singleness of purpose, at the end of the course they reach at the top.

That is only human and natural. Don't you see the same thing occurring all the time in commerce and the professions? Rockefeller said a long time ago that the first essential for success in business was patience. It is likewise one of the first essentials for success in this course.

Climbing the 'Wilder Kaiser'

A few summers ago, I started out to scale a peak in the Austrian Alps called the Wilder Kaiser. Baedecker said that the ascent was difficult and a guide was essential for amateur climbers. We, a friend and I, had none and we were certainly amateurs; so a third party asked us if we thought we were going to succeed. 'Of course,' we replied.

'What makes you think so?' he inquired.

'Others have done it without guides,' I said, 'so I know it is within reason and *I never undertake anything thinking defeat.*'

As an Alpinist, I am the merest, bungling novice; but that is the proper psychology for anything from essaying public speaking to an assault on Mount Everest.

Think success in this course. See yourself in your imagination talking in public with perfect self-control.

It is easily in your power to do this. Believe that you will succeed. Believe it firmly and you will then do what is necessary to bring success about.

FIVE

Delivering Your Talk

THE SECRET OF GOOD DELIVERY

There is something besides the mere words in a talk which counts. It is the flavour with which they are delivered. 'It is not so much what you say as how you say it.'

There is an old saying in the English Parliament that everything depends upon the manner in which one speaks and not upon the matter, Quintilian said that long ago when England was one of the outlying colonies of Rome.

Like most old sayings, it needs to be taken *cum grano salis*; but good delivery will make very thin matter go a very long way. I have often noticed in college contests that it is not always the speaker with the best material who wins. Rather, it is the speaker who can talk so well that his material sounds best.

WHAT IS DELIVERY?

What does a department store do when it 'do livers' the article you have bought? Does the driver just toss the package into the backyard and let it go at that? Is merely getting a thing out of one's own hands the same as getting it delivered?

The first essential of good talking is *a sense of communication.* The audience must feel that there is a message being delivered straight from the mind and heart of the speakers to their minds and their hearts. This matter of delivering a talk is, at the same time, a very simple and a very intricate process. It is also a very much misunderstood and abused one.

An enormous amount of nonsense and twaddle has been written about delivery. It has been shrouded in rules and rites and made mysterious. A modern audience, regardless of whether it is fifteen people at a business conference or a thousand people under a tent, wants the speaker to talk just as directly as he would in a chat. That is the same general manner that he would employ in speaking to one of them in conversation.

In the same *manner*, but not with the same amount of force. If he tries that, he will hardly be heard. In order to appear natural he has to use much more energy in talking to forty people than he does in talking to one; just as a statue on top of a building has to be of heroic size in order to make it appear of lifelike proportions to an observer on the ground.

Speak to the Chamber of Commerce just as you would to an ordinary individual. What is a meeting of the Chamber of Commerce, after all, but a mere collection of ordinary individuals? Won't the same methods that are successful with those men individually be successful with them collectively?

A good window does not call attention to itself. It merely lets in the light. A good speaker is the audiences so natural that the never notice the manner of speaking; they are conscious only of his matter.

HENRY FORD'S ADVICE

'All Ford cars are exactly alike,' said their maker, 'but no two men are just alike. Every new life is a new thing under the sun; there has never been anything just like it before and never will be again. A young man ought to get that idea about himself; he should look for the single spark of individuality that makes him different from other folks and develop that for all he is worth. Society and schools may try to iron it out of him; their tendency is to put us all in the same mould, but I say don't let that spark be lost; it's your only real claim to importance.'

All that is doubly true of public speaking. There is no other human being in the world like you. Hundreds of millions of people have two eyes and a nose and a mouth; but none of them look precisely like you. None of them have exactly your traits and methods and cast of mind. Few of them will talk and express themselves just as you do when you are speaking naturally. In other words, you have an individuality. As a speaker, it is your most precious possession. Cling to it. Cherish it. Develop it. It is the spark that will put force and sincerity into your speaking. 'It is your only real claim to importance.'

That is an easy direction to give. But is it an easy one to follow? Most emphatically it is not. It takes practice to be natural before an audience. Actors know that. When you were a little child, four years old, you probably could, had you but tried, have mounted a platform and 'recited' naturally to an audience. Yet when you are twenty-four, or forty-four, what will happen if you mount a platform and start to speak? Will you retain that unconscious naturalness that you possessed at four? You may, but it is dollars to doughnuts that you will become stiff and stilted and mechanical to draw back into yourself like a snapping turtle.

The problem of teaching or of training people in delivery is not one of superimposing additional characteristics. It is largely one of removing impediments, of freeing people, of getting them to speak with the same naturalness that they would display if someone were to knock them down.

Hundreds of times I have stopped speakers in the midst of their talks and implored them to 'talk like a human being.' Hundreds of nights I have come home mentally fatigued and nervously exhausted from trying to drill and force men to talk naturally. No, believe me, it is not so easy as it sounds.

The only way under high Heaven by which you can get the knack of this enlarged naturalness is by practice. As you practice, if you find yourself talking in a stilted manner, pause and say sharply to yourself mentally: 'Here! What is wrong? Wake up. Be human.' Then pick out some man in the audience, some man in the back, the dullest looking chap you can find and talk to him. Forget there is anyone else present at all. *Converse* with him. Imagine that he has asked you a question and that you are answering it. If he were to stand up and talk to you and you were to talk back to him, that process would immediately and inevitably make your talking more conversational, more natural, more direct. So, imagine that that is precisely what is taking place.

You may go so far as actually to ask questions and answer them. For example, in the midst of your talk, you may say, 'and you ask what proof have I for this assertion? I have adequate proof and here it is….' Then proceed to answer the imaginary question. That sort of thing can be done very naturally. It will break up the monotony of one's delivery; it will make it direct and pleasant and conversational.

Sincerity and enthusiasm and high earnestness will help you, too. When a man is under the influence of his feelings, his real self comes to the surface. The bars are down. The heat of his emotions has burned all barriers away. He acts spontaneously. He talks spontaneously. He is natural.

So, in the end, even this matter of delivery comes back to the thing which has already been emphasised repeatedly in these pages: namely, put your heart in your talks.

That is the secret. Yet I know that advice like this is not popular. It seems vague. It sounds indefinite. The average student wants foolproof rules. Something definite. Something he can put his hands on. Rules as precise as the directions for operating a Ford car.

That is what he wants. That is what I would like to give him. It would be easy for him. It would be easy for me. There are such rules and there is only one little thing wrong with them: they don't work. They take all the naturalness and spontaneity and life and juice out of a man's speaking. I know. In my younger days I wasted a great deal of energy trying them. They won't appear in these pages.

A speaker may follow the directions I have set down in this lesson and still have a hundred faults. He may talk in public just as he does in conversation and consequently, he may speak with an unpleasant voice and make grammatical errors and be awkward and offensive and do a score of unpleasant things. A man's natural method of every day talking may need a vast number of improvements. Perfect your natural method of talking in conversation and then carry that method to the platform.

PLATFORM PRESENCE AND PERSONALITY

Personality – with the exception of preparation – is probably the most important factor in public address. Yet personality is a vague and elusive thing, defying analysis like the perfume of the violet. It is the whole combination of the person, the physical, the spiritual, the mental; the traits, the predilections, the tendencies, the temperament, the cast of mind, the vigour, the experience, the training, the life. It is as complex as Einstein's theory of relativity, almost as little understood.

A personality is very largely the result of inheritances. It is largely determined before birth. True, later environment has something to do with it. But, all in all, it is an extremely difficult factor to alter or improve. Yet we can, by taking thought, strengthen it to some extent and make it more forceful, more attractive. At any rate, we can strive to get the utmost possible out of this strange thing that nature has given us. The subject is of vast importance to every one of us. The possibilities for improvement, limited as they are, are still large enough to warrant a discussion and investigation.

If you wish to make the most of your individuality, go before your audience rested. A tired man is neither magnetic nor attractive. Don't make the all-too-common error of putting off your preparation and your planning until the very last moment. Only then to work at a furious pace, trying to make up for lost time. If you do, you are bound to store up bodily poisons and brain fatigues that will prove terrific drags, holding you down, sapping your vitality, weakening both your brain and your nerves.

If you must make an important talk to a committee meeting at four, do not, if you can well avoid it, come back to the office after lunch. Go home, if possible, have a light lunch and the refreshment of a siesta. Rest – that is what you need, physical and mental and nervous.

When you have to make an important talk, beware of your hunger. Eat as sparingly as a saint. On Sunday afternoons, Henry

Ward Beecher used to have crackers and milk at five nothing after that.

'When I am singing in the evening,' said Madame Melba, 'I do not dine but have a very light repast at five o'clock, consisting of either fish, chicken or sweetbread, with a baked apple and a glass of water. I always find myself very hungry for supper when I get home from the opera or concert.'

I never understood this until after I became a professional speaker myself and tried to deliver a two-hour talk each evening after having consumed a hearty meal. Experience taught me that I couldn't enjoy a *filet de sole aux pommes nature* and follow that by a beefsteak and French fried potatoes and salad and vegetables and a dessert and then stand up an hour afterwards and do either myself or my subject or my body justice. The blood that ought to have been in my brain was down in my stomach wrestling with that steak and potatoes.

Do nothing to dull your energy. It is magnetic. Vitality, aliveness, enthusiasm: they are among the first qualities I have always sought for in employing speakers and instructors of speaking. People cluster around the energetic speaker, the human dynamo of energy, like wild geese around a field of autumn wheat.

Make sure your personal appearance is immaculate. An inquiry was sent to a large group of people by a psychologist and university president, asking them the impression clothes made on them. All but unanimously, they testified that when they were well-groomed and faultlessly and immaculately attired, the knowledge of it, the feeling of it, had an effect which, while it was difficult to explain, was still very definite, very real. It gave them more confidence; brought them increased faith in themselves; heightened their self-respect. They declared that when they had the look of success they found it easier to think success, to achieve success. Such is the effect of clothes on the wearer himself.

What effect do they have on an audience? I have noticed time and again that if a speaker has a sloppy appearance, an audience has as little respect for that man as he has for his own appearance. Aren't they very likely to assume that his mind is as sloppy as his unkempt hair?

A speaker is liable to be subject to the minutest scrutiny: he is under the magnifying glass, he is in the spotlight and all eyes are upon him. The smallest disharmony in his personal appearance now looms up like Pike's Peak from the plains.

Wear a warm, welcoming smile. 'He who cannot smile,' says a Chinese proverb, 'ought not to keep a shop.' And isn't a smile just as welcome before an audience as behind a counter? Attitudes are contagious.

Crowd your audience together. The fact is that no audience will be easily moved when it is scattered. Nothing so dampens enthusiasm as wide, open spaces and empty chairs between the listeners.

A man in a large audience tends to lose his individuality. He becomes a member of the crowd and is swayed far more easily than he would be as a single individual. He will laugh at and applaud things that would leave him unmoved if he were only one of half a dozen people listening to you.

If we are going to talk to a small group, we should choose a small room. Better to pack the aisles of a small place than to have people scattered through the lonely, deadening spaces of a large hall.

If your audience is scattered, ask them to move down front and be seated near you. Insist on this, before you start speaking.

Unless the audience is a fairly large one and there is a real reason, a necessity, for the speaker standing on a platform, don't do so. Get down on the same level with them. Stand near them. Break up all formality. Get an intimate contact. Make the thing conversational.

Keep the air fresh. In the well-known process of public speaking, oxygen is just as essential as the larynx, pharnyx and human epiglottis. So, when I am one of a number of speakers, before beginning, I almost always ask the audience to stand up and rest for two minutes while the windows are thrown open.

Flood the room, if possible, with lights. It is as easy to domesticate a quail as to develop enthusiasm in a half-lighted room gloomy as the inside of a thermos bottle.

Let the light strike your face. People want to see you. The subtle changes that ought to play across your features are a part and a very real part, of the process of self-expression. Sometimes they mean more than your words. If you stand directly under a light, your face may be dimmed by a shadow; if you stand directly in front of a light, it is sure to be. Would it not, then, be the part of wisdom to select, before you arise to speak, the spot that will give you the most advantageous illumination?

No clutter on the platform. And do not hide behind a table. People want to look at the whole man. They will even lean out in the aisles to see all of him.

Some well-meaning soul is pretty sure to give you a table and a water pitcher and a glass; but if your throat becomes dry, a pinch of salt or a taste of lemon will start the saliva again better than the Niagara talls.

You do not want the water or the pitcher. Neither do you want all the other useless and ugly impedimenta that clutter up the average platform.

The Broadway sales rooms of the various automobile makers are beautiful, orderly, pleasing to the eye. The Paris offices of the large perfumers and jewelers are artistically and luxuriously appointed. Why? It is good business. One has more respect, more confidence, more admiration for a concern housed like that.

For the same reason, a speaker ought to have a pleasing background. The ideal arrangement, to my way of thinking, would be no furniture at all. Nothing behind the speaker to attract attention or at either side of him – nothing but a curtain of dark blue velvet.

However, what does he usually have behind him? Maps and signs and tables, perhaps a lot of dusty chairs, some piled on top of the others. And what is the result? A cheap, slovenly, disorderly atmosphere. So clear all the trumpery away.

'The most important thing in public speaking,' said Henry Ward Beecher, 'is the man.'

So let the person stand out like the snow-clad top of the Jungfrau towering against the blue skies of Switzerland.

No moving distractions on the platform. I was once in London, Ontario, when the Prime Minister of Canada was speaking. Presently the janitor, armed with a long pole, started to ventilate the room, moving about from window to window. What happened? The audience, almost to a man, ignored the speaker for a little while and stared at the janitor as intently as if he had been performing some miracle.

An audience cannot resist – or, what comes to the same thing, it *will not* resist – the temptation to look at moving objects. If a speaker will only remember that truth, it can save some trouble and needless annoyance.

First, it can refrain from twiddling the thumbs; playing with the clothes and making little nervous movements that detract from the. I remember seeing a New York audience watch a well-known speaker's hands for half an hour while he spoke and played with the covering of a pulpit at the same time.

Second, the speaker should arrange, if possible, to have the audience seated so they won't have their attention distracted by seeing the latecomers enter.

Third, it should have no guests on the platform. When I, along with a number of others, was invited to sit on the platform while a well-known speaker delivered a series of talks, I declined on the ground that it was unfair to the speaker. I noted the first night how many of these guests shifted about and put one leg over the other and back again and so on. Every time one of them moved, the audience looked away from the speaker to the guest. I called the speaker's attention to this the next day. During the remainder of his evenings with us, he very wisely occupied the platform alone.

Master the art of sitting down. Isn't it well for the speaker himself not to sit facing the audience before he begins? Isn't it better to arrive as a fresh exhibit than an old one?

But, if we must sit, let us be careful of how we sit. You have seen men look around to find a chair with the modified movements of a foxhound lying down for the night. They turned around and when they did locate a chair, they doubled up and flopped down into it with all the self-control of a sack of sand.

A man who knows how to sit feels the chair strike the back of his legs, and, with his body easily erect from head to hips, he sinks into it with his body under perfect control.

Exhibit poise in appearance and speech. We just said, a few pages previously, not to play with your clothes because it attracted attention. There is another reason also. It gives an impression of weakness, a lack of self-control. Every movement that does not add to your presence detracts from it. There are no neutral movements. None. So stand still and control yourself physically and that will give you an impression of mental control, of poise.

After you have risen to address your audience, do not be in a hurry to begin. That is the hallmark of the amateur. Take a deep breath. Look over your audience for a moment; and, if there is a noise or disturbance, pause until it quiets down.

Hold your chest high. But why wait until you get before an audience to do this? Why not do it daily in private? Then you will do it unconsciously in public.

And what shall you do with your hands? Forget them. If they fall naturally to your sides, that is ideal. If they feel like a bunch of bananas to you, do not be deluded into imagining that anyone else is paying the slightest attention to them or has the slightest interest in them.

They will look best hanging relaxed at your sides. They will attract the minimum of attention there. Not even the hypercritical can criticise that position. Besides, they will be unhampered and free to flow naturally into gestures.

However, suppose that you are very nervous and that you find putting them behind your back or shoving them into your pockets helps to relieve your self-consciousness – what should you do? Use your common sense. If a man has something to say worthwhile and says it with contagious conviction, surely it will matter little what he does with his hands and feet. If his head is full and heart stirred, these secondary details will very largely take care of themselves.

After all, the stupendously important thing in making a talk is the psychological aspect of it, not the position of the hands and feet.

If you forget all else we have said about gesture and delivery, remember this: if speakers are so wrapped up in what they have to say, if they are so eager to get their message across that they forgets themselves and talk and act spontaneously, then their gestures and their delivery, unstudied though they may be, are very likely to be almost above criticism. If you doubt this, walk up to a speakers and knock them down. You will probably discover that, when they regain their feet, the talk they deliver will be quite flawless as a gem of eloquence.

SIX

The Content of Your Talk

THE FOUR MAJOR GOALS OF EVERY SPEECH

Every talk, regardless of whether the speaker realises it or not, has one of four major goals. What are they?

- To make something clear
- To impress and convince
- To get action
- To entertain.

Know your goal. Choose it wisely before you set out to prepare your talk. Know how to reach it. Then set about it, doing it skillfully and with science.

HOW TO MAKE YOUR MEANING CLEAR

Use Comparisons to Promote Clearness

As to clearness: do not underestimate the importance of it nor the difficulty. When the disciples asked Christ why He taught the public by parables, He answered: 'Because they seeing, see not: and hearing, hear not; neither do they understand.'

And when you talk on a subject strange to your audcence, can you hope that they will understand you any more readily than people understood the Master?

Hardly. So what can we do about it? What did He do when confronted by a similar situation? Solved it in the most simple and natural manner imaginable: described the things people did not know by likening them to things they did know. The kingdom of Heaven…what would it be like? How could those untutored peasants of Palestine know? So Christ described it in terms of objects and actions with which they were already familiar:

'The kingdom of Heaven is like unto leaven, which a woman took and hid in three measures of meal, till the whole was leavened.'

'Again, the kingdom of Heaven is like unto a merchant-man seeking goodly pearls…'

'Again, the kingdom of Heaven is like unto a net that was cast into the sea…'

That was lucid; they could understand that. The housewives in the audience were using leaven every week; the fishermen were casting their nets into the sea daily; the merchants were dealing in pearls.

And how did David make clear the watchfulness and loving kindness of Jehovah?

The Lord is my shepherd, I shall not want. He maketh me to lie down in green pastures, He leadeth me beside the still waters…'

Green grazing grounds in that almost barren country…still waters where the sheep could drink – those pastoral people could understand that. Sir Oliver Lodge happily uses this method when explaining the size and nature of atoms to a popular audience. I heard him tell a European audience that there were as many atoms in a drop of water as there were drops of water in the Mediterranean Sea. Many of the audience had spent over a week sailing from Gibraltar to the Suez Canal. To bring the matter still closer home, he said there were as many atoms in one drop of water as there were blades of grass on all the earth.

Use this principle henceforth in your talks. If you are describing the great pyramid, first tell your audience it is 150 feet, then tell them how high that is in terms of some building they see every day. Tell how many city blocks the base would cover. Don't speak about so many thousand gallons of this or so many hundred thousand barrels of that without also telling how many rooms the size of the one you are speaking in could be filled with that much liquid. Instead of saying twenty feet high, why not say one and a half times as high as this ceiling? Instead of talking about distance in terms of rods or miles, is it not clearer to say as far as from here to the union station or to such and such a street?

Avoid Technical Terms

If you belong to a profession that is technical – if you are a lawyer, a physician, an engineer or are in a highly specialised line of business – be doubly careful when you talk to outsiders, to express yourself in plain terms and to give necessary details.

I say be doubly careful, for, as a part of my professional duties, I have listened to hundreds of speeches that failed right at this point and failed woefully. The speakers appeared totally unconscious of the general public's widespread and profound ignorance regarding their particular specialties. So what happened? They rambled on and on, uttering thoughts, using phrases that fitted into their experience and were instantly and continuously meaningful to them; but to the uninitiated, they were about as clear as the Missouri River after the June rains have fallen on the newly-plowed corn fields of Iowa and Kansas.

What should such a speaker do? He ought to read and heed the following advice from the facile pen of Ex-Senator Beveridge of Indiana:

'It is a good practice to pick out the least intelligent looking person in the audience and strive to make that person interested in your argument. This can be done only by lucid statement of fact and clear reasoning. An even better method is to center your talk on some small boy or girl present with parents.

'Say to yourself – say out loud to your audience, if you like- that you will try to be so plain that the child will understand and remember your explanation of the question discussed and after the meeting be able to tell what you have said.'

An all too common reason why men fail to be intelligible is this: the thing they wish to express is not clear even to themselves. Hazy impressions! Indistinct, vague ideas! The result? Their minds work no better in a mental fog than a camera does in a physical fog.

Appeal to the Sense of Sight

The nerves that lead from the eye to the brain are many times larger than those leading from the ear; and science tells us that we give twenty-five times as much attention to eye suggestions as we do to ear suggestions.

'One seeing,' says an old Japanese proverb, 'is better than a hundred times hearing about.' So, if you wish to be clear, picture your points, visualise your ideas. Not every subject or occasion, of course, lends itself to exhibits and drawings; but let us use them when we can. They attract attention, stimulate interest and often make our meaning doubly clear.

Make your eye appeals definite and specific. Paint mental

pictures that stand out as sharp and clear as a stag's horn silhouetted against the setting sun. For example, the word 'dog' calls up a more or less definite picture of such an animal-perhaps a cocker spaniel, a Scotch terrier, a St Bernard, or a Pomeranian. Notice how much more distinct an image springs into your mind when I say 'bulldog' – the term is less inclusive. Doesn't 'a brindle bulldog' call up a still more explicit picture? Is it not more vivid to say 'a black Shetland pony' than to talk of 'a horse'? Doesn't 'a white bantam rooster with a broken leg' give a much more definite and sharp picture than merely the word 'fowl'?

Restate Your Important Ideas In Different Words

Napoleon declared repetition to be the only serious principle of rhetoric. He knew that because an idea was clear to him was not always proof that others instantly grasped it. He knew that it takes time to comprehend new ideas, that the mind must be kept focused on them. In short, he knew they must be repeated. Not in exactly the same language. People will rebel at that and rightly so. But if the repetition is couched in fresh phraseology, if it is varied, your audience will never regard it as repetition at all.

Use General Illustrations and Specific Instances

One of the surest and easiest ways to make your points clear is to follow them with general illustrations and concrete cases. What is the difference between the two? One, as the term implies, is general; the other, specific.

Let us illustrate the difference between them and the uses of each with a concrete example. Suppose we take the statement: 'There are professional men and women who earn astonishingly large incomes.'

Is that statement very clear? Have you a clear-cut idea of what the speaker really means? No and the speaker himself cannot be sure of what such an assertion will call up in the minds of others. The statement, as it stands, is entirely too vague and loose. It needs to be tightened. A few illuminating details ought to be given to indicate what professions the speaker refers to and what he means by 'astonishingly large.'

'There are lawyers, prize fighters, song writers, novelists, playwrights, painters, actors and singers who make more than the President of the United States.'

Now, hasn't one a much clearer idea of what the speaker meant? However, he has not individualised. He has used general illustrations, not specific instances. He has said 'singers,' not names of specific singers.

So the statement is still more or less vague. We cannot call up concrete cases to illustrate it. Should not the speaker do it for us? Would he not be clearer if he employed specific examples? Be concrete.

Be definite. Be specific. This quality of definiteness not only makes for clearness but for impressiveness and conviction and interest also.

Do Not Emulate The Mountain Goat

I recently heard a speaker, who was limited by a stopwatch to three minutes; begin by saying that he wanted to call our attention to eleven points. Sixteen and a half seconds to each phase of his subject! Seems incredible, doesn't it, that an intelligent man should attempt anything so manifestly absurd. True, I am quoting an extreme case; but the tendency to err in that fashion, if not to that degree, handicaps almost every novice. He is like a Cook's guide who shows Paris to the tourist in one day. It can be done, just as one can walk through the American Museum of Natural

History in thirty minutes. Yet neither clearness nor enjoyment results. Many a talk fails to be clear because the speaker seems intent upon establishing a world's record for ground covered in the allotted time. He leaps from one point to another with the swiftness and agility of a mountain goat.

HOW TO BE IMPRESSIVE AND CONVINCING

Aristotle taught that man was a reasoning animal – that he acted according to the dictates of logic. He flattered us. Acts of pure reasoning are as rare as romantic thoughts before breakfast. Most of our actions are the result of suggestion.

Suggestion is getting the mind to accept an idea without offering any proof or demonstration. If I say to you, 'Royal Baking Powder is absolutely pure,' and do not attempt to prove it, I am using suggestion. If I present an analysis of the product and the testimony of well-known chefs regarding it, I am trying to prove my assertion.

Those who are most successful in handling others rely more upon suggestion than upon argument. Salesmanship and modern advertising are based chiefly on suggestion. It is easy to believe; doubting is more difficult. Experience and knowledge and thinking are necessary before we can doubt and question intelligently. Tell a child that Santa Claus comes down the chimney and the child will accept your statements until they acquire sufficient knowledge to cause them to demur. Yet you and I, if we examine the facts closely, will discover that the majority of our opinions, our most cherished beliefs, our creeds, the principles of conduct on which many of us base our very lives, are the result of suggestion, rather than reasoning.

Not only does every idea that enters the mind tend to

be accepted as true; but it is a well-known psychological fact that it also tends to pass into action. For example, you cannot even think of a letter of the alphabet without moving ever so slightly the muscles used in pronouncing it. You cannot think of swallowing without moving ever so slightly the muscles used in that act. The movement may be imperceptible to you; but there are machines delicate enough to register that muscular reaction. The only reason that you do not do everything you think of is because another idea – the uselessness of it, the expense, the trouble, the absurdity, the danger or some such thought-arises to slay the impulse.

Our Main Problem

So in the last analysis, our problem of getting people to accept our beliefs or to act upon our suggestions, is just this: to plant the idea in their minds and to keep contradictory and opposing ideas from arising. He who is skilled in doing that will have power in speaking and profit in business.

Helps Psychology Has To Offer

Has psychology any suggestions that will prove helpful to you in this connection? Emphatically, yes. Let us see what they are. First, haven't you noticed that contradictory ideas are much less likely to arise in your mind when the main idea is presented with feeling and contagious enthusiasm? I say 'contagious,' for enthusiasm is just that? It lulls the critical faculties. When your aim is impressiveness, remember it is more productive to stir emotions than to arouse thoughts. Feelings are more powerful than cold ideas. To arouse feelings one must be intensely in earnest. Insincerity rips the vitals out of delivery. Regardless of the pretty phrases a man may concoct; regardless of the illustrations he may assemble; regardless of the harmony of his voice and the grace of his gestures: if he does not speak sincerely, these are hollow and glittering trappings. If you would impress an audience, be impressed yourself. Your spirit shining through your eyes, radiating through your voice and proclaiming itself through your manner, will communicate itself to your auditors.

Liken What You Wish People to Accept to Something They Already Believe

An atheist once declared to William Paley that there was no God and he challenged the English rector to disprove his contention. Paley very quietly took out his watch, opened the case and showed the works to the unbeliever, saying: 'If I were to tell you that those levers and wheels and springs made themselves and fitted themselves together and started running on their own account, wouldn't you question my intelligence? Of course, you would. But look up at the stars. Every one of them has its perfect appointed course and motion – the Earth and planets around the sun and the whole group pitching along at more than a million miles a day. Each star is another sun with its own group of worlds, rushing on through space like our own solar system. Yet there are no collisions, no disturbance, no confusion. All quiet, efficient and controlled. Is it easier to believe that they just happened or that someone made them so?'

Rather impressive, isn't it? What technique did the speaker use? Let us see. He began on common ground, got his opponent saying 'yes,' and agreeing with him at the outset, as we advised earlier. Then he went on to show that belief in a deity is as simple, as inevitable, as belief in a watchmaker.

Suppose he had retorted to his antagonist at the outset: 'No God? Don't be a silly ass. You don't know what you are talking about.' What would have happened? Doubtlessly a verbal joust – a wordy war would have ensued, as futile as it was fiery. Why? Because, as Professor Robinson has pointed out, they were his opinions and his precious, indispensable self-esteem would have been threatened; his pride would have been at stake.

Since pride is such a fundamentally explosive characteristic of human nature, wouldn't it be the part of wisdom to get a man's pride working for us, instead of against us? How? By showing, as Paley did, that the thing we propose is very similar to something that our opponent already believes. That renders it easier for him to accept than to reject your proposal. That prevents contradictory and opposing ideas from arising in the mind to vitiate what we have said.

Paley showed delicate appreciation of how the human mind functions. Most men, however, lack this subtle ability to enter the citadel of a man's beliefs arm in arm with the owner. They erroneously imagine that in order to take the citadel, they must storm it, batter it down by a frontal attack. What happens? The moment hostilities commence, the drawbridge is lifted, the great gates are slammed and bolted, the mailed archers draw their long bows – the battle of words and wounds is on. Such frays always end in a draw; neither has convinced the other of anything.

What Restatement Will Do

Restatement is another club that we can use to prevent contradictory and dissenting ideas from arising to challenge our assertions. However, we ought to be warned that in the hands of an inexpert speaker, it may prove to be a dangerous tool. Unless he has a fairly rich phraseology, his restatement may deteriorate into an unadorned and all-too-evident repetition. That is deadly. If the audience catches you at that, they will begin twisting in their seats, looking at their watches.

General Illustrations and Specific Instances

Used for the Purpose of Convincing There is little danger, however, of boring people when you employ general illustrations and specific instances. Interesting, easy to pay attention to, they are extremely valuable not only in making your talk clear, as we mentioned before, but also when the purpose of your talk is to impress and convince. They help to keep contradictory ideas from rising. People like to have a speaker give names and dates-something they can examine for themselves if they wish. That kind of procedure is frank, honest. It wins confidence. It impresses.

The Principle of Accumulation

Do not expect a hurried reference to one or possibly two specific instances to have the desired effect.

Call in Authority To Back You Up

As a boy in the Midwest, I used to amuse myself by holding a stick across a gateway that the sheep had to pass through. After the first few sheep had jumped over the stick, I took it away; but all the other sheep leaped through the gateway over an imaginary barrier. The only reason for their jumping was that those in front had jumped. The sheep is not the only animal with that tendency. Almost all of us are prone to do what others are doing, to believe what others believe, to accept, without question, the testimony of prominent people. Their words impressed. Their influence tended to prevent opposing ideas from arising. However, in quoting authorities, bear these points in mind.

1. *Be Definite.* Beware of beginning 'statistics show...' What statistics? Who gathered them and why? Be careful I 'Figures won't lie, but liars will figure.'

The usual phrase-'many authorities declare'-is ridiculously vague. Who are the authorities? Name one or two. If you do not know who they are, how can you be sure of what they said?

Be definite. It wins confidence. It demonstrates to the audience that you know whereof you speak.

2. *Quote a Qualified Authority Your Audience Trusts.* Ask yourself such questions as these: Is this person generally recognised as an authority on this subject? Why? Is he a prejudiced witness? Has he any selfish ends to serve. But even more importantly, is this someone my audience views as a trusted authority? Our likes and dislikes have more to do with our beliefs than most of us would care to admit.

HOW TO INTEREST YOUR AUDIENCE

If you were invited to dine at the home of a rich man in certain sections of China, it would be proper to toss chicken bones and olive seeds over your shoulder onto the floor. You pay your host a compliment when you do that. You show that you realise that he is wealthy, that he has plenty of servants to tidy up after the meal. And he likes it. You can be reckless with the remains of your sumptuous meal in a rich man's home; but in some parts of China the poorer people must save even the water they bathe in. To heat water costs so much that they must buy it at a hot water shop. After they have bathed in it, they can take it back and sell it second hand to the shopkeeper from whom they purchased it. When the second customer has soiled it, the water still retains a market value, although the price has softened a bit.

Have you found these facts about Chinese life interesting? If so, do you know why? Because those are very unusual aspects of very usual things. They are strange truths about such commonplace events as dining out and bathing.

That is what interests us – something new about the old.

There lies one of the secrets of interesting people. That is a significant truth, one that we ought to profit by in our every day intercourse. The entirely new is not interesting; the entirely old has no attractiveness for us. We want to be told something new about the old.

The Three Most Interesting Things in the World

What would you say they are – the three most interesting subjects in the world? Sex, property and religion. By the first we can create life, by the second we maintain it, by the third we hope to continue it in the world to come.

Yet it is our own sex, our own property and our own religion that interests us. Our interests swarm about our own egos.

Remember that the people you are to talk to spend most of their time when they are not concerned with the problems of business, in thinking about and justifying and glorifying themselves. Remember that the average man will be more concerned about the cook leaving than about Italy paying her debts to the United States. He will be more wrought up over a dull razor blade than over a revolution in South America. His own toothache will distress him more than an earthquake in Asia destroying half a million lives. He would rather listen to you say some nice thing about him than hear you discuss the ten greatest men in history.

How to be a Good Conversationalist

The reason so many people are poor conversationalists is because they talk about only the things that interest them. That may be deadly boring to others. Reverse the process. Lead the other person into talking about her interests, his business, her golf score, his success – or if it is a parent, her children. Do that and listen intently and you will give pleasure; consequently you will be considered a good conversationalist – even though you have done very little of the talking.

The Kind of Speech Material That Always Holds Attention

You may possibly bore people if you talk about things and ideas, but you can hardly fail to hold their attention when you talk about people. Tomorrow there will be millions of conversations floating over fences in the backyards of America, over tea tables and dinner tables – and what will be the predominating note in most of them? Personalities. He said this. Mrs So-and-so did that. I saw her doing this, that and the other. He is making a 'killing,' and so on.

The average speech would be far more appealing if it were rich and replete with human-interest stories. The speaker ought to attempt to make only a few points and to illustrate them with concrete cases. Such a method of speech building can hardly fail to get and hold attention.

If possible, these stories ought to tell of struggles, of things fought for and victories won. All of us are tremendously interested in fights and combats. There is an old saying that all the world loves a lover. It doesn't. What the entire world loves is a scrap. It wants to see two lovers struggling for the hand of one woman. As an illustration of this fact, read almost any novel, magazine story, or go to see almost any film drama. When all the obstacles are removed and the reputed hero takes the so-called heroine in his arms, the audience begins reaching for their hats and coats. Five minutes later the sweeping women are gossiping over their broom handles.

Almost all – magazine fiction is based on this formula. Make the reader like the hero or heroine. Make him or her long for something intensely. Make that something seem impossible to get. Show how the hero or heroine fights and gets it.

The story of how a man battled in business or profession against discouraging odds and won, is always inspiring, always interesting. A magazine editor once told me that the real, inside story of any person's life is entertaining. If one has struggled and fought-and who hasn't? This story, if correctly told, will appeal. There can be no doubt of that.

Be Concrete

Even though we have already covered the importance of being definite and concrete in previous sections, this principle is so important that we are going to cover it again in this section to try to lodge it firmly in your mind. We hope you will never forget it, never neglect it.

Is it, for example, more interesting to state that Martin Luther, as a boy, was 'stubborn and intractable,' or is it better to say that he confessed that his teachers had flogged him as often as 'fifteen times in a forenoon'?

Words like 'stubborn and intractable' have very little attention value. But isn't it easy to listen to the flogging count?

The old method of writing a biography was to deal in a lot of generalities, which Aristotle called and rightly called, 'The refuge of weak minds.' The new method is to deal with concrete facts that speak for themselves. The old fashioned biographer said that John Doe was born of 'poor but honest parents.' The new method would say that John Doe's father couldn't afford a pair of over-shoes, so when the snow came, he had to tie gunny sacking around his shoes to keep his feet dry and warm; but, in spite of his poverty, he never watered the milk and he never traded a horse with the heaves as a sound animal. That shows that his parents were 'poor but honest,' doesn't it? And doesn't it do it in a way that is far more interesting than the 'poor but honest' method?

If this method works for modern biographers it will work also for modern speakers.

Picture-Building Words

In this process of interest getting, there is one aid, one technique, that is of the highest importance; yet it is all but ignored. The average speaker does not seem to be aware of its existence. He has probably never consciously thought about it at all. I refer to the process of using words that create pictures. The speaker who is easy to listen to is the one who sets images floating before your eyes. The one who employs foggy, common-place, colourless symbols set the audience to nodding.

Pictures. Pictures. Pictures. They are as free as the air you breathe. Sprinkle them through your talks, your conversation; and you will be more entertaining, more influential.

Did you ever pause to observe that the proverbs that are passed on from generation to generation are almost all visual sayings? 'A bird in the hand is worth two in the bush.' 'It never rains but it pours.' 'You can lead a horse to water but you can't make him drink.' And you will find the same picture element in almost all the similes that have lived for centuries and grown hoary with too much use: 'Sly as a fox.' 'Dead as a door nail.' 'Flat as a pancake.' 'Hard as a rock.'

Interest Is Contagious

We have been discussing so far the kind of material that interests an audience. However, one might mechanically follow all the suggestions made here and speak according to Cocker and yet be vapid and dull. Catching and holding the interest of people is a delicate thing, a matter of feeling and spirit. It is not like operating a steam engine. No book of precise rules can be given for it.

Interest, be it remembered, is contagious. Your hearers are almost sure to catch it if you have a bad case of it yourself. A short time ago, a gentleman rose during a session of this course in Baltimore and warned his audience that if the present methods of catching rock fish in

Chesapeake Bay were continued the species would become extinct. And in a very few years! He felt his subject. It was important. He was in real earnest about it. Everything about his matter and manner showed that. When he arose to speak, I did not know that there was such an animal as a rock fish in Chesapeake Bay. I imagine that most of the audience shared my lack of knowledge and lack of interest. But before the speaker finished, all of us had caught something of his concern. All of us would probably have been willing to have signed a petition to the legislature to protect the rock fish by law.

I recently went to hear a speaker in London: after he was through, one of our party, a well-known English novelist remarked that he enjoyed the last part of the talk far more than the first. When I asked him why, he replied: 'The speaker himself seemed more interested in the last part and I always rely on the speaker to supply the enthusiasm and interest.' Everyone does. Remember that.

HOW TO GET ACTION

If you could have the power of any talent that you now possess doubled and trebled for the mere asking, which one would you select to have this mighty boon conferred upon? Wouldn't you very likely designate your ability to influence others, to get action? That would mean additional power, additional profit and additional pleasure.

Must this art – so essential to our success in life – remain forever a hit and miss affair with most of us? Must we blunder along depending upon our instinct, upon rule of thumb methods only? Or is there a more intelligent way to set about achieving it?

There is and we shall discuss it at once – a method based on the rules of common sense, on the rules of human nature, your nature and mine, a method that the writer has frequently employed himself, a method that he has trained others to use successfully. The first step in this method is to *gain interested attention*. Unless you do that, people will not listen closely to what you say. How to do this was dealt with at length above. The second step is to *gain the confidence of your audiences*. Unless you do that, they will have no faith in what you say. And here is where many a speaker falls down. Here is where many an advertisement fails, many a business letter, many an employee, many a business enterprise. Here is where many an individual fails to make himself effective within his own human environment.

Win confidence by deserving it. The prime way to win confidence is to deserve it. I have noticed time without number that facile and witty speakers-if those are their chief qualities-are not nearly as effective as those who are less brilliant but more sincere.

Speak from your own experience. The second way to gain the confidence of the audience is to speak discreetly out of your own experience. That helps immensely. If you give opinions, people may question them. If you relate hearsay or repeat what you have read, the thing may have a second-hand flavor. But what you yourself have gone through and lived through, that has a genuine ring, a tang of truth and veracity; and people like it. They believe it. They recognise you as the world's leading authority on that particular topic. As an illustration of the efficacy of this sort of thing, go to the newsstand and purchase a copy of any popular magazine today. You will find these packed with articles by men relating their own experiences.

Be properly introduced. Many a speaker fails to gain the attention of his audience immediately because he is not introduced properly.

An introduction – that term was fashioned from two Latin words, intro, to the inside and ducere, to lead – ought to lead us to the inside of the topic sufficiently to make us want to hear it discussed. It ought to lead us to the inside facts regarding the speaker, facts that demonstrate his fitness for discussing this particular topic. In other words, an introduction ought to 'sell' the topic to the audience and it ought to 'sell' the speaker. And it ought to do these things in the briefest amount of time possible.

That is what it ought to do. But does it? Nine times out of ten-no-emphatically no. Most introductions are poor affairs – feeble and inexcusably inadequate.

And what are we going to do about it? With all due humility of soul and meekness of spirit, go to the chairman beforehand and ask him if he would like a few facts to use in his introduction. He will appreciate your suggestions. Then tell him the things you would like to have mentioned, the things that show why you are in a position to talk about this particular subject, the simple facts that the audience ought to know, the facts that will win you a hearing. Of course, after being told only once, the chairman is going to forget half of them and get the other half all mixed up; so it is a good plan to hand them to him, just a sentence or two, hoping that he will refresh his mind before he introduces you. But will he? Probably not. And that is that.

Earnestness. The power of it is incredible – especially with a popular audience. Very few people have the capacity for independent thought. It is as rare as the topaz of Ethiopia. But all of us have feelings and emotions and all of us are influenced by the speaker's feeling. After you have won the audience's interested attention and their confidence, the real work begins. The third step then is to state the facts, to

Educate People Regarding the Merits of Your Proposition

This is the very heart of your talk, the meat. This is where you will need to devote most of your time. Now you will need to apply all you have learned in the section about Clearness, all you have learned in the section about Impressiveness and Conviction. Here is where your preparation will count. Here is where the lack of it will rise up and mock you.

Here you are on the firing line. Here is where you need to know a score of times more about your topic than you can possibly use.

If you are addressing a business group on some proposal that affects them, you should not only educate them; but you should let them educate you. You should ascertain what is in their minds-otherwise you may be dealing with something entirely beside the point. Let them express their minds; answer their objections; then they will be in a more placid state to listen to you.

Set One Desire to Fight Another

The fourth step in this method is to appeal to the motives that make men act. This Earth and all things in it and on it and in the waters underneath it, are run, not haphazardly, but according to the immutable law of cause and effect.

Everything that ever has happened or ever will happen has been, or will be, the logical and inevitable effect of something that preceded it, the logical and inevitable cause of something that follows. This principle, like the laws of the Medes and Persians, changed not. It is as true of earthquakes and the honking of wild geese and jealousy and the price of baked beans and the Kohinoor diamond and the beautiful harbor in Sydney – it is as true of those things as it is of putting a nickel in a slot and getting a package of gum. When one recognises this, he understands, once and for all, why superstition is unspeakably silly – for how can the unchangeable laws of nature be stopped or altered or affected in the slightest by thirteen people sitting at a table or because one breaks a mirror?

What causes every conscious and deliberate act we perform? By some desire. The only people to whom this does not apply are incarcerated in insane asylums. The things that actuate us are not many. We are ruled hour by hour, dominated day and night, by a surprisingly small number of longings.

All that means just this: if one knows what these motives are and can appeal to them with sufficient force, he will have extraordinary power. The wise speaker attempts to do precisely that. But the blunderer gropes his way blindly and to no purpose.

The man skilled in getting action sets one motive to war against another. This method is so sensible, so simple and so utterly apparent that one might imagine that the use of it was all but universal. Far from it. One often sees exhibitions that make him inclined to suspect that the use of it is very rare.

To cite a concrete case: the writer recently attended a noonday luncheon club in a certain city. A golf party was being organised to play over the country club course of a neighboring city. Only a few members had put down their names. The president of the club was displeased; something he was behind was about to fall; his prestige was at stake. So he made what he imagined was an appeal for more members to go. His talk was woefully inadequate; he based his urge very largely on the fact that he wanted them to go. That was no appeal at all. He was not handling human nature skillfully; he was merely unloading his own feelings. Like the irate father with the cigarette-smoking son, he neglected entirely to talk in terms of the desires of his hearers.

What should he have done? He should have used a generous supply of common sense; he should have had a little quiet talk with himself before he spoke to the others; and he should have addressed himself somewhat in this fashion: 'Why aren't more of these men going on this golfing party? Some probably imagine they cannot spare the time; others may be thinking of the railway fare and various expenses. How can I overcome these objections? I will show them that recreation is not lost time, that grinds are not the most successful men, that one can do more in five days when he is fresh than he can in six when his batteries need recharging. Of course, they know this already; but they need to be reminded of it. I will play up things that they ought to want more than they want to save the small expense connected with this party. I will show them that it is an investment in health and pleasure. I will stir their imaginations, make them see themselves out on the course, the west wind in their faces, the green sward under their feet, feeling sorry for those back in the hot city who live for nothing but money.'

Would such a procedure, in your opinion, have been more

likely to succeed than the mere 'I-want-you-to-go' appeal that the speaker used?

The Desires that Determine our Actions

What, then, are these basic and human longings that should mold our conduct and make us behave like human beings? If an understanding of them and a playing upon them is so essential to our success, then out with them. Let us have the light upon them, let us examine and dissect and analyse them – and tell a few stories about them. That, you will agree, is the way to make them clear, the way to make them convincing, the way to engrave them deep upon the walls of your memory.

One of the very strongest of these motives is-what would you say? You are right: the desire for gain. That will be largely responsible for a few hundred million people getting out of bed tomorrow morning two or three hours earlier than they would otherwise arise without this spur. Is it necessary to discourse further upon the potency of this well-known urge? Even stronger than the money motive is the desire for self-protection. All health appeals are based on that.

To make the appeal to this motive strong, make it personal. Don't, for example, quote statistics to show that cancer is on the increase. No. Tic it right down to the people who are listening to you, e.g., 'There are thirty people in this room. If all of you live to be forty-five, three of you, according to the law of medical averages, will die of cancer. I wonder if it will be you, or you, or you over there.'

As strong as the desire for money – in fact, in many people it is far stronger – is the wish to be thought well of, to be admired. In other words, pride. Pride with a capital P. *Pride* in italics. PRIDE in capital letters.

We are creatures of feeling, who long for comforts and pleasures. We drink coffee and wear silk socks and go to the theater and sleep on the bed instead of the floor, not because we have reasoned out that these things are good for us, but because they are pleasant. So show that the thing you propose will add to our comforts and increase our pleasures and you have touched a powerful spring of action.

Religious Motives

There is another powerful group of motives that influence us mightily. Shall we call them religious motives? I mean religious, not in the sense of orthodox worship or the tenets of any particular creed or sect. I mean rather that broad group of beautiful and eternal truths, of justice and forgiveness and mercy, serving others and loving our neighbors as ourselves. No man likes to admit, even to himself, that he is not good and kind and magnanimous. So we love to be appealed to on these grounds. It implies a certain nobleness of soul. We take pride in that.

Such is the power of the appeal to the religious emotions and convictions.

Part IV

LIFE CHANGING SECRETS FROM THE THREE MASTERS OF SUCCESS

Self-Evaluation Questionnaire

Now that you understand Napoleon Hill, Joseph Murphy and Dale Carnegie's three crucial life skills for breakthrough success, it's time to turn these ideas into action. And the best way to develop the right action plan is to begin with a thorough self-examination.

In the three-part questionnaire below, rate yourself on each question on a scale of 1 to 4:

1 = never or rarely

2 = seldom or sometimes

3 = often

4 = always or almost always

For any questions with parts a, b, or c, add the scores together and average them. If you really want to know yourself, as Napoleon Hill suggests, give this questionnaire to a trusted friend who cares about you enough to tell you the truth and have them fill it out on your behalf.

LIFE SKILL 1: CREATING A WEALTH MINDSET

Question **Rating (1-4)**

1. *Desire*. Examine your heart and mind. How strong and specific is your desire for wealth?
2. *Faith*. Do you truly believe that you can attain your desire? Is your faith sufficiently strong so that you not only expect to receive it, but you can truly see yourself in possession of it?
3. *Autosuggestion*. In pursuing your desire, do you daily follow Napoleon Hill's autosuggestion instructions listed on pages 67–70 (or their equivalent) in order to direct your subconscious mind

to attract what you desire? Do you follow this formula with the spirit of faith, emotionally believing in the statements as you repeat them, instead of just repeating them by rote?

4. *Specialised Knowledge.* Are you acquiring the specialised knowledge your field requires in order to be successful? (This may be in the form of formal schooling, training courses, Internet research, or direct access to trusted experts.)
5. *Imagination.* Do you truly believe that ideas are the source of wealth and not hard work alone? Are you using both your creative imagination and synthetic imagination to create ideas to transform your desire into money?
6. *Organised Planning.* Have you developed a specific plan for wealth based on your desire, specialised knowledge, ideas born of your imagination and approval by trusted advisors (your Mastermind group)?
7. *Decision.* Do you make your decisions promptly and change your decisions slowly?
8. *Persistence.* Do you channel your willpower towards persistence? Are you committed to persevere when following your plan results in temporary defeat and are you resolved to rebuild those plans based on what failure taught you and not to quit until you reach your goal?
9. *The Power of the Mastermind.* Have you assembled a Master Mind group of one or more people to work together in a spirit of harmony for the definite purpose of helping you execute your plan for wealth?
10. *The Mystery of Sex Transformation.* Have you mastered your sexual energy such that you can consistently harness and redirect it toward specific and creative effort in executing your plan for wealth?
11. *Your Subconscious Mind.* Do you give consistent wealth-building

instructions to your subconscious mind, using the principles of autosuggestion?

12. *The Brain.* Do you understand and believe that your brain is your most powerful asset? Are you committed to discovering and nurturing the full spectrum of its capabilities?
13. *The Sixth Sense.* Do you believe in a 'sixth sense': that there is intelligence behind all forms of matter and energy and those humans are equipped to tap into it? Do you structure your life to receive as much of its inspiration and intuition as possible? Do you act without hesitation upon receiving this intelligence?

LIFE SKILL 2: MASTERING THE POWER OF YOUR SUBCONSCIOUS MIND

Question **Rating (1-4)**

1. How strong is your 'health consciousness?' Do you believe that your thoughts affect your physical health in concrete, measurable ways?
2. Do you leverage the power of your subconscious mind to improve your health when faced with symptoms of illness?
3. How strong is your 'wealth consciousness?' Do you believe that your thoughts affect your financial situation in concrete, measurable ways?
4. Do you leverage the power of your subconscious mind to build wealth when faced with financial risk and opportunities?
5. When you have decisions to make or problems to solve and you're not sure of the next step, do you regularly open yourself to guidance from your subconscious mind?
6. When faced with difficulties in marriage (or significant

relationships, if you're single), do you fully believe you can have a mutually loving and supportive marriage/relationship, instruct your subconscious mind accordingly to have faith that what you have intended will come to pass, without worry?

7. When faced with difficulties in work relationships or friendships, do you follow the same process as above: believing in a full and ideal restoration of the relationship, instructing your subconscious mind accordingly and having faith that it will come to be at the right time and in the right way?
8. When someone wrongs you, how easily are you able to forgive them? Do you use the power of your subconscious mind to forgive in heart, mind and action?
9. Do you actively choose happiness in your life when adverse circumstances strike?
10. When facing mental blocks, emotional strongholds, or stubborn fears, do you regularly leverage the power of your subconscious mind to work on your behalf, instead of relying on extreme willpower and effort?
11. Do you believe that age is an asset and not a liability?

LIFE SKILL 3: INFLUENCING OTHERS IN FRIENDSHIP AND PUBLIC SPEAKING

Question **Rating (1-4)**

Building the Skills of Friendship

1. Do you rarely criticise, condemn, or complain?
2. Do you honestly and sincerely appreciate others? Are you fun to be with?
3. Are you genuinely interested in other people (do you pay

attention to them)?

4. Do you smile often?
5. Do you remember people's names?
6. Are you a good listener and encourage others to talk about themselves?
7. Do you talk in terms of the other's interests?
8. Do you make the other person feel important (sincerely)?

Developing Great Habits for Success

9. Do you regularly take inventory of yourself to know your strengths and weaknesses?
10. Do you grasp every opportunity for practicing your new resolutions with enthusiasm?
11. Do you consistently avoid making excuses for yourself?
12. Do you make definitive commitments?
13. Do you strive to consistently make a good impression with your personal appearance, your manner and your speech?
14. Do you regularly play games that require physical exertion or involve a matching of wits, such as sports, card games, chess or competitive video games?
15. Do you regularly do things for other people?
16. Do you focus on excellence in your work?
17. Do you exhibit poise in your speech and appearance, i.e.:
    a. Have you rid yourself of nervous habits?
    b. Rather than self-consciously focus on yourself, do you unfailingly focus on others?
18. Do you relax at least once an hour?
19. Do you get enough sleep?
20. Do you eat properly, according to your activity level?
21. Do you take care of your teeth and gums?

22. Do you organise your work daily to minimise distractions and maximise focus?
23. Do you rest before you get tired?
24. Do you allow yourself to heal when you get sick?
25. Do you live your life as if time is your most valuable possession?

Public Speaking

26. Do you have a strong and persistent desire to master the skill of public speaking to influence others?
27. When preparing to speak, do you know thoroughly what you are going to talk about?
28. Do you act confident when you address others (even when you don't feel confident)?
29. Do you practise frequently and consistently before you speak to groups?
30. Do you invest quality time in preparing your talk, following Dale Carnegie's steps in preparing your speech?
31. Do you understand and practise the principles of good delivery?
32. Do you understand and achieve the four major goals of the content of every speech:
    a. making your meaning clear,
    b. being impressive and convincing,
    c. interesting your audience and
    d. getting action from your audience?

After you (or your trusted friend) have completed the questionnaire, take note of where you're doing well (i.e., where you scored 3 or 4) and where you need some work (where you scored 1 or 2). Make a list of all items with scores of 1 or 2 and commit to using the principles of the mind and practical skills you learned in this book to strengthen these weak areas. Remember that knowledge is power. Then make a list of all items with scores of 3 or 4 and consider how you might take a greater leadership role and/or mentor others in these areas. Remember that you must give freely in order to receive.

No one can guarantee your success but you – it must be rooted in your own desire. What do you really want? Armed with a fuller self-awareness, develop a sound plan and pursue it. Use the full powers of your subconscious mind. And develop the skills of authentic friendship and public speaking to extend your influence and scale your success beyond what you ever thought possible. Your success already exists in the power of your mind – all that remains is for you to put it into action, one step at a time.